The VINEYARDS *of* CHAMPAGNE

Center Point
Large Print

Also by Juliet Blackwell and available from Center Point Large Print:

The Lost Carousel of Provence

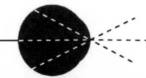

This Large Print Book carries the Seal of Approval of N.A.V.H.

The VINEYARDS *of* CHAMPAGNE

Juliet Blackwell

CENTER POINT LARGE PRINT
THORNDIKE, MAINE

This Center Point Large Print edition
is published in the year 2020 by arrangement with
Berkley, an imprint of Penguin Publishing Group,
a division of Penguin Random House LLC.

The text of this Large Print edition is unabridged.
In other aspects, this book may vary
from the original edition.
Printed in the United States of America
on permanent paper.
Set in 16-point Times New Roman type.

ISBN: 978-1-64358-621-2

The Library of Congress has cataloged this record under
Library of Congress Control Number: 2020932633

To Sergio
In losing you I lost my sun and moon
May you shine on, forever,
my diamond in the sky

In losing you I lost my sun and moon
And all the stars that blessed my lonely night.
. . . .
I lost the master word, dear love, the clue
That threads the maze of life when I lost you.
 —WINIFRED LETTS

The
VINEYARDS
of
CHAMPAGNE

Lucie

Reims, France
1916

The clicking of my mother's knitting needles is the metronome measuring the minutes, hours, months spent in the perpetually cool, dim caves. The sound reverberates off the chalk walls.

When there comes a pause in the shelling, the able-bodied dare to slip out into the aboveground world. To feel the sun on our faces, to breathe deeply of the air—however rank with smoke, it is better than the stale air within the caves— and to tend to the wounded. We comb through the charred ruins of our once-beautiful city for anything of use: an unbroken teacup, a child's toy, ripped blankets, or sweaters that can be unraveled for their wool.

My mother's hands were once soft from a lifetime of ease. Now those same hands reclaim old misshapen sweaters with an avarice that astonishes me, unraveling the yarn, winding it into a hank, soaking it in water to relax the crimp of the stitches, sometimes even dyeing it: pale yellow with onion skins or grayish purple with discarded grape musts.

Before, my mother taught me how to sit with my knees together, how to move gracefully, and when to smile. Those skills have no place in the caves. But another lesson I have learned from my mother: Yarn remains fundamentally unchanged, no matter its pattern. It is still wool. It might be singed, abandoned, stripped from a corpse. It might be unraveled altogether, a twisted, knotted rat's nest of fibers. But it can be cleansed and untangled and knitted back together again. It can take a new form. The shape may be different, but the wool is fundamentally the same.

The human spirit does not want to die; it is a resilient thing.

That first year of the war, without any hale young men, without the aid of decent horses or farm equipment, and with German bullets and shells raining down from the hills, we made up our minds to bring in the harvest. That first year, and the second, and the one after that. Every September, when the heat of summer begins to cede to the chill of autumn, when the cellar master declares the fruit has reached its pinnacle of sweetness, we venture out under cover of darkness to pick the grapes. We haul them below-ground, capture their juices, and lay the bottles to rest in the cool, dank caves.

We bring in the harvest, knowing that our beloved champagne will be drinkable only long after the war is over. A Victory Vintage to be savored in celebration of the end of war.

Women. Children. The elderly.

We bring in the harvest.

We make the wine.

Chapter One

Rosalyn

Napa, California
Present day

T here's one major problem with your little plan," said Rosalyn, patting the dossier Hugh had dropped on the desk in front of her. According to the itinerary, she was booked on an AirFrance flight to Paris departing from San Francisco the day after Christmas. She was to stay a couple of nights in Paris, then pick up a rental car that had been reserved in her name and head for Champagne, less than a two-hour drive northeast.

"What problem? I booked it myself." Hugh nodded and gave her an exaggerated wink. "First class—that's the ticket. Get it? The ticket?"

"But I don't like France. Or the French. Or champagne, for that matter."

"Are you saying you dislike *la Champagne*, as in the region of France," asked Hugh, "or *le champagne*, the bubbly nectar that is celebrated the world over?"

"Both, as you very well know. Not a fan."

Hugh's only reaction to her ill humor was a broad smile. Rosalyn's boss was a bear of a man who dwarfed the cramped winery/import office located in the lovingly renovated garage of his sprawling Napa Valley vineyard home. Standing several inches taller than six feet, the ironically named Hugh Small had the well-padded physique of a man who entertained frequently and enjoyed his own excellent cooking—and wine—a tad too much. His graying brown hair was wild and scruffy, and his clothes so sloppy that, if he hadn't been so well-known in the valley, the locals might have assumed he was one of the wanderers who camped among the vines, cruising the highways of Napa and Sonoma for dregs in bottles left on picnic tables by well-to-do tourists on wine-tasting jaunts.

Ten years earlier, Hugh had fulfilled a lifelong fantasy by purchasing a vineyard in Napa. He quickly realized just how hard it was to get established in the wine-producing business, and branched out into importing and selling select vintages from France and Spain through his company, Small Fortune Wines.

Hugh's favorite joke: "How do you make a small fortune in the wine business? Start out with a *large* fortune."

Today Hugh's light blue pullover sweater sported a moth-eaten hole over his heart. Rosalyn stared at it, pondering its significance. Hugh had more than enough heart for the both of them.

"Honestly, Hugh," Rosalyn persisted, trying to keep a lid on the vague panic simmering somewhere deep within her, "I know most people would jump at the chance to go to Champagne, all expenses paid, but I really don't enjoy traveling. You're sure you need me to do this?"

He nodded. "Andy's still at the hospital with his wife and their preemie; he couldn't possibly leave now."

"Couldn't *you* go? I could stay here and run the office."

"I need a wine rep in France," he said. "And you're a wine rep."

"Just barely."

"And you speak French."

"Just barely."

"And you've got a palate. Better than mine. Besides," said Hugh as he sorted through a stack of mail, tossing several envelopes into the recycling bin, "it's downright embarrassing that you've never been to France. What self-respecting wine rep has never been to France?"

"I *have* been to France."

"Once. And if I'm not mistaken you went to *Paris,* which is no more representative of France than New York City is of the United States. And admit it: You enjoyed your time there."

Snowflakes glittering on their scarves as they stood under the lamppost at the corner of Rue

17

des Abbesses and Rue Lepic. Tipsy on wine and after-dinner cognac. Giggling as they watched a man slip silently down the snow-covered cobblestone streets of Montmartre, their breath coming out in wispy clouds, mingling in the frigid air.

"It's our laughter," says Rosalyn, lifting her mittened hand as if to capture the mist. "Come back!"

Dash grabs her hand, warming it with both of his, kissing it. "Plenty more where that came from, Rosie. A lifetime of laughter for my beautiful bride. I promise."

Dash had lied.

"Of course I enjoyed it," Rosalyn said when she realized Hugh was still watching her, awaiting an answer. "It was my honeymoon. That was different."

"Dash went to France many times," Hugh pointed out. "He loved it there."

Rosalyn felt the usual sharp stab in her gut at the sound of her husband's name. Still, she appreciated that Hugh never hesitated to speak it aloud. It muted the pain, ever so slightly, each time someone talked about Dash as though things were normal; as if invoking his spirit, inviting his presence into this world. Most people tried to avoid any reference to him, or acted chagrined, as though they'd done something awkward and embarrassing by bringing him up.

"I like it right *here,*" insisted Rosalyn, gazing out the window at the twisty grapevines that marched along the rolling hills, their undulating lines interrupted only by an occasional oak tree. The sight of the parallel rows was soothing, as if a Zen master had pulled a giant rake through sand. "I defy anyone to come up with a more beautiful place than Napa."

"There's nothing wrong with seeking a refuge for a while, Rosalyn," said Hugh, his voice dropping, its gentle sincerity grating on her nerves. "But it isn't a life plan. If you decide to settle in Napa, it should be just that: a decision. Not an attempt to hide from life."

Rosalyn's eyes stung; nausea surged at the base of her throat. One hand fiddled with the silver locket that hung around her neck while the other reached for the travel dossier as she pretended to study the itinerary, hoping to distract herself, to stem the tears, to quell the incipient panic.

Breathe, she reminded herself. *Ten slow, deep breaths . . .*

"As you can see," said Hugh, his voice regaining its cheery tone as he pointed to a few items highlighted in bold script on the agenda, "you'll be representing Small Fortune Wines in Champagne for the festival of Saint Vincent, patron saint of vintners, which is held on the twenty-second of January. Until then, you'll meet with vintners, make nice, tour the caves—"

"Like I need to see any more wine caves in my life."

"You *do* need to see more wine caves in your life, Rosalyn," Hugh insisted. "The champagne caves are unlike any you've seen before; there are two hundred kilometers worth of *crayères* under Reims alone. An entire city, underground. Do you know the French moved whole schools and businesses down into the caves during the First World War?"

"Fascinating," Rosalyn said. "But is that why you want me to go? To attend a wine festival and tour some caves? That doesn't sound terribly cost-effective to me."

"No, no, no, you're also going to sign some new, smaller producers. It's the foundation of my vision."

"Your . . . what, now?"

Hugh returned her smile. "My vision to get people to stop thinking of champagne as a luxury, get them to drink a glass with appetizers as they do in France. Americans equate champagne with the big, expensive houses, Mumm and Taittinger. I want you to find and sign a few of the small champagne houses, the ones that don't charge a fortune for their wine. Step one is reconfirming our commitment with Gaspard Blé—you'll be staying at his vineyard. I've known Blé for years, but I heard through the grapevine—get it?—that Bottle Rocket's sending someone to the festival.

I wouldn't want to lose Blé to the competition."

Bottle Rocket was the Big Bad Wolf, Hugh's biggest competitor for the products of family-run French wineries.

Rosalyn nodded. Of course she would go to represent Small Fortune Wines in Champagne. She couldn't refuse Hugh anything; she owed him too much. Besides . . . maybe he was onto something. Maybe a change of pace was what she needed to pull out of the tailspin. Nothing else seemed to be working.

"So, how's Andy doing? And his wife?" Rosalyn belatedly thought to ask. "Is the baby out of the NICU yet?"

"Baby and mamma are doing just fine," said Hugh. "I brought them a gift basket yesterday, signed the card from all of us."

"That was nice of you." Rosalyn cringed inwardly. She used to be the one who bought the gifts, sent the cards, visited friends in the hospital. The Rosalyn-That-Was thought of other people, organized impromptu parties, never forgot a friend's birthday. Another unexpected indignity of grief: It had rendered her self-absorbed.

"It was no problem—any excuse to buy baby things," said Hugh. "Those little outfits are so *tiny;* hard to believe a human can come in a package that small, isn't it? Did you know they arrive in this world complete with teensy finger-nails?"

Rosalyn smiled at the note of wonder in his voice. "I've heard that."

"Anyway, Andy's not happy that he's missing out on this trip—that's for sure."

"I'll bet. I'll give him a call and check in before I leave."

Hugh tilted his head and fixed Rosalyn with a look. "Make the most of this, Rosie. Seriously. Sometimes a trip can shake off the cobwebs, open your eyes to new possibilities."

"I just got back from Paso Robles, remember?"

"Paso has its charm, but it's not exactly the French countryside."

"And yet Paso Robles has 7-Elevens, which, contrary to their name, are open twenty-four hours. That's a true gift to humankind, if you ask me."

"Champagne's the ticket, Rosie. Dash loved it there; I have a feeling you will, too."

Chapter Two

*D*amn Hugh, anyway.

The airplane seat belt sign had not yet turned off when, in a confetti-like explosion, the woman sitting next to Rosalyn dropped a folder full of papers and swore a blue streak that made the temporary denizens of the hushed first-class cabin turn their heads and stare. Even the perfectly coiffed, ever-poised AirFrance flight attendants were given pause.

"Let me help you with those," Rosalyn said, straining against the tight grip of the seat belt to pick up the yellowed papers scattered at her feet.

"Oh, *crikey*—yes, please. I can hardly move with this damned cast." The woman gestured in front of her to the leg sticking out, bound in an enormous cast that was brightly decorated with colorful swirls and interlocking paisley designs, done in a childish hand with Magic Markers. She was tall, probably fifty-something, with short, spiky peroxide blond hair. The woman spoke with a broad inflection that Rosalyn couldn't quite place: it sounded British, but not quite.

"The kids in the pediatric ward decorated it for me. Not bad, eh?"

"Very pretty."

"I'm Emma Kinsley, by the way, from Coonawarra. Do you happen to know it?"

"I'm afraid I don't."

"Would've been shocked if you did. Australia. Tiny town, really, located somewhere between Adelaide and Melbourne. And you?"

"Rosalyn Acosta. Nice to meet you."

"Sheesh, I'm such a drongo," said Emma, watching as Rosalyn gathered whatever papers she could reach without unbuckling her seat belt.

"Drongo?"

"Klutz, I should say. Look at this: History is scattered at our feet. There's a metaphor in there, wouldn't you say, Rosalyn?"

The papers appeared to be an assortment of handwritten letters, yellowed with age. Some were still in envelopes; others were loose; most were written in French, a few pages in English. But Rosalyn barely glanced at the correspondence. Instead, her heart fell at the thought of spending the next ten hours or so in forced companionship with a chatty seatmate.

I should have traded in the first-class ticket for an empty row in coach so I would have had privacy, Rosalyn thought.

It wasn't that there was anything particularly off-putting about Emma; it was just that, deep

24

down, Rosalyn didn't want to chat. With anyone. At all. Perhaps ever. *Anyone else in my situation would be happy,* Rosalyn reminded herself for the thousandth time. As everyone from Rosalyn's mother to the mail carrier had remarked, an all-expenses-paid trip to Champagne—with a couple of days in Paris, no less—sounded like a dream come true.

But lately stories of recluses had been resonating with Rosalyn: Emily Dickinson and Emily Brontë, J. D. Salinger and Henry Thoreau; various hermits in the history of numerous religions—there were a number of hermitic saints in Christendom, she knew, though she couldn't put names to them. Rosalyn certainly wouldn't describe herself as a person who emulated the saintly in any way, yet she would be willing to take the vow if it meant she could hide away somewhere in harsh monastic silence. No questions, no comments, no advice.

And yet here she was.

"So, tell me," Emma continued as Rosalyn handed her the last of the letters she had been able to gather. "What's waiting for you in France, Rosalyn? Business or pleasure?"

"I . . . I'm going on business," said Rosalyn.

The plane achieved altitude, the seat belt light pinged off, and a flight attendant came over and smoothly gathered the rest of the dropped papers, placing them in a messy stack on Emma's tray.

"What kind of business?"

"I work for a wine importer based in the Napa Valley. I'm going to Champagne to—"

"No!"

"Excuse me?"

"I'm going to Champagne, too!"

"Oh. How about that?"

"What a coincidence! Maybe we should commandeer the plane and make it land a bit closer to our destination. Don't you just *despise* landing after a long flight and then having to drive *another* couple of hours, with jet lag, no less? How are you getting there?"

"I have a rental car reserved."

"You should ride with me! I've got a driver picking me up: a very tall, dark, handsome man, not that I notice such things. But the Champagne region isn't that big. I'm sure we could drop you off with no problem."

This is a nightmare, Rosalyn thought. But then she checked herself: not a nightmare, not really, not in comparison with so much. Still, it was awkward. But as Dash used to say, *"Awkward never killed anybody."*

"I wouldn't want to be any bother," Rosalyn began. "I—"

"Nonsense. You'll come with me, and I'll drop you off." Emma started paging through the letters, shaking her head and muttering. "Just look at this mess. I had these in order by date, and now I have to start all over again. What a pain. So, where exactly are you headed?"

"A small town called Cochet, but—"

"*Cochet?* Good *God,* what's in Cochet?"

"A, um, champagne producer offered me use of his *gîte.*"

Gîtes were vacation rentals—sometimes a small cottage, sometimes a room in a house. Wine producers in France often kept accommodations for visiting buyers, or rented them out to tourists for a little extra cash. They had done so long before the advent of Airbnb.

"Tell me we're not talking about Blé Champagne, as in Gaspard Blé."

"Yes, as a matter of fact. You know him?"

"Ha! Blé's a . . . How should I say it? An associate of mine. Be careful with that one. Gaspard fancies himself quite the ladies' man, if you know what I mean."

"Is he really that bad?"

"Not actually." Emma waved her hand and chuckled. "He's charming. He's just a bit of an old-school-style rake."

"How do you know him?"

"I've been investing in the region for a while. Gaspard and I go back a ways . . . even had a brief fling, once, if I recall."

Rosalyn's eyebrows rose in surprise.

"Every once in a while a little Neanderthal energy can be fun in the bedroom." Emma

27

gave a knowing smile. "Anyways, I'm worried about you! There's absolutely *nothing* in that little town. One little store and that's it. Not even a *boulangerie*, and who's ever heard of a French village without a *boulangerie*? It's not even particularly charming—most of the older buildings were destroyed during the wars. In fact, as a general rule in Champagne, you won't find the kind of delightfully medieval villages that characterize the south of France."

"I'm not looking for charming villages. I'm going on business."

"Huh." Emma stared at her for a long moment. Rosalyn found her steady gaze disconcerting. Intelligence shone in Emma's dark eyes, and there was a level of perception beyond the norm that belied her casual words. "So what will you be doing there?"

"I'm supposed to be making some connections for my boss, Hugh Small, from Small Fortune Wines."

"Oh! You know who you should talk to? Comtois Père et Fils. Do you know them?"

"I don't know anyone yet."

"Jérôme Comtois is now the *fils*, the son, of Comtois Père et Fils. French to the core, though I imagine he speaks English well, thank the heavens. Used to be a professor of English literature at the Sorbonne, as a matter of fact."

"And now he grows grapes?"

Emma nodded. "Long story involving a rascal of an older brother who was supposed to take over the family business but instead ran off to be a beach bum in Thailand. At least that's the way I heard it. The whole thing was one big mess because the father had run the place into the ground, but since it's been in the family for generations, it carries the weight of history. So when his brother abandoned the family, Jérôme felt compelled to step in and take over. His wife at the time—an American like you, by the way—didn't like country life and returned to Paris. Rumor has it she had been having a fling with the older brother, which wouldn't surprise me in the least, but you didn't hear that from me. I'd hate to spread gossip."

Rosalyn realized that she was listening with rapt attention, her mouth hanging open. Chagrined, she closed it. "Is he . . . Do you know him well?" Rosalyn asked.

"Who?"

"Jérôme Comtois?"

"Oh, no, never met the man."

"Then . . . ?"

"You're wondering what his story has to do with *me*. Thing is, he inherited this collection of wine-making paraphernalia that his parents, grandparents, and *great*-grandparents had acquired over the years—according to what I've heard, there are ancient winepresses and old corks, a million things stored down in those cellars. I hesitate to call it a museum, but that's what the sign says—though last time I checked, Jérôme had taken the sign down. Supposedly there's also an old library chock-full of books and documents, including some items salvaged after the wars. I've been in touch with a historical archive in Reims, and the archivist suggested I take a look at the Comtois collection. I've tried to get Jérôme to give me permission to look through the place, but so far, no luck."

"Why do you want access?"

"Because of these letters." She held up the messy stack and let out a dramatic sigh. "I had everything organized by date."

Despite herself, Rosalyn was becoming intrigued by Emma's convoluted story. "So who are the letters from?"

"A French soldier in World War One, named Émile Legrand. His family had a farm on the outskirts of Reims, which I'm sure you know is the capital of Champagne."

Rosalyn noticed that Emma pronounced Reims in the French manner, which sounded like *Rance.*

"It's the correspondence between Legrand and my great-aunt Doris, who lived in Australia," continued Emma. "Doris was a real Francophile; from what I hear, she went to Paris on her honeymoon, and then traveled back to France after the war. But she never let on that she had a secret life. The little scamp."

"Maybe it was a secret romance."

"Perhaps, but I don't think so. I haven't made my way through many of these—there are hundreds of them. I suppose it's possible their relationship was romantic, though Doris was a lot older than Émile. Still, while the French don't mind the older woman–younger man dynamic—bless their Gallic hearts—I think it was more of a simple pen pal situation."

"How did they become pen pals?"

"Have you ever heard of the *marraines de guerre*?"

Rosalyn shook her head. Before Emma could explain, the flight attendant stopped at their row and offered them flutes of champagne.

"Ah! *Fantastique*! *Merci*." Emma accepted a flute with a grateful flourish. "I swear I was about to perish of thirst."

Rosalyn took a proffered flute and set it on the tray in front of her, watching the minuscule bubbles rising through the liquid gold. She wished she liked champagne. She wished she could enjoy the attentive first-class service. Mostly, she wished she were somewhere else. Some*one* else.

"So, have you heard of them?" Emma asked.

"I'm sorry—who?"

"The *marraines de guerre*? From World War One."

Rosalyn shook her head. "I don't know much about the First World War, except that it was supposed to be the war that ended all wars."

"Yes, we all saw how well *that* worked out. But you're in good company: The Great War has been overshadowed by the very war it was supposed to prevent. All the movies are about World War *Two,* not One. . . ." Emma trailed off as though pondering the significance of her own words, then took a hearty gulp of champagne. "Makes sense, if you think about it. *Nazis.* The perfect cinematic foil."

"So . . . *marraine* means 'godmother'?"

"Right. They were the 'war godmothers.' Sounds better in French. You speak French?"

"Some. I studied it in college, and I've been cramming while prepping for this trip, but I'm rusty."

"I find the key to speaking well is to drink plenty of champagne." Emma glanced at Rosalyn's untouched glass and held her flute up: "To champagne!"

With reluctance, Rosalyn raised her glass and they *tink*ed.

Dash's last New Year's Eve: the indoor rainstorm over the pool at the Tonga Room in the Fairmont Hotel, everyone laughing. Dash was the life of the party, as always, making instant friends with those dining at the neighboring tables. He had rented a luxury suite for the night.

32

No expense spared for his love, his bride, his girl.

Rosalyn imagined that the people sitting in economy were drinking their bubbly from plastic cups—assuming they were served champagne at all. She suddenly resented the formal, slick coolness of the first-class glassware. *Don't be ridiculous, Rosie,* she chided herself. *It's just a glass.* She took a sip. The wine tasted sour, the bubbles shocking her tongue, tickling her nose, annoying her.

Nope. Definitely not a champagne fan.

"So," Emma continued, seemingly oblivious to Rosalyn's lack of enthusiasm, "the *marraines de guerre* wrote to soldiers at the front to keep their spirits up. The soldiers were young men from all over France. Sometimes they didn't have family members to write to them, and sometimes the postal service from their hometowns was cut off. So the *marraines* filled in, writing to the boys and sending them occasional care packages of socks and baked goods. The idea was that the personal connection with folks back home would bolster morale, remind the men of what they were fighting for."

"Oh, that's"—Rosalyn searched for the words—"that's really sweet, but also sort of tragic."

"You want to hear something funny? At the time, the program was criticized—a lot of people thought it was immoral."

"Is that so? It sounds positively Victorian, if you ask me. I mean, they were pen pals; what could happen?"

"Never underestimate the ability of some people to fear something new," Emma said. "Many of the *marraines* were single, and critics suggested that the unmarried young ladies writing to young men would encourage disgraceful thoughts and behavior. How that would work wasn't exactly spelled out, but the war did bring about a lot of changes and a loosening of social traditions. Still, considering how many of the soldiers didn't make it out of the war alive, or at least whole, I suppose the point was largely moot."

The flight attendant stopped by to take their dinner orders. Rosalyn handed her nearly full champagne flute back and asked for a glass of red wine, prompting a subtle lifting of the eyebrows from the attendant.

Rosalyn felt Emma's eyes on her. She considered ending their conversation by claiming she needed to listen to her French-language podcast, but their dinner would soon be served, and she didn't want to be rude.

Besides, the topic they had been discussing intrigued her, despite herself.

"So, your aunt was a *marraine de guerre*?" Rosalyn asked.

"Yes. She was born and raised in Australia, but her mother came from France. Doris was very wealthy, with patriotic feeling for France, as well as Australia, which had entered the war alongside Great Britain. I never knew her—she was actually my great-*great*-aunt, I guess, the sister of my great-grandfather—but according to family lore she was a strong-minded woman, a wealthy widow, accustomed to getting her own way. She didn't have children, so maybe this was her way of showing maternal affection. However she managed it, she and Émile kept up their correspondence throughout the war."

"I noticed one of the letters was in English."

"When she first began the correspondence, Doris composed her thoughts in English before translating them into French. But I suppose she became more confident about her French over time and stopped writing the English drafts, or if she still did, I couldn't find them. Émile mentioned he carried Doris's letters with him, in a bundle in his knapsack, and put them in a safe place whenever he returned to Reims. I'm hoping I might be able to find them."

"That's why you're interested in the Comtois collection?"

Emma nodded. "It's a long shot, I know, and that generation is long gone, but I was hoping there might be some reference to them in the museum. I'm no historian, but don't you think this story would make a fascinating book, with both sides of the correspondence?"

"It would. But didn't you say Jérôme Comtois has closed his museum?"

She looked pensive. "I'm hoping he's just being ornery. He's a bit prickly, doesn't like tourists. Then again, he had the family business foisted upon him, so perhaps he'll mellow over time."

"So that's the reason you're going to Champagne? To find your aunt's letters?"

Emma waved a hand in the air. Broad and slightly bony, it was a hand seemingly more suited to hard work than to manicures. "No, I'm checking on a few vineyards I've invested in."

"Champagne vineyards? I'm impressed."

She shrugged. "Sounds fancier than it really is. As I'm sure you know, vineyards are just farms, after all. And it's in the blood; I was raised in the wine business in Australia. You're Californian?"

"How did you know?"

"You mentioned Napa. Also, the accent."

"We Californians like to say we don't have an accent."

Emma's laugh was loud and bold, a raucous party. "*Everybody* has an accent. So, surely you're not just *working* in Champagne? Meeting a lover, perhaps?"

A pang, deep in her belly. *Climbing the steps to the Basilique du Sacré-Coeur, strolling hand in hand past artists' galleries, poking through the Montmartre cemetery. Imagining Picasso and Degas, Toulouse-Lautrec and Renoir, wandering those same cobblestone alleyways, now swamped with tourists. Shivering while eating gelato in the park, because even though the day was freezing, the ice cream was too good to resist. Dash bought a silver necklace from a tiny, abandoned-looking jewelry store hidden in a courtyard; the handmade locket hung from a delicate-looking chain. He fastened it around her neck, his nimble hands warm on her skin. From that moment, she had never taken the locket off.*

The sheer romance of feeling safe and taken care of, in love with the man who had just become her husband. She had felt so proud, so vital.

She had been so young.

Once again, Rosalyn felt Emma's eyes studying her and forced herself back to their conversation. This was a classic sign of grief brain, a frequent topic of conversation in the support group she met with for the young bereaved. Jumping from one topic to the next, having difficulty maintaining a train of thought, losing the threads of conversations. It had faded over time but was still there, lurking at the edges of her consciousness, rearing its head especially when she felt stressed or tired.

"No, just business," Rosalyn said. "I'll be checking in with some champagne producers, and representing Small Fortune Wines at the festival of Saint Vincent."

"Oh, that's great! I'll be at the festival, too. It ought to be cracking."

"I'm sure," Rosalyn said, accepting with an appreciative sigh her glass of red wine from the flight attendant.

"But you're not looking forward to it." It was a statement, not a question.

"It's not that, not exactly. I'm just not really a party person."

"An introvert, eh?"

"Something like that."

Emma's dark eyebrows rose. "And yet you're in the wine business?"

Rosalyn let out a wry chuckle. "So it seems."

Emma smiled, her eyes searching Rosalyn's face. After a long moment, she asked, "Were you always an introvert? Or only since your heart was broken?"

The breath caught in Rosalyn's throat. When she spoke, her voice was strained. "Excuse me?"

"It's all over your face, poor thing."

Suddenly Rosalyn was drowning, her eyes stinging and filling with tears. She scolded herself—*not now not now not now*—wishing she were back home, ensconced in her little cottage in the vineyard, where she could curl up on the cold tile of the bathroom floor and keen into one of Dash's old T-shirts, even though they'd long since lost the scent of him.

She took a long pull on her wine, gulping twice,

breaking any number of rules of etiquette about taking small, graceful sips in order to appreciate the full flavor.

Ten long, slow breaths.

Rosalyn felt a surge of gratitude when the older woman turned her attention back to the letters. It would only make things worse if Emma reached out to rub her shoulder or grasp her hand, asking her what was wrong—or, worse, apologizing for making her cry. That always made Rosalyn feel as if *she* should apologize for making the other person feel bad in the first place. C. S. Lewis wrote that grief felt a great deal like fear: the fluttering in the stomach, the repeated swallowing, the impulse to flee. That was all true, but to Rosalyn, it was so much more. Still, in a strange way, the grief itself helped her cope; it muted everything so that she could rarely summon the energy to dwell on all she had lost.

Not just Dash, but the life they'd had together. The future they had dreamed of. Even their past.

Rosalyn had lost the person who had accompanied Dash to Paris.

She had no idea who she was anymore.

Chapter Three

I t's going to take forever to put these back in order," Emma muttered as she opened one set of folded sheets. "Listen to this: 'April 26, 1916. "Lucie says the blind woman must be granted the prettiest teacup, because who understands beauty more than those who have lost their sight?"' Isn't that lovely? By his own admission, Émile Legrand was not an educated man, but if you ask me, he had the soul of a poet."

"You mentioned he was a farm boy," Rosalyn said, grateful for the distraction. "I'm surprised he was so well-read."

"Émile's fascinating. I wonder whether he was this charming in person, or if he simply had a way with the written word. He wrote two or three letters a week to Doris; I have the sense they were an important outlet for him, helped him survive the trenches."

"Who is the Lucie he mentions?"

"Mademoiselle Lucie Maréchal. She was living in the caves under the city of Reims."

"Why was she in the caves?"

"During the war, Reims was surrounded by the

German army, which shelled the city for years. Something like ninety percent of the buildings were destroyed, and thousands of civilians were killed. A lot of the citizenry sought shelter in the caves beneath the champagne houses. You've never been to Reims?"

Rosalyn shook her head. "Just Paris." *The lamppost on the corner, shaking off snowflakes. "A lifetime of laughter for my beautiful bride. I promise."* "So, what are you going to do with the letters?"

"At the moment, I'm just curious to see how many I can find. My grandmother used to tell me stories about Doris when I was little, and for whatever reason, I've always felt a special connection to her. I'm going to try to find a historian or someone to write a book about their story."

"Why not write it yourself?"

Emma smiled. "Prose—not to mention organization—is not my strong suit. And it will take a lot of work to get everything translated. But I figured while in Champagne, I should search the archives. And I've put out some feelers with a few people who will let me root through their attics; and there may still be some Legrands in the area. It's a long shot, but in my experience a lot of Frenchies have ancient family homes that are passed down through the generations, and since they never throw anything away, it's entirely possible something might be tucked away in some corner of a dusty attic. Maybe even some photos; can you imagine? It would mean the world to my mother, if I could find them. She's a nut for family history."

"Your mother's still with you?" Rosalyn asked.

Emma nodded but said nothing; her lips pursed slightly.

"Did . . . did Émile survive the war?" Rosalyn asked, suddenly sure she knew the answer.

Emma hesitated. "I don't know. I haven't found an official announcement from the war bureau, or anything like that. But like I said, I haven't gotten to the last letter. Not even sure where it is. I started to put them in order, but it's not easy reading with that stylized script and fading ink, not to mention the censorship."

"I noticed bits and pieces of the letters are cut out, or blacked out."

"Yup. Wartime correspondence was subjected to 'Anastasia's scissors.' The *poilus* weren't allowed to tell anyone where they were, or where they were headed. Anything that even *hinted* at their location or destination was censored. Every once in a while some of the letters slipped past the censors, but it was rare."

"Sorry—who were the *poilus*?"

"The French soldiers—the regular boys, not the officers."

"Doesn't *poilu* mean . . . ?"

" 'Hairy,' " Emma confirmed with a nod. "Living in the trenches for days or weeks or months at a time, it was hard to shave or get a haircut, so the soldiers started to wear their hair as a badge of honor. Being hairy was associated with masculinity, being fierce and brave."

By now Rosalyn had part of the stack in front of her and was trying to match the free pages with their envelopes, putting the military envelopes in order by the dates stamped on the front or, in the case of stamps too faint to read, by the dates written on the letters. It was oddly calming, holding history in her hands. She imagined the words being carefully jotted down on the fragile onionskin paper in muddy trenches, the likelihood that Émile had never made it home from the front. The agony of his loved ones upon hearing the news.

It was profoundly unsettling to find other people's misfortunes comforting. Whenever she spotted a cemetery, Rosalyn would stop and meander through, hungrily searching the headstones for evidence of young men dying in the prime of life. It wasn't schadenfreude—she would never wish this pain on another—but rather the recognition of a fellow sufferer. A strange, fathomless kinship.

She wasn't the only one. Others had survived far worse.

Some, for instance, were forced to live in

caves to escape the hell raining down upon their city.

"Anyway, I had planned to check in with my wine producers and vineyard managers, and then do some snooping around in attics." Emma gestured to her cast, shook her head, and let out a sigh worthy of a martyr. "But now *that* plan is a bust. Old French homes aren't exactly built for the disabled."

"I'm sorry to hear that. What happened to your leg?"

"An unfortunate encounter with a taxi on Bush Street, right outside the Chinatown gates. Ruined a damned fine pair of jeans. But I suppose it could have been worse."

Rosalyn nodded and turned her attention back to the letters. Emma was right. They weren't easy to read, but with the aid of the dictionary on her computer, she made out a few snatches of lines: ". . . The air is thick with grenades and trench mortars. These last are a diabolical kind of toy. Their explosion feels like ten earthquakes rolled into one."

"Intriguing, aren't they?" Emma asked.

"They are." Undeniably so. It wasn't just what the words said that captivated Rosalyn. It was the ghostly presence of the hand moving across the paper a century ago, the lingering stories of lives long gone. A tangible remnant of the past.

The crumbling letters left tiny bits of brown

and yellow dust on her tray and the pads of her fingers. Traces of a long-ago life.

"The letters don't paint a very pretty picture, though, do they?" said Rosalyn, as she tried to decipher a description of life on the front. "A bunch of hairy men living in muddy trenches—can you imagine the smell?"

Emma laughed that boisterous laugh again. "Smelling good was the least of their worries."

"I'm curious, though," Rosalyn continued. "If things were as bad as all that, how was there mail delivery to and from troops?"

"The French government made delivering the mail a priority. Most of the fighting was on the western front, near France's borders with Germany and Belgium. But the soldiers came from all over France. It was a dreadful war, with a tragically high casualty rate. In order for the *poilus* to risk their lives for *la patrie*—and accept that they might be injured or die—they needed to maintain their connection to the folks back home. That wasn't always possible, though. Reims, for example, was so cut off from the outside world that some of the businesses that still operated issued their own currency in lieu of banknotes. I doubt the postal service could get in or out."

"I wonder what happened to Lucie. Her story could make a very interesting part of your book."

Emma nodded. "I hope to see if I can find any descendants of Lucie Maréchal in the area.

Émile's letters create quite the vivid portrait. As I said, it's likely that Émile died—along with a million and a half others—but if not, I might be able to find his descendants."

It did seem like a long shot, Rosalyn thought. Still, while the Great War seemed like ancient history, it really was only a few generations in the past. It wasn't unreasonable to think that letters and other documents remained tucked away in family albums or attics. Rosalyn had left old school papers and other relics at her childhood home until her mother moved recently. It could happen.

The flight attendants began the dinner service, and Rosalyn was disappointed when Emma tucked the letters back into their inadequate folder. The meal was delicious—nothing at all like the airplane food people used to complain about, back when complimentary meals were offered on most flights. Rosalyn had to admit that the French knew how to do air travel—at least in first class.

Rosalyn was on her third glass of wine when Emma suddenly said, "Hey! I don't suppose you'd like to go on the hunt for me? I'll pay you, of course—I'm quite wealthy."

"Oh . . . thanks, but I have a job."

"But you don't like it."

Rosalyn let out a startled, breathy laugh.

"Doesn't hunting down old letters sound more interesting than what you're doing?"

"Well, yes, but there's also . . ." A debt to be repaid, a debt that could never be repaid. Hugh had done so much for her. "I'm only in France for a few weeks, and I have to fulfill my obligation to my boss."

"I can work with that. Just change your return ticket and stay a few more weeks. I'll make it worth your while."

"I really don't think so. But thanks for the offer."

Emma shrugged and mopped up the last of the sauce on her plate with a dinner roll. "It was worth a shot. I suppose I could see if there's a local I could bribe. It's just that you speak English, thank God. Speaking French is such a *burden*. And I like you. I think we're on the same wavelength."

Rosalyn looked at her with surprise. Emma was so open, so seemingly eager to embrace life in all dimensions. Rosalyn was the opposite: a cardboard cutout masquerading as a person.

Emma leaned into her slightly. "I'm not saying we're *alike,* Rosalyn. I'm saying I think you understand me. It's not just because we're both native English speakers—I spent a year at the Sorbonne and speak French passably well, but that does not mean the French and I understand each other. They are an odd lot, aren't they? Fabulous, but odd. They treat you like a leper if you want to make a meal out of a bag of chips,

47

for instance. Americans, on the other hand, I feel a certain kinship with. Might be the British-colonial thing—you Americans have a lot in common with us Aussies."

"Maybe so," said Rosalyn with a smile.

"Your attitude toward smoking, on the other hand . . ." She trailed off, popping a piece of Nicorette gum. "Can't believe we can't smoke on planes. Is there no civilization anymore? Did you know that the French are so antiauthoritarian that smoking rates went *up* after it was banned from public buildings? They also cut in lines. You Americans, on the other hand, are far too puritanical in that regard."

"When it comes to line cutting or smoking?"

"Both, but I was thinking of smoking."

"Not sure we can blame the Puritans for that one. I think it has more to do with lung cancer rates."

Emma waved her off. "Never underestimate your history of puritanism. Like how obsessed you Yanks are with sex, but get freaked out at nudity."

"We're a puzzle, all right," Rosalyn mumbled, then downed the last dregs of her wine and wished she had more. She had no desire to indulge in a battle of cultures, nor did she want to represent all Americans to the French—or to the Aussies, for that matter. Weren't we all individuals, after all? And besides that . . . Rosalyn didn't feel capable of representing anyone at the moment, much less an entire nation. She was a bubble-wrapped Christmas ornament, ready to shatter.

After dinner, the flight attendants whisked away all evidence of their meal, and the captain dimmed the lights.

"Well, then," said Emma as she fetched earplugs and an eye mask from the pocket in the seat in front of her. "France is nine hours ahead of California, which means they're asleep right now, and so should we be." She popped a pill, then held the vial out to Rosalyn. "Want one?"

"Oh, no, thank you."

"Suit yourself. *Bonne nuit*, Rosalyn. See you in Paris."

Chapter Four

Rosalyn closed her eyes in hopes of getting some rest, but quickly gave up. It was a struggle for her to sleep in her own bed, let alone in public.

She read a novel for a while, but although the bestselling true story of a plucky woman's fight against the violence and corruption in an inner-city school had Hollywood blockbuster written all over it, it failed to hold her interest. Then she scrolled through the selection of in-flight movies, but the stories seemed trivial: the comedies puerile, the dramas unremarkable.

Finally, Rosalyn eased Emma's bright yellow folder of letters over to her tray. Peeking inside, she gently grasped a fat military envelope. It was foxed with mildew, the scent reminding Rosalyn of a used bookstore.

It dawned on her that sorting through musty old letters probably wasn't routine in first class. As if on cue, the well-dressed man across the aisle glanced at her, his elegant nostrils flaring. Rosalyn ignored him.

The onionskin paper crackled as she slipped

it out of the envelope. The handwriting was as before, with that peculiarly French upright script.

Rosalyn used her French travel dictionary as well as her computer to translate, but there were words she didn't recognize and couldn't find in the reference book or online—she imagined they were names of weapons or otherwise war related. The ink was faded in spots, and the stylized cursive was difficult to decipher. And with the occasional phrase cut out or blacked out, it was slow going.

Still, she managed a few paragraphs.

> Lucie tells me that one morning the bombing began again, and the clock was chiming nine o'clock, but it did not have a chance to finish. . . . A xxx burst in through the wall, covering all in dust and chunks of plaster. . . . The tinkling of broken glass . . . The shock of concussion is so hard to describe; it makes one feel injured, even when whole.

Rosalyn perused the abused pages, struggling to understand the language, imagining a long-ago war-torn world, until her eyes grew heavy, and she slept.

She dreamed of the medicine cabinet.

Kneeling on the aqua blue bath mat in front of

the open cabinet, Rosalyn wondered if the medications within would be sufficient to kill her.

She felt strangely detached from the question, and even more so from its implications. When Dash died, Rosalyn had fractured. Something deep down had broken, fragmented, splintered into pointy, stabbing shards. She was a shattered mirror. She was seven years of bad luck.

If it wasn't for bad luck, I wouldn't have no luck at all.

The words of the old song came to Rosalyn's mind, crooned in Dash's husky voice. He wasn't a morning person, but if she gave him his space, he would be humming by the time he emerged from the shower, singing disparate lines of old and new songs, mostly the blues, laughing at the absurdity of the lyrics because, as he had declared on their wedding day—an extravagant affair held outdoors among the grapevines—Dash considered himself to be the luckiest man alive.

His prescriptions were lined up in neat rows on the shelf: amber vials and bottles and bubble packs of painkillers that had cost every cent they had, and then some. All marked with the name of the man Rosalyn had married six years ago and lost two and a half years ago and still loved: Dashiell Anthony Acosta.

Take with food. Do not crush or chew. Take as needed.

What if she crushed *and* chewed them, popped handfuls into her mouth on an empty stomach, *as needed?* She could wash them down with a lovely bottle of Napa Cabernet, as Dash had suggested he do toward the end, when he was trying to celebrate his thirty-eighth birthday—knowing he would never have another birthday—but was too sick to hold anything down. Good reminder: Rosalyn should take an antinausea pill before the others.

This was the sort of thing a person learned when watching her husband struggling to survive, to eradicate murderous cancer cells through chemotherapy and radiation and surgery and drugs and prayer and sheer force of will. Not that any of it mattered in the end.

Ninety-seven days—that was all it took.

Ninety-seven days, from diagnosis to death.

Chapter Five

Upon landing in Paris, Emma and Rosalyn exchanged business cards.

"I'm sure I'll see you in baggage claim, or passport control, or customs," said Emma, urging Rosalyn to go on ahead while she waited for an attendant with a wheelchair. "Sorry to say, none of us is getting out of this airport quickly."

Rosalyn disembarked to the terminal, stopping in a restroom to comb her hair and splash water on her face. She snuck a look at herself in the bathroom mirror and immediately regretted it. Not that anyone looked their best after a transatlantic flight, even in first class. Still.

The face staring back at her was haggard and wan, dark circles underlining her sherry-colored eyes. Her mother would have been appalled, but then, that was nothing new. The Rosalyn-That-Was would have primped for an airplane voyage; she would have kept a makeup bag close at hand. Today's Rosalyn wore no makeup to take the edge off. Her dark brown hair was shaggy and badly in need of a trim; she should have taken care of it before this trip, but the thought of being trapped in a salon chair while a chatty hair stylist fussed over her had been too much to contemplate.

Now she wished she had toughed it out. Somehow it felt worse to look so unkempt in France, among Parisians known the world over for their sense of style. The women at the mirrors on either side of her were well-coiffed and chic, stunning in spite of the harsh fluorescent lighting. Rosalyn hoped standards might be more relaxed out in the countryside, in Champagne.

She practically fell asleep on her feet as she waited, glassy-eyed and bovinelike, in the swollen line for immigration control. Later, at baggage claim, she spotted Emma.

"Still time to change your mind," Emma said as she directed her escort to grab her many bags. "Want to ride with me?"

"I really do appreciate the offer, but I need my own car. I'll be driving all over the region, visiting wineries. And I'm booked in a hotel in Paris for the first couple of days anyway."

"Well, I can hardly argue with Paris. But Champagne's a small place," said Emma. "I'll be staying in Épernay, which is a ways from Cochet, but I feel sure we'll cross paths. If not, give me a shout. Honestly, I would love the company. If for no other reason than that it would be nice to speak English over dinner."

Rosalyn thanked her. On the one hand, she

didn't have the bandwidth for any new "friends." On the other, as Hugh tried to hammer into her, the wine business was all about socializing. She really should inquire about tasting the wines from Emma's vineyards, if they weren't yet represented in the U.S. market. And . . . she would love to find out what had happened with those letters.

"It was really good to meet you," Rosalyn said.

Emma stilled, fixing Rosalyn with that disconcertingly direct gaze. "I try to stay away from giving unsolicited advice, Rosalyn, but believe me when I say: You'll muddle through. Life's not easy, and it sure as hell isn't fair. But we're survivors, you and I. Just keep putting one foot in front of the other."

Rosalyn watched as Emma, the wheelchair, and her escort were swallowed by the crowd milling about the spinning luggage carousels. A second man trotted behind, pushing a trolley loaded high with Emma's matching luggage.

If she hadn't felt so empty inside, Rosalyn would have sworn that she felt bereft.

Almost as if she had lost her only friend in France.

Just keep putting one foot in front of the other.

Emma's parting words reverberated in Rosalyn's mind as she progressed through customs and finally departed from the main terminal to find the taxi stand.

This was the same thing her grandmother had told her at Dash's memorial service, and as far as advice went, it was helpful. Far better than "You'll meet someone else someday," or the ever-popular "He's in a better place; at least he's no longer in pain." Much less the exquisitely painful: "It's a shame you didn't have children so you'd have someone to remember him by."

For the past two years, Rosalyn had been putting one foot in front of the other, like a good soldier marching off to war.

The directive had kept her upright and working, with only intermittent sessions on the bathroom floor, gazing at the medicine cabinet. One foot in front of the other kept her functioning while she settled Dash's estate and came to understand the full extent of her disastrous financial situation. It kept her going while she represented Hugh's wine selection to restaurants, grocery outlets, and liquor stores; pretended to enjoy an occasional get-together with friends; and now landed in France on a trip most would envy.

One foot in front of the other had kept her marking time. Feeling more and more isolated with each passing day, not only from her life with Dash but from the world as a whole. From herself.

Rosalyn had practiced meditation and

breathing exercises and yoga. She had hiked in the redwoods and strolled by the ocean. She had tried journaling but stayed away from art projects—it was too raw, too emotional, to return to the creativity that had once sustained her but now served only to remind her of what it had been like to be happy.

She had stopped going to therapy when the counselor mentioned—tossed off in an almost passing way—that "In this life, pain is not optional, but *suffering* is."

"What the hell is that supposed to mean?" had been the response screaming inside Rosalyn's head. *Suffering is optional?* She had rolled the concept around in her mind for a few days but couldn't absorb the meaning. It felt too much like blame.

Rosalyn canceled her next appointment and didn't go back.

The truth was that there was no remedy to losing a loved one. No way to reframe it, no matter how talented the therapist. No one could say anything to make it better; nothing could be done about it. It was just *there,* hunkering down, a malevolent, unbearable weight she was forced to carry.

"I'm still alive, aren't I?" Rosalyn felt like saying to anyone who suggested she wasn't coping well. It was just that . . . mere survival didn't feel like enough anymore.

One foot in front of the other.

Chapter Six

Lucie

In the before time, the time of sweet oblivion, we had no idea what was to come.

I recall once I threw quite a fit of pique because the pink of my ribbon was not the right hue. I had wanted the ashes of roses of a woman, not the brash, rosy pink of a little girl. After our home was destroyed, I found the length of ribbon in the ruins and used it as a tourniquet on a young soldier whose leg had been blown off by a mortar.

I am quite certain he did not mind which shade of pink was the ribbon.

After war was declared, my father insisted I finally accept an offer of marriage, and so I acquiesced to a young man from a fine family. Like everything else, he was taken away by the war. He rarely writes, or if he does, the letters don't come through. It is hard to imagine him on a battlefield; he had soft hands and an easy, dandified way about him. He is now an officer with the army, but when here in Reims, he had enjoyed parties and dancing and dressing just so.

In the before time, we couldn't believe our

German neighbors to the north would decide to take possession of us. It would be like someone in the house next door, a friend and colleague, coming by and announcing: "This is now *my* house. You will stay and serve me, or you will die." The invasion seemed just that absurd.

Under whose authority does a country, a people, a government, decide such things? Back when my father taught me lessons as I idly spun the big globe in the corner of his study, he would explain that war was terrible but was sometimes necessary.

Father was wrong. This war is indeed terrible, but it is in no way necessary.

I remember the first shell that smashed through the walls of our house. I had been descending the stairs—the massive spiral stairs of which my father was so proud—and the clock on the wall was chiming to tell us it was nine o'clock. It had struck only four chimes when the world exploded.

My ears rang, and I saw but could not hear the tinkling of the shattered windows, shards of glass raining down upon me. I fell several steps down, covered in the white plaster dust of a wall that had disappeared.

Concussion is so . . . *odd.* It leaves one feeling sure one is dead, even without showing any apparent injury. I could not believe I remained whole.

Later, my nose would bleed and my head would ache, perhaps from injury, or maybe my mind itself was damaged and scarred. Later, I would muffle my cries in a pillow while *Maman* carefully picked out the hundreds of tiny splinters of glass embedded in my skin. Later, she would apply her special salve of thyme and lavender, telling me my young flesh would heal with very little trace of the wounds I had suffered.

Much later, I realized that I had survived a shelling, probably by inches. Had I been one step higher or lower on the stairs, I might have lost my legs, or worse.

But at the time I could think only: Am I dead? Have I died this easily?

Papa was too old and frail to join our boys who went to fight; our sweet Henri does what he can, but he, too, was rejected by the military as unsuitable.

So we all remained at our poor, wounded house—a home once so fine it had its own name: Villa Traverne. Several refugees helped us to cover the gaping holes with tar paper to protect us from the rain, and we stayed living there, as though in a giant dollhouse, pretending it was normal to mount stairs that no longer had a wall.

Ours was not the worst on the block. What had once been an esteemed neighborhood now lay open and vulnerable like a stripped carcass, its streets clogged by piles of masonry and broken furniture, and even the bodies of friends and neighbors.

Our homes, our haven, our Reims, in ruins.

In September of 1914, the Germans shelled us for half an hour even though they had already taken control of the city. They wanted to frighten us, make us small. And they did. The streets looked like an artist's conception of hell: iron girders contorted into tortured angles, massive wooden beams splintered into kindling. I am still haunted by the doors and windows that remained, even when all around them had been destroyed. Naked stairways leading into the sky, into the void.

My father begged us to evacuate, but my mother refused.

Maman is unusual for a woman of station. Eugénie Dubois was raised as the daughter of a farmer in the hills outside of Besançon, and learned from her own very humble grandmother how to make salves and ointments from herbs and oils. Though she took on the airs of a fine lady after marrying my father, war changes things. She started knitting sweaters and scarves for the children when the first war refugees arrived in Reims; later, when our neighbor's son showed up on our doorstep in need of care, she took him in and tended to his wounds.

Word spread quickly, and soon enough our

once-fine Villa Traverne became a makeshift clinic, providing refuge to those unable to fight but not so gravely injured as to be evacuated to the military hospital.

My mother taught me to wash wounds with salt water and honey; she applied plasters made of mustard and calendula. We concocted salves from lavender and beeswax, and balms with olive oil and thyme. Rosemary, yarrow, and comfrey leaf reduce itching and scarring; Saint-John's-wort helps with aching joints and nerve pain. Teas of slippery elm bark, sage, and peppermint cure all manner of intestinal ailments, and a shot of pear brandy from our rapidly dwindling cellars was always appreciated.

We didn't have much, but we brought the poor, aggrieved soldiers bowls of soup, crackers with honey, slices of *pain ordinaire au levain*. I do not care for nursing, and am not by nature a physician, but more than anything, these unfortunate men, some merely ailing while others are permanently *mutilés*, needed rest and recuperation, so the nursing was not strenuous.

Through it all, my father left his study less and less; his wool business had included a robust trade with our neighbors to the north, and was now abandoned. Some of our fellow *Rémois* had looked upon us with suspicion because of those German ties, but now none of that matters.

After the invaders marched into Reims, two

soldiers pounded on our still-standing door and demanded to know why we had not evacuated with the others. I explained, in their own language, that we were tending to the sick. They laughed, less interested in the fate of the "dirty French *poilus*" than in the fact that I spoke German. They thought it was a fine thing, and suggested that I could teach the children of Reims to be good German subjects.

I barely refrained from spitting on them.

After a mere eight days, our valiant French forces wrenched control of Reims away from the *Boches*, but the invaders squatted down on the surrounding hills and pelted us with their weapons from afar.

What they could not hold, they were determined to destroy.

Chapter Seven

According to the itinerary Hugh had prepared, Rosalyn was to take a taxi from the airport to a small hotel in the Saint-Germain-des-Prés neighborhood of Paris. She would spend a couple of days getting over jet lag while playing tourist, and then pick up a rental car and drive to Champagne.

Even wrapped in her heavy winter coat, Rosalyn shivered as she dragged her luggage to the taxi stand and joined the long queue. But as she progressed toward the head of the line, her heart started to pound. Nausea roiled in her belly.

Who turns down a free stay in Paris?

Rosalyn, that's who. She simply couldn't stomach the memories. Rosalyn abandoned her place in line, got herself a double shot of espresso, lugged her things over to the rental car counter, and spent half an hour changing her reservation to start right away. Gaspard Blé was out of town, but his office manager had sent an e-mail with the code that opened the door and assured her she was welcome to arrive at any time and make herself at home in *Chambre Chardonnay*.

She entered Blé's address in Cochet into the GPS on her phone, but after tracking down the dark red Renault rental in the dimly lit parking garage and loading her bags, Rosalyn studied the proposed route on a paper map to orient herself.

The old map was soft with wear, tearing at the corners. Hugh had plucked it out of a pile of papers in a dusty corner of his office with a flourish, declaring, "*Here* she is!" Rosalyn ran her fingers along the furred seams, sparing a smile for her occasionally pushy but mostly delightful friend Hugh, wondering how long he had had this map and on what adventures it had accompanied him. It had always amazed her that Hugh was still single; once when Dash teased him about it, Hugh remarked that all the interesting women his age were already taken, and joked that not everyone could marry their young interns.

Charles de Gaulle Airport sat well northeast of Paris, en route to the Champagne region, which meant Cochet was less than two hours away. It took nearly that long to drive from Napa to San Francisco on bad traffic days.

Then again, in California, Rosalyn didn't have to deal with roundabouts. Jittery from the strong espresso, Rosalyn went round and round the first few times before figuring out her exits. The route was a confusing alphabet soup of roads: take D401, also called E50, toward the A4. From there, D23E5 to D23 to D24. *What's wrong with exit numbers?* she thought grumpily. *Better yet, signs reading, "Rosalyn, it's this way"?*

Once she made it to the autoroute, driving became easier and she could relax a little. Soon the outskirts of the city fell away, replaced by lush green forests and farmers' fields.

The light began to dim along the horizon, the cold winter sun going to bed. The flight had arrived a little after three; it had taken a while to retrieve her bags, pass through customs, and rent the car, so Rosalyn hadn't left Paris until after five. There were numerous stops along the autoroute advertising fuel and snacks, but she kept going, determined to reach Cochet before it was pitch-black.

But once she exited the autoroute, Rosalyn started getting truly hungry—a ravenous, panicky emptiness amplified by lack of sleep and the body's confusion induced by jet lag.

Out in the countryside, there was no fast food and, as she'd assumed, certainly no 7-Elevens. Rosalyn passed through one small village after another, their *boulangeries* and butchers long since closed for the night. Hugh's voice whispered in her ear: she should have gone to Paris, where businesses and restaurants stayed open late.

She drove past acre upon acre of vineyards and other crops—wheat and alfalfa, she guessed—

rimmed by tall trees. The landscape was studded with ponds and streams, the fields interrupted now and then by stone farmhouses, some featuring steep turrets and colorful roofs tiled in patterns.

There were no food options at all, apparently, so Rosalyn munched on almonds and a PowerBar as she drove, reflecting upon the irony of being so hungry in what was pretty much universally acknowledged as the culinary capital of the world. Why hadn't she grabbed something besides espresso in the airport? She began torturing herself with the thought of hot, glistening *pommes frites*, or a luscious *pain au chocolat*. Perhaps a nice duck *à l'orange*, or . . . what other dishes were the French famous for? Crêpes, maybe? She didn't know that much about French food, when it came down to it.

Dash had done the ordering for her while on their honeymoon. Mostly, she remembered the bread.

Patches of snow and ice gave testimony to the season, and leftover Christmas decorations, limp and sagging from weather, still adorned the town squares. Homes were dark, their wooden shutters not for show the way they were in Napa—these were actually closed at this hour, giving the villages an unfriendly, stockaded look. Green neon pharmacy signs flashed vulgarly on sleepy main streets, an incongruous modern touch.

Old town houses with shared walls—*maisons de village*—came right up to the street, with at most a tiny walkway separating them from narrow cobblestone roads. The roofs were made of earth red tile; the jagged stone was golden or gray, some partially covered in a mellow yellow stucco.

This is going to be all right, Rosalyn told herself as once again she drove round and round in a roundabout, trying to decipher road signs. Even with the GPS—featuring a polite British voice that asked her to "Please bear right"—it was hard to figure out which exit to take. But what was the worst that could happen? She might wind up sleeping in her car, which would be not great but doable. After all, this was France. Nothing bad happened in France, right?

Just one world war after another.

She had a sudden mental image of Émile Legrand in the trenches, and Lucie Maréchal surviving underground.

One foot in front of the other.

In an effort to fend off sleepiness, Rosalyn went over what she knew about Champagne the region, and champagne the wine. After Hugh had taken pity on her and offered her a job as a wine rep, she had taken classes in viticulture at night school.

She had learned that the region of Champagne was tightly controlled by panels of representatives

69

who dictated everything from when the grapes were ready for harvest to how much inventory each winemaker must keep on hand for reserve, how much they were allowed to sell, and even the use of pesticides.

Le champagne vient de la Champagne; champagne (the drink) comes from the (region of) Champagne. Those who loved the bubbly concoction waxed on about the contrast of the masculine with the feminine: the region's chalky, difficult soil giving rise to one of the world's most delicate beverages. Rosalyn had also learned that a series of international treaties meant that the French owned the designation "champagne" and had a coronary whenever people outside the geographical region applied the term to their sparkling wines. The U.S. hadn't signed on to the treaties at the time due to Prohibition, leading to a persistent sense of resentment among the *Champenois*.

At long last, Rosalyn spotted a small sign: COCHET.

Emma Kinsley hadn't been kidding: there wasn't much to it. Surrounded by farmers' fields, the town consisted of a collection of houses, an old stone church, a *mairie*—a town hall—a small school, a grocery store, and a mechanic's shop, all of which were shuttered.

Rosalyn kept her eyes peeled for the address of Gaspard Blé's *gîte*, but before she knew it, she had left Cochet behind. She realized this not only because she was once again surrounded by fields, but also because French town limits were indicated by a road sign with the name of the town bisected by a huge red line: a vivid indication that you were no longer in the town.

Having continued until coming to a small turn-out, Rosalyn carefully navigated a change of direction—no small feat given the deep irrigation ditches that ran along both sides of the narrow road, which had neither bike lanes nor shoulders. She had been warned that the French drove fast on these rural highways. Flustered, she made her many-pointed turn as quickly as possible, and headed back into Cochet.

Finally, she spotted Blé's address at a sharp turn in the road. She proceeded slowly down a gravel lane, her tires popping and spitting, until she reached a courtyard surrounded by several disappointingly modern buildings, not unlike what she might have seen in Napa. There were no lights on, and no cars in the lot. A building to the left sported a large sign: BLÉ CHAMPAGNE/SALON DE DÉGUSTATION/TASTING ROOM. A building to the right had a small entryway with a glass door, and as the headlights illuminated within, she could see signs over the interior doors: CHAMBRE CHARDONNAY, CHAMBRE PINOT MEUNIER.

Fingers numbed by the cold, she struggled to

input the code on the electronic keypad to the left of the entry, praying it wouldn't lock her out if she got the password wrong too many times, like her bank's ATM seemed to enjoy doing. Clearly there was no hotel in Cochet, and now that she realized just how cold it was, sleeping in the car was not an option.

Success. The door buzzed, and she entered into a blessedly warm tiled foyer.

Rosalyn opened the door to *Chambre Chardonnay* and flicked on the lights to reveal a large room with a tiled floor and pristine cream-colored walls. Near the entry stood a tall chest of drawers and a round oak table with four chairs, and at the other end a double bed and two nightstands. There was an en suite bathroom with a large shower and a separate toilet room, as well as an empty closet with shelves and a rod.

That was it. Nice, and roomy, but . . . sterile.

One large window would look out onto the courtyard and parking area, Rosalyn imagined, except that a rolling shutter was closed over it, the type shop owners used to keep thieves at bay. A button on one side of the window presumably operated the shutters, but no matter how she pressed it, nothing happened. Despite the bright overhead lights, the room felt dark, almost cavelike.

On the table was a bottle of champagne, atop

a note written in a distinctive upright French script:

> Dear Madame Acosta,
> I am very sorry I am not here to greet you properly. Our man Pietro Santini will come if you need anything. His number is by the telephone. Please to help yourself to anything from the kitchen—and to champagne! It is located in the building next door. The code is 1914. The code to access the Internet is 2343sf532fhlik58089bxjk5.
> Cordially,
> Blondine Blé, daughter of Gaspard Blé

Waves of fatigue washing over her—it had been a *very* long travel day—Rosalyn propped the main door open with her purse while she unpacked the car, her ungloved hands freezing. After rolling everything inside, she pulled the door shut tightly and set about organizing her home for the next few weeks. She cranked up the heat, stashed her clothes in the closet and her toiletries in the bathroom, and set up her computer on the table, plugging it into an outlet to charge, using the foreign adapters Hugh had reminded her to pack.

Now what?

Rosalyn perched on the edge of the bed and ate

half of another PowerBar, washing it down with tap water, wishing for junk food and a bottle of red.

She had been a stickler about her diet until Dash got sick, at which point she had alternated between eating nothing at all and periodically stuffing herself with junk. In her experience, hospital vending machines were stocked with exactly the kinds of rubbish foods that landed so many people in the hospital in the first place, ironically enough. In an effort to use this trip to modify her habits, Rosalyn had packed only healthy snacks. She glared at them now with distaste; eating well had seemed like a much better idea when she wasn't hungry. At the moment, she yearned for potato chips, chocolate, the salty-sweet temptations of a PayDay bar.

What a rotten time to decide to be virtuous.

Hunger temporarily if unsatisfactorily sated, she kicked off her shoes and reclined on the bed. The quilt was filled with fluffy goose down, and she sank into its softness with a sigh, closing her eyes, grateful to be horizontal.

Unbidden, images flashed through her tired mind: the medicine cabinet in her little cottage in Napa; Dash in his last moments, pale and cruelly shrunken on the hospital bed; the way she had run from the room. She thought of how desperately she longed no longer to put one foot in front of the other.

She was weary. Depleted. Desperate.

In France.

A country apparently devoid of twenty-four-hour convenience stores.

Damn Hugh, anyway.

Chapter Eight

Rosalyn had come to know when sleep was a lost cause. After half an hour she climbed out of bed, crossed over to the little table, started up her computer, and opened her Internet browser.

There were a few work e-mail messages waiting for her, but nothing pressing. She sent notes to Hugh and her mother to let them know she had arrived safely. None of the local champagne vintners had returned the messages she had sent earlier asking to arrange tastings, so she rooted through her shoulder bag to find the longer list of producers Hugh had suggested she meet with in Champagne.

Her hand stilled when she came across one of Emma's old letters stuck in a side pocket.

The envelope was stamped January of 1915, by which point Émile and Doris had been corresponding for a few months. As she had on the plane, Rosalyn studied the letter with a wordless sort of reverence: the military envelope, the yellowing onionskin paper, the ink fading to a rusty brown at times so faint she could barely make it out. Dark splatters of some substance—mud? Coffee? Blood?—marred one edge.

She brought out her travel dictionary, opened the bookmarked website that translated French into English, and began to decipher the letter as best she could. There were words she didn't know, phrases she didn't understand—but at least very little had been cut out or censored.

It was laborious but fascinating work. From time to time, the faded ink was so hard to read that she had to squint to decipher the letters, or resort to an educated guess based upon the meaning of the rest of the sentence. Other words and phrases were legible but unfamiliar, necessitating a thorough search of the dictionary and website, cross-referencing to be sure she understood their true meanings in context. Most challenging were the idiomatic expressions, which conveyed great meaning but defied word-for-word translations—she marked those with the placeholder "xxx."

She brought out her journal and began a list of unknown words and mysterious phrases; maybe she could figure them out later, or find a native speaker who could help.

My dear Marraine, Madame Whittaker,

I do hope my meaning won't be lost or altered by the censors. But word has come down that the censors have been xxx with too much mail to analyze, so now it is a lottery to see what shall make it through!

Shall I tell you the difficulty that sometimes exists between poilus and the officers? They are men from higher classes, no more attuned to war than we poor farmers. Some are decent types, but others xxx. There have been mutinies, soldiers tried for treason and shot down dead with French bullets, not for cowardice but for the sin of not wishing to face bullets and poison gas, shielded only by their too fragile human flesh. (If Anastasia's scissors are sharpened, I'm sure none of that will survive.)

One of the officers is affianced to a young lady from Reims, named Lucie Maréchal. I will not mention the gentleman's name, which would mean nothing to you, of course, but he was known to me in Reims. He and his brothers xxx and xxx were in the habit of hunting in the fields not far from our home, on the outskirts of the city. Often he would stop to purchase a jar of my honey—my bees were known to produce among the finest honey in the region—and he was always trying to negotiate me down from my standard price.

With communication with Reims disrupted, he has been set upon by the fear that the young lady in question is being unfaithful, or perhaps has been harmed or xxx in some way. It seems she declined to evacuate the city when she had the chance; I cannot understand why.

I did not have an acquaintance with this young lady, but because I know Reims, and he and I were known to each other, the officer has sent me to the city to gather intelligence—and to carry a gift and letter to his beloved. He claims he is unable to leave his important post, though I believe it is more likely he fears the treacherous trip in and out of the city. Risking my life to pass through the dangerous zone for an invented purpose xxx as ridiculous as so much else in this war; as I'm sure you know, it is never guaranteed that one will survive the expedition.

Refusing a direct order is not possible, so I went, and took heart from knowing I would be able to see for myself as to the well-being of my old neighbors and my beloved city. My own dear family has evacuated to the south, thank the heavens, but I was happy to return to Reims, if only to indulge in a bottle or two of my region's famous bubbly nectar. In the trenches our only luxury is our daily ration of wine and brandy. When in Reims I felt sure I would be able to imbibe at will.

I will not describe for you at present what I discovered in the formerly handsome streets of my city. My heart is still broken at the scandalous devastation, not only of the homes and businesses, but even the great cathedral, where the kings of France have been crowned through the ages, where Joan of Arc rode in to savor her victory.

The Huns have done their best to destroy it, and along with it, our very spirit as a people. Whether they will succeed is xxx.

Well, my dear Marraine, what shall I tell you about the young lady in question? I found her in her family home, which had been badly injured by a mortar, losing half the wall that had enclosed a grand staircase. She and her mother were nursing a dozen soldiers along with only one maid. I am certain it was quite a shocking change from their previous life, before the war.

The mademoiselle is beautiful, to be sure, the sweetness of her countenance most welcome after months in the rotten gray muck of the trenches. There is a grace about her, as if she would smell like flowers despite the mud on her face.

I was certain she would be silly and vain, as so many young ladies of her class are. I will admit, with shame, that I was angry at having been sent for such a frivolous reason, and upset at the state of my fair city, and did not mask my feelings around her.

She did not flinch under my harsh words. On the contrary, she smiled and asked what the officer in question had sent her.

It was an intricately carved comb for her long chestnut hair. She laughed when she saw it.

"What good is a comb? A wheel of cheese would have been more welcome."

I was surprised, and pleased at the same time.

When not nursing the soldiers, the mademoiselle's mother knits incessantly and gave me a present to take with me: a knitted balaclava for the officer from Reims, and two pairs of thick wool socks for me. This might seem a small thing. But clean, dry socks are a balm to the poilu, who stands day and night in the muck.

We shared a bottle of champagne—the young lady, her mother, and I. Perhaps it is the contrast of what I have seen these last months, but never have the bubbles tickled my nose in such a joyful fashion, never has the nectar tasted so sweet.

Obviously, since I am writing you this letter, I made it back to my xxx in one piece. Still . . . I think it will take me some time to understand all I saw and felt on my trip back to the city that I once called home.

Rosalyn sat back in her chair and stretched when she came to the end of the letter, feeling a sense of accomplishment. Glancing at the clock, she realized hours had passed while she had been immersed in Émile's world, translating, struggling to understand.

He had signed the missive to his pen pal, *Je vous prie d'accepter, Madame, l'expression de mes sentiments distingués.* She smiled at the oddly formal closing: "I pray you accept, Madame, the expression of my distinguished sentiments." His signature was bold, penned with a flourish:

Émile Paul Legrand

"It's likely that Émile died—along with a million and a half others," Emma had said.

Rosalyn felt a deep pang for all those who had lost their sons, boyfriends, husbands, loved ones during that horrific war. At the same time, she felt solace in their bereaved company.

She hated that.

Rosalyn searched for Emma Kinsley's business card so she could let her know that she had one of her precious letters, but of course she couldn't put her hands on it. Once upon a time, Rosalyn had been an organized person, almost compulsively so. Now, no matter how orderly she started out, things were soon topsy-turvy. Like everything else in her life.

She gave up after a brief search. She would look for the business card in the morning, after she figured out how to open the window and let some natural light into the room.

For now, images of Émile and Lucie's meeting in her head, Rosalyn lay back down under the fluffy duvet and was finally able to fall asleep.

Chapter Nine

Lucie

Let me tell you about the house I grew up in: Villa Traverne.

The walls were made of the finest stone, a gold-veined travertine, and the wood throughout was mahogany, polished to a high sheen. It was four stories tall, with steep roofs of gray slate and tall windows made of blown glass that opened to delicate wrought iron balconies.

The grace of a ballerina combined with the sturdiness of a fortress.

Inside, the walls were stenciled and gilded, Art Nouveau and neoclassicism engaged in an uneasy truce. Columns topped with cupids studded the entry, elaborate mantels crowned every doorway, and carved stone fireplaces warmed each bedroom. Oak floors were inlaid with a Greek key design, covered in thick Turkish rugs.

My older sister, Marguerite, and I used to run through the wide halls, our little brother, Henri, limping behind. We would play hide-and-seek, or pretend we were characters in a novel. Our favorite was *Alice's Adventures in Wonderland*;

we would chase the white rabbit up and down the stairs, ducking into niches or behind curtains, ignoring our nanny's attempts to curtail us.

It has been said that fortunate children take things for granted, and that certainly was the case for me. I didn't see the beauty at the time, much less understand the indescribable pleasures of having enough to eat, a clean, warm bed in which to sleep. In truth, I was a spoiled child who did not appreciate the great privilege into which she was born.

When Marguerite was twelve, she fell ill with scarlet fever. I snuck into her death chamber, wanting to see her, talk to her, certain I could rouse her with a "fairy wand" made of a twisted beech branch that Marguerite had always insisted contained magic. The horrified adults shooed me out, and I never did get to say good-bye. But later from the pile of her belongings meant to be burned, I took a lace shawl I had always admired and wrapped it around me, thinking of Marguerite. I fell ill within a few days, but I did not die. I am quite sure I passed the sickness on to my brother; he, too, recovered, though it took him much longer. Henri had been frail ever since he was injured in a carriage accident at the age of five. I do believe I was responsible for that as well; he had been chasing me when he ran across the street.

Henri survived the fever, but ever after, his

joints ached and he became forgetful and slow. He had to be cared for like a child after that.

One day a soldier arrived on our doorstep dirty, weary, and hungry, much like any other *poilu*.

But he was angry as well. It turned out he was *Rémois*, and this was the first time he had witnessed the destruction of our beloved cathedral. He had sought me out in particular, which made me think he needed nursing. But he looked whole enough, standing on what was left of our porch at the Villa Traverne. When I said so, he seemed confused.

"My name is Émile Legrand," he said. "Your fiancé sent me."

"My fiancé? Has he been wounded?"

"No, mademoiselle. He was well enough when I left him. He has been worried about your welfare."

I held his gaze for a moment. His face was young under the whiskers and dirt, but his eyes looked a thousand years old. They were eyes of war, as I was coming to understand. Eyes that had seen too much. If only the ears were as expressive, for they had no doubt heard too much, the flesh felt too much . . . but it was the eyes that revealed the pain.

The understanding of things that should not be understood.

"You'd better come in out of the cold," I said,

inviting him into our once-fine foyer. The gilt ceilings soared twelve feet, but the winding staircase behind us, of course, was partially open to the sky, covered only in part by what tar paper and planks we could find.

Despite our devastated staircase, Monsieur Legrand was clearly unaccustomed to such a home, and paused, checking his boots for mud. I waved off his concern.

"Oh please, monsieur," I said. "Come into the next room and you will see what we are dealing with every day."

In the parlor-turned-sickroom, my mother was tending to a man with a leg wound infested with maggots.

I called to her to join us, and we moved into the kitchen for a cup of tea and a hunk of our last loaf of bread, with marmalade from the final jar put up last year. Most of the help had evacuated the city; we kept only one housemaid, Honorine, who now assisted us with the injured.

Monsieur Legrand held out a package. It was a gift from my fiancé.

A comb, I thought dully when I opened it. *I would just as soon cut my tresses off.*

"He would better have sent a wheel of cheese," I said with bitterness, earning a sharp look from my mother. I sweetened my tone. "Please, monsieur, if you would be so kind as to wait a few moments, I'll write a thank-you note."

Monsieur Legrand nodded. Other than thanking us earnestly for the tea and toast, the poor fellow hadn't uttered a word since he had entered the house.

"Are you sure you're not injured?" I asked finally. "Your tongue, perhaps? We once had a man here, a *poilu*, with just such an injury. But that poor soul had also lost his nose."

"No, of course not," he said with a frown.

My mother gave me another sharp look, and suggested we open a bottle of champagne. Our cellar was nearly empty of preserves and jams, of the last canned peaches and cherries.

But we still had champagne, enough to share.

From the way his weary eyes lit up, I concluded Monsieur Legrand had gone far too long without tasting our beloved bubbly brew.

Chapter Ten

Rosalyn awakened with a jolt. After the initial shock of disorientation, she remembered she was in Gaspard Blé's *gîte* in Cochet. She got out of bed and tried to peek through the tiny cracks of the metal shutters, but it appeared to be pitch-black outside.

It was also pitch-black *inside.* She groped around the bedside table but couldn't find the light switch, so she grabbed her phone. It was blinking five o'clock. Disoriented, she wondered whether it was five in the morning or five in the evening. *Probably morning,* she thought. Europe used a twenty-four-hour clock to indicate time instead of a.m. and p.m., and her cell phone would have made the switch automatically.

Turning on the phone's flashlight, she padded across the room to the switch for the overhead light by the door. Then she fiddled with the shutter over the window and finally, through pushing some combination of buttons, she managed to get it to scroll up halfway. Better than nothing.

She needed coffee.

Rosalyn grabbed her regular flashlight, put her coat on over the T-shirt and flannel pants she had slept in, pulled on the snow boots Hugh had insisted she take with her, checked the door code for the kitchen next door, and went out into the dark early morning.

The cold struck her like a body blow.

The chilliest nights in Napa were never like this. This was a cutting, painful frostiness that reached into her body, grabbed her bones, and shook her, the wind pummeling her face and head with tiny pinpricks of sleet. She shivered uncontrollably, the beam of the flashlight jumping spasmodically as she punched numbers into the keypad of the building.

The door opened onto a loading dock, which wasn't exactly warm but was at least sheltered from the wind. The walls were stacked with hundreds of empty wooden crates, cases, and packing materials. A forklift was parked in one corner.

One unmarked door led to a utility closet; the next opened onto a divinely heated hallway, which led to an office area and then, just beyond, to a large tasting room that was separated from a full kitchen by a huge granite counter. Half a dozen round tables were encircled with chairs, leafy green plants enlivened the corners, and colorful framed maps of the Champagne region adorned the walls.

Dash had described how charming tastings were in France: They were usually held in tiny closetlike rooms in the sides of buildings, across simple wooden counters. You would drive down a gravel drive, perhaps tap the horn once or twice, or merely call out a greeting. An elderly man or woman—often a grandparent minding small children—would eventually emerge from a house and come pour tastes of the one or two wines the family produced. No money changed hands. In comparison, in Napa, tastings had become slick, orchestrated events where tourists happily shelled out ten or twenty dollars—or more—for a few sips of a flight of wine.

As Rosalyn cast an eye over this brand-new facility, it appeared to her that Gaspard Blé had built his tasting room for the American tourists.

Rosalyn had told Emma on the plane that she had come to Champagne for business, not in search of French country charm. Still, the newness and sterility of the facility were disappointing. Why take the time, and pony up the expense, of traveling to a faraway historic place when you could have the same experience at home?

Gazing about the tasting room, she was reminded of one of the worst arguments she and Dash had ever had. Dash had wanted to live in a new condo development, in a unit with wall-to-wall carpeting, top-of-the-line appliances,

91

and a pool and a workout room on the premises. Rosalyn had had in mind a charming little bungalow with a small yard and a few shade trees, a home they could paint and fix up a little, make their own. Dash had won the argument, of course, and they had moved into the condo.

When Dash got sick, they ended up in exactly such a cottage, when Rosalyn, now in charge of their finances, learned they were deeply, desperately in debt. When Hugh found out they were on the verge of being evicted, he offered them the old caretaker's quarters on his property. The cottage that housed the medicine cabinet.

She shook off the memory. *Focus.*

Blé's tasting room might have been frustratingly modern, but it was deliciously warm and Rosalyn breathed a sigh of relief as sensation returned to her fingers. A quick tour of the kitchen turned up a loaf of bread and assorted fruit on the counter, and in the small refrigerator she found a bowl of pale brown and green eggs, small cartons of plain yogurt, a package of cured ham known as *jambon de Paris*, a large square of butter, a small glass bottle of cream, and an assortment of cheeses on a plate covered with a dome.

She opened yet another door to reveal a large pantry, where numerous tote bags and wicker baskets hung from pegs. The shelves were lined with jars of confiture, honey, olives, and nuts, as well as boxes of crackers. She didn't see a coffeemaker, which was a disappointment, but she did find a box containing packets of instant espresso. It wasn't what she had been hoping for on such a cold, dark morning, but it would do in a pinch. She filled the electric kettle with water and switched it on.

While waiting for the water to boil, she completed her inspection of the kitchen: bottles of oil, jars of spices, all the basic kitchen staples. And champagne. Bottles and bottles of champagne. In the fridge, on the counter, in the pantry—the sparkling concoction was everywhere.

Pity she wasn't a fan; she could have had quite the party for one.

Rosalyn emptied two packets of the instant espresso into a sturdy earthenware mug and assembled a small plate of bread, cheese, ham, and fruit, covered the plate with a thick cloth napkin, and hurried back through the freezing predawn to her room.

Taking a seat at the table, Rosalyn opened her laptop and started checking e-mail, mindlessly taking bites of the food. Then the flavors hit her. The bread couldn't have been terribly fresh, but the crust was crispy and the tender middle— what the French called the *mie*—was soft and chewy. She couldn't even imagine how good this bread must taste straight from the oven; no wonder the French gorged on carbs. The *jambon de Paris* had just the right amount of saltiness, enough to satisfy but not so much that it overwhelmed the taste of the meat. And the cheese was a stinky, soft variety she had never heard of called Langres; it oozed over the chunk of bread, delivering a burst of intense yet mellow flavor that left her wanting more.

Even the clementine, which she had taken more as a concession to good health than from any desire for fruit, was amazing. As she peeled the small orange, its citrus scent perfumed the air, a hint of spring in the middle of winter. Tart but sweet, the juice ran down her chin before she could catch the drops with her napkin.

She sat savoring her meal for so long that her computer went to sleep.

Finally sated, she sipped her instant espresso—not great, and certainly not what she had hoped for in coffee-loving France, but she'd had worse—and returned her attention to her e-mail. None of the local producers had yet responded to her e-mails, but that was no surprise; many were out of town over the holidays.

Hugh had sent a chatty note asking how she was doing, attaching a photo of Andy's new baby, and updating her on several of her accounts. He ended with: "By the way, thanks to you I'm $5 richer. I made a bet with Andy that you wouldn't make it to Paris! In any case, enjoy Champagne. I know you will."

Rosalyn shut the computer and turned to Émile's letter.

She really should unearth Emma Kinsley's business card and let her know she had one of Émile's letters, but she was strangely reluctant to part with it. Maybe she had been too hasty in refusing Emma's offer of short-term employment. Had Emma been serious? Was she really willing to hire Rosalyn to track down more letters, and maybe to start translating the rest of them?

First, Rosalyn had been sent to France to sample and buy champagne, a wine she didn't even like, and then she had been offered a job searching for fascinating old letters. Rosalyn felt as if she were in a play with an oddball script, one in which the world had gone off its axis.

But then, that was nothing new. Once upon a time, she had set up her easel among rows of grapevines, where she was visited by humming-birds, tiny spirits come to sanctify her. She remembered looking up at the sunset-streaked skies and feeling grateful that God, or the fates, or *whoever* was running things, had sent such beauty and grace her way. She used to relish opening her paint box, sorting through the pig-ments: phthalo blue, red lake, pale ocher. She stood among the vines in her linen apron, a floppy hat on her head to ward off sunburn, trying to capture the scene on canvas over different seasons: the lush fruit in summer and fall, then the leaves turning yellow and brown, falling off to display the twisted cane, vulnerable-looking and yet so very strong. In the evenings, she would make dinner while Dash opened a bottle of wine and exclaimed over her latest paintings, talking about the art show they would put together when she was ready.

Rosalyn had believed—she had *known*—that she was blessed, that she was living a fairy-tale life.

Then came the diagnosis, and then Dash started vomiting up his pills and falling on the floor, and finally she had betrayed him by fleeing from his hospital room, unable to witness his final departure, unwilling to bear the moment the magic left this world just as surely as the light left his eyes.

She hadn't painted since. The color had been leached out of her life.

Outside, it was still dark. Rosalyn glanced at the clock: six in the morning, and she was wide-awake. How strange that jet lag should affect her this way. California was nine hours behind France, so her body should think it was nine in the evening. Probably she'd be dead on her feet in a few hours, just as the French were beginning their workday.

What now? Going back to bed was out of the question; in fact, she felt strangely energized.

Rosalyn bundled up in layers and her big coat,

hoping to ward off the cold. She wound a scarf around her neck and head, then pulled her orange wool hat down over her ears. The hat had been knitted by one friend, the scarf and her gloves crocheted by another. As she pulled them on, she thought to herself—not for the first time—that painting was surely the least useful of all the arts. Knitting and crocheting made it possible to give the tangible gift of warmth.

It amazed Rosalyn that she still had friends at all. Those few patient souls who waited for her to come back, to return to her old self. She wondered how long they would wait, and suspected they should not make the effort. Rosalyn was beginning to doubt it would ever happen; her old self had died, had disappeared just as surely as Dash.

One foot in front of the other.

Literally, in this case. Feeling overstuffed and unwieldy in the unaccustomed layers, she left the building and stepped carefully, fearful of slipping on patches of ice. *If I fall, I might start rolling and never stop,* she thought wryly. *I'll become the subject of a limerick: There was a young woman from Napa . . .*

Her snow boots crunched as they set down on the cold, hard earth. Otherwise, the silence was broken only by the occasional barking of a dog or the distant rumble of a car engine. Fog transformed the landscape into countless gradations of gray. Her breath came out in clouds, joining the mist.

The village was still silent, still shuttered. A few homes glowed gold from within, but there wasn't a soul on the street. Pity there was no *boulangerie* in town. Didn't bakers start work at four in the morning?

In the center of the village was a tiny plaza dominated by a stone monument inscribed, "*Mort pour la France*," and dedicated to villagers who had died in the two world wars as well as in the Algerian war. Rosalyn took a moment to read through the long list of names, most young men, most in their late teens and early twenties. A statue of an eternally serene and vigilant Mary, her palms facing out, watched over the plaque. Overhead, a holiday garland sagged, defeated by the rain, and one shiny red Christmas ornament lay cracked on the cobblestones.

Pinpricks of sleet stung her cheeks. She shrank into her coat, breathing through her scarf, reveling in the warmth of her own breath. The ground was spotted with patches of snow—not the pretty white powder of greeting cards, but dirty, hard, and crusted over. The weather felt strangely fitting, reflecting as it did her bleak interior world. The typically sunny, mild climate of Napa, topped by cartoonishly blue skies and puffy white clouds, often felt like a cruel jab, mocking her pain.

A hand-lettered sign in the window of the town's lone grocery store stated that the shop was closed for the holidays and would reopen on January 2.

The tour of the village didn't take long. Emma hadn't been kidding when she said there wasn't much to Cochet. Aside from the main square with its monument, there was an old stone church, the store, an auto repair shop in the garage of an ancient-looking house, and an elementary school. Otherwise it was simply a clutch of small homes, surrounded by fields of grapevines.

On the outskirts of the village there were no streetlights, and though the sky was lightening, it was still dark out. Rosalyn had always liked long winter nights, even when Dash was alive. She reveled in the mystery and possibilities of the dark.

At the moment, though, she wondered whether she was foolish to walk along the highway in the predawn duskiness. There was no shoulder to speak of, much less a proper sidewalk, just the pavement with deep ditches on either side. The fog sank into an otherworldly mist, hanging low to the ground. Maybe it was the jet lag, but Rosalyn started to feel entirely isolated from the world: not a soul knew where she was or what she was doing. She could disappear into the fog, let it swallow her whole, obliterate her physical presence just as the life she had dreamed of had been erased.

The sound of an approaching engine awoke her from her trance.

Startled, Rosalyn escaped the road by leaping across the ditch, landing on a narrow footpath that ran along the rows of staked grapevines. Only then did she realize the sound was coming not from the highway but from within the vineyard. A very old truck slowly made its way down a rutted, muddy lane that ran along the vines, its headlights illuminating the area just in front of it. It came to a halt with a rattle of the engine and the squeak of old brakes.

A tall man climbed out of the cab, leaving the truck's headlights shining. He wore a wool knit cap, fingerless gloves, and a heavy parka over jeans. His big rubber boots sank into the mud. Unheeding, he strode into the vines and crouched down, as though inspecting the plants.

One side of the man was lit by the harsh light of the headlights, the other by the mellow glow of the sun, which was just beginning to rise. Clouds of mist eddied and flowed in the glow of the headlights, hovering above the earth like a swirling ephemeral blanket.

Suddenly the man stilled, then looked around, still crouching. When he spotted Rosalyn, he slowly straightened.

Belatedly, Rosalyn realized that she might be trespassing by standing to the left of the roadside ditch, on the edge of the vineyard itself. She was too far away to see the expression on the man's face.

She opened her mouth to speak, but he beat her to it.

"*Bonjour, madame.*"

"*Bonjour, monsieur*," she replied.

"*Ça va? Est-ce que je vous peux aider?*" He asked her if everything was all right, if she needed help. His voice was deep, resonant.

"*Oui, ça va. Pardonnez-moi.*" Yes, it's fine. Excuse me, Rosalyn answered, trying to remember how to say, "I'm taking a walk." After a moment, she blurted out: "*Je suis au promenade.*" I am on a promenade. That probably wasn't the proper way to say it, but she hoped it made sense.

Rosalyn thought the man frowned, but she couldn't be sure from this distance. She doubted he encountered many strangers strolling along the highway in the predawn hours. In Napa, some of the homeless tramped up and down the highways for days and weeks and months at a time. Was that the case here in Champagne as well? And if so, did this farmer imagine Rosalyn was a wanderer making her way along the vines? She liked that idea, somehow. Playing a part that wasn't her, catching a glimmer of a life she didn't lead.

Finally, Rosalyn waved an awkward good-bye, leapt back across the ditch, and hurried back toward town.

Chapter Eleven

The sun rose higher in the sky with each step. On impulse, Rosalyn stopped by the central square and picked up the cracked Christmas ornament, then pinched off a few small sprigs from an evergreen tree.

Back in her room at Blé's place, she arranged the evergreen branches on the table and placed the ornament in the center, like a Christmassy bird's nest.

In Napa, she had done her best to ignore the holidays, spending her nonworking hours roaming the vineyards, eating dinners of microwaved egg rolls and streaming show after depressing show from Netflix. Her mother had invited her to join her and her new husband in Palm Desert for Christmas, but Rosalyn had declined, citing the need to prepare for her trip to France. It wasn't the holiday itself she wanted to avoid but the holiday spirit—the ever-present reminder of the joy of loved ones reunited, the pressure to pretend that she was enjoying herself, too.

It was agony, sometimes, donning that mask.

After making herself a cup of tea, she sat at the table and took out the big leather-bound journal she had brought with her. A grief counselor had urged her to get the journal, to write to Dash, to allow her thoughts and feelings to spill out onto its smooth white paper. Rosalyn abandoned the project after filling only ten pages. Writing her feelings hadn't helped; nothing did. Still, Rosalyn had brought the journal with her to France, partly from a sense of obligation and partly from the hope, scarcely recognized, that perhaps here the feelings would be easier to access.

Instead, she brought out a regular number two pencil—it was the best she could do without any true artist implements—and scrawled a quick sketch, smudging and crosshatching and erasing until she got the effect she wanted on the paper. She drew the stark black of tree branches against the slowly brightening sky, the man crouched down inspecting his twisty vines bathed in the old truck's headlights, the light streaming through the parallel lines of barren-looking stalks, the mist hovering low to the ground like an other-worldly presence.

Lost in her sketch, Rosalyn was startled at the sound of a car pulling up outside.

She crossed over to the window—having finally figured out how to open the shutter, she was now unable to close it—and saw a man in his fifties climb out of a pickup truck. He was short and dark featured, his face tanned and lined from years of working outdoors.

Rosalyn lifted a hand in greeting. He reared back, as though shocked to see her. She passed through the entryway and out the main door.

"*Bonjour, monsieur*," she said, already trying to formulate a few sentences in her mind. "*Je m'appelle*—"

"*Bonjour*! You must be the American? I'm so sorry. I thought you were arriving tomorrow." He spoke French with a strong Italian accent, giving the melodious language a charming singsong quality. "I am Pietro Santini."

"I arrived early," said Rosalyn, searching for the words in French. "I was originally scheduled to spend some time in Paris but changed my plans. I had the code for the door, so I made myself at home. I hope that's all right—I should have called."

"Not at all. It is fine. You are most welcome. I am just sorry I wasn't here to greet you. No one is in the office over the holidays, either. Look here. I bring you some baked things from my wife." Pietro spoke slowly, but his scarred hands gesticulated energetically. "And she sends some eggs from our chickens, and homemade pâté, and jam."

"That is so kind. Thank you," Rosalyn said, accepting the gifts of food. "It all looks wonderful."

"You find everything okay in the apartment? My wife, she make the bed and clean. You are the first guest!"

"Everything is lovely. Thank you."

"This is a nice house, not like the old places here, made of cold stone. This is new and nice, eh?"

She smiled and nodded. "It's very nice."

"We are very small here in Cochet, not even a *boulangerie*. There is one in Salpot, my wife likes the best. Others prefer the *boulangerie* in Foucrault. Also there is a butcher there, and also a pharmacy—people get sick on flights, eh? And with this cold . . . Does the heat work all right?"

"Yes, thank you. It's very comfortable."

"Please, would you like to join my wife and me for dinner tonight?"

"Oh, I . . . Thank you so much for the invitation, but I'm still suffering from jet lag. I'd rather rest for a few days."

"What will you eat?"

"You just brought me such lovely food."

Pietro looked troubled. "But that is not a proper dinner. . . ."

"I'll be fine. Thank you."

"All right, but if you need anything else," he continued in his singsong French, "you call me, eh? You have my number?"

Rosalyn nodded. "I do. Thank you."

"It is a quiet time now in the village, but soon will be New Year's, and then Epiphany, and then the festival of Saint Vincent, and all will change," Pietro said, returning to his truck and starting the engine. "You will see. Good thing you are staying awhile. But for now I hope you enjoy the peace. Maybe you relax a bit, eh?"

"Yes, thank you. I think I'll do exactly that."

After nabbing a fresh-smelling poppy seed muffin from the basket and stowing the rest of the food in the kitchen next door, Rosalyn returned to her room, and finally located Emma's business card. She sent her an e-mail:

Dear Emma,

It was a pleasure meeting you on the plane. I hope you're doing well, and that the jet lag has waned. I am writing you because somehow I ended up with one of your historic letters. My apologies; I am not sure how that happened. I will be happy to return it to you if you will send me an address. I translated it—it was a good workout for my French! I'm attaching a copy of the translation to this e-mail, in case you're interested.

Sincerely,
Rosalyn Acosta

She then sent a few e-mails to producers she was hoping to meet with in Champagne, and once more checked in with Hugh. Business concluded, she turned back to her drawing, trying a few more versions based on her vivid memory of the predawn scene, before going into the kitchen to fix herself two of the farm-fresh eggs Pietro had brought.

The day was cold but sunny and clear. At a loss for what to do next, Rosalyn climbed into her rental car and went for a drive, familiarizing herself with the region. She passed through several sleepy villages with *boulangeries* and butchers, pharmacies and greengrocers, all closed for the holidays.

Memorials for those *mort pour la France* studded the landscape: she noticed them in plazas, in forest copses, in cemeteries, out in the middle of nowhere. Clearly, the *Champenois* lived side by side with their dead. Rosalyn stopped alongside several roadside markers to read about battles that had taken place there, running her fingers over the lists of names of *les morts*. The dead ranged in age from seventeen to fifty-four, but most were around twenty.

Where had Rosalyn been at twenty? At college in Sonoma, majoring in marketing and design. Going to parties, dating a little, discovering a life outside of her Central Valley hometown of Fresno. By the time she was twenty-two and a senior, she had landed an internship with Dash's company; they eventually got married, and that was that.

Imagine being so young and watching your friends and fellow soldiers dying at your side, felled by bullets and disease. Looking out across the frozen but picturesque landscape, Rosalyn tried to envision these fields crisscrossed with barbed wire and trenches dug deep into the sticky mud.

She felt an intense urge to read more of Émile's letters. To know what it was like.

Back at the *gîte*, Rosalyn had nothing but time on her hands. When the sun went down, she poured herself a glass of Bordeaux and scoured the Internet for information about the Champagne region during the First World War. She studied photographs of soldiers in the trenches, searching their young faces. The old film showed everything in shades of sepia and gray, though of course in reality there must have been the light blue of the soldiers' uniforms, the browns and greens of the mud and surviving vegetation, the pale chalk of the open ground.

The deep red of blood.

When Rosalyn researched the caves, or *crayères*, under the champagne houses of Reims, she found mostly tour information. There were a few references to the *Rémois*—the townsfolk from Reims—moving underground during the war, bringing their schools and businesses with them, as Hugh had mentioned. But the information was limited and she couldn't find any photographs.

Finally, Rosalyn looked up Anastasia's scissors and found a number of ugly caricatures of a bespectacled old woman wielding an enormous pair of shears. According to one article, twenty members of each army corps were assigned to open and inspect letters, and any statements deemed "subversive," or that revealed army locations or future plans, were *caviardés*—blacked out by pen or cut out altogether. The censors lived under the threat of losing their relatively cushy desk jobs and being sent to the front if they allowed anything to slip past, so while some edited with a light hand, others were downright draconian.

In one song written by a patriotic soldier, a mother tried to talk her son out of going to fight on the front. He replied:

> I can only live as a *poilu*.
> If I die here I die without glory.
> My country first!—My dear child!—
> You are only mamma. My mother is
> France!

Despite the patriotic fervor of the song, it was suppressed by the censors for expressing an "unbearable appreciation of a mother's feelings."

An unbearable appreciation of feelings. Rosalyn deliberated on the phrase, rolling it over in her mind. What a sentiment. It was accurate, though; if people knew what it felt like to lose a beloved one, if they truly understood the agony, the unfathomable waste of a life cut short, they wouldn't be able to support the war.

It would be, quite simply, unbearable.

Two days after writing her, Rosalyn logged on to her e-mail and found that Emma had replied:

> My favorite AirFrance seatmate! How wonderful to hear from you! I've been offline for a few days, but I won't bore you with *that* story—especially when I have so many others!
>
> Please don't worry about sending the letter by mail. Too easy for it to get lost, and it's irreplaceable. I'll come pick it up, or I'll send my aide-de-camp, André. Expect us when you see us!
>
> And since we're on the topic . . . You're staying at Gaspard Blé's gîte, right? It's on the ground floor, right? No stairs? Are all the rooms occupied? Is Gaspard still out of town? So many questions, so little time . . .

Rosalyn smiled at Emma's straightforward enthusiasm, and answered: As far as I can tell, no one else is staying here, so either the room next door is unoccupied or whoever is there is creepily quiet. Ground floor, no stairs. Yes, Gaspard is still out of town. A very nice man named Pietro Santini is watching over the place, and brought me food so I wouldn't starve. You were right, of course; there's not much in Cochet, and what little is there is closed for the holidays.

Rosalyn paused, surprised at how much she was enjoying the exchange with Emma, the odd closeness she felt with a near stranger. Maybe it was as Emma said: They really were on the same wavelength.

She continued: In fact, nothing's open in the surrounding towns, either, which makes me wonder where the locals shop. Or do they spend the holidays churning butter at home? Probably they plan ahead, unlike some of us. The whole area is shuttered and quiet. It's been very restful. I like it.

Her fingers hovered over the keys for a moment. Finally, she typed, I've been putting one foot in front of the other, and hit SEND.

Rosalyn turned her attention to other e-mails, and was surprised and pleased when, a few minutes later, Emma responded:

Good old Pietro. He's a treasure. If there's anything nicer than a French accent, it's a French accent with an Italian twist. How cute is that? And remember, if you get bored buying champagne, my offer of a research job still stands. What could be more interesting than poking around old French attics?

Other than a few chatty e-mails from Hugh and her mother and a couple of friends in Napa, Rosalyn felt very removed from the world. Very alone.

But she did not feel lonely. In fact, it was only when she was by herself that she did *not* feel lonely.

She'd finished the three paperbacks she'd brought with her, and tried reading more on her computer but her eyes glazed over. Her e-reader had broken the day before she left California, when she set it on the roof of her car while searching for her keys, forgot it, and drove off. Yet one more example of not paying attention, of breaking things, tripping over nothing, walking into walls. Grief brain.

The village of Cochet remained quiet, the only signs of life the occasional workers guiding tractors through the fields.

She continued to wake early in the morning,

which made no sense. Her body should have adjusted by now. But perhaps it already had; when she was at home, Rosalyn frequently woke up before dawn. Dash had died at four twenty-seven in the morning, and for months afterward, she had startled awake at that moment, precisely. Perhaps it was as simple as that.

On a few occasions when she walked in the cold silence of dawn, Rosalyn saw the same farmer tending to his vines; the two exchanged waves.

Feeling as if she should be working, Rosalyn continued to send out e-mails, leave voice mails, check inventory, and respond to inquiries from Hugh's other reps, who were watching over her accounts while she was out of town. But her phone calls and e-mails to local producers went unanswered. Hugh seemed unfazed, and urged her to relax and enjoy her time away.

Time slowed down. Sometimes annoyingly so.

At last it dawned on her: This was what she had wanted. To be alone, surrounded by silence. No questions, no comments, no one to answer to.

Her very own hermitage in the French country-side.

As she began to embrace the solitude, Rosalyn felt an urge to capture some of the local scenery on paper and started sketching close-ups of the barren grapevines in winter, landscapes of the gently rolling hills, the villages tucked into shallow valleys. She drew the man on the tractor at dawn, the memorial in the village square overseen by the Madonna, and a grave marker she found near a pond in the woods.

Rosalyn had always preferred painting to drawing; with paint she could lay down swaths of color versus the hard lines of the pencil.

But now she had no taste for color. The harsh contrast of the dark graphite against the creamy white paper suited her mood as she worked at capturing the myriad hues of gray.

Although she didn't catch another glimpse of him, Pietro kept the kitchen stocked with the basics. Food simply appeared, as though delivered by an Italian elf: a plump farm-raised chicken one day, thick pork chops wrapped in white butcher paper the next. Baskets of winter vegetables, squash and kale and potatoes.

For the last few years, Rosalyn had lived on takeout, frozen food, leftovers from office functions—anything that didn't require time in the kitchen. Cooking was something she had done for Dash, and it was so central to their life together that she couldn't bear the thought of preparing meals just for herself. But now, faced with fresh food, a large kitchen, a huge stove, and no fast-food options, she put some music on, grabbed a sharp knife, lit the stove, and started chopping. Adhering to the old adage "When in Rome," she tried her hand at a classic French dish from a recipe she found on the Internet: *coq au vin*. It was surprisingly simple, and Pietro had provided her with all the ingredients: bacon, pearl onions, *champignons de Paris*—button mushrooms—and thyme. She found an inexpensive burgundy in the cupboard to use for the sauce.

Soon the kitchen/tasting room was filled with the homey aromas of food bubbling on the stove. She felt self-conscious sitting down to such a formal dinner all by herself but was pleased by the results of her labor.

Later, as she lay in bed, Rosalyn realized she had enjoyed the act of cooking again. It did not feel like betrayal; it didn't feel like anything more significant than a good dinner.

The next day she drove to Reims to check out the capital of the Champagne region. A few stores were open, but by and large the town was as sleepy as Cochet and the other villages. There were similar soggy leftover Christmas ornaments, though on a larger scale. The massive Gothic cathedral reminded her of Paris's famous Notre-Dame; she almost stopped to take a look inside, then decided against it.

Dash holding her hand as they climbed the winding steps to visit the gargoyles at the top of Notre-Dame, making the whole tour group laugh by calling out for "Sanctuary!"

As Rosalyn toured Reims, she drove past the impressive mansionlike façades of the Mumm,

Veuve Clicquot Ponsardin, Taittinger, and Ruinart champagne houses. In Champagne, the major wine houses were located in large towns rather than in the vineyards, as they are in Napa and in the rest of France.

The Pommery champagne house—now called Vranken Pommery Estate—was a vast gray-and-red Elizabethan-style mansion, complete with turrets. It was closed to tourists for the holidays, of course, but Rosalyn pulled her Renault up outside the tall iron gates and spent a few minutes studying the formal buildings and manicured grounds.

Somewhere under these buildings was where Lucie Maréchal had sought shelter from the German bombardment.

Rosalyn tried to imagine what it would be like to move one's whole life underground. Had the moment of decision been borne of panic? Or had it been the only sensible option, given the circumstances? Had entire neighborhoods relocated? Why hadn't they already evacuated the city?

Or, she wondered, was the decision assumed to be a temporary solution to an immediate problem that had, instead, altered their lives in untold ways?

Chapter Twelve

Lucie

First the Reims Cathedral, and then Villa Traverne.

Thinking back on the home that was Villa Traverne, I still find it hard to believe that such a fine, sturdy building would collapse.

But then, even great stone castles fall under the constant barrage of a wartime siege, do they not?

Once upon a time my father, Raymond, taught me about such things as we sat in his study, reading and studying the globe. But no more.

On February 22, 1915, more than a thousand shells were showered on Reims, sometimes as many as ten every minute. The Germans called it "watering the city." An incendiary bomb set Villa Traverne on fire, and our once-fine house burned for fully a day, until there was nothing left but charred ruins.

We had no choice but to leave. We were barely able to get our injured soldiers out in time; later they were evacuated by the army, and the rest of us were left standing, dazed and smudged with soot, in the rubble-strewn street. Honorine left to try to find her sister.

Nothing remained of the life our family had lived.

All my father's books, his precious tomes, gone.

Only the globe stood, a blackened tribute to what once had been our world.

Now my father passes his days in silence, staring at the walls. Papa had remained strong through the maiming of my brother and the death of my sister.

But this final blow, the loss of Villa Traverne, has rendered him mute.

It was up to *Maman* and me to find a new situation.

Despite all the destruction and chaos rained down upon Reims, there were still neighborhoods that remained intact. We moved into a small house that had been abandoned by an evacuated family, in the southern part of the city. Some clothes and cookware had been left behind, and we availed ourselves of them though my mother insisted we show the items the utmost respect so the family might find their things intact upon their return.

If they returned.

Chapter Thirteen

Rosalyn was on her way back to Cochet when she noticed her gas gauge was nearing empty. *Damn it.* She tried to remember if she had seen a gas station once she had left the autoroute on her way to Cochet that first day.

Soon enough the fuel light blinked on, ratcheting up her nervousness.

She pulled over to the side of the road, took several deep breaths, and turned to her phone for help. Its software directed her to a nearby village, where she found two gas pumps in the parking lot of a small convenience store. The store was closed for the holidays, of course, but to her great relief the pumps took credit cards.

Rosalyn tried one card, then another, then another. Each time the pump's digital display demanded a code. *What* code? She didn't have codes for her credit cards. She had a PIN for her debit card, but the pump didn't recognize that card and spat it out.

She felt like crying.

An engine rattled as an old truck pulled up on the other side of the island. She recognized the vehicle, and the driver: He was the farmer she had encountered in the field during her predawn walk that first day, the same one she had seen several times since. They waved each time, but always at a distance. Seeing him now, up close, she realized he looked very . . . *French.* Full lips, pouting, the top lip as full as the bottom, as though poised to say something, or to kiss someone. He had unbearably sad, downward-tilting gray-green eyes. Her mother would have said he "looked like trouble," with his scruffy, short-cropped beard, but Rosalyn sensed sorrow more than anything else.

He inserted his card into the other gas pump, tapped in a code, and immediately started fueling up his truck.

"*Bonjour, monsieur,*" Rosalyn said.

"*Bonjour,*" he said, his eyes on the digital readout.

"*Pardonnez-moi,*" she continued. Although the man projected an air of "Don't bother me," desperate times called for desperate measures, so she asked him if he would help her: "*Est-ce que vous pouvez m'aider avec le machine? J'ai besoin de pétrole.*"

He let out a long sigh, practically rolling his eyes, and spoke in rapid-fire French, which she couldn't follow.

"*Je suis désolée. Je ne comprends pas,*" Rosalyn apologized, and asked him to speak more slowly. *"Est-ce que vous pouvez parler plus lentement?"*

He stared at her for a moment, then asked in clipped English: "It is an American card?"

"Yes."

"The American card does not work here. You have to have the chip."

"It *has* a chip."

"And a code."

"What code?"

"A personal code." The man yanked the fuel nozzle out of his truck, returned it to its resting place in the pump, and flipped the gas door closed with smooth, efficient movements.

Damn it. What now? "And there's no way to pay cash, right?"

"The store is closed," he said. "As you can see. Most of the businesses are closed this time of year."

Rosalyn nodded, trying to figure out her next step. Maybe she could make it back to the *gîte* on fumes. If not . . . did they even have taxis or ride-share services in this part of France? Too bad she hadn't thought to bring Pietro's phone number with her.

You'll be fine, she assured herself. If worse came to worst, she was probably close enough to Cochet to walk home.

Rosalyn felt the man's eyes on her.

"You are the one walking before dawn," he said, a frown creasing his brow.

"*Oui, c'est moi.*" She felt oddly vulnerable to be recognized, as though her cocoon of privacy had been cracked open. Rosalyn had enjoyed the anonymity of their predawn encounters, the infinite possibilities and the absolute lack of expectations.

"Why do you do this?" he asked. "Why do you walk before dawn?"

"*C'est à cause du décalage horaire,*" Rosalyn responded, blaming the jet lag.

"Speak English. It is easier for you."

She was simultaneously relieved and insulted. "Thank you. I'm visiting Cochet until the festival of Saint Vincent. I'm staying at Gaspard Blé's *gîte.*"

The man was silent for a moment, then walked around to her side of the gas pump, inserted his card, and tapped in a code.

"It will work now," he said, handing her the nozzle.

"Oh, thank you. I can't tell you how much I appreciate this. I'll pay you back in cash. I have euros."

He shrugged, now looking amused.

The machine hummed as it filled the Renault's tank. They waited without speaking. As she watched the digital numbers speed by, Rosalyn's anxiety rose. Liters were smaller than gallons, she knew. But how many liters did her car hold? She did have enough euros to reimburse him, didn't she? She tried to remember where she had last seen an ATM.

"You start work awfully early," Rosalyn said to break the silence.

"I practice biodynamic agriculture. Things have to be done on a certain schedule."

"Is that the same as organic?" Rosalyn recalled from her college courses that in France organic produce is called "bio," or *biologique*.

"No." He did not elaborate.

The numbers were mounting fast, along with her apprehension that she would not have enough cash to cover it. Sure enough, when the tank was full and she put away the nozzle, she was several euros short.

"I'm sorry. I'm a little short on cash, after all," she said, holding out all the money she had. "I think I saw an ATM in Reims. I'll go there right now and get the rest I owe you."

He glanced at the wad of bills in her hand and shook his head. "Don't worry about it."

"Of course I will pay you back. Should I stop by your home, or . . . ?"

He gave a firm shake of his head. "Consider it a New Year's present. *Bonne année*."

And with that, he turned and walked to his truck, hoisted himself into the cab, turned on the engine, and drove off.

Until that moment Rosalyn hadn't realized it was New Year's Eve.

And she didn't even know his name.

Rosalyn declined Pietro's invitation to join the townspeople at a small New Year's Eve fete in the *mairie*, though from the solitude of *Chambre Chardonnay*, she could hear the sounds of laughter and revelry.

Rosalyn had wanted a hermitage, and she got it. French countryside style.

She sat gazing out the window, watching as light snowflakes fell in the parking area and on the trees beyond, and fiddling with the empty locket around her neck. She had always meant to find tiny photographs of her and Dash. She always assumed they would have plenty of time.

At midnight, the church bells rang out slowly—one, pause. Two, pause. Three, pause . . . When the twelfth bell sounded, loud cheers and the honking of noisemakers filled the air.

A new year.

Yet another year further away from her life with Dash. Another year from the person Rosalyn had been with Dash.

Chapter Fourteen

Like Hugh and so many other recent arrivals in Napa, Dash had invested in a winery with money earned in the computer industry, abandoning the high-tech campuses of Santa Clara for the deceptively rural fields of Napa.

Rosalyn had fallen for him the first time she saw him. He and a few other local winery owners had visited Sonoma State University to interview potential interns, who would earn academic credit for their work in the industry. With his brilliant smile and easy laugh, Dash was enthusiastic and inspiring. Competition for the coveted internships was intense, and after applying and interviewing for several, Rosalyn was thrilled to land the one she wanted most: at Dash's company, Domain Acosta.

But she didn't kid herself that Dashiell Acosta paid her any particular attention. The dynamic winery owner rarely came into the office, and when he did, Rosalyn was one of a half dozen eager interns. Though he was unfailingly polite and encouraging, she knew he saw them for what they were: enthusiastic but young, inexperienced, unpaid workers.

Rosalyn worked nights busing tables at an upscale restaurant in downtown Napa to help pay her way through school. The first time she saw Dash at the restaurant, two of the waitstaff were out with the flu, and she'd leapt at the chance to pick up a cocktail shift. It was a plum assignment—tipsy Napa socialites and day-trippers from San Francisco tended to be big tippers, and she would end the shift with a nice wad of cash.

That night her mind was on a class project due the next morning, a label redesign that she would have to finish when she got home after her shift. Distracted, she forgot which man had ordered which drink, and hesitated a moment at their table.

Dash looked up at her, his head cocked slightly. "I know you."

"Just barely," she said with an embarrassed smile. Figuring she had a fifty-fifty shot at getting their orders right, she set the highball glasses down in front of them.

His tablemate, a hearty-looking fellow she had heard Dash call Hugh, gave her an indulgent smile. She was no model, but she was young, with long hair and big eyes, and older men had a way of gazing at her with a mixture of benevolence and vague flirtatiousness.

The two men swapped glasses.

"Oh, my apologies," Rosalyn said.

"We're good. Thanks. Where do I know you from?" Dash asked.

That stung. Rosalyn didn't expect the winery's big boss to remember her name, not really, but for him not to be able to place her at all? It was a blow. Apparently she truly was beneath his notice. *Rich people,* she thought to herself. *The rest of us matter, too, you know.*

"I'm an intern at your winery, from Sonoma State," she said, refilling their water glasses. "Anything else I can get for you? Your server will be by in a moment to take your food order."

"Wait. You're an intern in *my* office?" Dash sounded surprised.

"Dash." Hugh shook his head and let out an exasperated sigh.

Rosalyn nodded, outwardly pleasant but impatient to end this awkward conversation. Table four needed water, and the toddler at table six had tossed several utensils on the floor. This was the bane of anyone in food service: pretending you had all the time in the world as customers hemmed and hawed over the menu or asked you to describe the food and how it was prepared, all while you were acutely aware that others were waiting for your attention.

"For how long?"

"About a month now. If there's nothing else . . . ? Excuse me." She rushed off.

As she worked that evening, she kept an eye

on the table. The men enjoyed their meal and ordered a second bottle of wine. They were in high spirits, laughing and engaging nearby tables in a raucous discussion. How she yearned to sit at one of these tables, to rest her sore feet, to enjoy delicious food, to relax and be able to order whatever she wanted, to indulge in as many bottles of wine as she wished.

Someday, she thought as she carried a loaded tray of cocktails to a table of rowdy business executives. *Though clearly not today.*

An hour later she was leaving the women's rest-room after a quick break when she encountered Dash in the narrow hallway.

"Do you have a moment?" he asked politely.

"I'm sorry. I have to get back to work."

"I'm guessing from your reaction earlier that you've been working hard in my office, and I'm a jackass for not realizing that."

She blushed and looked away.

"I apologize. I'm what I like to call . . . a sort of hands-off manager."

"There's really no need to apologize," she said.

"That's very kind of you. But tell me—why are you working here if you already work for me?"

Rosalyn's mouth fell open. Was he serious? "Because you don't pay your interns—that's why."

He looked surprised. "Ah."

"I'm not complaining," she added quickly,

afraid of offending him. She needed a good evaluation so her faculty adviser would sign off on the internship for academic credit. "We do it for the hands-on experience. I didn't expect to be paid."

"Still . . ."

Rosalyn was eager to end this conversation—her break was over, and her manager would not be pleased to find her chatting in the hallway with a customer.

"That's a lot, isn't it?" Dash continued. "Working at my company during the day and serving drinks here at night. When do you find time to go to class, do homework, and get some sleep?"

"I make it work," she said. "And speaking of work, I really need to get back to it. Excuse me, Mr. Acosta."

"Call me Dash, please. Oh, excuse me—I'm in your way, aren't I? I apologize," he said with a smile, stepping aside. "No one should ever stand in your way."

"Thanks." She hurried back to the bar.

After Dash and Hugh left, Caitlyn, one of the other servers working that night, called Rosalyn over to give her a share of the tips. The restaurant's custom was for the food servers to split their tips with the bartender, busser, and cocktail waitress.

"This is for you," Caitlyn said, handing Rosalyn

some cash. "Table three left me a huge tip—and specified that this"—she added another bill—"was for the 'hardworking cocktail waitress.' "

Rosalyn stared at the bill. "A *hundred* dollars?"

Caitlyn raised an eyebrow. "Not bad for a round of cocktails."

"Oh, I gave them more than a round of cocktails," said Rosalyn.

"No way! I *thought* I saw you hanging out with one of them by the restrooms!" She lowered her voice. "What else? Do tell!"

"I kept their water glasses full, too."

Caitlyn looked disappointed, then laughed. "C'mon, Super Server," she said. "There's a lot still to do before we can blow this joint."

Rosalyn studied the crisp hundred-dollar bill, and smiled.

The next day, Dash caught Rosalyn asleep at her desk.

She hadn't gotten home until after two in the morning, at which point she drank a strong cup of coffee, then spent three hours finishing her class project. Around dawn she tried to get a little sleep—which didn't work, thanks to all the caffeine—before rushing off at ten o'clock for her first class of the day. By three her classes were over, and she headed to the winery for her internship. Business was slow, she was alone in the warm office, and . . . she nodded off, right there at her desk.

Slowly, Rosalyn came to consciousness, realizing with dread that someone was watching her.

"Oh, sweet Jesus . . . ," she whispered under her breath.

"It's Dash, actually. Looks like we should fit a cot in here for nap time."

"I'm so, so, *so* sorry," she said, surreptitiously wiping a little drool from the corner of her mouth and reaching for something, anything, to say that would make the situation better. "I was up late last night . . . and I'm . . . I'm just so sorry. I don't have an excuse."

"Sure you do," he said, his voice kind. "You're exhausted."

"That's no excuse."

"Sounds like a good one to me." He shrugged. "Anyway, I was just looking for the sales numbers for the two thousand fifteen Zinfandel."

"Oh, they're right here," she said, pulling the file from a stack on her desk and handing it to him.

Dash half turned as if to leave, then paused. "If it's not too personal, may I ask: What kept you up so late last night? The restaurant?"

"That was part of it. But when I got home, I had to finish a label design for one of my classes."

"What kind of label design?"

"For you, actually." She blushed. "I mean, for your Zinfandel. I chose to redesign it for a class project."

He raised one eyebrow. "What's wrong with my Zinfandel label?"

"Everything," Rosalyn blurted out.

He looked surprised.

"Oh, I can't believe I said that out loud. I'm still half asleep. I'm so sorry."

"You do a lot of apologizing around me. How about we stop that?"

"Of course. Sorry."

He smiled, and little crinkles appeared at the corners of his eyes. He carried himself so easily, she noted, was so at home in his skin, as if he were the king of the world. She supposed he was, at least the king of his small domain here in Napa.

"What I meant to say," Rosalyn continued, "is that I thought it should be more eye-catching, to differentiate it from all the other bottles on the store shelves. According to the sales figures in that file, your wines sell best in the upscale wine shops whose clients are less concerned with price, and where the shop owners are probably recommending your wines. And that's great, of course, but in the larger outlets your bottles need a distinctive label to catch people's attention. Your average buyer judges a bottle based, at least in part, on its label."

He tilted his head. "And you have a better label design?"

She blushed again. "I do. I mean, it's just an

idea. It's silly, really. I'm a marketing-and-design major, so I'm supposed to think about these things."

"May I see it?"

"Oh, I don't know. . . . It's just a rough idea. . . ."

"Are you going to deny me a peek at my own Zinfandel label, Rosalyn?"

"I . . . Of course not." As she pulled it up on the office computer, he came around to her side of the desk, put one hand flat on the desk blotter and the other on the back of her chair, and leaned in to study the screen.

She caught a whiff of soap and something masculine, a subtle blend of sandalwood and moss she would later learn was the signature scent of a cologne imported from Paris.

"You did this?" he asked, staring at her label.

She nodded, trying to ignore his closeness, and the fact that her heart was pounding. For the redesigned label, Rosalyn had blatantly ripped off a Mucha painting of a woman and depicted her with a basket of grapes, in the Art Nouveau style. It was derivative, but she liked the result: romantic and evocative, a nod to the past while still contemporary.

"This is good," he said. "Really good."

"It's just—"

"I like it. No need to be modest, Rosalyn. I really should be paying you."

"Speaking of which, thank you for that huge tip last night. I don't know what to say—it was completely unnecessary."

He shrugged. "What's money good for, if not to give it away?"

I wouldn't know, Rosalyn thought.

"You keep at it, Rosie girl. Get some sleep, and maybe I'll see you tomorrow."

Two nights later, Dash returned to the restaurant, this time by himself. He hung out at the bar, telling stories and making the bartender and the patrons laugh. Rosalyn could feel his eyes on her as she hustled here and there, taking orders and fetching drinks. They exchanged nods a few times, and she grew warm under his gaze. At one point he waved her over to order a half dozen Tomales Bay oysters and a tasting plate of local artisanal cheese. She made sure the oysters were freshly shucked and properly chilled and the cheeses were at room temperature, and brought them to him with a small basket of fresh sourdough bread.

"This looks wonderful, Rosalyn. Thank you."

"My pleasure," she said with a nod, returning to work. For the next half hour, two large tables of families celebrating birthdays kept her busy, and by the time she glanced over at the bar, Dash was leaving. She chided herself for feeling disappointed when he slipped out of the restaurant without saying good-bye.

The bartender Phil waved her over.

"Those must have been some oysters, Rosalyn," he said with a wink, handing her two crisp hundred-dollar bills. "He specified that these are for you."

"He what? This is for me?" she asked. "There must be some mistake."

Phil shrugged. "You ask me, somebody's got an admirer."

She ran out to the parking lot and spied him opening the door of his late-model Lexus. "Wait, Mr. Acosta—"

He stopped, and turned toward her. "It's Dash. Please."

"Dash, then." She held the money out to him. "Look, I appreciate the thought. I really do. But I did nothing to deserve this kind of money."

"I'm a big tipper."

"Not this big. Not usually, I'll bet. Is it because of what I said yesterday, about the unpaid internship? Because I'm serious. I knew it was unpaid when I accepted the position. I'm doing it for the experience."

"It's not about that."

"Then . . . why?"

"I want to make you happy."

She paused. "Why would you want to do that?"

He stepped toward her, his dark eyes studying her hair, her eyes, her mouth. For a moment she thought he was about to lean down and kiss her, and her heart started to race, her breath coming quickly.

Then he flashed a jaunty grin, ducked his head, and said, "Shouldn't we all want to make each other happy?"

"I . . ." She was at a loss for what to say, but handed him the money. "Seriously, I wouldn't feel right about keeping this. I wasn't raised that way."

"You weren't raised to earn money? What are you, a trust fund baby in disguise?"

She laughed. "Not exactly, no. But two hundred dollars for serving two appetizers is a bit much."

He let out a loud sigh, looked at her a moment, and said, "Split the difference?"

She hesitated, then nodded and handed him one of the bills.

"You drive a hard bargain, Rosie."

She felt his eyes on her as she returned to the restaurant.

The next few times she was in the winery office, Dash came by, greeted her with his easy smile, and went about his business. Rosalyn found herself dwelling on thoughts of him. The way he dressed in jeans and a sport coat, like a cross between a farmer and a businessman. The way his dark hair curled at the collar, a bit longer than she usually found attractive, but in his case she made an exception. She wondered where he lived, how old he was, if he had a wife or a girlfriend. One day he gave her and the other two office interns a book on wine. Hers was dedicated: *Hope this makes you happy.*

When she mentioned she loved to paint, he asked what her favorite pigment was. The next morning, she found on her desk a tube of natural ultramarine, a precious—and expensive—blue pigment, decorated with a cheesy bow. She liked the bow almost more than the paint.

"Ultramarine blue was the most precious color to the Renaissance painters," she said, admiring the tube. "It's made of ground lapis lazuli stone."

"I didn't know that."

"And it's a darn sight more appetizing than 'mummy brown,' which was actually made of pulverized mummies."

"Now you're pulling my leg."

"I'm not! It's true."

"You are a veritable font of information, Rosie. Where do you learn all this stuff?"

She shrugged, hesitating to make up a story. The truth was that when she was ten years old, her father left, and Rosalyn had escaped the harsh summer heat of Fresno—and her mother's devastation—by hiding out in the public library. She loved painting, so a kind librarian showed her the section on fine art, including one thick tome that listed dozens of pigments, along with their histories and qualities. Ever since, it had become a kind of game; in her mind she would run through the exotic-sounding pigments like a mantra.

Dash smiled. "How did Shakespeare put it? 'Young in years, in judgment old'?"

"I think it goes 'young in limbs,' but I'll take it," she said, returning his smile.

He started to drop by the office more frequently. Was it her imagination, or did he pay a little more attention to her than to the other interns? Some days Dash would bring a sandwich and offer to share, lingering as though he didn't have a business to run, and they would chat about art and painting and wine. Rosalyn told him how her mother had advised her that she would never be able to make a living with her art, so she should either acquire a professional skill—like marketing—or marry rich.

He threw back his head and laughed at that one.

She started to think about Dash all the time. She obsessed over his distinctive scent, his slapdash handwriting. She yearned for the slightest hint of him. Alone in bed at night, she wondered what it would be like to kiss him, to touch him. It was a ludicrous infatuation, she knew, but she couldn't help herself.

She began a project to redesign all of his labels, one after another. Rosalyn told herself—and Dash—that she could use them as class projects, but the truth was that spending time with his products made her feel closer to him.

One Saturday morning, she was doing her weekly wash at the Laundromat in town when she spied Dash going into a restaurant across the street, accompanied by a beautiful woman. Frozen, Rosalyn watched as he held the door for his companion, who smiled as she looked up at him. They disappeared inside, the door closing behind them. Shutting Rosalyn out.

She felt as if she had been punched in the gut, so visceral was her reaction.

"Don't be ridiculous, Rosalyn," she scolded herself. *"He's your boss—that's all. You're suffering from a schoolgirl crush. He's not yours, and never will be."*

But she couldn't stop thinking about him. Her classmates at the university—bright, healthy young men full of optimism and promise for the future—now seemed callow in comparison. A few discreet questions to the office manager revealed that Dash was from Phoenix, had been married but was divorced four years ago, had no children, and was thirty-four years old—twelve years older than Rosalyn.

She tried directing her energies into her studies, where they belonged. Besides, Rosalyn reminded herself repeatedly, at the end of the semester her internship would be over and she would likely never see him again. Unless he came by the restaurant. But still . . .

It didn't help.

One Thursday Dash and his friend Hugh were again at the restaurant, at her table. She tried to act casual as she greeted them and took their cocktail orders.

"If I leave you three hundred this time, will you follow me out into the parking lot again?" Dash asked.

She laughed. "*No,* and you certainly don't need to buy me, Dash."

"Did you hear that?" He put his hands over his chest and exclaimed to Hugh: "She called me *Dash!* That's progress."

"Will you please just ask the woman out already?" said Hugh, smiling at her. "Though I can't imagine why she'd agree. She's worth twice as much as you, easily."

Rosalyn's pounding heart seemed to still as she and Dash stared at each other. As if she were in a movie, everyone else in the restaurant—the diners, the waitstaff, the barflies—seemed to fade away.

After a long moment, Dash said: "Rosie girl, you have gotten under my skin. If you say yes, I honestly think I could offer you a lifetime of laughter."

Sometimes, when the pain was especially intense, Rosalyn tried to remind herself of the annoying things Dash had said and done.

Like the way he had commandeered their only

bathroom each morning so that Rosalyn had to jump out of bed before him if she wanted privacy to quickly pee and brush her teeth. Or the way he insisted on watching the Tour de France, *all* three weeks of it, every damned stage, all the while lecturing her on the *peloton* and what the different colored jerseys represented. He teased her for liking the polka-dotted jersey best, and for wondering aloud why scantily clad models stood onstage with the athletes as they received their awards.

He had a habit of loudly clearing his throat when he was thinking. At first she had found it endearing, but soon it became irritating. He liked wall-to-wall carpeting—and it had to be *white* carpeting, which she thought singularly impractical for someone who bought, sold, and drank so much red wine.

He insisted on renting an expensive condo in a posh new development and leased a luxury car. He spent hundreds of dollars on new clothes instead of purchasing perfectly stylish but used garments from the consignment shop in Petaluma, as she always did.

Dash had spent freely, assuming he had plenty of time to earn more money, until his time ran out and Rosalyn was left a widow, deep in debt.

But then she would remember Dash's husky voice crooning to her, making her feel safe and loved, and she would collapse in a heap on the aqua blue bath mat in their cottage bathroom, stifling her sobs with the T-shirt that no longer smelled like him, wishing more than anything that she could hear him clear his throat just one more time.

Chapter Fifteen

O n the second of January, Rosalyn awoke as
excited as a kid on Christmas morning: This
was the day the village grocery store reopened.
It wasn't as though Rosalyn *needed* anything—
Pietro kept the little kitchen well stocked. But
it was a signal that everyday life was resuming,
awakening after a long holiday nap.

Still an early riser, Rosalyn arrived at eight in
the morning, just as the store opened.

"*Bonjour, madame*," Rosalyn said to the stocky
woman in her fifties who sat on a stool behind
the checkout counter. The woman's hair was cut
in a no-nonsense short do, and she wore a bright
orange work smock over a heavy sweater and
jeans. She had her nose in a paperback novel.

"*Bonjour, madame*," said the shopkeeper.
"*Bonne année.*"

"*Et bonne année à vous*," Rosalyn responded.

It felt funny to hear her own voice after so
many days of near-monastic silence. Other than
to Pietro and the man at the gas station, she
hadn't uttered a word in a week.

Slinging a plastic basket over one arm, she

meandered through the aisles of the small store, poking around and getting her bearings. Gazing at the assortment of salamis, pâtés, and cheeses, Rosalyn had to admit that Cochet's store offered a higher-quality selection than her local 7-Eleven in Napa. Too bad it wasn't open twenty-four hours a day.

The store sold a variety of breads, presumably since the town didn't have its own *boulangerie*. Probably the average French person would look down her Gallic nose at convenience store bread, but Rosalyn was happy to find it.

She lingered over a dainty display of round cakes decorated with frangipane, called *galette des Rois*, cake of kings. They were set upon delicate little glass stands lined with doilies, and though she wasn't going to buy a whole cake just for herself, she was tempted.

Instead, she selected a simple baguette, some *pâté de campagne*, a ripe-looking Camembert, a bag of potato chips, some olives, a chocolate bar, and—this last was necessary—a package of toilet paper.

The woman behind the register placed her battered paperback facedown by the register when Rosalyn approached.

"*Bonjour*," Rosalyn said again as she placed her basket of goodies on the counter.

"*Bonjour, madame*," said the cashier with a nod, ringing up her items.

Rosalyn's eyes fell on the book the woman had been reading. She formulated a sentence in her head before asking: "*Y a-t-il une bibliothèque dans le village?*" Is there a library in town?

"*Pas en Cochet.*" Not here in Cochet, the woman answered, her voice rough and deep, a smoker's voice. "There is one in Trefeaux, and a beautiful one in Reims. They are on holiday hours now, though."

"Holiday hours" meant "closed," Rosalyn suspected.

"Sometimes the bus comes through," the woman continued in French.

"The bus?"

"It's a portable library bus."

"Do you know if they have books in English?"

The cashier didn't respond. The look on her face said plenty.

By now there were two people in line behind Rosalyn: a deeply tanned young woman wearing a very short skirt, high-heeled boots, and tights, and a woman in her sixties wearing a puffy purple down coat. They didn't seem particularly friendly, but they waited patiently. It might have been in her imagination, but Rosalyn thought the younger woman was staring at the baguette in her basket.

Finally the young woman said: "Excuse me. There is a *boulangerie* in Salpot, not ten kilometers from here. It has much better bread."

The cashier cast the woman a glare. "This bread is perfectly good."

The woman in the short skirt arched her delicate eyebrows, pursed her lips, and looked away.

"I forgot something," she mumbled, swore under her breath, and returned to the refrigerated section.

"That bread is perfectly good, very fresh," the cashier assured Rosalyn. She looked at her expectantly. "You have no bag?"

"I . . ." Rosalyn suddenly understood why there were so many tote bags hanging in the pantry at Gaspard Blé's place. She should have made the connection since in California shoppers were supposed to bring their own bags to stores, too, though it was no big deal if a person forgot—just a dime for a paper bag. That didn't seem to be an option here. "No, pardon me."

"Then you must buy one."

"All right."

"There is one there for one euro." The cashier gestured to a stack of reusable tote bags in the same bright orange as her smock and printed with one giant sunflower.

"Thank you," said Rosalyn.

The woman handed her a small device, with her card stuck into one end of it. "Please put in your number."

Again with the code.

"It's a credit card. It has no number," Rosalyn said with a shake of her head, feeling so flustered that she defaulted to the Spanish word for number—*número*—instead of the French.

"You must have a code, *madame*."

"I'm sorry. Apparently the American cards don't have codes."

Letting out a long sigh, the cashier reached beneath the counter and came up with an old-fashioned credit card machine, the kind that made an imprint of the card using carbon paper. She placed Rosalyn's card on the metal plate, laid a charge slip on top of it, rolled the metal arm over the two, and then filled out the slip with the amount owed.

Rosalyn felt like a bumbling tourist in a town unaccustomed to outsiders. But surely in the summer months, tourists came to Cochet in search of champagne, right? Surely she wasn't the first American to arrive in town with a credit card but no code.

"You are staying here in Cochet?" the woman asked as she handed the charge slip to Rosalyn to sign.

"Yes. At Gaspard Blé's *gîte*."

"He's out of town," she said, tearing off the top copy, slipping it in the cash register drawer, and handing the carbon paper and bottom copy to Rosalyn. "Did Pietro let you in?"

"Yes." Rosalyn began to pack her own groceries

in her new bright orange bag. The cashier seemed to approve.

As Rosalyn was placing a bag of chips on top, the shopkeeper said: "I am Dominique Cheveaux. A friend of Gaspard's. That was his daughter, Blondine, there, talking about the *boulangerie*—she'll be back *tout de suite.*"

"Oh . . . I'm Rosalyn Acosta. Nice to meet you."

"You are Portuguese?"

"Excuse me?" Rosalyn wasn't sure she understood her properly.

"You sound Portuguese. You look Portuguese."

"I'm from California. But I speak Spanish, and sometimes my Spanish comes through instead of French when I speak. Well, nice to meet you."

Rosalyn turned to leave.

"*Attendez, s'il vous plaît.*" Dominique asked Rosalyn to wait. She called toward the refrigerated section: "Blondine, this is the American from your *gîte!*"

"Coming," called a muffled voice from the other side of the store.

Dominique started ringing up the middle-aged woman's purchases while Rosalyn waited at one side, feeling awkward.

"Do you know the man who has fields to the north of town, the one who practices biodynamic agriculture?" Rosalyn asked.

"Of course. Everyone knows him," said Dominique. "Why?"

"I owe him some money—he helped me out the other day. Do you know how I can get in touch with him?" Rosalyn supposed she could try to connect with the man on one of her early-morning walks, but there was something almost sacred about that predawn hour; she hesitated to sully it with such prosaic concerns.

"*Oof*, that one," said the woman in the puffy purple coat. "He has been in a bad mood since his wife left."

The woman in the short skirt joined them, and nodded. "He keeps to himself," she said. "But you are staying in my *gîte*? You are the American Rosalyn Acosta?"

Rosalyn nodded.

"I am going there right now. My name is Blondine. I am the daughter of Gaspard Blé." She kissed Rosalyn on each cheek. "*Enchantée*."

"It's so nice to meet you," said Rosalyn. "I got your note."

An elderly man joined the line. "I hear she brought him the boy, at least."

"Who?" demanded Blondine.

"She's asking about Jérôme," said the older woman in purple.

"He isn't . . . Are we talking about Jérôme Comtois?" Rosalyn asked.

"You know him?" Blondine asked.

"No, though I do owe him some money."

"How do you owe money to someone you do not know?" Blondine asked, sensibly.

"It's sort of a long story. . . ."

"He never wanted the place," said the man, his voice loud. "But his brother ran off, and he had to step in. That Raphael never was any good. He was a sneaky little kid, too."

All three women nodded.

"I hear Raphael took off with the wife," said Dominique.

"That's just gossip," said the woman in purple, gesturing to Rosalyn. "But she went back to Paris, for sure. She's like you."

"Like me?" Rosalyn asked.

"She means American," said Dominique. "Jérôme's wife was American."

"This sort of thing happens with Americans," said Blondine. "They think all of France is Paris, and when Jérôme brought her to the countryside, she was not pleased. She did not like village life."

The group at the checkout stand gazed at Rosalyn, as though expecting her to explain the actions of a fellow American.

"Personally, I'm not that fond of Paris," Rosalyn said.

The villagers burst out laughing and spoke quickly among themselves. Rosalyn couldn't follow the conversation, but the tone sounded complimentary.

Blondine then introduced her to the other two townspeople, and Rosalyn tried to commit their names to memory: the elderly man was Gilbert Schreyer, and the woman in the puffy purple coat was Valérie Trepot.

"Please wait for me," Blondine said, still in French, "and we'll walk back together."

So Rosalyn waited for Blondine to purchase her groceries, bade *au revoir* to her new acquaintances Dominique, Valérie, and Gilbert, and began walking with Blondine back to the *gîte*.

Seeing Blondine in the natural light, Rosalyn guessed she was probably in her early thirties, older than Rosalyn had initially assumed. Her blond hair was cropped in a flapper style that curled under her chin, and her high-heeled leather boots tapped out a smart tempo. Blondine's short skirt and frenetic energy would have fit in perfectly in New York, Rosalyn thought. She seemed out of place in this sleepy French village, carrying a woven basket of groceries.

Rosalyn tried to keep up with Blondine's confident stride, carefully navigating the cobblestones, wary of patches of snow and ice that glistened here and there. Strategically placed metal posts were the only things standing between them and a car careening too quickly through the narrow streets of the village.

"I must beg your pardon for not meeting you

when you arrived," said Blondine. "My father is furious with me."

"No, it was my fault." Rosalyn was pleased to be able to understand Blondine's French, but felt awkward responding, her lips and tongue tripping over the pronunciation. "I changed my plans and arrived early. And Pietro checked on me and brought groceries. It was nice to have time to settle in."

"Oh, that's good. I could not resist the chance to visit Mallorca. A friend of mine invited me to stay in her place . . . and I think I'm still hungover. Have you been?"

Rosalyn shook her head.

"It is so beautiful there," Blondine said with a dramatic sigh, casting a jaundiced eye at the cold gray of the village. "Not like here. Spain is warm and sunny, even in January. Probably like it is in California. You must cry to be here in this season."

"It's not so bad. I don't mind the cold."

Blondine frowned and made a *tsk*ing sound.

"Honestly, it has been a nice change of pace," Rosalyn continued. "The only problem is that I'm not getting any work done. No one seems to be around."

"We allow the vines to rest from mid-December to mid-January, so a lot of people leave town for the holidays. Like me! It is a tyranny, working on the farms, following the agricultural schedule.

I don't know why anyone would go into this business."

"Aren't *you* in this business?"

She twisted her mouth. "Only because I have no choice, really. There is a great deal of pressure to keep the family business going. And my father . . ." She shrugged. "You will see. Gaspard is a bit of a despot."

Rosalyn was concentrating on understanding the French, and wasn't sure she caught everything. "What do you mean—he is a despot?"

"You will see soon enough, when you meet him. Besides, I am the only one who can speak English with our clients."

Rosalyn couldn't help but notice that, so far, Blondine had spoken only in French to her.

"My father will return soon to prune and tie up the vines; he likes to begin early, when he can get a good crew together. We will show you."

Rosalyn nodded, though she wasn't especially interested; she had seen plenty of vines being tied up in Napa every season. But listening to Blondine made Rosalyn realize just how far away Napa and the Small Fortune Wines office were. She was in daily e-mail contact, and had been gone only a week, but it seemed like more. Cochet felt like another world.

She was a jumble of contradictory emotions: On the one hand it was a profound relief to be somewhere new and foreign, where she wasn't a widow, where people didn't know about the sorrow she carried. At the same time, she was loath to let go of the grief. It felt like her last tangible connection to Dash.

Rosalyn realized she had lost the thread of what Blondine was saying, though it appeared not to matter. Blondine seemed to leave no thought unarticulated, and rarely required a response. As they walked along, she pointed out the house of this person and that, complained about how few services there were in town, and bemoaned the lack of a *boulangerie*. The nearest gas station was the one that Rosalyn had found two villages over, where she had encountered Jérôme Comtois.

They passed the old stone church with a small cemetery, surrounded by a walled garden. Rosalyn noted that the slabs of stone and crypts were aboveground, similar to those she had seen on a trip with Dash to New Orleans. Many were topped with silk flowers and framed photographs of the lost beloved.

"Nearly every village in France, no matter how small, has a church," Blondine explained, noting her interest. "But things have changed; there are not enough priests to go around, or enough old people to attend services, so we have to share priests—that's why mass is celebrated here only every four or five weeks. You can drive to different villages if you want to attend mass each Sunday."

"Are all French people Catholic?" Rosalyn asked.

"*Bien sûr,*" she answered quickly. "Of course. At least, in the countryside. We are raised Catholic, though we're not all *Catholic.* Not like the old days. Now we get married and buried in the church—that's about all. Not many people go every Sunday, mostly just the old people. There are a few Protestants . . . but most are still Catholic."

Blondine pointed out the auto repair shop as they passed by. "An old priest runs that auto repair shop."

"Really? A priest?"

"An ex-priest, I suppose, though once a priest, always a priest. But he was asked to leave the church."

"What did he do?"

"He fell in love," Blondine said with a little sigh. "I think this is very romantic. Don't you? Imagine leaving the church for the person you love."

Rosalyn smiled. "I suppose it depends on how one feels about his commitment to the church. I don't know much about it. I wasn't raised Catholic."

"You weren't? What are you?"

"I'm . . . not much of anything, I guess. My background is sort of generalized Protestantism."

Rosalyn said this last, "generalized Protestantism," in English since she couldn't fathom how to translate it.

Blondine turned to her, a frown marring her smooth brow. "*Je ne comprends pas*."

Rosalyn relapsed into French, saying: "It doesn't matter. I didn't grow up in a churchgoing family. So, the priest was asked to leave the church because he fell in love with a woman?" Rosalyn asked, hoping to change the subject. "That seems harsh."

"Oh no, the reason it was so shocking wasn't that he fell in love, but that he fell in love with a *man*." She lifted one eyebrow and gave Rosalyn a significant glance. "I don't think I have to tell you that this is not California. These things are still whispered about in small towns here. . . ." She let out a sigh. "But *I* think it's a romantic story, to give up so much for the one you love, whether woman or man."

"Are they still together?"

She shook her head. "It is very sad. His love was killed in the Algerian war."

"But the priest stayed here, in Cochet?"

She nodded. "The garage belonged to his love's family. I don't think he makes much money, but the shop is part of his house. And even though he's very old, Monsieur Bonnet is still good with cars. He served in the military as well."

Blondine then switched subjects and told Rosalyn she had come to Dominique's store this morning because she had forgotten the vanilla for the *crème anglaise*, which her mother had promised to teach her to make tonight. Her parents had separated when she was a teen, she said, though they were not divorced. She had two brothers and one half sister, but none of them showed any aptitude for wine. Blondine sold wine for her father's vineyard, but what she really wanted to do was to become an independent agent and, above all, to visit the wine-producing regions of the United States.

"But to get a work visa? Impossible . . ." She trailed off with a shake of her head. "It is impossible. The United States is worse than France, and we're *terrible.* Tell me, what are the men like where you are from?"

Rosalyn's first thought, as always, was of Dash, but that wasn't fair. Dash was one of a kind. More typical were the boys she had known in college, often sweet but unfocused and unsophisticated, or the surfer dudes, who acted as if there was sand between their ears as well as between their toes. The Silicon Valley sorts were young and ambitious, and though often bright and hardworking, many were socially immature, as though their parents had never taught them how to do their own laundry.

And yet to a Frenchwoman raised in a small town by a farmer, perhaps hipsters who couldn't cook but were willing, if not eager, to spend hundreds of dollars on fancy cocktails and meals in farm-to-table restaurants would seem glamorous.

"Why don't you come to Napa and see for yourself?" Rosalyn said, having given up on describing American men.

"Really? I would love that!" Blondine said, then added, deflated, "But I don't know if my father would allow it."

Rosalyn opened her mouth to ask why a grown woman needed her father's permission, but refrained.

Blondine gave her a sidelong glance. "I know. It sounds strange, does it not? My father is very demanding. Anyway, here we are, *chez vous*. How do you like the *gîte*?"

"It's lovely," said Rosalyn.

"But you ran out of toilet paper," Blondine said, peeking into Rosalyn's bag of groceries, as if taking notes. "I must stock more. We haven't rented the room out yet, so you are the first. Please, tell us if you need anything different. I have heard that Americans are very particular about their bathrooms. We made the shower after an American design."

"It's really quite nice," Rosalyn assured her, wondering if she had somehow been too free with the toilet paper.

"But you Americans always say that, and then you don't return or you leave a terrible review on the Internet. I have been warned this is how you are. Why are you afraid to tell us to our face? I'm not sure I like this."

Again, Rosalyn felt odd speaking on behalf of all Americans. *There are more than three hundred million of us,* she felt like saying. *We're a diverse lot.* But perhaps Blondine was right about the strange politeness face-to-face, with an Internet bomb lobbed afterward. It wasn't the sort of thing Rosalyn would do, but she could imagine others might.

"You really want to know?"

"Yes, I asked you already."

"Okay . . . I could use more towels, and a hair dryer would be great. Maybe a hot pot and tea or coffee service so a guest doesn't have to go to the kitchen just for a hot drink? And the lights aren't very convenient—you have to switch them off at the door rather than from the bed. Also, I can't figure out how to make the shutters go up and down very well." Rosalyn was glad she had looked up the word for "shutters," thinking to ask Pietro how to operate them: *les volets.* "In fact, some curtains would be nice."

"This is a lot." Blondine frowned. "I thought you said everything was fine."

Rosalyn let out a startled chuckle. "And I meant it—but you asked me to tell you everything that wasn't perfect, so I did."

Blondine shrugged. "Show me."

They went into the *gîte*. Rosalyn cringed when she realized she had left the bed a tangled mess of sheets; there was a damp towel hanging on the back of a chair and yesterday's clothes were in a pile on the floor.

Blondine didn't say a word, crossing to the shutters and showing her how to work the controls. "You don't have shutters like these in America?"

"Not really. Some businesses have them, but not homes. Is it . . . Is theft a big problem here?"

"No. Why?"

"They look like high-security shutters."

"Huh." Blondine brought the shutters all the way down so that it was completely dark inside. "This way you can sleep. You see?"

"But it's so disorienting not to know what time it is because it's always dark. Especially when you have jet lag. If you added some curtains, a visitor could choose how much light they wanted. It's just a suggestion. But since you asked: Americans like choices, especially when they're on vacation."

Blondine nodded, and seemed to make a mental note. "What else?"

"Maybe some art on the walls? Something to remind guests that they're in France."

"I keep meaning to get to that. Oh, these are nice," Blondine said, moving over to the table, where a few of Rosalyn's drawings were propped up against the wall.

"Those are just sketches. . . ."

"Of the grapevines, yes? We should put up art that shows grapes and things, I think. If I leave it to my father, he'll put up photographs of muddy tractors."

Rosalyn smiled. "I think you're right. The average tourist would prefer looking at grapevines rather than tractors. But it should be something colorful, not black-and-white like these pencil drawings. Maybe some champagne glasses, bottles, that sort of thing? You could keep with the theme. Have fun with it."

"Do you want to paint the walls with things like that while you're here?"

"Oh, I don't . . . I don't know."

"These are good suggestions. Thank you," Blondine said, apparently done with the conversation. "Your decoration is broken," she said, gesturing to the broken ornament. "I'll get you a new one."

"Oh no, thank you. I picked it up like that. I like it that way."

Blondine raised one eyebrow, made that little *tsk*ing sound again. "This evening, you must come with me and my mother to dinner at my aunt's house."

"Oh, that is so kind of you, really, but . . ." As much as she had looked forward to the opening of Dominique's market, socializing with strangers—and stumbling along in French—had tired her out.

She couldn't imagine sitting through a French family dinner, most likely falling asleep over her escargots. All she wanted at the moment was to hide away for a bit, maybe watch something on her computer, get a little work done, and not have to talk to anyone.

Maybe she truly *was* becoming a hermit.

"You do not want to come?" Blondine demanded in English.

"Thank you, but I have some work to do, and I bought some things for dinner. . . ."

"You will eat alone?" Blondine cast a doubtful eye at the potato chips that were peeking out of the orange tote bag Rosalyn had placed on the table.

Self-conscious, Rosalyn stood up straighter and tried to pull in her stomach.

"Truly, Blondine, I am so appreciative of your generous hospitality, but I am very tired. Also, the office in California is still open, and because of the time difference, I need to spend the evening making phone calls and answering e-mails for work."

Blondine pursed her lips, and then nodded, reverting to French as she led the way back out into the courtyard.

"All right, but at least let me make you something to eat now. It is early—have you eaten yet? I know you Americans are accustomed to big breakfasts."

"Oh no, there's no need."

"Please, you will be doing me a favor. My father will kill me if I don't take care of you."

They both looked up as the sound of crunching gravel signaled the arrival of a car in the drive. It was a large, shiny black vehicle with tinted windows. As it pulled up, one of the windows rolled down with a smooth hum, and a head popped out.

Emma Kinsley.

Chapter Sixteen

Lucie

Every day the explosions—and the path of destruction—come nearer. I suppose it is human nature to become accustomed, and some even lay bets on which neighborhood has been hit as we listen to the racket.

A curfew was imposed, from six in the morning to six at night. Six in the morning was usually when the shelling began, since the people walked out into the streets to try to work or find food or simply interact with other humans. But it was the nights that were unbearable. After six in the afternoon, it was dark, as we had no gas or electricity, and our pipes shattered from the cold. There was no firewood, and all the trains that used to bring supplies are now used to transport troops and munitions. We could not light candles or oil lamps after dark, for fear the lights would attract a sniper's attention, and we blacked out windows so the enemy couldn't determine which areas of the city were still inhabited. We were so cold and damp that many dropped from illness.

Still and all, there were few complaints. If

anyone laments the situation, someone always says, "Just imagine the poor *poilus* in the trenches!"

We passed a few miserable weeks in our borrowed home. One day I was standing in line for bread, hoping the wretched *Boches* would hold off on the shelling for another twenty minutes at least, when a boy who used to garden for us told me people were seeking refuge in the caves under the House of Pommery. He said some shops were moving underground as well, and many accepted barter instead of proper francs.

Father had taught me that long before housing bottles of champagne, the *crayères* had been a sanctuary for Christians hiding from the Romans; it made a certain kind of sense that now they offered a haven to the *Rémois* escaping the bombardment.

The prospect of finding refuge belowground, where one could ignite a lamp without fear and the temperature never fell below that of a chilly evening, was like turning on a light within me. Warmth flowed through my veins, reaching even to my fingers, which were numb with cold as I ran through the streets, staying close to the walls so as not to present an easy target, the precious baguette tucked under my arm.

My mother at first was appalled by the idea of sheltering underground "like vermin." But as she was saying this, the ground shook, and Henri rushed in, barely escaping a renewed round of shelling that took down a neighboring house. We gathered the few things we had managed to save when we fled Villa Traverne—my mother's knitting needles, some photos, a few books—and presented ourselves at the top of the steps leading down to the Pommery caves.

The Pommery champagne house had been a fine, proud mansion built in the style of an Elizabethan manor. But now most of the buildings had been damaged by the shelling; some were now nothing but smoking piles of rubble. Many employees already had been killed.

As I descended those hundred sixteen steps into the Pommery cellars for the first time, the chill entered my bones. But it was the sour smell that most impressed itself upon me. Hundreds, perhaps thousands, of women and children, a few elderly or infirm men, were crowded into the tunnels. They had the blank, staring-into-space visages I had come to know from those who had experienced the bombs, had seen bloody limbs left in the street, had witnessed the wholesale destruction of Reims. They shared the otherworldly sensation that the world was no longer what we knew.

The air was stale and smoky from oil lamps and candles, vinegary from too many unwashed people and too little fresh air. One old blind woman had brought her bird in a cage, and it sang, still; there were a few potted plants and some colorful bits of bric-a-brac salvaged from the ruins. But those were the only bits of cheer.

The malaise, the dispiritedness, hit me like the concussion of a bomb: ours was a last-ditch effort to survive. To live.

It was a shadowy, surreal hell. But it was a refuge from the shells and sniper fire.

As we advanced deeper into the caves, my mother whispered: *The world has turned upside down.*

Chapter Seventeen

"Emma! What are you doing here?" Rosalyn went over to the car to greet her friend.

"You mentioned Gaspard Blé, and I realized it had been ages since I stopped by. Also, because of this busted leg of mine, I need a place to stay without stairs and with an accessible shower. I thought his new *gîte* might be just the thing."

"But you said there was nothing to do in Cochet."

"There really isn't! But I have a car and a driver after all. This is the estimable André, by the way. My irreplaceable assistant. Heaven only knows where I'd be without him."

A tall, attractive man climbed out of the driver's seat. He looked like a model, with jet-black hair dyed platinum blond at the tips.

"*Bonjour, mesdames*," he said to Rosalyn and Blondine with a nod, and opened the car door to help Emma out. She hopped on one foot, and André steadied her with one hand while passing her a pair of crutches.

"Blondine! My love! How are you!" effused Emma.

Blondine did not look pleased to see Emma. "What do *you* do here?" she demanded in English.

"Just stopped by to say hello, and thought I'd stay a spell. Rosalyn and I met on the plane, if you can believe that luck."

"My father is in Spain."

"Oh good! Even better. I already called and talked with Pietro, and he told me I could have the *Pinot Meunier* room, gave me the codes for the doors and everything. André will stay upstairs in *Pinot Noir*."

Blondine muttered under her breath.

"Don't let her fool you." Emma caught Rosalyn's eye. "She adores me. This is just the way the French are. They show their love with gruffness. They try to be an aloof culture, but they don't quite pull it off. Am I right, Blondine?"

Blondine shot her a look, then turned back to Rosalyn. "Come. I will make you an omelet."

"Honestly, please don't trouble yourself," said Rosalyn.

"Nonsense." Blondine punched the code on the keypad next to the door leading to the kitchen/tasting room, and went inside. Rosalyn held the door for Emma, who instructed André to stow their luggage in their rooms and then go relax.

"Isn't your man hungry, too?" asked Blondine.

"André isn't 'my man,' sad to say. And he does his own thing—he'll be fine," said Emma.

"As opposed to you," said Blondine, leading the way into the kitchen. She turned to Rosalyn. "Anywhere there's food, this one will show up. We can't get rid of her."

Unsure whether she understood the French, Rosalyn asked: "You're trying to get rid of Emma?"

"Of course. She comes and eats our food and drinks our wine and doesn't think about it."

Emma grinned as she leaned her crutches up against the counter and hoisted herself up onto a stool. "I'm going to put this place on the map. Just wait and see. Hey, please make this old woman's heart happy and tell me you have a chilled bottle of bubbly in that little *frigo* of yours." She gestured to the small refrigerator.

"*You* are going to put Champagne on the map?" Blondine demanded. Though she sounded annoyed, Blondine did as Emma wished, taking a bottle from the fridge and setting it on the counter. "We are already world famous for our sparkling wine."

"That's true of champagne in general, but decidedly *not* true of Blé Champagne in particular." Emma turned to Rosalyn. "You should see their pamphlets, and the website. *Someone's* English is not up to snuff."

"I would be happy to look over things while I'm here," Rosalyn offered, taking a stool beside Emma. "If I can do anything to help . . ."

"I speak very well the English," insisted Blondine. "I study this for many years." She reverted to French with a sullen shrug. "But it is difficult to understand the differences between English spoken in England, in Australia, and in America. Also, there are other countries where they speak your language, too. It is very complicated. Good thing champagne is a universal language, eh?"

"Indeed it is. To champagne," Emma said, easing the cork out of the bottle with a soft sigh, and pouring the pale golden liquid into a flute. "Just a bit to start the day. Would you like some?"

"Isn't it a little early for champagne?" Rosalyn said, glancing at the clock.

"See what I mean about the puritanical outlook of Americans?" said Emma.

"It's not that. It's just . . ." Rosalyn looked toward Blondine. "Is it customary to drink champagne with breakfast?"

Blondine rose one eyebrow. "Only for the old folks, like my father and Emma."

"I am impervious to insults, dear girl," Emma said. "When the great Noël Coward was asked why he drank champagne for breakfast, he answered: 'Doesn't everyone?' And *he* was a freaking genius."

The room filled with the aroma of fresh baked goods as Blondine took several plump croissants out of a bag and placed them on a large platter. Their flaky layers glistened with butter. Despite her earlier protestations that she wasn't hungry, Rosalyn's mouth watered.

"These are from the Boulangerie Julien. Like I said, it is the best."

Blondine bent down to extract butter from the small refrigerator. She cracked several eggs into a bowl, added a dollop of cream and some fresh chopped herbs, and whisked them together with a practiced hand.

"So, when is your father due back?" asked Emma.

Blondine made a face. "Soon, I think."

"Gaspard's a character," Emma told Rosalyn. "He's what I like to call a 'great man.' "

"I thought you said he was a little . . ." Rosalyn held back in front of Blondine.

"I don't mean 'great man' as in a great humanitarian. He has 'great man syndrome,' thinks his you-know-what doesn't stink. Like all those artists and authors who walk around like they're God's gift, and never acknowledge all the women in their lives who do the cooking and the cleaning and the raising of children so the menfolk can focus on themselves. Pablo Picasso, Ernest Hemingway—you know the type. Larger than life. Gaspard expects everyone around him, including his darling daughter Blondine, to do what he says, when he says it, and to accommodate him so he can continue with his great, important work."

"I don't know about this," said Blondine with a shrug. "But it is true that he is . . . a character."

They fell silent. Rosalyn changed the subject. "So, seriously, is it typical to drink champagne for breakfast here?"

"Only on special occasions," said Blondine. "It is more common for lunch."

"And for apéritif, and with dinner, and after dinner . . . ," added Emma.

"Back home, we associate champagne with celebrations," said Rosalyn, "though we're hoping to change that by getting more bars to offer it by the glass."

"We drink it for celebrations as well," said Blondine. "But really, for us it is our local wine, like that of any other region. Bordeaux, Burgundy, *Vin Jaune* in the Jura. The locals drink it with everything, actually."

"So how did it become associated with celebrations?"

"Ah, good question," said Emma. "That was the work of Madame Jeanne Pommery."

"As in the Pommery Champagne House?" asked Rosalyn.

"Yes," said Blondine, pouring the egg mixture into a hot pan greased with a mixture of butter and olive oil. "Champagne used to be very sweet, so sweet that it was said only the British would drink it. No offense."

"None taken," Emma said. "She's American, and I'm Australian. No Brits here."

Blondine shrugged, as if it was all the same to her. "Anyway, Madame Pommery was the one to stop adding so much sugar. She invented brut—you call it dry—champagne. She was a young widow and took over the business from her husband, just like the *veuve* Clicquot, who also had children to support. They both became major players in the champagne industry in the nineteenth century."

Veuve meant "widow," Rosalyn knew, but she had never really thought about the meaning of the famous champagne named Veuve Clicquot.

At least Rosalyn had no child to worry about when Dash died, though that always felt like a double-edged sword. *"Too bad you didn't have children to remember him by."*

Grief brain again. Rosalyn forced herself to refocus on the conversation between Emma and Blondine. Although Emma had claimed her French was bad, and even Rosalyn could hear she had an atrocious accent, she displayed a good command of the language.

"In Champagne we say that we would be nowhere without the widows," said Blondine.

"That's a saying?"

"Oh, sure. *Les veuves* Clicquot and Pommery,

and later Lily Bollinger, too," said Emma. "And England's Queen Victoria—another widow—was one of Pommery's best customers, and helped to popularize champagne in Britain. The history of champagne is a history of widows."

Rosalyn wasn't the only one.

"Emma, didn't Lucie and the others take refuge in the caves of the Pommery winery?" Rosalyn said.

Blondine tilted her head, a questioning look on her face.

"From my letters," said Emma, explaining to Blondine the correspondence between Émile Legrand and her aunt Doris. "Lucie is the name of a young woman Émile mentions often. She and her family took shelter in the Pommery caves during the German bombardment."

Blondine waved off the idea. "I don't like war talk. The old people always go on and on about the war."

"Wrong war," said Emma. "This was the *First* World War, the Great War. Meant to end all wars."

"They got that wrong," said Blondine.

"They did, indeed."

"I did always hear about the smiling angel of Reims, though," said Blondine, taking the pan off the heat. She tilted it with a practiced hand, and the omelet slid smoothly onto a platter. "I think that was from the First World War."

"Do I want to know what happened to the

smiling angel of Reims?" Rosalyn asked, wincing slightly.

"Her head fell off," said Blondine, drawing a finger across her neck in a dramatic gesture, "during the bombings."

"She never stopped smiling, though," said Emma. "Talk about a metaphor."

"The Reims Cathedral was bombed by the Germans," said Blondine, dividing the omelet in three and placing the slices on plates, garnishing them with chopped parsley and a croissant, and setting the plates on the table nearest the counter. "It was a scandal, a true outrage, that such a monument should be destroyed. All of the kings of France were crowned in the Reims Cathedral, and even Joan of Arc came there in her triumph. It was barbarous of them to destroy such a treasure, the whole world agreed."

"It's true," said Emma in English as they all sat down to eat. "The German destruction of such a beautiful and historic building was used as anti-Hun propaganda—Germans were said not to respect religion, or art. But to me the worst part was that the cathedral had been used as a makeshift hospital, with the wounded sleeping on straw on the floor. The incendiary bombs caught some scaffolding on fire, which melted the lead from the roof and rained molten metal down on the wounded, lighting the straw on fire. It was a bloodbath."

"That's horrifying," said Rosalyn. The food on the plate in front of her lost its appeal.

"Enough war talk," said Blondine. "With the festival of Saint Vincent coming up, you will see bottles opened to accompany breakfast—that is sure."

"Speaking of celebrations, Rosalyn, you'll want to investigate the region before the craziness starts," said Emma. "These sleepy little villages will be inundated in a few weeks, and you won't even be able to park."

"That's why I came early," said Rosalyn. "I was supposed to connect with François Martin, and reach out to a few other producers, before the festival."

"Martin is in Martinique," said Blondine. "A lot of the producers leave after the Christmas celebrations, because things are quiet in the vines."

Not for the first time, Rosalyn wondered why Hugh had booked her on a flight departing immediately after Christmas. He had to have known that everyone she was supposed to meet in France would be somewhere else during the holidays. Now that she thought of it, why had he made all the travel arrangements himself, instead of having her do it, as he usually did? Had he understood, better than she had, that she'd needed a break—and thought he knew just what kind of break she needed most? Typical Hugh.

Bless him.

"Speaking of the festival," said Blondine, "you'll need a costume."

"Excuse me?" Rosalyn's heart sank. She wore a mask every day; if only they knew. "I'm not what you would call a costume person."

"Don't worry. I will help you. It's simple: a skirt and a blouse, a red cape, and the lace cap. It's traditional, and maybe seems silly, but we all do it."

"So, I was thinking . . . ," said Emma.

"You see? I knew she had something up her sleeve," said Blondine. "She thinks because she is rich she can do whatever she likes."

Emma just smiled, Cheshire cat–like, and continued addressing Rosalyn. "You said you didn't want to work for me, and I respect that. But you're looking for small champagne producers, right? Jérôme Comtois mostly grows grapes for others, but he has started to make his own champagne—a small vintage, but I hear it's quite good. What if you went to talk to him about representing his champagne in the United States?"

Rosalyn blinked. "I sort of met Comtois already, though he wasn't what I'd call overly friendly. And I got the feeling from the folks at the store today that he doesn't care for Americans."

"They were gossiping about him at Dominique's?" Emma asked. "It figures. There's no café or bar in the village, so the store's gossip central."

"You forgot about the auto repair shop," mentioned Rosalyn.

"Monsieur Bonnet does not allow gossip at his shop," said Blondine, her tone grave. "He was a victim of it himself."

"Comtois might not like Americans," said Emma, "but that doesn't mean he wouldn't like *selling* his champagne to Americans. Business is business."

Blondine stuck out her chin. "This is not a bad idea. Everyone likes the idea of being represented in the American market. Americans can be strange, but they are good customers."

"But . . ." Rosalyn couldn't think of a reason to object, except that she still cringed at the thought of what had happened at the gas station. On the other hand, it would provide the perfect opportunity to pay him the money she owed him. "I really do have other work to do."

"Like what?" Emma asked. "Martin is out of town, and according to Blondine, he's a real pain in the ass anyway."

"Never did I say this," Blondine denied, in English.

"You didn't have to; everyone knows it's true," said Emma. "Anyway, Rosalyn, what could it hurt? You've got time, and Comtois is around. He was sighted at the co-op outside Reims last night."

"How is it you know so much?" Rosalyn asked. "You just arrived in town."

"She's rich," quipped Blondine in a dismissive tone.

"I have an inquiring mind," Emma said. "And a lot of friends. So, it's a plan, then: Rosalyn will go talk to Comtois about representing his wine, and then cleverly work the conversation around to his collection."

Rosalyn raised an eyebrow. "Sure, that's a natural segue—from asking about his wine crop to inquiring as to the whereabouts of a century-old bundle of your aunt's letters."

"You're a smart girl. You'll figure it out."

"Why don't you ask him yourself?"

"Because everyone here knows her," said Blondine. "She is not popular."

"Now you're hurting my feelings." Emma's chuckle belied her words. "The *Champenois* don't particularly like foreigners and they don't like interlopers, and I fear I have a reputation as both. But I like to think I'm exceedingly popular, all things considered, for a foreign interloper."

"That reminds me," said Rosalyn. "I should ask: Is *your* champagne represented in the U.S.?"

"Of course. For years now. How do you think I got so rich?"

"Oh, good for you, then," Rosalyn said as she carried their dirty plates into the kitchen sink to wash them. "Thank you for the omelet, Blondine. That was delicious."

"*De rien*. It is nothing."

"One more thing, Emma," said Rosalyn. "Let me give you back your letter, before I forget."

Emma seemed to sense her reluctance, her hawk eyes never leaving Rosalyn's face.

"I have a better idea. You're not doing much at the moment, right? Whereas I am involved in a whole *bordel*." Emma waved a big hand in the air. "Really, it's not worth going into, but suffice it to say that it's a real pain in my ass. Anyway, since you've got all the time in the world—"

"Emma, I already told you: I'm not looking for a job."

"I get that. But you enjoyed reading the letters, didn't you? What if you start reading through the rest of them, put them in order for me, maybe continue to translate them or at least make a few notes as you read? You did such a good job on the one you e-mailed me about."

"Oh, I don't know. . . ."

"It would be great for your French."

"Yes, I'll have a great vocabulary the next time I want to chat about bombs, blood, and barbed wire. But honestly, Emma, you're asking me to take on a lot of responsibility. What if . . . what if something happened to the letters?" asked Rosalyn. "They're irreplaceable."

"What would happen to them?" asked Blondine.

"I don't know. . . . They could get wet, or burned, or . . ." Rosalyn trailed off with a shrug and reverted to English. "I'm such a klutz lately. The other week, I left my e-reader on my car roof and drove off. What if I spilled coffee on them, or left them in a café somewhere?"

"What is 'klutz'?" Blondine asked.

"*Empotée*," said Emma. "*Maladroite*."

"Huh. *You're* a klutz?" said Blondine. "Emma's the one with the broken leg. And last time she was here, she had a cast on her arm."

"Can't argue with that." Emma laughed. "Anyway, Rosalyn, that's catastrophic thinking, and that's not good for anybody. Nothing's going to happen to the letters, and if it does—well, that's the way the cookie crumbles. They've been scanned into the computer, so you could read them that way if it would make you feel better. But I warn you: The letters are a *lot* easier to read in person, what with the faded ink, the old-fashioned handwriting, and the holes and deletions from the military censors."

As Emma spoke, Rosalyn silently agreed. It was the feeling of the letters in her hands, the tangible connection to history, that had attracted her to them in the first place. Reading digitized images on a computer screen wouldn't be the same.

"Besides," continued Emma, "you saw what happened to them on the plane. If they're going to be damaged or destroyed, it's much likelier to happen when they're in my possession than in yours. At least you have two good legs. Blondine's right. I'm like Calamity Jane."

More like the Unsinkable Molly Brown, Rosalyn thought to herself.

"At the very least we should put them in plastic sleeves to protect them," said Rosalyn.

"My father has a whole bunch in the office that we use for our wine tastings," said Blondine. "Want me to get some?"

"They're not archival quality," said Emma. "But they'll do in a pinch."

And so the three women spent the next hour carefully inserting old letters into protective plastic sleeves, until Emma had to leave for an appointment and Blondine needed to cover the phones in the office. Later that morning, André brought another two boxes full of letters down to *Chambre Chardonnay*. As Emma had said, there were hundreds, spanning years.

It dawned on Rosalyn that, what with Emma and André sharing the *gîte*, Blondine now at work daily in the office, and Gaspard Blé arriving soon, her peculiar countryside hermitage had come to an end.

Strangely enough, the realization didn't cast her into despair.

Chapter Eighteen

Rosalyn couldn't help herself: she dove into the letters, and spent the rest of the day struggling with the French and reading the faded—and often censored—words.

She started with an easy one: Doris's first letter. The script was slanted and florid, with decorative swirls and bobs that looked lovely but were difficult to decipher, like ornate calligraphy. But at least it was in English.

> November 13, 1914
>
> Dear Monsieur Legrand:
>
> It seems odd to be writing to someone I have never met, and am unlikely ever to meet. Allow me to introduce myself. My name is Doris Dickinson Whittaker, and I live near a town named Coonawara, in Australia. Although half the blood in my veins is French, thanks to my dear departed mother, I learned her native language in school rather than at her knee. I am therefore committing the great sin of composing this letter in English first,

and then translating it into the French as I remember from school, with the loyal but occasionally unreliable assistance of the great, fat dictionary that sits upon my desk.

A friend of mine told me about the *marraines de guerre*, the women who write to boys on the front, to boost their spirits and remind them of home and country. And yet you, my poor Émile, must be content with an Australian *marraine*, one who can't possibly remind you of home and hearth and country! But I hope that our correspondence may remind you, at least in part, of what you are fighting for.

For I am with you brave French boys, in heart and soul.

Doris

Australia
1914

Doris sat back in her fine leather chair, the unfinished letter on the gleaming mahogany desk in front of her. She gazed at the ornate grandfather clock and the carved marble mantelpiece, the tasseled velvet curtains and the embroidered silk pillows adorning the velvet love seat. The things her husband had provided for her.

Beautiful things, made more so by contrast with the scorch marks that ran along the foundation of her sitting room. Doris had had most of the interior rooms gutted and repaired, but intentionally left that one corner unretouched, the soot and burn marks reminding her of the life she had nearly lost, along with her home.

The phrase "war godmothers" did not sound nearly as romantic as *marraines de guerre*, Doris thought, and wondered if it was merely a function of the translation, or whether the French language was inherently more beautiful than English. She didn't like that the English phrase used "god" in the title. Since this war had begun, Doris sometimes doubted whether He had ever existed at all, or whether He had merely grown tired of human antics and forsaken them.

She could hardly blame Him, if so.

It was unusual for an Australian woman to be a *marraine de guerre*—as she had just penned to the young Monsieur Émile Legrand, most *marraines* were French. But Doris had not hesitated to use her money to make it happen; one way or another, she would do her part for the war effort.

And she had always wanted a child to pass her wisdom on to. Not that she had much wisdom, but she supposed some inevitably came with age, no matter how one tried to hide from it. What else was money for, after all? To find the name and essential military address of one Émile Legrand, a simple farm boy from the outskirts of Reims, in the region of Champagne, in the north of France, not far from the borders with Germany and Belgium. The site of the fiercest fighting.

What else should she tell her new "godson" about herself? Doris leaned over the desk once again and reached for her pen, the kind that had a reservoir of ink inside the barrel, the clever thing. Her husband had insisted on buying these extravagantly priced fountain pens, preferring them over the dip pens that stained so easily. She supposed that was yet another thing she should thank him for.

She started to write, then hesitated, her pen held aloft. Her girlhood friend Caroline Bickley had urged Doris not to reveal her wealth or marital status, for fear she might be taken advantage of. *A soldier may be fighting for a noble cause,* Caroline had said sternly over the rim of her teacup. *But that does not mean that all soldiers are noble.* And indeed, the flyer that described the ideal *marraine* underscored the importance of not becoming too personal—some of the public already considered correspondence between unmarried men and women without benefit of chaperones a touch unsavory.

People were ridiculous.

I am so sorry that you have been compelled to go to war at such a young age. I imagine you garbed in your uniform of sky blue trousers and jacket, as we have seen described in our newspapers. The traditional uniform of bright red trousers was very smart, though I understand it made you more visible to those dastardly Huns!

I am sure you are very brave, but I know you would rather be dressed in your simple muslins, guiding the plow and bringing in the harvest. Please tell me what you can about your life before the war, and even now; perhaps it would be a solace to you to share your experiences with a "mother" so very far away.

I assure you, I am not a delicate flower, and I read every account of the war that comes to us, no matter the wretchedness of the violence. I do not fear the darkness. If it is any succor to you to share with me, please describe to me your life in the trenches.

Doris caught a glimpse of herself, distorted in the reflection of the curved glass doors of an intricately inlaid curio cabinet imported from England.

Her father had always instructed Doris to make

the most of her winsome good looks, and ever the obedient child, she had obeyed, catching the eye of the richest man in the county, Richard Whittaker. For all the good his fortune had done her. She was scarred now, not from a fist but from a life of bitterness. Her plump, youthful face had not aged well, and over the years, it had settled into the hard angles and sharp planes of disappointment and resentment. No children, no husband, sitting in her fire-damaged mansion with a staff who cared for her because she paid them to. Her once-lithe figure was now heavy and clumsy, due to her fondness for pastries and tea cakes. Food and wine were her last indulgences.

Her only other source of happiness was her collection of dollhouses.

There was a Cotswold cottage, a Venetian town house, a Tokyo home with small rice paper doors. And within, tiny mothers and fathers, even tinier children. Pets and grandparents. Families. Symbols of lives Doris would never live, but could fantasize about.

She peeked into the windows of her newest acquisition: a petite French farmhouse, complete with stone walls. She had asked the doll maker to build it when she read about the victory of the Marne, followed by the siege of Reims and the bombardment of the cathedral. Inside the farmhouse, three miniature baguettes sat on the big wooden kitchen table, alongside a mound of diminutive produce and petite baskets of apples. The mother worked in the kitchen; the father brought home a rabbit for dinner. Bundles of herbs—thyme and lavender—hung from the rafters. A fiddle sat in the corner; she imagined the father played in the evenings, when the family gathered around the stone hearth, a large iron pot of simmering stew hanging from a hook above the red-orange embers.

It was a simple house, a happy home.

Doris thought of the invading Germans—the "barbarian Huns," as the English and Australian press had started to call them—marching across the fields of Belgium and France, tipping over the water troughs for the horses, slaughtering the cows and sheep to feed themselves, terrorizing the children. Turning the neat green fields red with blood . . .

Best not to think about that. The French—with the British and Australians and other allies—would fight valiantly against the invading hordes. And they would be victorious.

They *had* to be victorious.

After finishing her letter to Émile, Doris would take on the unpleasant task of writing to influential friends in the United States, telling them in no uncertain terms that their nation must not stay neutral but must rally to the support of their good friends France and England.

Doris thought of the day the messenger came

to the door with the news of her husband's death. He had shot himself, the drunken fool, when his pistol fired as he climbed over a fence chasing a black cockatoo he was convinced had insulted him. It was a stupid and entirely avoidable act of an idiot, and exactly the sort of thing she had come to expect of him. Doris referred to her husband's untimely demise with the polite fiction "a hunting accident," and those who knew the truth tactfully pretended they didn't.

As Caroline Bickley had swathed Doris in the customary widow's weeds, she counseled: "Chin up, my dear. There is something peculiarly compelling about a widow who has found her voice."

Finally, Doris concluded her letter to Émile, the simple French farm boy, with a quotation:

> The American writer Edgar Allan Poe wrote: "In the Heavens above, the angels, whispering to one another, can find, among their burning terms of love, none so devotional as that of 'Mother.'" I am sure you have a true mother who is thinking of you, and I have no intention, still less the ability, to replace her, but I thank you for allowing me to be your *marraine de guerre*, just for now. Just until the nightmare is over.

Once the missive was composed, Doris set about the onerous task of translating it into her finishing school French—something else she should thank her husband for. She had come to him a "diamond in the rough," as he'd liked to say, and he'd said it often. They met when she was fifteen, and he nearly forty. With her parents' enthusiastic approval, Richard sent her to finishing school to be trained and molded into the proper society wife he believed he deserved. Doris had been willing enough at the time—she was barely more than a child, she reflected—and she had learned many things during those years.

Quite enough, her dear brother, Louis, liked to say, to ensure Doris would never become a proper wife.

She stared at the letter, once again hesitating. Finally, she signed it:

Yours truly,
Mrs. Doris Dickinson Whittaker

Chapter Nineteen

Rosalyn riffled through the first group of letters, the ones Emma had carried with her on the flight to Paris. They seemed to be the earliest correspondence, most dating from late 1914 or the winter months of 1915.

Of course, back in the day of snail mail—mail that had to pass through a war zone, no less—Émile might well have been answering questions Doris had written in several previous letters. If he was writing a few times a week, there wouldn't be a straightforward tie between letters received and letters answered. It would take weeks or even months for a letter to go from France to Australia, and back again.

After searching through stacks of envelopes, Rosalyn discovered one from Émile stamped December 28 that seemed to be his response to Doris's first missive:

> My esteemed Mrs. Whittaker,
> I was so very pleased to receive your kind and fascinating letter. It is an amazing thing in our modern world, to be

able to correspond with someone so very far away. Someone from another country, across the vast ocean, in Australia! My imagination is set afire just thinking of the voyages by carriage, train, and sea, the exploits and adventures through which our letters must pass to arrive in our hands!

Please rest assured that your French is very good. Perhaps better than my own. Though I enjoy reading, I cannot claim to be a well-educated man.

We are so grateful to have Australian troops fighting by our sides; I have met many, and they are always very cheery. Though I cannot understand their English, I have been led to believe that they, along with the British troops, are disappointed in the beer of the xxx region. If only we were in Reims, I would serve them our famous champagne. How I miss it—the bubbles, the effervescence, the effusive joy.

But enough about that. You asked about my home. My family has some land in Reims, on the outskirts of town. We have vines and sell our grapes to the large champagne houses of Pommery and Taittinger. I am also an apiarist, and I keep several beehives. My mother kept a kitchen garden as well, though it has long been abandoned, along with my hives.

I think of my bees often, and hope they have escaped the poison gases; I think perhaps they fled to the deep forests. Bees are far more intelligent than most people assume. Sometimes I think they are a good deal smarter than the humans I know.

I wonder if you have heard about the bombardment of Reims. The Germans entered the city in September, and held it for only ten days. But after being expelled from our city, they remained on the surrounding hills, shelling the city from the heights. It is a thing of horror, to see the buildings tumbling into the streets in a great cloud of brick and plaster dust. They appear quite like living things as they moan and groan and fall to their knees, spilling their contents into the streets like viscera.

There are also snipers awaiting the citizenry. They make no distinction between soldier and civilian, between a legitimate target and an innocent child.

Everywhere the land is strewn with bodies, as neither side dare stop to bury their fallen soldiers. It is an atrocity, what is happening to my region. Trenches and barbed wire crisscross the once-green fields of xxx; there are mortar shells and gas, and corpses of human and animal alike poison the creeks.

But enough of that. I have not been back to Reims in many months; it is difficult from here. I prefer to think of my city as I left it. And of my loved ones safely tucked away in their homes.

I am so very pleased to know that you enjoy poetry. One of my favorite countrymen is Charles Baudelaire— in fact, he translated Edgar Allan Poe into my language. Do you know his *Les Fleurs du Mal*? In it he wrote, *je suis un cimetière abhorré de la lune*. One of your countrymen has translated it into English for me: I am a cemetery shunned by the moon.

At night, trying to sleep in the trenches, I often feel like that, as though plagued by the gutted silence of a cursed cemetery whose ground is too cold for even the moon to plate with its silver light.

The savagery of this war is a thing of nightmares.

Thank you, my esteemed *marraine*, for writing to me. The postal system has been disrupted in Reims, encircled as it is by the enemy, and we rarely receive mail from our families and loved ones. Your letter was a true balm to my soul, sweeter than the salve my mother used to concoct in her kitchen. She applied it to me once, after an accident with the thresher. It smelled of olive oil and thyme, honey and myrrh, and the arnica and herbs gathered in the high mountains.

Sometimes at night I imagine the scent lingers on my skin; I conjure it when my nostrils are filled with the noxious odors of death.

But again, I apologize for my baroque language, my tendency toward hyperbole. This must be why I am so drawn to Mr. Baudelaire's writing. My fellow *poilus* find me difficult to comprehend, at times.

I sincerely hope you will not share their opinion of me!

Je vous prie d'accepter, Madame Whittaker, *l'expression de mes sentiments distingués.*

Émile Paul Legrand

Chapter Twenty

Although her countryside hermitage had been invaded by Emma and Blondine—and Emma's assistant, André, who generally kept to himself—Rosalyn did not feel suffocated.

On the contrary, she rather enjoyed stumbling into the kitchen in the morning to find Emma slouched over a mug of steaming coffee, perusing *Le Monde* and chuckling at the latest antics of French politicians. Or André materializing at just the right moment to open the door for her, nodding politely. Or Blondine dropping by *Chambre Chardonnay*, rapping smartly on the door, and sharing a croissant and coffee before starting work in the office.

Rosalyn was at last able to connect with some of the growers and winemakers who were returning to the region and invited her in for tastings. She sampled their effervescent offerings, explained Small Fortune's marketing plans, signed one producer, and arranged for a few others to send samples to Hugh in Napa.

Throughout, she could hear Hugh's voice in her head: In any kind of business interaction, ongoing human-to-human contact was key, and the small, family-focused wine growers of France, perhaps more than most, took relationships seriously.

It was certainly easier than trying to convince busy wine shop owners or restaurateurs in the Napa Valley to buy the wine she was *selling*, Rosalyn reminded herself as she drove from village to village, parking alongside muddy, freshly plowed fields. Here, in Champagne, she was the buyer, the U.S. representative whom the wineries wanted to impress so that they might export their wine to the American market.

Still, each time Rosalyn pulled up to a new winery, she would take a long moment to take ten deep, slow breaths, psyching herself up for the interaction. She tried to remember what it was like to feel happy and carefree, to be her old self, friendly and outgoing, the affable American representative.

Over and over, she donned the mask.

She spent one afternoon in Épernay, the second largest city in Champagne and home to the famous champagne houses of Moët & Chandon, Perrier-Jouët, and Pol Roger. But she preferred the small villages, most boasting at least one or two small producers of champagne. She stopped at informal tasting rooms, chatted with winemakers, and was taken out to lunch by aspiring vendors, and when she limped back to the *Chambre Chardonnay* at night, grateful to be done for the day, she reminded herself—for the thousandth time—how many people would have loved to have her job.

Hugh had offered Rosalyn the position out of friendship, and probably to the surprise of both of them, she wasn't bad at it. But she wasn't a great wine rep, either, and she never would be because she wasn't by nature a salesperson. Emma was right. It leached something out of her soul.

But if I didn't work for Hugh, she thought to herself, a slight panic fluttering deep in her belly, *what would I do?*

She couldn't *not* work. More than two years after Dash died, she was still paying down their debts, slowly and painstakingly digging herself out of the pit of financial obligations and bad credit that Dash had left her in. Rosalyn had long since reconciled herself to the fact that she would have to work at any decent-paying job she could get, not to mention she would never have the lavish art show Dash used to talk about. She never painted anymore, anyway.

Her fairy tale had had a far too real ending.

The only thing she really wanted to do right now was to dive back into Émile's letters. She sat at the table in her room at the *gîte*, heedless of the passing hours as she deciphered words and phrases, checking their meanings with translation sites online, as well as lists of French slang and idiomatic expressions, striving to capture not just the definitions of the words and phrases but their true meanings, and the nuances of expression.

The dates were out of order, but she didn't care.

January 14, 1915

My dear *marraine*, Mrs. Whittaker,

We are now situated in xxx, not far from xxx. When last I wrote I promised next to tell you of how it all started. The beginning, as we *Rémois* experienced it.

The euphoria over the victory of the Marne ceded to the somber fear of the approach of the invaders. At first there was a great exodus from the city, as those with means—and many of those with very little—slept at the train station with hopes of finding a space to ferry them south, away from the threatened onslaught.

I remember marching off to war, the citizens thronging the bridge of Laon to toss flowers to the convoys of us *poilus* heading to the front, smiling and singing as we went.

We *Rémois* were confident we would defeat the *Boches* and return in time for Christmas. What made us think this, I still don't know, except that it seemed so absurd that anyone should try to take our country from us. We were full of a brash confidence that now feels like arrogance, or ignorance, or a pathetic mixture of both.

Christmas has passed and we are in a New Year, but we *poilus* celebrate the holiday as we celebrate every day, hunkered down in our trenches of mud, leaning against sandbags and even our fallen comrades, as we have neither the time nor the ability to remove the poor broken remnants of men, sons, friends, fathers. I hesitate to tell you these things, my dear *marraine*, but you repeatedly assure me I should tell you all the truth, as I see it. It is a horror, and surely not appropriate for a lady.

I hope you will not think badly of me when I tell you that despite the dreadfulness that fills my daily existence, there are moments of strange and glorious beauty. I seize upon them eagerly: a startlingly clear night, the stars twinkling and beckoning with their immaculate shine, untouched by the terror of bullets and shells, safe even from the poison gases.

A violent bombardment that leaves everyone shaken, yet somehow, miraculously, alive.

Or the Christmas Eve miracle—have you heard of it?

Truthfully, I don't know whether or not to believe it actually happened, but I choose to. It is too wonderful a story not to. It was told to us by a medic who claimed he witnessed it firsthand.

This is the way he told the story:

Those of us who live in the trenches are at times only a few meters—or less—from the enemy ensconced in their own pits. When it is quiet, we sometimes speak to one another, or even barter for small items such as cigarettes. We are young men trying to stay alive, and when the enemy shows his human face, we are reminded that we used to be neighbors, relatives, fellow farmers, and merchants.

So, on Christmas Eve, while in his trench, a British soldier began to sing "Silent Night," his sonorous voice filling the quiet void. You may know, my dear *marraine*, that this is a song originally written in German. Other soldiers joined in, and when they finished, the Germans answered in kind, singing *"Stille Nacht"* in the original German. From then on the singing continued, and as darkness fell, candles were lit along the line. Some say there were even some gifts exchanged, and an informal cease-fire allowed each side to collect their dead from No Man's Land in peace.

So, there you have it. A brief break in the fighting, in recognition of our shared humanity. I imagine the officers in charge wouldn't like the idea of us seeing such humanity in our foes.

And when the night was over, the slaughter recommenced.

Your friend,
Émile Legrand

June 1, 1915

My dear *marraine*,

I asked Lucie why she did not flee the city when she had the chance, and she told me a very long story. It was as though she needed to tell it, for someone to hear, to understand.

It was in August of 1914 that the refugees from the north began to arrive, a flood of Belgians, and those from Mézières and Rethel and Givet. They came by ox-drawn wagon and wheelbarrow, in carts loaded with a mishmash of furniture and other household objects, farm tools and children's dolls.

"It was the dolls that seemed most poignant to me," said Lucie. "Those simple little poppets, which usually bring solace and joy, were the only objects they were able to save."

They flooded into the once-beautiful squares and parks of Reims, camping where they could. Much of the citizenry came out to cook for them and feed them. The plaza in front of town hall, which later became a scene of carnage, was full of children playing, happy to experience a respite in their journey. Their parents' faces were deeply lined in worry; they were not able to enjoy themselves in the same way.

Within two weeks they heard the first guns, and within two days of that, the Germans arrived. They insisted a French prisoner show them the way to the *mairie*, but as he was not from Reims he misled them. Then they picked up another Frenchman, who might well have misled them on purpose. In any case, the *Boches* were enraged by the time they found the *mairie*. Perhaps that is why they set about shelling the city for a full half an hour, destroying several buildings and terrifying the populace—even though they had already conquered the city.

Eight days later the French soldiers returned and drove the Huns out of

Reims in a glorious victory. The invaders retreated to the heights and began to bombard the town, determined to destroy what they could not have.

We have yet to see if they will succeed, if our beloved Reims will fall in on itself like so many other villages and towns, to become a city fit only for the dead.

Sending you kind wishes and respectful thoughts,

Émile Legrand

April 2, 1916

My dearest Mrs. Whittaker,

I wonder about the educational system in your country. Here in France, schools used to be run by convents and monasteries, but after the revolution, the state took over the charge of developing good citizens. Still, the teachers approach their work with no less selfless dedication than did the nuns and monks. Even after the evacuation orders, even after the Germans invaded and were in turn expelled, only to hide in the hills "watering" the city of Reims with showers of shells, every teacher stayed. If children remained, they said, they would remain to teach them.

A teacher's profession is a consecration.

Early in the shelling a bomb crashed into the house of Monsieur Forsant, Inspector of Primary Education. He was not at home, fortunately, but he took it as a harbinger of what was to come. And so even though the schools were scheduled to open two weeks after the incendiary bombs destroyed our cathedral, Monsieur Forsant finally decided to delay the opening to an undetermined date in the future.

After much of the citizenry had fled to the shelter of the *crayères*, the caves that run under the city, an intrepid teacher named Madame Deresme asked for permission to open a school in that dank, dark, but relatively safe place.

Monsieur Forsant came to inspect the scene. He encountered there a bitter smell, the sight of unwashed, unkempt, and dejected women, children, and grand-parents huddling together. He had to climb over beds and push aside chairs to pass, as many of the refugees had brought all their worldly goods down into the tunnels, such as they could.

It was clear the people were suffering from the physical and moral wretchedness of the loss of their possessions, their loved ones, their safety. There is a certain abasement of the spirit that accompanies invasion and war, my dear *marraine*, the likes of which I sincerely hope you will never experience. It is in some ways more difficult than the outright terror of the trenches, or at least it is a more insidious adversary.

In France the teachers do not believe in pampering children. The youth must learn the moral courage that is necessary to face life's difficulties. The children are taught that they are doing their best for France, that they are displaying their patriotism, by focusing on their studies and learning well.

And do you know that first Christmas, hundreds of pairs of new shoes were sent to the children by people all over France? And a soldier managed to bring a Christmas tree through the dangerous section. They lit candles and sang patriotic songs, and the children recited poems. The soldiers billeted there in the caves were the appreciative audience, along with the mothers and grandparents.

When Lucie described the vivid scene, I was reminded of the Christmas Eve armistice. I take comfort in the way humans insist on creating moments of meaning, and peace, and joy, even in the most trying of times.

As Lucie says: The human spirit does not want to die; it is a resilient thing.

With all my best wishes,
Émile Legrand

After reviewing the website for Blé Champagne, Rosalyn realized Emma had a point—the website's English version was at best awkward, and often downright wrong. She approached Blondine about it, and the two of them quickly developed a routine: Many mornings Blondine would rap on her door with croissants and coffee in hand, and they would sit at the table and eat breakfast while Rosalyn suggested changes to Blé Champagne's website as well as to other marketing materials.

In exchange, Blondine helped Rosalyn work through the rather gruesome list of unknown vocabulary she had gleaned from Émile's letters.

Blondine winced in distaste at the ghastlier descriptions, and some phrases she was unable to decipher, but she knew many others: *obus* meant "shell, bombardment." *Une abeille*, or a bee, referred to a bullet. *Un Boche* was a German. *Un crapouillot*, a little toad, was a small mortar. *Un groin de cochon*, a pig's snout, meant a "gas mask." *Le séchoir*, the clothesline, referred to the rolls of barbed wire that crisscrossed the battlefields—it had earned the nickname because soldiers became entangled on the wire as they ran, and remained hanging there, even in death.

"No time for language lessons today," Blondine declared one morning. "I have been remiss—I must show you our facilities here. You run around all of Champagne, but haven't yet seen our own operation. My father will kill me to know this. So, after *le petit déjeuner*, we shall take a tour, yes?"

After they had enjoyed flaky, butter-soaked croissants and downed rich coffee, Blondine showed Rosalyn their champagne-making process and the chilly storage caves built directly into the hill behind the loading dock.

"Probably you know all about the *méthode champenoise*," said Blondine.

"As you know, I'm more of a red wine connoisseur. I would love a refresher course."

"The *méthode champenoise* involves the deliberate initiation of a second fermentation, which is responsible for the bubbles," Blondine explained as she pointed out the wine-making equipment. "Primary fermentation takes place in tanks to transform the juice into wine. Bottle fermentation, known as the *prise de mousse*, is when the wine begins to effervesce."

The bottles were capped with metal tops, like soda. Then the wine was carefully cataloged and allowed to rest for several years in A-frame racks called *pupitres* that positioned the bottles on an angle, nose down. The bottles were regularly "riddled," or turned a bit to collect the debris produced by the yeasts and sugars, which would otherwise cloud the wine.

"It was the *veuve* Clicquot who figured out how to get rid of the deposits." Blondine pointed to a demonstration bottle that was mounted in front of a light. When she whirled it, sediment floated around within it. "Once the sediment has collected in the neck of the bottle—which takes a long time—it is *dégorgées*."

"*Dégorgées* means 'disgorged,' right?" Rosalyn asked, unsure of the translation.

Blondine nodded. "We freeze just this last part of the neck. Then the bottle is pointed nose down, and the cork or cap is removed very rapidly. The frozen liquid containing the sediment is forced out by the pressure, and then the bottle is corked again before too much fizz or champagne is lost."

"That sounds . . . tricky," Rosalyn said, remembering how replacing the watercooler bottle in Hugh's office involved the combined efforts of the entire office and sales staff, and they still managed to spill half the contents on the carpet.

"It takes a lot of skill. Now most of it is done by machine, but it was done by hand for centuries, and sometimes still is. A professional riddler can jiggle fifty thousand bottles a day, and a good disgorger is worth his weight in gold."

"I'll bet." Rosalyn tried to imagine a business card printed with *Professional Riddler* or *Experienced Disgorger*. "And then the missing wine is replaced by the *dosage*?"

"*Oui*. The *dosage* is a fortified wine with a little sugar and sometimes a special ingredient. This is the winemaker's secret. See the markings set on the piles of bottles over there?" She gestured to a small A-frame sign atop a stack of champagne. "That is a secret code known only to the winemaker. In the larger cellars such as Pommery and Mumm, the winemakers ride through the caves on bicycles. It is the only way they can get around to check on the inventory. It is very prestigious to be a cellar master in Champagne."

As Blondine spoke, Rosalyn recalled the lectures from her oenology classes. Champagne was made of only three grape varietals: Chardonnay, Pinot Meunier, and Pinot Noir; and when made exclusively from Chardonnay grapes, it was called *blanc de blanc*. There were different levels of quality: Grand cru was the best, then premier cru, and finally *appellation Champagne*.

"Some of the smaller producers sell most of their crops to the big champagne houses but make their own champagne as well," said Blondine. "It is more distinctive, since they are much smaller operations."

"Have you tasted the champagne from Comtois Père et Fils? Do you think I should try to represent it back home?"

Blondine paused for a moment. "I haven't tried it, no. But his family's wine-making collection is impressive. Comtois has the biggest collection of corks in France, or so they claim."

"That's a lot of corks."

"It is," said Blondine with a nod, perfectly serious.

"Why doesn't Jérôme want to open his collection to the public?"

Blondine shrugged. "Who knows? Everyone says he's been in a bad mood ever since his wife ran off, but I think he must be overwhelmed. Jérôme is doing everything himself, with a very small staff. If he cannot produce enough grapes or wine, he cannot save the winery. The historic collection must be the last thing on his mind."

"Well, that makes sense."

"Also, he has never been fond of tourists, and naturally the collection brings tourists to him. His father spent most of his time and his fortune on the collection, buying ancient winepresses and transporting them to the Comtois cellars. I think Jérôme resented this, and I don't really blame him. It must be hard to be expected to give up your career in Paris to come back to this small village to save the business your father has nearly bankrupted."

"It sounds like you know Jérôme well."

"Not really, but Cochet is a small village. We were raised here, went to the primary school and played together as children. But then he went off to university in Paris, and after that, we rarely saw him anymore. No one expects him to stay long." She checked the readout on her phone. "Now I must go to work in the office. My father will arrive soon, and we will have a special dinner in celebration of the Epiphany. So you cannot eat potato chips for dinner tonight."

"Thank you for the invitation," said Rosalyn. "I am looking forward to it."

And truth to tell, she was.

Chapter Twenty-one

Lucie

L iving in the caves is a kind of death. But no, that is not apt.

Death, the priest assures us, is a land of milk and honey, a wondrous promise of rewards for a life well lived. Living underground is a slow torture of the spirit, a thousand cuts to the soul, countless jarring shocks to the natural order of things.

This war has turned the world upside down. Poison gases waft on the gentlest summer breeze; warm blood seeps into the earth to nourish the roots of the ancient grapevines. Soldiers in trenches gnaw on hardtack as unyielding as stone while their feet turn doughy with rot. Women and children tend the grapevines under the cover of night, but remain shrouded in cool darkness during the brightest hours of day.

The dead lie unburied and unconsecrated aboveground, while the living cower deep beneath the surface of the earth.

The world, upside down.

Ours is a constant search for light. The caves

are dim, lit only by precious oil lamps or candle stubs. In the largest pits there are pyramid-shaped skylights at the very top; there is always a competition to stand beneath these, to be able to look out to the sky and search for the bright blue of day, the fluffy white of clouds, an occasional passing bird.

Of course, in the case of a direct hit, the poor soul underneath will be pierced by glass shards. Such is our lot.

Madame Pommery named several sections of the caves in homage to her best customers: Rio de Janeiro, Dakar, Havana, Bruxelles. My mother, father, and brother and I have made a place for ourselves in the Dakar niche, shifting stacks of bottles and *pupitres*—the special racks used to keep the bottles neck down—to serve as partitions. Privacy is one of the many luxuries we have lost in this war.

There is a hole nearly hidden at the back of Dakar, in the wall of our niche, and I crawl through with my candle in hand, feeling very much like Alice in Wonderland. My mother says it is inappropriate, that only rats crawl through holes in the ground. But it is difficult to keep up such arbitrary standards, even for her; she scolds me, but her attention is soon diverted by her knitting, and she is once again lost in the world of her wool, purling and counting stitches.

On the other side of the small opening is a

series of crude stairs carved out of solid chalk. At the top of the steps is another small room, this one big enough only for a blanket. A couple of small shafts allow for air circulation, but nonetheless it feels a bit like a tomb. I have squirreled away several books I rescued from the rubble, and a couple I was able to salvage from our old house, from our old life: Jane Austen's *Orgueil et Prévention*, a volume of *Les Contes des Frères Grimm*, several novels by George Sand, and, of course, *Les Aventures d'Alice au Pays des Merveilles*.

I share my little cave within a cave with a gargoyle that was felled by the bombardment of our great Cathedral of Notre-Dame de Reims. I have named him Narcisse, for my favorite flower and the saint's day that falls on my birthday, October 29. Narcisse is squat and ugly, and not very large, luckily for me; he was a heavy-enough load to carry and maneuver through the hole in the wall.

When the fighting is over, the grim little fellow must be returned to take his place with the other gargoyles that guard our cathedral and watch over our city; but for now I enjoy his companionship. His scowl makes me think of my own countenance. I have placed a piece of broken mirror on a rough chalk ledge—despite my mother's protestations that it would bring bad luck—and it shows just such a grim set to my own features, which I hardly recognize these days.

I try to smile, especially for the sake of the children. But I cannot deny that it hurts. At times my face feels as though it will crack with the strain, shattering like a mirror, as though struck by a mortar.

When we lived in Villa Traverne, I barely noticed the stencils, the gold and silver gilt, the paintings and portraits and statuettes. In fact, I resented them; I once was severely punished for running in the hall and breaking a fine Limoges figurine.

But now, in the caves, it is a different story. Many years ago, when Madame Jeanne Pommery was left a widow, she decided to extend these caves, first carved by the Romans as they excavated stone to build their cities. She transformed giant chalk pits and quarries by uniting them with graceful galleries and niches, tunnels and passages, to age her bottles of champagne.

But that wasn't enough; she also added art.

There are sculptures engraved on the cellar walls, and bas-reliefs of Bacchus sculpted in the soft chalk. The soldiers and cellar workers sometimes carve their initials or graffiti into the walls; I enjoy trying to read the messages, though some are in English, which I don't understand. I have begun my own small gallery in my little cave within a cave, carving creatures imagined from the Grimms' fairy tales and other mythology, especially sirens. I've always wanted to visit the sea. The idea of sailing away is enticing; perhaps I could find a land of peace.

Now a tall rabbit is engraved in the wall, standing right at the mouth of my little refuge; he wears a vest and is checking his pocket watch for the time.

Now I see. Art is our sanctuary, our momentary escape from a world in which the bombs rain down, the injured arrive, and even the *petits enfants* are killed and maimed.

But one can gaze at the bacchanalian scene—which my mother deemed inappropriate—and imagine lolling in the peaceful forests, drunk and dancing and gay for all time.

One can spend the day scraping and spewing dust, thoughts lost in the attempt to bring forth a rabbit from the chalk walls.

My mother says there is beauty in necessity.

I say there is a necessity *of* beauty.

Chapter Twenty-two

That afternoon Rosalyn had planned on visiting a producer in the village of Le Mesnil-sur-Oger, but gray storm clouds were rolling in and she was loath to give up her warm, dry room. Instead, she checked her e-mail and found an invitation to a "Gathering of Vintners" to be held in the caves under the House of Vranken Pommery. The invitation reminded guests to dress appropriately for the chill of the caves.

Even with her stomach quailing at the thought of attending a party, Rosalyn was excited by the prospect of seeing Lucie's underground refuge.

Outside, the storm seemed to be building. Rosalyn fixed a cup of hot tea, sat down at the table in her room, and sorted through more of Émile's letters. The missives now littered her room, spread out over every horizontal surface—the table, the cabinet, and even the floor.

June 17, 1916

Dear Mrs. Whittaker,

There is a famous sculpture on the Cathedral of Reims. Do you happen to know it? It is an angel with a sweet smile, a relic of a long-ago sculptor who had lost patience with the stoic bishops and angels of his commission. There she has stood for centuries, looking down upon royalty, upon brides and grooms, upon cardinals and bishops, upon the peasants and farmers, artisans and workers, who have streamed through the church's doors in search of salvation and beauty and peace.

She is called the Smiling Angel, or sometimes simply the Smile of Reims.

She was decapitated in a German attack on the cathedral, her smiling visage rolling at the entrance and cracking into pieces. Lucie says the pieces were collected by the Abbot Thinot the day after the cathedral fire, and squirreled away for safekeeping. With the grace of God, she will be restored after this cursed war is over.

I have seen friends fall at my side. I have carried in baskets the torsos of men who have lost all their limbs. I was once buried alive by a collapsing trench, and am regularly doused with poison gas. These are hellish things to experience.

So why is it that the destruction of our Smile of Reims seems to me the most barbarous act of all?

At the roar of an engine outside, Rosalyn went to the window to see pulling into the parking lot a large truck towing a trailer loaded with four Jet Skis. A man in his sixties climbed down from the cab. He was handsome in the way of some rugged outdoorsmen, with a tanned face and an air of self-assurance.

Her genial host, Gaspard Blé, she presumed.

Rosalyn ran a comb through her hair, pulled on her coat, gloves, and scarf, and went out to meet him.

"What do you think?" he said without preamble. "I can sell these for a nice profit."

"Very nice. But . . . is there a big demand for *Jet Skis* in Champagne?" Rosalyn asked, racking her brain for bodies of water in the area. As far as she knew, Jet Skis were used on the ocean, and the ocean was a long way from landlocked Champagne.

The rain had died down but the wind was picking up, and the afternoon sky was an ominous slate gray. Rosalyn was clad in three layers of clothes under her parka, but still shivered. Gaspard, in contrast, wore a flannel shirt over a T-shirt, jeans, and boots, and didn't seem to notice the cold.

"Not so much, no. But also absolutely *no* supply, so I'm golden on that score." He leapt off the trailer and kissed her once on each cheek. He smelled of tobacco. "You must be the lovely

Rosalyn Acosta. I am Gaspard Blé, at your service."

"Nice to meet you," said Rosalyn. "I appreciate being able to stay in your *gîte*. It's very comfortable."

"I'm glad. You're the first guest. I had another place, but we wanted to step up the facilities to accommodate American tourists. We want to lure them away from the big cities, into small villages like Cochet. Be sure to tell Blondine about anything you don't like; you'll be doing us a favor."

"I will. Thank you."

He started rearranging some boxes on the trailer.

"That's nothing," said Blondine, joining them. She looked cold in a lightweight jacket and short skirt, her arms folded tightly across her chest. "You should see his warehouse. It's full of all sorts of crap."

"Hey, that's your inheritance, young lady. I'm having a sale next Saturday. Should make a pretty penny."

"You import items for sale?" Rosalyn asked. "And here I thought you were a winemaker."

"I am a man of many talents, and vision."

"Did you drive straight through?" Blondine asked. "What time did you leave Tarragona?"

"This morning."

"It's a twelve-hour drive."

He flashed a jaunty grin. "*Very* early this morning. And we were up late last night, celebrating our last night in Spain. So Epiphany had better be good! Now"—he rubbed his hands together—"when's *apéro*? Kings' dinner tonight, right? Because the king, he has arrived."

Gaspard patted himself on the chest and gave Rosalyn a wink. Blondine rolled her eyes.

The storm arrived in earnest before evening, but though the air felt frigid, it didn't snow. Instead, wind blew black branches into violent tangles, rattling the windowpanes, and the rain fell in sheets. André waited for Rosalyn by the door with an umbrella, which was caught by the wind and turned inside out by the time they dashed the twenty feet to the loading dock door and let themselves in, shaking off as much of the water as they could.

"Quite a storm," said André, staring at his ruined umbrella.

"Indeed," said Rosalyn. "Very dramatic. Sorry about your umbrella."

"Plenty more where that came from."

They found Blondine in the kitchen, unpacking groceries from what looked like half a dozen tote bags. Emma was seated on her usual stool, opening a bottle of champagne. The cork left the bottle with the muffled *snick* of a practiced hand—a connoisseur of champagne, Rosalyn

225

had learned, never opened the bottle with the dramatic *pop* so common to celebrations back home. It wasted too much of the precious bubbly.

"May I help?" Rosalyn asked Blondine as she moved toward the kitchen.

"There's a lot to do," mumbled Blondine.

"And she's running late, as usual," said Emma with a smile. "No worries, Blondine. We'll wait. We have champagne, after all."

Rosalyn found an apron in the closet and tied it on over the outfit she had worn for the special occasion. Unsure how fancy Epiphany dinners were, she had upgraded from her usual jeans and sweater to a knit wrap dress and nice leather boots.

"What can I do?" she asked Blondine. "I've worked in restaurants for years."

"*Vraiment*?" Blondine asked.

"Mostly I served cocktails. But I know my way around a kitchen well enough. I'll be your sous chef."

"You'll save my life," said Blondine. She explained the evening's menu: it began with *apéro* of petite crab brioches and slivers of dried salami. Dinner was a leg of lamb—*gigot d'agneau*—in wine and onion sauce, *bouchée à la reine*, and potatoes *au vapeur*, followed by a green salad with mustard-shallot dressing. Dominique was bringing dessert.

The wine pairing was easy: Each course would

be served with copious amounts of champagne.

Unfortunately, Blondine was not the best at delegating tasks, and tended to talk to herself instead of to Rosalyn.

"She's feeling pressure because of her father," Emma said to Rosalyn, before turning to Blondine. "*Calme-toi*, Blondine. Your father is just a man, like any other. And you're a wonderful cook, so why don't you have a drink of this delicious *cru* and relax? An unhappy chef will make unhappy food. That's simple science."

Blondine hesitated, then accepted the flute of champagne Emma held out to her.

"We should make a toast," suggested Rosalyn.

"But of course we must!" said Emma. "Suggestions?"

"To the Epiphany?" suggested Blondine.

Emma snorted. "Too conventional."

"How about to the three of us?" said Rosalyn. "We're not all that conventional, when it comes down to it."

Emma laughed. "Brilliant! All right, you wenches, to the three fairest flowers of France, Australia, and the United States!"

"*Santé!*" Blondine and Rosalyn chimed in as they touched glasses. Rosalyn took a sip, to fulfill the toast.

Blondine downed half her glass and returned to the kitchen to adjust the oven.

"Here," said Rosalyn as she handed Emma a

small chopping block, a knife, and some carrots. "Make yourself useful."

Emma grinned and said to Blondine, "This one's getting awfully cheeky, wouldn't you say?"

Rosalyn smiled. Still lacking direction from Blondine, she started chopping onion and garlic on the assumption that they would be needed in one dish or another.

"Hey, André!" Emma called out, and he immediately appeared from the direction of the office.

"*Oui, madame*?"

"Do be a doll and put some music on for us, will you? Something French and atmospheric. None of that Europop crap."

"*Oui, madame*." He slipped back into the other room, and within seconds, French music came on over the sound system: Jacques Brel, then Lara Fabian.

"How much do you pay him to stand around, waiting for orders, like that?" Blondine asked Emma the question that had been on Rosalyn's mind.

"A *lot*," Emma said. "And he's worth every euro. He runs my office in Épernay, but when I come to France, he's on call pretty much twenty-four seven—more so this trip, since he has to drive me everywhere."

"Must be nice to be rich," grumbled Blondine.

"Oh, it *is*. It certainly is," said Emma. "*Much* better than the alternative, I always say."

"Rosalyn, help yourself to more champagne," Blondine said.

"Oh, um . . ."

"Save your breath," said Emma. "Rosalyn doesn't like champagne."

Blondine whipped around to gape at Rosalyn. "What do you mean, she doesn't like champagne?"

"Ask her yourself," said Emma.

"Rosalyn, is this true?" Blondine was clearly scandalized.

"It's not that I dislike it, as much as I just . . . prefer red."

"You prefer red."

Rosalyn nodded.

"*Huh.* Champagne is famous the world over."

"I realize that."

"But the bubbles . . . It is lively and effervescent. . . . It is liquid gold."

"Champagne is very beautiful," Rosalyn agreed, blushing and wishing Emma had kept her big mouth shut. "It's celebratory and all that. I'm just more of a red wine fan."

Blondine let out a long, loud sigh and turned back to rolling out dough on the counter. "There is a rack in the pantry with some Bordeaux, if you prefer."

Rosalyn widened her eyes at Emma in a *what the hell?* look, to which Emma responded with a shrug.

"We like what we like, right? Nothing wrong with that," said Emma, "though it's a good idea to stay open to new things. You never know when your tastes might change."

"That's true. So," Rosalyn said in a blatant bid to change the subject, "have you tracked down any descendants of Émile or Lucie?"

"Not so far. I've been making phone calls, and found two Legrands outside of Épernay, but neither of them knew of an Émile from that era. No nibbles on Lucie Maréchal yet, though it's tougher because women change their names with marriage." She poured herself more champagne and downed a couple of pills, then gave Rosalyn a wink. "I always take my vitamins with champagne."

"That's the spirit," said Rosalyn with a smile.

Emma held her glass up in yet another toast. "Here's to locating the descendants!"

Rosalyn and Blondine joined in the toast, and for the next half hour, the women focused on preparing the evening's meal, accompanied by the strains of classic French ballads, the tattoo of rain on the roof, and the occasional rumble of thunder. Emma recounted a funny story of a standoff with a cranky kangaroo during an ill-advised foray into Australia's outback, and Blondine waxed poetic describing her recent trip to Mallorca. Rosalyn mostly listened. She didn't want to talk about Napa, and certainly not about

Dash. She felt buoyed at the chance to set aside the burden of grief for a few hours, like an ant dislodging a load several times her weight.

For the moment Rosalyn was living in a parallel world where she was nothing more than a run-of-the-mill wine rep cooking an Epiphany feast with friends.

"Forgive my ignorance, but I wasn't raised Catholic," Rosalyn said when there was a lull in the conversation. "What does the Epiphany celebrate, exactly?"

"It is the day the wise men came to find Jesus and offer him presents," said Blondine. "Traditionally this was when children were given gifts, though now most people celebrate on Christmas morning or eve. But we still like to mark the day with the *galette des Rois*."

"I saw those in the store the other day," said Rosalyn.

"Dominique will bring one tonight, but not one of those from her store. She should have made it herself. It is tradition, but she's no baker. She'll buy the cake from the Boulangerie Julien. I insisted. It is a wafer cake, with frangipane inside, very good."

"She's leaving out the best part," said Emma. "When the cake is served it is customary to *tirer les rois*—decide who is king for the day. A porcelain charm called *la fève* is baked into the cake, and whoever gets the slice with *la fève*

231

is declared king—or queen, in our case—and guaranteed a good year."

"Also they have to bring the *galette des Rois* the following year," said Blondine.

"Well, that seems like a good system," said Rosalyn.

Blondine pulled the hot crab brioches out of the oven just as Gaspard arrived accompanied by two men, a father and son from Spain, whom he introduced as Raúl and Augustín Santiago. The Spaniards were cork makers in town selling their *bouchons*. From Blondine's startled reaction, Rosalyn realized Gaspard's invitation must have been a spur-of-the-moment decision and she took more salad out of the small *frigo*.

"I've always wanted to see an actual cork tree," Rosalyn said. The main character from her favorite children's book, *The Story of Ferdinand*, used to sit under just such a tree, smelling the flowers. In her child's mind, the tree had consisted of hundreds of actual corks, stuck together.

"Then you must come visit us in La Mancha," said Raúl, the elder Santiago. He was plump and short, with the dark sloping eyes so common among the Spanish. "It would be our pleasure to show you how we make our *bouchons* from the bark of the cork trees."

Rosalyn passed the tray of brioche and salami to the men, who had gathered at the counter, trading tales with Emma and drinking freely of champagne. Spirits were high, the music was playing, and André had rejoined them and helped himself to champagne.

It was after eight, and dinner was nowhere near ready. Rosalyn's stomach growled, and she snuck another brioche. Blondine didn't miss much.

"You are accustomed to eating earlier in the U.S.," she said flatly.

"I am, yes. But I'm more than fine with this brioche."

"I hear Americans eat as early as six in the evening!" said Gaspard. "How are you not too hungry in the morning?"

"I never really thought about it. Maybe that's why a lot of people eat big breakfasts," Rosalyn said.

"That's because they go do real work," Emma teased. "Not like you effete Frenchies with your tiny espressos and crusts of bread."

"You look at us vintners and tell me we don't work hard," Gaspard said, pounding on his chest, then splaying out his hands. "Look at these calluses. We are *Champenois*, true, and so we laugh and joke; we celebrate life with champagne. But we also work hard to coax the vines from this difficult soil."

"My father eats only a piece of chocolate and coffee in the morning," said Blondine, gesturing with a knife in hand. "I cannot live without

233

my croissant, but I don't think I could eat an American breakfast. Sausage and beans for breakfast?"

"You're thinking of *English* breakfasts," said Emma, nabbing a slice of glistening salami. "As I've mentioned before, Rosalyn's American, and I'm Aussie—thank you very much—and we're nothing like the English. Though honestly it couldn't make the slightest bit of difference."

"Then why did you bring it up?" asked Gaspard.

"Habit," she said with a smile. "Don't like being mistaken for something I'm not."

"We will eat in an hour or so," said Blondine as she put the *gigot* of lamb on to simmer. "We are expecting more guests."

Soon Dominique arrived with a rumpled younger man named Dani. They set a large pink bakery box atop the counter, shook the water from their hair, and hung up their raincoats. Dani appeared young enough to be Dominique's son, but there was something about the intimacy of their interactions that made Rosalyn wonder if theirs was a romantic relationship. *None of your business,* she chided herself. Staying in a small town seemed to have brought out her inner gossip.

It was nearly ten o'clock in the evening by the time they sat down to dinner.

Rosalyn's mouth watered. The leg of lamb had

been simmered to perfection in a silky wine-and-onion sauce. Accompanying the lamb was *bouchée à la reine*, or "Queen's morsel," a puff pastry shell filled with mushrooms in a delectable gravy, and alongside this were simple steamed potatoes—*au vapeur*—doused in butter and sprinkled with parsley. Hunks of fresh, chewy baguette sat directly on the tablecloth, the crumbs ignored.

After so much time eating simple meals and snacks, Rosalyn had to admit that the formal dinner was wonderfully satisfying. She relished every bite.

The conversation was lively, with Dominique talking about visiting family in Provence over the holidays and Gaspard telling stories of partying in Tarragona. To Rosalyn's ears, Gaspard's exploits sounded like those of a frat boy on spring break, not a farmer in his sixties. But Gaspard laughed easily and was charming and play-ful. André, as was his wont, smiled pleasantly and remained almost entirely silent, a quiet but welcome presence.

When Rosalyn expressed interest in the history of using corks for bottling wine, Raúl spoke passionately about the sacrilege of introducing plastic corks to the market.

"Corks used to be made of whole hunks of the tree, but now we mash together bits of cork with glue and silicone. But in essence, they have been made the same way for hundreds of years, just like glass bottles," said Raúl. "Plastic corks have no place near fine wine, just as plastic bottles have no place. Just imagine!"

"In case you haven't noticed yet," said Emma to Rosalyn in a low voice, "the Europeans tend to be rather traditional."

"Of course we are traditional," said Gaspard. "When you make a perfect product, it is a sacrilege to change."

"Champagne corks are different from other wine corks, of course," said Augustín. "King Louis XV issued an edict regarding champagne bottling back in the eighteenth century. Back then, corks were wedged in by hand, with three pieces of twine holding them in place."

"Even so, the corks could explode without warning," said Raúl. "Sometimes taking out an eye of a cellar worker. It earned champagne the nickname 'devil's wine.' "

"Many's the winemaker who has gone down to the *cave* to find entire rows popped, a lake of wasted champagne at his feet," said Gaspard.

"Or *her* feet," Blondine grumbled under her breath.

Gaspard rolled his eyes. "You start making your own champagne, young lady, and we'll talk."

"Now we use metal caps, like I showed you in the cellars," Blondine explained to Rosalyn, "until it is time to put in the second dosage, which is when the cork is put in and tied down with the wire hood called a *muselet*."

After the dinner dishes were cleared, a simple green salad was passed around. Rosalyn was more than full by then, and because the *galette des Rois* was still on its way, she helped herself to only a couple of leaves. It seemed to her the salad was an excuse to rest and pause before the final course.

"I'm sorry we don't have a cheese course," announced Blondine as they finished their salads. "The *fromagerie* closed early today. Unless anyone would like some local Chaource or Langres? I have both here."

They demurred and then everyone—with the exception of Rosalyn and Blondine—brought out their cigarettes and lit up.

After an interlude, Blondine went to the kitchen and returned with the cake.

"Do you have these in America?" asked Dominique. "The round shape symbolizes the sun or, some say, the crowns of the kings."

"It's beautiful," said Rosalyn as she helped Blondine pass out dessert plates.

"If only we had some children here," Gaspard said, glaring at Blondine.

"They usually crawl under the table to distribute the slices," Emma told Rosalyn. "Tradition is all well and good, but it's a little disconcerting having children crawling under tables, if you ask me."

"Are we expecting anyone else tonight?" Rosalyn asked, noting that Blondine laid out a serving in front of an empty chair.

"*Ça, c'est la part du Bon Dieu,*" said Dominique.

"The piece of a good God?" Rosalyn translated and looked at Emma, who nodded.

Dominique explained: "It is tradition to put out a piece for a stranger, or a poor person. This is very important. In case they come by, there is a place waiting for them."

Rosalyn glanced out the sliding-glass window, imagining there wouldn't be a lot of people passing by in the storm, asking for cake.

"That's a lovely tradition."

"This is a celebration of the wise men, Melchior, Caspar, and Balthazar," said Gaspard as he poured more champagne into their flutes. "This is why we give gifts, because the wise men brought gifts to the baby Jesus."

Gaspard stood and raised his glass in a toast. "*Pluie des Rois, c'est blé jusqu'au toit et dans les tonneaux, vins à flots!*"

Rosalyn caught most of the words, but not the meaning, and was grateful when Emma leaned over and translated: " 'Rain of Kings'—on Kings' day, Epiphany—means 'grain up to the roof and wine overflowing from the barrels.' Gaspard thinks it's funny because his last name means 'grain.' "

Thunder shook the building, and Emma let out a gasp. Rosalyn turned to see an old man standing at the glass door, umbrella held aloft, like an apparition.

Chapter Twenty-three

Blé let out a curse under his breath. "Who invited *him?*"

"*I* did," said Blondine, her chin edging up a notch in a defiant slant. The move earned a fond look from Augustín.

Blondine hurried to the door and let the man in, handing him a towel.

"*Bonsoir*," he said in a gravelly voice, stashing his umbrella in the stand and thanking Blondine for the towel as he tousled his gray locks. He was a small wrinkled man with sad blue eyes, who appeared shrunken in his too-large clothes.

"Please let me introduce Monsieur Michel Bonnet," said Blondine. "Monsieur Bonnet, this is Mesdames Rosalyn Acosta from America and Emma Kinsley from Australia, and Messieurs Augustín and Raúl Santiago from Spain. I believe you know the others. Quite an international party, *non*?"

"*Bonsoir, messieurs-dames*," he said, with a nod.

Michel Bonnet, Rosalyn recalled, was the former priest Blondine had told her about the day they walked back from the market, and as she gazed around the room, she felt as if she were in a fairy tale or a joke: "An ex-priest, two Spanish cork makers, and a winemaker walk into an Epiphany party . . ."

She forced her attention back to the discussion at hand. Gaspard looked disgruntled at having Bonnet at his table, but Dominique and her young man greeted him as a dear friend, and if the Spaniards noticed Gaspard's attitude, they were too polite to say anything. Monsieur Bonnet took the extra place setting while Emma filled his flute with champagne, Blondine put on a pot of strong coffee, and Dominique served everyone a slice of cake.

"Actually, Michel and I know each other. Don't we, Michel?" said Emma. "That's what comes of investing in Champagne. I tell you, I know everyone at this point."

"Not everyone," Blondine pointed out.

"Quite right," Emma said. "I still need to get to Jérôme Comtois."

"I can get to him," said Gaspard.

"So you keep saying," Emma replied. "But I haven't seen any evidence of it so far."

"What is it you wish to learn from Jérôme?" asked Dominique.

"I have these letters, correspondence between a great-aunt of mine and a young soldier from World War One named Émile Legrand. I was hoping to find her part of the correspondence in the Comtois collection."

"Letters from a hundred years ago?" Dani asked.

"It's a long shot, I know, but I want to try," replied Emma. "I'm also looking for any families by the name of Legrand or Maréchal; I've had a few hints, but so far nothing's panned out. You wouldn't have any leads for me, would you, Michel?"

Bonnet smiled, revealing crooked teeth. "I am old, but that was before even my time. World War Two, now, that's a different story. I was a boy when the Germans invaded, and I remember four years later, when the Allies marched through this valley and kicked them out."

They all drank to France's liberation, and dug into their Kings' cake. It was flaky and light, with a delicate almond paste at the center, more like a pastry than what Americans considered to be cake, Rosalyn thought, and she enjoyed every bite. The table was quiet as they savored the dessert.

"There was an orphanage built by one of your type after the Great War, though—this I know," Bonnet said suddenly to Emma.

"One of my type? By which you mean what?" Emma asked. "Charming? Intelligent? Endowed with savoir faire?"

"A wealthy Australian woman."

Emma looked surprised. "Is that right? Around here?"

"Oh yes, of course, not twenty minutes from here. You know, the First World War left more than a million orphans in France. Just imagine."

"Terrible," Dominique said, and Dani nodded.

"You're saying an *Australian* woman founded an orphanage around here?" Emma continued. "What was her name?"

Bonnet shook his head. "This, I do not know. I assumed you did, and that there was a connection of some kind. It was perhaps why you chose to invest in our region."

"No, that wasn't why," Emma said, looking nonplussed. "I just like champagne."

"Well, Michel," said Gaspard. "Congratulations: I don't think I've ever seen Emma at a loss for words."

"Did I say something wrong?" Bonnet asked.

"On the contrary," said Blondine, "I imagine Emma will want to look into this orphanage. Where is it?"

"The Vieille Ruche, I believe it's called."

"The big old house outside of Vurgren? I love that place!" said Blondine. "Very beautiful, very bourgeois."

Rosalyn knew that in French, "bourgeois" was not an insult, as it often was back home— or, at least, in the part of California where she was raised, where it meant having a shallow

243

attachment to worldly goods and conventionality. In France, the word simply referred to individuals of a certain stature and wealth.

"The Germans occupied Vieille Ruche as a command post during the Second World War," Bonnet explained. "That's why I know about it—it was a scandal when the Nazis forced the orphans out. A Madame Bolze lives there now. Her husband's family made a fortune in glass."

"Is she of the Bolze bottle makers?" asked Raúl. "They are well-known."

"She is indeed. As you may imagine, bottles are a big item around here," Gaspard explained to Rosalyn. "They were especially hard to come by during the war years."

"Does anyone know this Madame Bolze?" Emma asked. "I'd love to contact her, see if she might know anything about this 'wealthy Australian woman,' or have any records dating back to the orphanage."

"Why would she keep such old stuff?" Blondine asked.

"Many people find history interesting," Bonnet said, looking amused. "As we grow older, we tend to appreciate the past more. Perhaps you will as well."

"Hmph," Blondine replied, clearly unconvinced.

"I will introduce you to her," said Gaspard.

Emma's head whipped around. "You will?"

"You see? What did I tell you?" Gaspard said to no one in particular. "Emma always under-estimates me. But I am an official with the Archiconfrérie de Saint Vincent now, and I sit on the *comité*. Madame Bolze will take my call."

Emma raised her champagne flute and gave him a warm smile. "A mistake I will be sure not to make again."

"There is one little problem with your plan, *ma chère* Emma," Gaspard said.

"What's that?"

"The Vieille Ruche is a four-story manor," he pointed out. "Unless André is willing to cart you up and down the stairs, this will not be possible."

"I value André much too highly to subject him to anything quite as dangerous as toting my not-insubstantial self up four flights of stairs," Emma said. "But fortunately, there's a work-around—my good friend Rosalyn. What say you, Rosalyn? Care to explore with me?"

Rosalyn smiled. "I'd be happy to."

"It's settled, then," Emma said. "More cham-pagne!"

As Rosalyn was about to take another bite of her cake, she noticed something nestled within the layers of pastry. It took her a moment to realize: She had been served the piece with *la fève*.

"Look what I found," she said, holding up a little figure of a baby.

"*Voilà*, you are king for the day!" said Gaspard.

"And you must bring the cake next year," said Dominique.

"Do you have any royal edicts, as king?" asked Bonnet.

"As a matter of fact, I do," said Rosalyn. "Tonight, the men do the dishes, and no more smoking indoors."

The group dissolved into laughter as Rosalyn stood to help Blondine clear the table, and the others lit their cigarettes.

Rosalyn teased that as king, she would have their heads cut off for their impertinence.

Chapter Twenty-four

By the time Emma, André, and Rosalyn headed back to their bedrooms at the *gîte*, the storm had passed, but the fallen rain had frozen. The courtyard looked like something out of a movie: icicles hanging like Christmas ornaments from branches and eaves, a thick sheet of ice frosting every surface. Gaspard threw handfuls of rock salt on the walkway, but they still practically skated all the way back, arriving intact only with André's considerable help.

After several effusive *bonne nuits* at her door, Rosalyn slipped into *Chambre Chardonnay*. She caught a whiff of evergreen from the sprigs she had placed on the table, in the little nest for the shattered ornament. She leaned down and put her nose to the branches, inhaling deeply. The scent reminded her of Dash. Or, more precisely, of Dash's cologne, which she had noticed the very first time she got close to him. It was subtle but intoxicating.

When she came home from the hospital that last time, after running from his room, Rosalyn had thrown the bottle against the wall, where it shattered, spewing glass shards and its fragrant contents on the carpet.

More than two years later, the cottage still smelled of him.

Rosalyn positioned a chair in front of her one big window and looked out over the sparkling scene outside, an enchanted landscape painting come to life. As a native Californian, she was fascinated by the winter weather—especially since she was safe and warm, inside looking out.

Wind buffeted the window, stirring frozen branches that *tink*ed together, sending icicles crashing to the ground. What would a storm of this intensity have meant for the soldiers in the trenches? Would they have been exposed to all the elements, desperate for new wool socks? At least those living in the caves under Reims were protected from changes in the weather; it was a constant, cool temperature down in the bowels of the earth, hovering around fifty-five to sixty degrees Fahrenheit. Perfect for champagne. Chilly for humans, though nothing a good wool sweater couldn't fix.

Rosalyn fiddled with the *fève* she had found in her slice of Kings' cake. She had experienced a childish surge of giddiness upon discovering the tiny baby figure nestled in the layers of pastry. It was just a silly tradition, but Rosalyn had never won *anything*. No Girl Scout lottery, no premovie drawing, rarely even a card game. Dash used to tease her that she was "unlucky at cards, lucky at love."

Not so much, in the end.

She stared at the tiny baby, thinking of what Lucie had said about the youngest refugees carrying their dolls. Feeling the familiar pang, deep down. Rosalyn had wanted to start a family. Dash's response was "someday, all in due time," but Rosalyn had known that "someday" meant "never." She'd briefly considered allowing herself to get pregnant "by accident," but decided that would be unfair and underhanded, a thorny premise on which to invite a new life into this world.

Dash liked children—but he enjoyed other things more. He wanted to go out to dinner and dance, to remain unencumbered by the needs of little ones. It was the same reason he didn't want Rosalyn to get a full-time job; she taught a few art classes to children, but mostly she painted and played house during the day, remaining free to join Dash at the drop of a hat. He wanted to hold impromptu parties, to hop into the car and drive wherever, whenever the whim struck. Up the coast to Timber Cove, down the coast to Santa Barbara. One weekend he and Rosalyn took off to London, just for fun; other times, they flew to Mexico or Hawaii. Theirs was a life others had envied: a whirlwind of fine dining, four-star hotels, the best wines, and the liveliest company.

Until it wasn't.

Rosalyn sometimes tortured herself, wondering: Had Dash made himself sick, somehow? The drinking, the rich food, the indulgent lifestyle. During the day while she was painting in the vines, lost in sweet oblivion, he attended to business but also lingered over three-hour lunches with clients and potential investors.

Later, when the terrible truth set in, that their lifestyle was built on credit, that he—that *they*—were deeply in debt, Rosalyn realized that Dash had not been attending to business after all. At the very least, not well.

She had wanted to believe him when he said he had everything under control; she trusted him to handle their finances while she spent her days among the rows of vines, reveling in her palette of sap greens and raw siennas and hints of vermilion. Dave's gray and phthalocyanine, viridian green. Lost in the shape and form of the hills, the blue of the sky, the fluff of the clouds outlined in gold.

She had given her life over, part and parcel, to Dash.

Now, as she slipped *la fève* into the locket, where it was a snug fit, and turned back to Émile's letters, Rosalyn tried to remember: Had he even asked for it?

March 27, 1915

Dear Madame Whittaker,

Once again I have been sent to Reims. My poor, devastated city is even worse than before. I am so sorry to say it. After looking the lady Lucie Maréchal up at her Villa Traverne, only to find there nothing but charred ruins, I discovered through a passerby that they had moved to another house, to the south of the city.

But there, another ruin stood.

In truth I began to panic, thinking of the terrible things that might have happened to the young lady and her family. Though I see the death of my fellow soldiers every day, it is harder to cope with the violence done to civilians.

At long last, and with great relief, I found the lady in question, along with her mother, father, and brother, hiding down in the *crayères* of Pommery. They have taken shelter there, along with so many others, and have made a little niche for themselves into a strange kind of home, under the sign of Dakar.

I don't quite know how to describe Mademoiselle Lucie Maréchal. The first time I met her, her words and attitude surprised me; she was not the spoiled girl I had expected. But now . . . she has given up her fine silks for simple muslins, her soft kid shoes for the wooden clogs worn by women who work in the fields. She does not seem embittered, but merely determined. There is a stubborn set to her chin that makes even this battle-weary soldier believe that she will survive and do as she pleases, within the confines of her war-scarred world.

Already the others in the caves look to her for guidance. She forms groups that go out to scavenge for useful items—and to help the wounded—in the rubble after shellings. A little orphan girl named Topette follows her around and sleeps by her side at night.

Many of our brave troops are bunked down in the caves under xxx, mostly French but some British as well. I find myself wishing, fervently, that I could remain here to fight alongside them. At times they become emboldened with champagne, and I find myself fearful that they might bother the young ladies. It is something quite akin to jealousy, though I realize it is not my place.

The tunnels have been extended far out under the vines on the hillsides. Into No Man's Land, a hell of trenches and soot, shell holes and *séchoirs*. That the vines survive the gas and bombardment is a testament to [unreadable], and, I like to think, to the spirit of the *Rémois*.

Please always know I think of you with *le coeur toujours chaud.*

Respectfully,
Émile Legrand

My dear *marraine*,

Many of my battalion have been dropped not by bullets but by disease. I think the flies have something to do with it, as well as the heat and the still-unburied bodies. There seem to be millions of flies here in xxx, and they are all over everything. Put a cup of tea down without a cover and it is immediately covered; when you open your mouth to speak or to eat, in they pop. It is a gruesome sort of game.

Where we are now must have been a "No Man's Land" because there are no houses or buildings of any kind to be seen, and except for the flies, the only living things are rats and lizards and occasionally brave little canaries.

You asked about our rations. We get plenty of bully beef and army biscuits, but bread and fresh meat have become a luxury, and it is not possible to buy anything. Last winter flour was in such short supply that bread was being made with dried ground turnips, but it was better than nothing. Once, a few weeks ago, a *boulangerie roulante* appeared; you cannot imagine the jubilation to have a few slices of *pain au levain*! I believe I will never again take such things for granted.

Lately we have been fed on pea soup with a few lumps of horse meat, if we're lucky. I don't complain, as I know the kitchen staff eats the same as we do, and theirs is not an easy job. Not long ago one cook was hit by a sniper while out scouting for nettles and dandelion greens to add a little flavor to the soup.

I find the worst part is that the kitchen staff has only two large vats, in which everything is prepared, and here in xxx it is difficult to wash our bodies, much less the dishes. Thus everything we eat tastes of something else; our tea often smells like potatoes and onions.

When last I visited Reims, Lucie took me to a little café that had been set up underground, in the caves. There were little tables, and we all seemed to be taking part in a play, as though we were outside at a sidewalk café. We shared a tea cake and some champagne; the cake was stale and made of something other than flour—it is best not to wonder—but it was ambrosia nonetheless. The champagne shimmered like the nectar of the gods, as always.

And the lovely Lucie, sitting before me, was like an angel from heaven (a very determined, stubborn angel) that has been assigned to purgatory for some unspoken sin, trapped beneath the earth, within the caves.

Yours with all affection and respect,
Émile Legrand

Chapter Twenty-five

Lucie

When first we landed in our underground lair, the overwhelming feeling was one of relief. But that did not last long.

Soon enough I came to understand that the gravest danger was no longer the shells that dropped—though they sometimes shook us even deep within the cave—but the prodigious degradation of spirit.

There are soldiers billeted in their own sections of the *crayères*; they have extended the tunnels so they can travel for many kilometers into No Man's Land without ever exposing themselves to the outside world.

Though they do not live among us, their military presence means that the world at large has learned about the pitiable, brave *Rémois* living underground. Journalists and sometimes even politicians and famous performers appeal to the military authorities for special passes to come visit the strange and remarkable "underground cities" that now house the populace of Reims under the celebrated champagne houses of Clicquot, Taittinger, and Pommery.

It feels more and more like we are, indeed, living in Alice's wonderland, that we have fallen down the rabbit's hole.

I care less about visiting dignitaries than I do about my own stomach. When the dangerous zone is relatively clear, the soldiers are able to bring in food and other necessities. Occasionally presents arrive from concerned citizens in sections of France relatively untouched by war, and some by admirers from faraway parts of the world: One year the children were sent new shoes, and another time thousands of cut flowers filled the caves, lending us their garish colors and heavenly scents for a few days.

Oil for the lamps is always in short supply and we suffer the indignity of using "latrines"—buckets that must be taken out and dumped—for our most basic needs. We have to line up for food, but at the very least, we know we will not starve.

Indeed, businesses spring up in the caves. When he has access to flour, the baker can make *pain au levain* and *pains-biscuits*, sending warmth and the mouthwatering aroma of baking bread through its section of the cellars; the grocery often has a stock of vegetables and canned goods, and very occasionally offers grapes, apples, or even pears for sale.

Somehow, Monsieur Émile Legrand found us

down there, in Dakar. He brought a note from my fiancé, and another present: This time it was a wheel of cheese, so I suppose he was listening. He sent a postcard, telling me he was well, and wishing me better.

In the caves a small café proffers coffee and tea, and even champagne and brandy; the woman in charge sets out little tables and chairs so we can pretend we are sitting outside, enjoying the air.

Monsieur Legrand and I took a glass of champagne there, feeling quite daring. He told me he was sorry to see my family living down in the caves, but was happy to know we were safe. At my heartfelt urging he spoke of his life in the trenches; he said he felt like an animal, poking his head above the earthen rim of his ditch only to feed and to kill.

I told him we made quite the pair, both running to ground to survive.

He told me that he writes several times a week to his *marraine*, a woman who lives in Australia, which is a country clear on the other side of the world, where no bombs fall. He laughed when I asked whether he had ever seen the ocean, and whether we might sail away to that land of peace, after the war.

Before leaving, he asked if he could leave a bundle of his *marraine*'s letters with me for safekeeping; he invited me to read them at will.

When I stood I remarked that I thought the champagne was going to my head. He smiled and quoted his favorite poet, a man named Charles Baudelaire:

> One must always be drunk. That's it—that's the only question. In order not to feel the horrible burden of time that weighs on your shoulders and bends you to the earth, you must be drunk without pause. . . . But drunk with what? With wine, with poetry, or with virtue, as you wish.

I made him write it down for me. To be honest, I am not sure whether my head was affected by the champagne or by the man himself.

This time, I nearly cried to see him go.

My family fell into a pattern: Upon rising and sharing tea, my mother and I would tidy our niche, which meant folding our blankets, dusting, and sweeping up the chalky white powder that sifted down incessantly from the walls and ceiling. Henri would venture deeper into the caves to find out through the grapevine whether any new supplies were expected that day and, if so, where we were supposed to line up. My father would remain mute, sitting on a scavenged chair and staring at the bottles that provided us a modicum of privacy.

He was not the only one; I would venture to say that the great majority of those dwelling in the underground shared that same vacant stare, beset by the treacherous malaise that attacks one who has lost too much.

The children, meanwhile, ran wild.

Had I been only a few years younger, I'm quite certain I would have joined them—most likely I would have led the little gang, running through the tunnels and mounting crude stairs, discovering hidden niches and tunnels within tunnels, exploring galleries that led onto wider galleries or narrow passages or dropped into steep pits, pretending to be in Alice's world.

But as it was, my mother drew me aside and told me I must do something to help.

"What am I to do about it?" I asked. "No one else is doing anything."

"You must," she said. "You are able, and therefore you must."

My mother was not a woman to be gainsaid. And it was clear she was right; this was no way to live.

First, I joined the small groups that waited for a pause in the shelling, and then went to sift through charred remains, searching for anything of value: unbroken chairs, serviceable blankets, even pretty little items that would remind us of the before time. We raided the ruins of a pharmacy and helped to stock the "hospital" that had been set up in a large quarry pit; a soot-covered Madonna was rescued from the cathedral, cleaned, and brought down to grace our underground chapel. We scavenged from a damaged interior decorator's shop, and were able to embellish parts of the cellars with wallpaper and figurines; it may sound silly but it provided a degree of normalcy to some family niches and well-used sections of the caves.

The bravest children were able to help, slipping through openings too small for adults and reaching into crevices between the rubble to extract items of value. Though it was hazardous to be outside, we learned to stay close to standing buildings, to dart quickly across open areas, and to listen for shells and bullets.

One little girl of seven years, Topette, began to follow me around. She has no idea what happened to her family; as far as she could explain it to me, she last saw her parents at the train station, when they were waiting for permission to evacuate. Her father had to go back to their home to retrieve some important papers, but when he did not return, her mother ordered her to stay right where she was, by the pillar closest to the track; her mother disappeared into the crowd, and that was the last time she saw her. Through her tears, Topette told me she stayed by the pillar as long as she could, but night came and went, her stomach hurt, and she wet her pants. Finally she disobeyed her mother and ran home, but their house was now no more than a bombed-out crater.

Topette and I were mending privacy curtains one day when Monsieur Albert Corpart, the long-time vineyard manager of Pommery champagne house, came down to the caves.

He announced he was looking for help to bring in the harvest.

Dull eyes turned to him, wondering if it were true. The vines were now on the front line of the fighting; how could he expect us to bring in the grapes?

But Monsieur Corpart is well-known to all for his *entêtement*, his pigheadedness. After working in Pommery's vineyards and nurturing the plants for nearly thirty years, he was not about to abandon his precious vines to the vicissitudes of war.

"The winery has no access to proper money since the banks closed," Monsieur Corpart explained, "but workers will be paid in vouchers that can be used at any local businesses, and after the war, Pommery promises to make good on the markers. All of our healthy young workers have gone to battle the *Boches*, but you women and children, and anyone else feeling well enough, can wage war against the enemy in the classic way of the *Rémois*: You can help make champagne."

He was asking us to bring in the grapes, to lay up bottles of a Victory Vintage that would develop bubbles and be ready to drink only after this wretched war was over. For some reason I thought of Monsieur Émile Legrand; I imagined sharing a glass with him in peacetime, long after the war.

Despite the bombs, despite everything, Monsieur Corpart was asking us to make the wine.

I was the first to raise my hand.

Chapter Twenty-six

Madame Bolze was not only willing to talk but was delighted at the prospect of visitors, and invited them to come on Tuesday at eleven o'clock. Blondine wasn't about to miss a chance to see the inside of the Vieille Ruche, and she offered to drive so that André might have a day off.

"Works for me," Emma said. "But be fore-warned: I'm a backseat driver of the first order."

"Backseat . . . ?" Blondine asked.

"She means she's going to tell you what to do every step of the way," Rosalyn said.

"This is supposed to be news?" Blondine said. "We'll leave at nine."

"I'll be ready," said Rosalyn. "But why so early? Michel said it was only a twenty-minute drive."

"We have stops to make. We will need a basket with fruit and pâté, and we must stop at the *boulangerie*. We cannot arrive empty-handed."

The next day Rosalyn helped Emma into the front passenger's seat and climbed in the back with Emma's crutches.

At the butcher a few towns over, Emma and Blondine argued over which basket to buy and which pâté was superior: the *pâté de campagne* or the truffled mousse. At the fruit stand, Emma and Blondine argued over whether to buy apples or pears, clementines or Valencia oranges, or dried fruits like plums, apricots, and dates.

And that was nothing compared to the long, drawn-out discussion at the counter of the *boulangerie*. Blondine insisted on bread that was *pas trop cuit*, not too cooked, which engendered yet another heated discussion with Emma, who was staunchly of the opinion that a well-browned baguette was best. Soon the baker emerged from the rear of the store to weigh in on the proper degree of doneness of a perfect baguette, and several other customers waiting their turn to order chimed in.

Rosalyn stayed out of it, relishing the opportunity to examine the baked goods on display. The *boulangerie* wasn't a *pâtisserie*—a shop that specialized in pastries and desserts—but nonetheless sold delectable-looking *choux*, or cream puffs, as well as éclairs, madeleines, macarons, meringues, and *tartes aux fruits*, which were miniature open-faced fruit-and-custard tarts. How in the world did the French stay so skinny?

The *boulangerie* smelled like heaven, and Rosalyn hoped the scent would linger on her clothing the way the cigarette smoke had after the Ephipany party.

The disputants in the Great Baguette Debate at last called a truce—neither side had convinced the other, though all agreed the proprietor of the *boulangerie* had the best bread in all of Champagne—and, to appease Emma, Blondine bought several baguettes in varying degrees of doneness, as well as an assortment of other breads to bring home with them.

Back in the car and once again en route to visit Madame Bolze, Blondine ripped off the heel of a baguette and handed it to Rosalyn.

"It's called *le quignon*, the bit you eat on the way home," she explained.

"There's a name for that?" asked Rosalyn, and took a bite of the delicious fresh baguette.

"You don't even want to know how many words the French have to describe all types of bread, bread creation, and bread consumption," said Emma, letting her head fall back on the headrest and breathing out a weary sigh. "I'm telling you, it's a religion."

The ice from the other night had long since melted, but a heavy mist hung over the fields of cereal grains, lucerne, and wheat. Old fences, tractors, and other farm equipment studded the landscape. Doors to caves were nestled at bottoms of hills, like Hobbit houses. Tucked into the valleys of gentle, rolling hills were little villages full of stone houses topped with red roofs.

Rosalyn gazed out at the passing countryside and felt . . . if not happy, then at least not terribly *un*happy.

The moment she became conscious of it, guilt washed over her. Thoughts of Dash flooded back: their honeymoon in Paris, walking hand in hand through the Napa vineyard, how proud he was of her painting, how much he loved her eyes. Most piercing was the memory of how she had run from his hospital room that last time.

She forced her mind away from that image, focusing instead on the old letters she had been reading, on the idea of these very same villages burned and bombed by the invading German armies. What would it have been like to see enemy soldiers marching through these cobble-stone streets? She imagined the chalky blue and green shutters shut tight against aggressors, giving the houses the look of charming fortresses or sleeping hulks.

They passed a marker, this one a stone angel, no doubt standing over yet another list of war casualties. There was something calming about being in a place that had experienced so much suffering, yet refused to forget.

"Emma," Rosalyn heard herself say, "you and Blondine mentioned that this area owes its success to the widows. Do you suppose it was *because* they were widows that they accomplished what they did? Or were they just extraordinary women regardless of their marital status?"

"Good question," said Emma. "I read that Madame Pommery set up a retirement fund for her workers, and founded a mother's fund. That was pretty forward-thinking of her, and I would assume it had to do with her own understanding of the precarious economic situation facing women and children at that time, especially when the husband died."

"Madame Pommery founded an orphanage, as well," Blondine said. "It wasn't uncommon for wealthy widows. I agree with Emma. I think they understood the special challenges women and children faced. And back in the day, *veuve* was a respected form of address—especially for women of means. Widows had much more freedom than women with living husbands."

"Some champagne producers put *veuve* in front of their names, just for the status of it," added Emma, "even if they didn't have any widows in the family—or, at least, none who were involved in the business."

"Scammers from the start, huh?" said Rosalyn.

Emma waved a hand in the air. "You have no idea. This place was chock-full of scammers—producers would find some ditch digger named Pérignon, and establish a new 'house of Dom Pérignon.' Champagne has tried to reinvent itself as a very classy area, but its history was a bit wild."

"I had no idea *la Champagne* was so full of drama."

Emma snorted. "Wherever there are people, there will be soap operas."

Rosalyn smiled and gazed out the window, pondering the irony of her landing in Champagne, of all places, the land of widows.

"But yes, it's all about the widows here in Champagne," Emma continued.

Rosalyn opened her mouth to tell Emma and Blondine that she, too, was a widow. It wasn't a secret, exactly, so much as a private thing. But she hesitated. Her loss weighed her down like a stone, and it was relaxing not to have to think about it, not to *be* a widow, every moment of every day.

"I'm excited to see the house," said Blondine. "But I remember there were rumors that the Bolze family collaborated with the Nazis during the war."

"How old is Madame Bolze?" Rosalyn asked.

"She's in her eighties now, which means she was just a child at the time. But still. What would it be like to know your wealth comes from such a history?"

"Today she's just an old lady who might be able to help us with something. Anyway, there are always rumors about such things," said Emma, and turned to Rosalyn. "There was a shortage of glass during the war, and it's possible the Bolze bottle makers sold to some people they shouldn't have. But the truth is, there's always someone somewhere making money off war."

"That's sad but true," said Rosalyn. "They say war's great for commerce."

"I'm not sure they can be condemned for cooperating with an occupying army," said Emma. "What was the alternative?"

"My father's uncle was a teenager during World War Two who was shot and killed for helping to blow up a German supply train," Blondine said fiercely. "*That* was the alternative. You Australians and Americans have never been invaded and had to fight to free *la patrie*. You do not understand."

"Girl's got a point," Emma said, and Rosalyn nodded. "But since we've arrived at our destination, may I suggest we set aside seventy-five-year-old innuendo and keep an open mind?"

Blondine turned onto a gravel driveway. Ahead of them, visible through ornate wrought iron gates, the Vieille Ruche house loomed. Surrounded by a large stone wall, it was four stories tall and built of multicolored stone in shades of red, ocher, and green.

A boy of about ten ran to greet the car as they pulled up. "*Bonjour*! You're the friends of Madame Bolze?"

He opened the gates, and Blondine pulled through; then he closed them carefully behind them.

"She lets us come play here sometimes," said the boy. "My mom does work for her. *Bonne journée!*"

Madame Bolze opened the door and stood in the threshold to greet them. She was short and round and unsmiling, with close-cropped silver hair. Dressed in pants and a tunic, she had the aura of a farmer's wife more than of a grande dame.

Rosalyn helped Emma out of the car, then handed her the crutches. Emma swayed, supporting herself on the doorframe.

"Are you okay?" Rosalyn asked.

"Sure. Just a little dizzy. Got up too fast." She gazed at the tall house. "Good thing I'm not the one who has to climb up there, right?"

Fortunately there were only three shallow steps leading to the front door landing.

"*Bonjour, madame!*" Emma called out. "We are your visitors—and we come bearing gifts!"

The basket of pâté, fruit, and fresh bread seemed to smooth over any awkwardness, as Madame Bolze spent a while inspecting the contents.

After introductions, she waved them in. "Come in, come in. It's cold outside."

They stepped into a cramped foyer with

several doors, and one small hallway leading to a twisting staircase. A grandfather clock, two credenzas, and a coat stand crowded the space.

"Put your coats there." She indicated an overloaded rack.

"Thank you so much for having us," said Emma, gesturing with her crutches. "As you can see, I'm a little worse for wear, so I brought these two with me to be my legs."

"Of course." Madame Bolze opened a door to a large light-filled sitting room, fronted on one side by a glassed-in solarium. They were immediately enveloped in the heat of the radiators and the sunroom.

Everywhere were books and furniture and boxes of papers and photographs and miscellaneous items. Scattered on a small coffee table were postcards, baby photos, and documents with blocks of print and seals that looked like important legal papers. A mélange of abandoned craft projects cluttered a large round table, and knitting needles stuck out of half-finished sweaters and scarves. The walls were covered in religious icons, landscape paintings, and antique mirrors.

The room was crowded with too many tables and chairs, and yet there was nowhere for the four of them to sit comfortably without rearranging things.

"I need to get organized," said Madame Bolze.

"The mother of the boy who opened the gates comes to help me a couple of times a week, but even so, I never seem to have time to get through all of this. It's a lifetime's worth of stuff."

Rosalyn wondered if everyone would become a hoarder if they lived long enough—then remembered her mother's biannual purges, during which she threw out just about everything that had been inspired by the latest fashion trend. The echoing rooms then "forced" her to go out and buy new stuff, which might well have been the point.

The jumble made Rosalyn more optimistic that they might actually find papers from World War One somewhere in the clutter.

"This used to be a dovecote," said Madame Bolze as she gestured to one section of the living room, where ancient stone steps led up to a closed-off space. Books were stacked on the steps, and within the alcove was a massive wooden desk covered with papers. Perched along a half wall that divided the room were green glass wine bottles, from the tiniest to the largest Rosalyn had ever seen.

"And that was my husband's office. He ran his business from here."

Rosalyn wondered: Had the papers been sitting there, just like that, since Monsieur Bolze died, just like Dash's pills in the medicine chest at home? Another fruitless attempt to make time stand still.

"So, tell me again what you girls are looking for?"

"Monsieur Bonnet mentioned that this house used to be an orphanage," said Emma.

"That was before my time. I'm not *that* old."

"Of course not—I didn't mean to suggest otherwise," said Emma with a soft chuckle. "But you mentioned on the phone that you might have some papers from back then. The thing is, Monsieur Bonnet is certain the orphanage was founded by an Australian woman, and I have reason to think she might have been a relative of mine. My great-grandfather's sister."

"I remember the Nazis marching in," said Madame Bolze. "They came right down the main road of the village. I was at school, taking an exam, and was relieved when the teacher told us all to go home. I had no understanding of what was to come. But I know very little about the Great War."

"We understand," said Emma, glancing at Rosalyn. Was Madame Bolze a little fuzzy with the details, or was she simply not paying attention? "Why don't you tell us what you remember about World War Two? We would very much like to hear your stories."

Emma had an innate ability to put people at ease, to get them to talk, Rosalind thought. She would have made an excellent investigative journalist. Or a truly charming inquisitor.

"I remember the bombings, and with poor Reims just barely digging out from the previous war, according to my father. He told me about the Smiling Angel."

"I heard about that," said Rosalyn. "What a shame."

"It's become a symbol of the brutality of war around these parts," said Emma with a nod. "But I should note that the Angel of Reims was decapitated by a bomb. It's not like soldiers scaled the cathedral façade with broadswords, or anything."

"Still, they are barbarians," Blondine sniffed. "I don't trust the Germans."

Bolze gave her a startled look. Rosalyn had noted the number of German-sounding surnames in the area and among the champagne houses. She had assumed that the animosity over the wars had faded, what with the passage of time and developments such as the European Union. But clearly history was alive and well in the minds and hearts of the French—and no doubt the Germans as well.

"During the war, even paper was scarce," Madame Bolze said as she led the way into the kitchen, crowded with a table and chairs, and decorated with painted blue and white tiles. "A lot of old papers were used to line trunks, or to start fires."

"People burned historic documents?" asked Emma.

"They did what they had to do to survive. I'm just saying, don't expect too much." Madame Bolze opened a pie safe and extracted from a cookie jar a large key ring full of old skeleton keys.

"If there's anything to be found, my friends here will find it. In the meantime, I'll wait here, if that's all right." Emma nodded toward Blondine and Rosalyn. "Thanks, *mes amies*."

The key ring clanked as the elderly woman returned to the small hallway, grasped the banister, and started hoisting herself up the stairs.

"Please, madame, we can go by ourselves," said Blondine. "You don't need to be climbing these stairs."

"Nonsense," Madame Bolze said, her progress slow but steady. "It is what has kept me alive this long."

As they slowly mounted the steep, twisting, creaky stairs, Madame Bolze kept talking, telling them about being estranged from a daughter and a son, and the family fights over the estate. She spoke about when she and her husband used to go to Spain for vacation, to a small town on the Costa Blanca called Calpe, how they had a boat and bought cheap goods at the *pulga*, or flea market.

"I still have some of those sweaters," she

boasted, and it wasn't hard to imagine the fifty-year-old jerseys tucked away in one of the numerous wardrobes, plastic bins, clothes racks, or chests that lined the narrow passageways. "Moroccan wool—it is the best."

Rosalyn didn't catch everything Madame Bolze was saying, focused as she was on Blondine's legs in front of her. Blondine was wearing chic high heels, as usual. How did she manage, first on the ice, now on these stairs? It might have been very American of her, but Rosalyn was glad she was wearing comfy boots.

Finally they arrived at the fourth floor, which the French counted as the third floor. Madame Bolze tested a locked door handle. "I keep it locked. There are a lot of family heirlooms up here."

Rosalyn tried to imagine the intrepid thief who would make his or her way up to this level, past all the rest the house contained.

Madame Bolze tried several keys in the ancient lock until she finally found the right one. She pushed the door open and stuck her gray head in, as though to be sure they weren't disturbing anyone. After a moment, she stepped back.

"*Bon*. There an old black steamer trunk in the corner. It has been there since before we moved in. I do not know if it contains what you are looking for, but my father-in-law bought this house after the Second World War, so . . . it is possible."

Madame Bolze turned and began her slow descent down the stairs, holding tightly to the metal banister, the treads creaking underfoot.

Blondine and Rosalyn looked at each other.

"Do you suppose there's someone living in here?" asked Rosalyn in a low voice.

"It sort of felt like she was checking for someone, didn't it? Probably just ghosts."

"I ain't afraid of no ghosts," Rosalyn said in English, parroting a film from childhood.

"*Comment*?" Blondine asked.

"Never mind. You don't have earthquakes in this area, do you?" Rosalyn asked. Everything about the old house suggested it would tumble down at the slightest provocation—if not because of the crooked timbers, then due to the sheer tonnage of junk on every floor.

Blondine shook her head. "I'm more worried about fire, myself."

"Oh great," said Rosalyn, realizing there was no way out of the house other than the cramped stairwell, or a window. "Now I am, too."

"Good thing we don't smoke, eh?" Blondine said. "*Allons-y*."

Chapter Twenty-seven

The attic space itself was like the rest of the house, but more so: Objects were piled high, a few covered with sheets, most not. They zigzagged their way between piles of musty books and old magazines, cardboard boxes and decrepit small appliances, the air smelling of dust and abandonment.

Rosalyn moved a box aside and jumped back in alarm.

"A mouse?" Blondine asked.

"No . . . a painting."

A stern-looking older woman stared out of a gold-framed oil painting, tight curls on the side of her head, lace at her throat and wrists.

"Speaking of the *veuve* Clicquot," said Blondine, peering over her shoulder. "That looks very much like a famous portrait of her. She was . . . *intimidante*."

"This one certainly looks intimidating. In English we would say 'formidable,' but that word means something different in French."

"Back in the day, women in portraits were either young and beautiful or old and scary."

Blondine gazed at the portrait, her head tilted to one side. "I'm not sure what that means, really, but maybe this woman was also a widow, ready to rule the world."

"And more than a little annoyed," said Rosalyn.

Blondine laughed. "Yes, more than a little annoyed. I said those wealthy widows were impressive, not that they were a lot of fun to be around."

They made their way farther into the cluttered attic room, pushing aside a sewing mannequin, a baby's cradle, and a stack of dining chairs.

Blondine picked up what looked like a large scrapbook that was sitting on a small cupboard. "Oh, my grandmother had one of these."

"What is it?" Rosalyn came to see the book, which held embroidered scraps of linen.

"A young woman's journal, from nineteen twenty-seven. These are samples of how to fold napkins for different sorts of occasions. It's the sort of thing a well-brought-up young lady was expected to know before marriage. Can you imagine a life like that?"

"It's a far cry from Pilates classes and Netflix marathons—that's for sure. But it's also sort of sweet, thinking of a girl putting that book together."

Blondine nodded and replaced the scrapbook where she had found it.

Part of Rosalyn wanted to flee the dusty attic—

now that Blondine had put the fear of fire in her head, she felt a certain sense of urgency—but another part of her wanted to sit and sort through these boxes. Because while it was junk, it was old *French* junk.

"We are looking for a big black trunk, yes?" Blondine asked, noting her distractedness.

"Right. According to Madame Bolze, it should be in the corner."

"There are four corners."

"True. Divide and conquer," Rosalyn replied. "I'll take these two corners and you take those two."

At long last, they located the steamer trunk hidden beneath a pile of old curtains.

It took both of them to lug the heavy trunk a few inches away from the wall so they could open the lid. Rosalyn unlatched the big clasp, then paused.

"What are you waiting for?" asked Blondine.

"I don't know, really. I just needed a moment."

"Take your moment, then," Blondine said. "But the sooner we open it, the sooner we can get out of this firetrap."

"Fair point," Rosalyn said, and lifted the lid.

The trunk was packed full of items, which they lifted carefully, one by one, and set aside. There were books, journals, and old papers; several pairs of black leather button-up baby shoes; a christening gown of silk that now hung in shreds;

carefully folded linens and quilts that had once been beautiful but were now decaying.

"I think we found what we were looking for," Rosalyn said as she perched on a footstool and started sorting through a stack of antique documents bound with ribbon. Many were written on ornate letterhead marked: *Orphelinat de Champagne: pour les orphelins de guerre.* "The Orphanage of Champagne: for the war orphans."

"I don't see any letters from an Australian woman," said Blondine, digging deep into the contents of the trunk. "Isn't that what Emma was hoping for?"

"Yes, though I'm not sure why they would have ended up here, anyway," said Rosalyn. "I think we're looking for any link at all to her great-aunt, Doris Whittaker. Yet another wealthy widow."

"Oooh, look at this," said Blondine, paging through a thick leather-bound ledger. She handed it to Rosalyn. "It's a roster of the orphans."

Rosalyn balanced the ledger on her knees and skimmed the handwritten entries. As in Émile's letters, the old ink was fading and at times was hard to read, but at least the ledger hadn't been subjected to Anastasia's scissors.

"All those poor children," said Rosalyn, running her fingers lightly over the dozens— hundreds?—of names meticulously recorded: *Louise Rose Beaulieu; Reims. Paul Marc Martin;*

La Neuville-aux-Larris. Clement Luc Laurent; Épernay. Jean-Claude Travers; unknown origin; Augusta Page Mercier; Cuchery. Some entries included the names of deceased parents and other family members, or the names of those who adopted the children; others simply listed the child's name and origin, with no clue as to what had happened to them.

"Sometimes I think we'll never get over it," said Blondine. She set down an ancient pair of baby shoes and came to join Rosalyn, who was flipping through the pages. "So many of these little ones grew up and were sent into battle in the next world war, just two decades later. And the young adults who survived the First World War had to send their own children to fight—and to die—in the second. Something like that must live on in the national consciousness, don't you think?"

"Yes, of course. To be occupied, and brutalized over two generations . . . That's got to leave a scar. A deep scar."

"Champagne has always been a theater of war. There were the Gauls and Romans, and then the Hundred Years' War, the Napoleonic Wars, the Franco-Prussian War, and then two World Wars. All of them right here, on these lands. Some say this is why the grapes began to fizz, to bring us joy, to balance things out."

Blondine dove back into the trunk, leaning over,

ostrichlike, rummaging through the contents.

"Look at this!" Blondine handed Rosalyn a manila envelope full of ancient sepia-toned photographs.

There were several of children playing in the courtyard of what was now Madame Bolze's house, and a few individual photos of children with their names scrawled on the back. Most astonishing was a handful of photographs of the schoolrooms that had been set up in the champagne caves.

"These are amazing," said Rosalyn. "I tried looking this up online, but I didn't find anything like this. So they really did have schools in the caves."

"Can you imagine? It must have been so hard down there, no electricity, no fresh air. . . ."

"And no plumbing."

Blondine wrinkled her nose. "I never thought of that."

"I imagine things got pretty basic at times," Rosalyn said, studying a photograph of a school-teacher. She was unsmiling, clothed head to toe in black, but she stared at the camera with a steady gaze, a determined tilt to her chin. "But they persevered. They taught the children. They brought in the harvest. They didn't just survive. They *lived*. Astonishing."

"Why would these photos be included with the papers from the orphanage?" said Blondine.

"Maybe some of the teachers came here after the war, to continue taking care of the children?" suggested Rosalyn.

"That would make sense. Hey, look at this." Blondine opened a silk pouch that contained several long knitting needles. "Do you suppose needlework was part of the curriculum back then?"

Rosalyn had learned the word *tricoter*, French for "to knit," while reading Émile's references to Lucie's mother knitting socks and sweaters.

"Maybe so, especially if you consider they were still training girls to fold linen napkins according to the occasion."

"Aha!" said Blondine, suddenly straightening, holding a framed certificate in one hand.

The fancy scrollwork made it hard to read, but they could make out the roster of the orphanage's board of directors. The first name listed was *Doris Dickinson Whittaker, veuve.*

"So Emma was right. Her aunt was involved with the orphanage," said Blondine. "I thought she was making it up."

"Why would she do that?"

Blondine shrugged. "I never know with Emma. But then, we don't see that many Australians around here, so I suppose it makes sense."

Satisfied that there were no letters from Doris in the trunk, Rosalyn and Blondine gathered the most interesting items—the ledger, the certificate with Doris's name on it, the silk pouch of needles, and the photographs of cave life—and carried them downstairs, carefully picking their way along the crowded stairs, stepping around the piles of books and magazines.

"I can't believe how well you navigate in those heels," Rosalyn said.

"How do you mean?" asked Blondine.

"I'm a klutz in heels," said Rosalyn, realizing she had learned this word—*empotée*—from Emma. If she were to stay another few months in France, she might actually begin speaking the language with confidence.

"Did you lock the door?" asked Madame Bolze as Blondine and Rosalyn entered the sunny living room.

"*Oui, madame, bien sûr,*" said Blondine, placing on the table what they had found and handing Madame Bolze her keys. "Thank you for letting us go up there. Look at what we found! There were no letters from your aunt Emma, but we did find her name on a certificate listing her as one of the directors of the orphanage. Truthfully, though, there's lots more stuff up there, so one never knows."

Madame Bolze wrinkled her nose. "They smell funny."

"Just the smell of old papers," said Emma, picking up the certificate. "This is amazing. I knew she loved France, but I didn't know about all this."

"It makes sense that she would want to help after the war," said Rosalyn. "She understood better than most how the region had suffered. According to Émile's side of the correspondence, at least, they seemed close."

"We also found these photos," said Blondine as she spread the photographs out on the table. There were several portraits of women with names on the back.

Emma held one up. "Look! On the back it reads: '*Lucie Maréchal, dans les crayères du Pommery, Dec. 1916. Assistante.*'"

"*Lucie?*" Hungrily, Rosalyn studied the image of the dark-haired, pale young woman she had read so much about. Lucie Maréchal wore a black high-necked dress and stood with a young girl at her side; they were both unsmiling and almost seemed to be glaring at the camera. The expression on Lucie's young face was resolute, unyielding.

"Not what I expected," said Emma, voicing Rosalyn's thoughts. "Émile describes her as soft and young, with the sweetest face."

"She had been through a lot by then," said Blondine, taking the photo from her and gazing at it. "War isn't kind to people. Deprivation, responsibility, the weight of grief . . ."

Rosalyn nodded; she barely recognized herself in the mirror anymore. Her face was that of a stricken stranger, her eyes—the feature Dash swore had been the first thing he'd noticed about her—were open wounds. She shrank from having her picture taken nowadays.

Madame Bolze picked up the silk pouch and unfurled it atop the table. She ran gaunt, blue-veined hands over the selection of tools.

"Now *these,* I remember. Bone needles."

"*Bone* needles?" Blondine asked.

"They were made of bone back when I was a child. Cow bone, I think. These were for knitting, and these were for crocheting—see the hook? And these"—she held up the smallest-gauge needles—"were for tatting. Not many people know how to do that anymore. But these were precious instruments, and not just for making decorations like lace. Being able to make or repair sweaters or garments was sometimes the difference between life and death back when I was a child. Every girl was expected to know her needlework."

"Madame Bolze, did you ever hear about the schools in the caves beneath the Pommery champagne house during World War One?" Rosalyn asked.

She nodded her gray head. "A lot of people moved into the caves for safety, to escape the bombs. It must have been dreadful down there; I don't even like spending much time in my own cellar. I have a few friends from school whose parents lived under Reims as children; I remember them sharing stories about it in class."

Emma leaned forward eagerly. "I don't suppose you know anyone by the family name of Legrand or Maréchal?"

"I believe I knew a Legrand at one point, but he moved away. But you know, my memory is not as good as it used to be." Madame Bolze shook her head and gazed down at the things Blondine and Rosalyn had brought down from the attic. "These things . . . they really do need to be organized, don't they?"

"They're of great historic value, Madame Bolze," said Emma. "Would you be willing for us to take them to the archives in Reims so they can be properly cared for and made available to others?"

The elderly woman's hand fluttered to her chest, and she avoided their eyes. "Oh, I don't know. . . . I would have to go through them first. I'll go through them, and I'll think about it. I know I need to get organized. . . . My memory isn't so great sometimes."

"You're too modest," said Emma, gesturing toward the display of bottles on the half wall of the living room. "Tell them the names of the bottles."

"Mignonette and piccolo," Madame Bolze said for the two smallest. "This is . . . chopine, I think? And then demi, of course, though sometimes called *filette* in the Loire Valley. Then there's the standard-sized bottle, the magnum, the Marie-Jeanne or Dame Jeanne. . . ." She trailed off.

"I know the Jeroboam, and the Rehoboam," said Emma. "But that's the extent of it for me."

"Methuselah, Salmanazar, Balthazar," said Madame Bolze suddenly, as though just now remembering. She smiled, pleased with herself. "I don't have examples of the Nebuchadnezzar, Melchior, Solomon, Sovereign, or the Melchizedek. Those are too large to be moved, even when they are empty. I don't think they're ever used."

"Never used, but they were invented and named?" asked Rosalyn.

Madame Bolze nodded. "They were in our catalog, but as far as I know, we never produced them. My husband always wanted people to have any bottle they wanted."

"Now *that's* impressive—am I right?" said Emma, switching to English: " 'Name the wine bottles'—a great party trick for wine nerds."

Chapter Twenty-eight

That night Emma, Blondine, and Rosalyn sat around the table in the *Chambre Chardonnay*, sorting through Émile's letters and chatting about what they had found—and what they *hadn't* found—in Madame Bolze's attic. As they spoke, they kept their hands busy slipping aged papers into protective plastic jackets.

"There's probably a lot more to be discovered in that house," said Blondine. "If one had the time and energy to go through everything."

"Madame Bolze just 'needs to get organized,'" Emma said with a sigh. "But yes, I'll bet you're right, Blondine. I wish I had been able to talk her into letting us take the things with us. My powers of persuasion failed me just when I needed them most."

"I can't get over that photograph of Lucie," said Rosalyn. "I feel almost like I know her at this point, through Émile's letters."

"I know the feeling," Emma said softly.

"I wish Madame Bolze had let us have the papers and photographs, and the orphan asylum's ledger," said Rosalyn. "You're right. They should be given to the archive and taken care of."

"And besides, you want to look at them some more," said Blondine. "I know. I feel the same. I am not sure why, but your obsession is rubbing off on me. I blame you both. I never cared about boring old history before."

Emma chuckled.

"This upright cursive of the French . . ." Rosalyn's eyes blurred as she tried to make out a paragraph of the letter in her hands. "It's so hard to read. It's distinctive and beautiful, done with such flair and polish, and yet at times it's nearly indecipherable."

"Rather like the French themselves," Emma said.

"*Calligraphie*, it's called," said Blondine, ignoring Emma's comment. "This is the way we are taught to write. The *maîtres* in school are very strict, very rigid, and we were in for a scolding if we got it wrong. We practiced on little *tableaux noirs* at our desks."

"What are *tableaux noirs*?" Rosalyn asked. "Black . . . surely not 'tables.' "

"Chalkboards," translated Emma. "Slates, I think we'd call them. Told you they were old-fashioned."

"I'm still amazed the *Rémois* were able to hold school in the cellars during the war," said Rosalyn. "I can't wait to see the Pommery caves for myself."

"They're not open for tourists yet," said Blondine. "Too early in the season."

"And the public only gets a quick tour," said Emma. "It's fun to go down all those steps, and to see the graffiti and imagine what life might have been like, but for what we'd like to see, such as where Lucie and her family lived, we'd have to poke around a bit. I'm working on my contacts at the vineyard to get unfettered access to the caves, but it's slow going. The proprietors of the champagne houses tend to be a bit protective; like a lot of people here, they want to advance the image of Champagne as a glamorous wine region rather than remind people of their painful past. But I'll keep working on it."

"I received an invitation to a party in the Pommery caves," said Rosalyn. "A 'Gathering of Vintners,' they call it."

Emma snorted. "*Dreary,* I can already tell you. I went last year, and they kept all the really interesting parts of the caves cordoned off. Also, it's more than a hundred steps down, so I think I'll skip it this year."

Rosalyn's heart fell at the thought of attending the party by herself, meeting all those strangers, but she reminded herself that this was her job. And she wanted to get a sense of the caves, at least.

"Anyway, those photos, and that register of orphans," said Rosalyn, going back to their earlier subject, "I hate to think of them up in that moldy attic full of ghosts."

Emma's eyebrows shot up. "You saw ghosts up there?"

"No," said Blondine with a quick shake of her head. "But if there *were* ghosts, that's where they would live."

"Can't beat that logic," Emma said wryly. "But I suspect Madame Bolze is haunted by nothing but a long life that is not ending well. While you two were upstairs bothering the ghosts, she confessed how sad she was to be estranged from her children. So we decided she's going to Tours to see her daughter, and afterward she'll try to reconcile with her son."

"That's wonderful," said Rosalyn. "Did you have to talk her into it?"

"It didn't take much. I told her I would ask André to take her if she didn't have any other way to get there." Emma blew out a long breath, and stood to go. "Anyway, I'm done in, going to take a nap."

As Emma rose and grabbed her crutches, Blondine said, "Madame Bolze must be so lonely, rambling around that huge old place by herself. At the very least she should have some grandkids running around, playing hide-and-seek, don't you think?"

"The Vieille Ruche would be a *great* house for hide-and-seek," Rosalyn said, though the threat of a fire still gave her pause. "But . . . maybe we should buy her some rope ladders for the upper floors. Just in case."

After Blondine and Emma left, Rosalyn sat down to sketch Madame Bolze's attic while the chaotic image was still fresh in her mind.

As she drew, her mind wandered. What were ghosts, after all? Our wishes, our desires, our regrets and nostalgia?

Rosalyn *wanted* to be haunted by Dash. She sought out signs, hoping he would reach out to her from beyond the gossamer wall that separated them.

As a child, Rosalyn had been drawn to the mystical in children's books: worlds full of fairies and elves and faraway enchanted lands where magic was real. Even as she grew up she still believed, not in fairies per se, but in the magic of a hummingbird, the enchantment of the woods. At times the sunset would strike her as a gift from beyond; a happy coincidence would feel like the universe reaching out to her.

Her time with Dash had seemed like just such a fairy tale, a charmed life of love and connection and beauty and happily ever after.

But when he died, the magic had been replaced with a void, an absence. For the first time, she envied others their religious faith; it would have been far better to imagine there was someone in charge, someone with some sort of plan that required Dash's death and Rosalyn's agony. Surely there was a reason. There had to be a reason.

Dash sent no signs. There was no magic. Hummingbirds were on a desperate hunt for food; the woods were no more enchanted than she was. And the most glorious sunsets were caused by air pollution or smoke from wildfires.

The more she chased her husband's ghost, the farther away he felt.

Chapter Twenty-nine

Lucie

Now that my life has become a whirlwind of scavenging ruins, cleaning wounds, organizing children, and picking grapes at night—not to mention how difficult it is to find enough water and privacy to bathe—I have grown weary of dealing with my long tresses.

Maman always says a woman's hair is her crowning glory. Though I love and respect my mother, I fear her ways no longer apply; they have disappeared as surely as the Villa Traverne and our neighbors, the parties and society functions that once made up our lives.

The world has turned upside down, and I with it.

So I took a set of shears and bobbed my hair. Women are doing it all over; I saw pictures in one of the dog-eared magazines passed around from one denizen of the Pommery caves to the next.

Predictably, my mother is furious to the point of tears, and wonders aloud what has become of me, what is to become of us all; but her protests dissolve into prolonged coughing spells. She has developed a worrying hack, and no matter how much tea of anise I make her, she does not seem to improve.

On his last visit, Émile told me he quite liked my new hairdo. He said I looked posh, and modern. This time my fiancé sent a present of earbobs—which are wholly impractical but look grand with my newly cropped hair—but Émile brought me something I truly treasure: a translation of a book of stories by an American author named Edgar Allan Poe.

Émile and I stroll the lengths of the *crayères* together as I tell him about bringing in the harvest, and list for him what we have lately been able to scavenge from the ruins. He exhorts me to be careful on my expeditions, but I remind him that I have stayed alive this long, and have no intention of dying anytime soon.

At my urging, Émile tells me of the lice and the flies and the rats plaguing the soldiers, of the death and blood and destruction. He confides that his fellow soldiers have begun to see ghosts, and that he, too, sometimes feels an otherworldly presence come to stand beside him on the battlefield. He hopes I do not think less of him for telling me this.

And through it all, his sad, beautiful eyes tell me something else altogether.

I have been proposed to several times; I know when a man is falling in love. It is my own heart that takes me by surprise.

Chapter Thirty

The next morning on her walk, Rosalyn again spotted Jérôme Comtois in his fields, this time on a tractor. He wore a scarf and heavy gloves, dirty jeans, and muddy boots, and was topped by an army green parka-length jacket.

Owning a vineyard sounded like fun, but Rosalyn knew that the reality was one of hard, constant toil. Grape producers were farmers, pure and simple; they spent long days tending to the earth and the plants, enveloped by mud, sun, and wind. They might clean up for a wine tasting, but at their cores were farmers.

As Rosalyn watched Jérôme, she decided he was more rugged than handsome. She found it hard to picture him teaching in a classroom at the world-famous Sorbonne, so perfectly did he fit working in his fields. He put her in mind of the Frenchmen who had gone to California in search of gold, back in the day, and left their mark with such place names as French Creek and French Canyon, and, of course, the French wineries of Napa.

"Bonjour, monsieur."

"*Bonjour, madame.*"

"I owe you money," she said in French, reaching into her pocket to extract the envelope she had been carrying around in case she saw him.

"It is not necessary. I told you not to worry about it."

"I'm not worried about it. But I still want to pay you back. Rumor has it you already don't think highly of my people, and I don't want to give you more cause to dislike us."

He pressed his lips together, turned the engine of the tractor off, and climbed down. He pulled off one glove, accepted the envelope with a quick nod, and shoved it into the back pocket of his jeans. Then he started fiddling with a knob on the side of the tractor.

"So," Rosalyn said, "I hear you have a museum."

"Yes," he replied in English. "But we are only open to tourists during the summer."

"Actually, I'm here on business. I represent a small American champagne importer."

He didn't reply but for a moment ceased his incessant fidgeting. The dawn air was so cold, their breath left traces of mist before them; Rosalyn watched his hands, amazed that he could feel anything with his bare fingertips.

"You should speak to the co-op," he suggested. "I make only a very small vintage."

"I'm aware of that. I've been told it's excellent."

He straightened, placing his hands on his hips and studying her. "Why is an American importer here at this time of year?"

"I got here a little early, I guess. I didn't realize everything would be closed. It's . . . a little different where I come from."

"Where is that?"

"Napa, California."

He nodded. "I've been there. It was a long time ago."

"Did you enjoy it?"

"Not particularly, no."

"Oh. Well. I . . ." She trailed off, unsure how to respond. The French could be so very blunt.

"Madame—"

"Rosalyn," she said, thrusting out her hand. "Rosalyn Acosta."

He gazed at her hand for a moment before grasping it and shaking. "Jérôme Comtois."

"*Enchantée.*"

"Madame Acosta—"

"Rosalyn, please."

"Rosalyn, *bon*. I am sorry to sound impatient, but I have much work to be done."

Do your freaking job, Rosie, she thought. *It's now or never with this guy.* She had dealt with reluctant clients before. Usually she was on the other end of this transaction, trying to sell the wine she represented to a retailer or restaurateur, but in many ways it was a similar dynamic.

"Please, just hear me out. Two minutes of your time?"

Jérôme sighed, but nodded.

"My boss, Hugh Small of Small Fortune Wines, specializes in importing from small family wineries. We currently represent a very high-end champagne, but are in the market for more affordable wines to be served by the glass. We'd like to introduce Americans to smaller French wineries, to make champagne more of an every-day pleasure."

He studied her for a moment. "That sounds like a practiced speech."

She shrugged. "It's my job, Monsieur Comtois."

"Why?"

"Excuse me?"

"I wonder why you are in the wine business, why you are here, shivering in the cold, when everyone's out of town."

"Oh, I, uh . . ."

"You love champagne—is that it? Went into the business because it sounded like a romantic Hollywood film? Wine making is not romantic, madame. It is standing out in the cold, checking on plants, fighting frost and hail and bugs and wind. It is a cycle of never-ending neediness of the vines. The reason no one is in town now is because this is the only time in the entire year they can leave for a week or two. It is *not* romantic."

"I never thought it was. I went into this business because I needed a job," she said. "My . . ." Her voice caught, and she stopped, afraid of breaking down in tears. *My husband died and left me in terrible debt, and I needed a job. Everyone says it's a dream job, I'm so very lucky, but I hate it. I hate my job.*

Tears stung, but did not fall. Rosalyn had promised herself after Dash died that she would not be ashamed of crying. And she wasn't—she cried in grocery stores, in her car, in public restrooms—but she despised how tears brought conversations to a halt, especially with men.

And crying was hardly professional behavior. If she couldn't get a grip on her emotions, she really would have to find another way to make a living, and where would that leave her? Back to waiting tables? If she had to move back in with her mother, even temporarily, she would shrivel up and blow away on the dry wind.

Grief brain. She forced herself to focus on the situation at hand.

"I apologize, madame." Comtois looked alarmed, and a muscle worked in his jaw. "I did not mean to upset you. My ex-wife tells me that sometimes I am brusque to the point of rudeness."

"It's not your fault, and I'm not upset." Rosalyn cleared her throat and joined him in staring at the rows and rows of grapevines planted along the rolling hills. She knew that the vines nearest the forest would produce grapes with a unique flavor, just as those grown on the hillside would be distinct from those grown on the flats. Variation within a vineyard was especially pronounced in France, where vintners did not irrigate the vines. Instead, they believed the struggle of the roots searching through layers of chalk and limestone to find water improved the taste of the grapes and, eventually, of the wine.

"I mean, I obviously *am* upset, but not because of anything you've done or said. . . . I'm at something of a crossroads in my life, I guess you could say."

The moment she blurted it out, Rosalyn cringed.

A moment of silence passed between them. She stared at his mud-covered boots, wondering why she felt so comfortable standing in the fields with this gruff farmer.

"Look, this is silly," she said. "I really *would* like to try your champagne, and possibly rep your wine in the United States, but I also wanted to return your money, and to ask a favor."

"Another favor?" Comtois said, and she could not tell if he was serious or teasing.

"Emma Kinsley is a friend of mine, and she would like very much to access your family's collection. It's a long story—and certainly a long shot—but she's looking for some letters from World War One, and thought there might be something tucked away in your collection, in some corner of your caves. . . ."

He nodded slowly. "She's been in touch, but I told her I don't think I have anything like what she's searching for. My father collected artifacts, such as corks and winepresses. There are a few books from the World War One era in the library, but I haven't seen any personal paperwork or correspondence."

"Well, I said it was a long shot."

A crinkle showed between his eyebrows when he frowned. "Emma Kinsley sent you here to ask me that?"

"I'm honestly in the area scouting for small champagne producers. But she asked me to mention it if I saw you. You're . . . a little hard to pin down."

"You seem to catch me in the fields rather frequently."

"I suppose most people aren't out at five in the morning."

He gave her a ghost of a smile, his tongue playing with his cheek.

"I suppose not. But at the moment, I really do need to get back to work. Madame—"

"Rosalyn."

"*Rosalyn,* the so-called museum is a mess, with issues with electricity and water damage. It's too dangerous for someone to go poking around looking for family heirlooms. If I can,

I'll get it cleaned up and ready to visit by tourist season, though I can't promise even that. Please tell Madame Kinsley she will be welcome to go through the place at that time."

Chapter Thirty-one

I'm afraid my meeting with Jérôme Comtois was a bust," Rosalyn said later that day when she found Emma outside in the parking lot, smoking. "On all scores. He's not interested in being represented by yours truly, either."

Emma stood at attention. "You talked with him? What did you say? What did *he* say?"

"I gave him my standard spiel about wanting to rep small French champagne producers, and he said, in a nutshell, 'Thanks, but no, thanks.' He even said it in English."

"What about the collection?"

"Apparently there are electrical and water issues that need fixing before he's willing to let anyone in, and that wouldn't be before the tourist season. He said that in English, too. I'm starting to believe he doesn't think highly of my French."

Emma coughed into her hand, then gestured to her cigarette. "I know, I know. I smoke too much. So, where did you find Comtois?"

"I see him sometimes in his fields when I walk early in the morning. I didn't realize it was him at first, but I finally put it together. Anyway, I owed him some money, so I was carrying around the cash in case I saw him."

"You owed Jérôme Comtois money?" asked Emma. "I thought you didn't even know who he was."

"It's a long story involving an American credit card."

"Ah, couldn't get the card to work at the gas pump when the store was closed, huh?"

"Okay, I guess it's not that long a story."

With Gaspard back in town, Blondine cooked a formal multicourse dinner every night. The amount of planning, shopping, cooking, and cleaning was daunting to the typical American sensibility.

One night the feast began with butternut squash soup, which was followed by *coquilles Saint-Jacques* in wine and butter sauce with rice, and *île flottante* for dessert. The next it was duck *confit* and *cassoulet*, green beans in butter, salad, and an elaborate cheese course. After that was *dos de cabillaud*, lentils, potatoes cooked in duck fat, and vanilla panna cotta covered in fruit and topped with an almond cookie. Everything was accompanied, of course, with plenty of crusty bread and champagne.

In regular attendance were Gaspard, André, Blondine, Emma, and Rosalyn. Occasionally they would be joined by Dominique and Dani, and twice by Pietro and his wife, Colette. Sometimes another friend from town would stop by—usually with no advance notice. Blondine seemed to expect it, and always made extra.

One night Gaspard announced, "I have invited Jérôme Comtois to the Gathering of Vintners in the Vranken Pommery cellars this weekend."

"He never comes to such things," said Blondine.

"He will this time," said Gaspard. "I made sure. I am not without influence in this town, especially now I am on the *Comité Champagne*."

"My hero!" said Emma. "But I'm not sure it will do much good. He doesn't seem willing to let me into his collection."

"Try again, though I'm not sure how you expect to get to the party since it is being held in the cellars."

Emma swore. "It's true. These old buildings weren't exactly built with broken legs in mind. But never you mind." She let out a sigh. "I'll figure out a way."

"There are one hundred and sixteen steps leading down to the *crayères* of Pommery," Rosalyn pointed out. "And the same number back up."

"Good thing I'm rich," said Emma with a grin.

The following night Gaspard announced he was dining with friends in Reims, Blondine planned on spending the evening with her mother, and André had the night to himself. Emma and Rosalyn were on their own for dinner.

Feeling like defiant teenagers, they decided to have a "colonial dinner," which consisted of all the snacks they wanted and absolutely no cooking. They laid out a feast of a crusty baguette, two kinds of pâté, a chicken terrine, olives, potato chips, smoked salmon, and, in concession to good health, two prepared *salades* the French seemed very fond of, one of grated carrots and the other of lentils. Luscious Swiss chocolate bars were dessert.

It was fun to speak in fluent English; Emma and Rosalyn had developed a patois around Blondine, conversing primarily in French but switching to English here and there when Rosalyn couldn't think of a word, or when Emma wanted to be sure Rosalyn understood something.

"I knew it," said Blondine when she arrived late that evening and took in the detritus of their feast on the table. "You should have come to my mother's house for a proper meal. My father will be angry."

"We ate some *salade*," said Rosalyn, feeling like she was caught going off her diet by her mother.

Emma had no such guilt issues and waved her off. "Gaspard is running around with his new ladylove. Not to mention, the man has absolutely no say over our nutrition, or lack thereof. Rosalyn and I are from the colonies; we could live on popcorn and PowerBars for a year. It's our superpower."

Rosalyn smiled. "This is true."

"However," Emma added, "if it will ease your mind, know that I have no compunction about lying to Gaspard and saying we ate a sumptuous meal with you. Make up a menu and we'll go with it. *Steak frites*, perhaps?"

"I made *coq au vin* once," said Rosalyn, "in this very kitchen."

Blondine pressed her lips together. Rosalyn imagined that on an older person, the gesture might seem bitter or angry, but on Blondine's young face, it was adorable, somewhere between a pout and defiance.

"Did you want to go through more letters?" Rosalyn asked.

"No, I am just here to pick up some files from the office," said Blondine. "I have to go visit some accounts tomorrow before the party."

Rosalyn's stomach fell at the reminder of the winemakers' gathering tomorrow. Here was her chance to see the caves where Lucie had lived, but the thought of meeting all those people . . . At least now Emma would be going, she consoled herself.

"You have something to wear?" Blondine asked Rosalyn.

"Are you saying you don't like my wardrobe?" Rosalyn asked with a slight smile.

"It's a very nice event," said Blondine. "Also, it is cold down there."

"As a matter of fact, I brought a dress for such an occasion. In fact, I brought a few. I have a nice sweater I can pull on over it." Rosalyn ran her hand through her hair. "But you don't happen to know a decent hairdresser, do you? I didn't get a chance to get my hair trimmed before leaving."

"There is a woman who comes to houses and does it," said Blondine.

"Hairdressers make house calls?"

"There's a lot of that around here," said Emma, "especially in the small towns. There aren't many shop fronts, but lots of people have skills. They mostly work off the books, to avoid taxes."

Blondine nodded. "But she's out of town now."

Of course she is, Rosalyn thought with a sigh.

"I could do it for you," said Blondine, assessing Rosalyn's hair.

"You could?"

"Do you trust her?" asked Emma.

Blondine *tsk*ed loudly, and Emma chuckled.

Before Rosalyn quite knew what was happening, she found herself wrapped in a towel and sitting on a tall stool in front of Blondine, who was armed with a comb and a huge pair of shears. Emma drank champagne, barking out the occasional piece of unnecessary advice, until

Blondine stopped and yelled at her, making them all laugh.

With a start, Rosalyn realized it was the first time she had laughed like this since Dash died.

She felt disloyal. She felt relieved. And just as she had in the car, she felt a fleeting moment of . . . not *happiness,* exactly.

But not *un*happiness, either.

Chapter Thirty-two

Lucie

Laboring in the vines is hard work, but I relish the chance to leave the dank caves.

Unfortunately, we have to sneak out of the cellars under the cloak of night, so as not to attract the attention of the enemy. Still, breathing deeply of the damp soil, feeling the dew under our fingers, seeing the stars and moon overhead, make us feel alive again.

Many of the fields are furrowed with trenches and pockmarked from shells, and coils of barbed wire mar the view. But the surviving vines are heavy with fruit.

We stoop, kneel, and bend for hours without speaking; the only sound besides the crickets and frogs is our *sécateurs*, snapping like locusts. The trick is to find just the right stem to cut with one hand so the cluster of grapes will fall freely into the other hand. Then the grapes are placed carefully in a basket, so as not to bruise the fruit. Monsieur Corpart could not stress this enough: Unlike many other wines, champagne must be made from undamaged fruit.

Some of the children are quite good at the job, their small hands quick and nimble. But of them all, Topette is the star. She likes to compete with me to see who can pick the most.

Topette lives with my family in Dakar now, and I have even shared with her my secret cave within a cave. When we return after working half the night in the fields, my mother rubs ointment into our sore muscles, and then we fall exhausted onto my pallet of blankets.

Terrible news filters down from the champagne makers aboveground: Monsieur Corpart tells us the cellar master of Pol Roger suffered a serious head injury when struck by shrapnel, and several workers were killed while loading a wagon when a shell landed in the courtyard at Krug. At Ruinart Père et Fils, André Ruinart became ill after working in his flooded cellar for months.

But still, the champagne must be made.

What a joyous day it was, when we finished bringing in the harvest with only minor injuries to two women and one old man, all struck by shrapnel when they did not throw themselves to the earth in time.

The grapes still have to be pressed for their juice, then filtered into vats, and later bottled and put to rest neck down in the *pupitres*. But our harvest is complete.

Émile arrived just in time for the end-of-harvest feast for the fieldworkers.

My mother accuses me of having quite forgotten my fiancé, and I do believe she is correct. Émile brought me another note from that gentleman; it was short and full of instructions for what I must do to remain a lady under wartime circumstances.

I asked Émile to sit beside me at the harvest party. *Maman* frowned when she saw Émile brush my hand with his, but then, coughing into her handkerchief, she looked away, and with the rest of us, she offered up a toast to the end of the war.

This time I sent a much longer note with Émile for him to give to his commanding officer, my fiancé. I thanked him once again for the earbobs, the comb, and the cheese, and with a sincere apology wrote that the war had changed everything and that I was breaking off our engagement.

One day a Madame Deresme, an experienced *maîtresse*, stopped by Dakar. With her was an older gentleman I had heard of but did not know personally, a Monsieur Forsant, superintendent of schools for Reims.

Superintendent, now, of ruined and empty schools.

Madame Deresme had the idea of opening a school right here, in the caves. What was needed, she said, was a routine, a schedule, a semblance of regular life that would take our children into the future.

The caves go on for many kilometers, so even though they are already housing thousands of troops and civilians as well as a hospital and a bakery and a grocery and a café and a winery operation, there is plenty of room to set up a school.

There are different chambers for classes and an exercise yard or gymnasium. The so-called gymnasium is considered especially important so that the children, deprived as they are of fresh air, will not fall ill and can express a child's natural enthusiasm and energy.

We build partitions from the cases of champagne and cover the chalk walls with straw matting decorated with wallpaper rescued from a ruined interior decoration shop. We bring in potted plants that wilt soon enough from lack of sun, but nonetheless brighten the corners. Desks and chairs are scavenged from the ruined schools aboveground. We put up the flag of France, as well as those of our allies, the British Union Jack and the Australian Union Jack with its Commonwealth Star.

The school under the House of Pommery is named for General Manoury. It is a mix of boys and girls, and our little scholars follow a strict daily routine based upon the national curriculum. One could almost fool oneself that things were normal, except that unlike a typical school, six cows are stabled nearby to provide milk—my brother, Henri, has discovered his talent as a milkman—and there is a gas mask at the ready for each and every student.

Though I was never particularly attentive to my own school studies as a child, I now work as an assistant to Madame Deresme. I help the children with their history and geography, remembering the lessons as my father once taught me. Among my daily duties is to be sure there is always a lamp left burning in the deepest caves, in case of further evacuation. We are ever fearful that a shell might collapse the highest floors of the cave system.

While I doubt my letters reach Émile, I write to him to tell him what I am doing. He loves books of all kinds. He would be pleased.

I do believe my little Topette is proud to see me there, as well, standing at the head of the class. Like me, she is not a natural student, more suited to action than to contemplation. But as Madame Deresme tells the children every day, it is their duty to study hard so that they may lead France into the future.

They are like the champagne, encapsulating the hopes of a nation. We must wait for them to mature so they can lead us toward the future.

Chapter Thirty-three

The next day Rosalyn put on a long-sleeved silk wrap dress and topped it with a long cashmere sweater, sprinkling her wrists with lavender oil, and tried to psych herself up for the party. She felt hypersensitive and fragile, as though she were dressing a wound.

What kept her going was the image of Lucie living down in those caves. Rosalyn wanted to see where the young woman had spent the war years, to see if she could discover any sign of her, maybe even find the little niche that she and her family had claimed for their own.

Emma dashed those hopes as André drove them toward Reims.

"We can poke around a little tonight, of course. But they'll have most of the tunnels cordoned off—don't want wayward guests getting lost down there, or stealing vintage secrets or whatever it is they're afraid of. No, we'll have to get permission to explore if we want to find where Lucie really was. But for now, how about a quick tour of Reims?"

Emma pointed things out as they navigated the

city. "As you can tell, a lot of the architecture is relatively new, as so many buildings had to be rebuilt after World War One. The Second World War was somewhat kinder to our poor Reims, but left its mark, as well. The *Rémois* have been put through it."

They drove by picturesque parks and peaceful squares; Rosalyn tried to imagine them full of refugees and the injured.

"The Cathedral of Notre-Dame de Reims," said Emma as André pulled up by the vast church. "It is as impressive a Gothic tour de force as the Notre-Dame in Paris, in my view. It even has a similar, massive stained-glass rose window and the lacy stone details common to the style. Lord, I hope they're able to repair Notre-Dame de Paris as well as they did this one. André, let us out here, if you don't mind, and we'll get the wheelchair out of the back. Rosalyn simply must see inside."

Climbing to the top to see the gargoyles, the winding stone staircase with grooves in the center of the treads from centuries of footsteps, Dash right behind her. Goofing around on the wooden staircase that led to the great bell, imagining the hunchback hanging from the rope. Kissing while overlooking all of Paris, feeling—literally—on top of the world.

The memory brought the familiar pang of loss and regret, but it also made her smile.

"Hard to imagine it was destroyed in the war," Rosalyn said a while later, as she pushed Emma in the wheelchair down the main aisle of the cathedral. "It looks so whole."

"It was a wreck," Emma said. "I'm sure there are photos in the gift shop, but just imagine it without a roof, or anything else made of wood. It all burned."

Rosalyn studied the ornate ceiling overhead, the intricate woodwork forming the choir loft, and the ornate pipe organ.

"The main structure remained basically intact because it was made of stone," Emma continued. "But it was just a shell. After the war the Rockefeller Foundation stepped in and contributed a lot of money for it to be refurbished. Don't know if you noticed, but we drove by a Carnegie library on our way into town. Rockefeller and Carnegie, two millionaires who used to compete in philanthropy. Those were the days, huh?"

Rosalyn imagined the scene as Emma had described: the molten lead raining down, setting the thresh on fire; the wounded men, the nurses, and the townspeople scrambling for safety. What utter, horrifying mayhem.

"And all these stained-glass windows had to be replaced, of course," Emma said as they reached the apse in the back, off of which radiated several small chapels. Late-afternoon sunlight spilled through the glass, splashing bright jolts of color onto the gray stone floors. "This group was designed by Marc Chagall, and those are by Imi Knoebel."

"Beautiful," Rosalyn murmured, her mind not on the stunning stained glass but on what it must have been like within the cathedral during the bombardment that smashed through the glass.

"Enough with the sepulcher air in here," said Emma. "It's sunny out. Let's go check out the façade."

They had entered the cathedral from a rear door, so they skirted the building toward the north portal of the west façade of the church.

"More than two thousand sculptures grace this place," said Emma. "Literally *tons* of angels and royalty—I think only Chartres Cathedral has more."

"And more than a few gargoyles, as well," said Rosalyn.

"Yes, aren't they charming? These aren't nearly as famous as the ones of Notre-Dame de Paris, but then Victor Hugo never wrote a book about this place. Still, they're pretty cool. Apparently a lot of them fell off during the shelling. The townspeople retrieved them and kept them safe, and then they were remounted after the war."

"That's a lot of sculptures, all right," said Rosalyn, her eyes skipping over the numerous huge figures, almost twice life-sized, set in rows along the façade. They weren't posed stiffly; on the contrary, some appeared to be chatting among themselves, while others tilted their heads down toward the visitors.

"I take it that's the famous Smiling Angel of Reims?" Rosalyn asked when her eyes alit on a winged seraph with a full smile on her—or his?—face.

"I find it a tad creepy," said Emma, gazing at the angel. "But don't tell anyone; they take their Smile very seriously around here."

"Well, it's been through a lot. Hard to keep smiling after your head's been cut off."

"Oh, I don't know. Seems to me that's the mark of a true stoic." Emma checked her phone. "Speaking of stoicism, looks like it's time we headed over to the champagne house. We're fashionably late. Ready to party?"

"I don't know about the party," said Rosalyn, "but I'm more than ready to see those caves for myself."

"You go on ahead," said Emma as they passed through the large reception area ahead of the entrance to the caves. Works of art were scattered throughout, including a giant sculpture of an elephant standing on its trunk. "I'm going to look for a freight elevator. Otherwise, I'll have to hire some strong folks to help André carry me down those steps."

"Are you sure?" Rosalyn asked. One hundred sixteen steps sounded daunting enough with two good legs; she couldn't imagine trusting someone to carry her down them.

"The party's in the caves," said Emma. "Therefore, I am going into the caves. Don't look so worried, Rosalyn! I'll be fine. I'll see you down there. Go!"

Rosalyn went, eager to see—and especially to *feel*—the caves for herself. The broad stone steps led straight down, the chalk ceiling arched over them. What must it have felt like to descend these steps with the sounds of your city being bombarded in the background?

Blue lights flashed as she descended more than one hundred steps into the belly of the earth. The lights gave the disconcerting sensation of entering a discotheque or an underwater cave, but the stagnant air told another story. The chill set in about halfway down; she pulled her sweater tight.

Cables running along both sides held baskets, which were now simply used as a display, but in the old days this was the way bottles were sent up to the surface.

Rosalyn had read that there were more than eighteen kilometers of caves under the Vranken Pommery house alone, and a total of two hundred fifty tunnels and wine cellars under Reims as a whole. When she looked left and right, noting dim corridors radiating off the main tunnels, it wasn't hard to believe.

As Emma had predicted, many areas were cordoned off, and greeters stationed regularly along the way shooed tonight's visitors toward the party. As she walked slowly toward the event, Rosalyn took in everything she could: piles of bottles topped with specially coded placards, and hundreds of *pupitres* holding champagne bottles nose down. Modern art installations studded the tunnels: everything from an upside-down bouncy castle to huge mobiles made of reflective glass.

Graffiti had been carved into the chalk walls: dates, names, slogans, drawings. Markings by those who had dwelled in this perpetually cool, damp place.

Rosalyn ran her fingers along the wall, which coated her fingertips in a damp white film. In some areas water dripped through the walls and ceilings, wetting the floors and creating stalactites overhead. The caves were reinforced with brick and concrete here and there, but primarily they were pure chalk and limestone.

The sounds of music and conversation drifted down the *crayères* from the party venue, but Rosalyn took her time, drinking it all in.

She wished she were alone down here, free to explore . . . with an excellent flashlight.

Chapter Thirty-four

The Gathering of Vintners was held in one of the larger pits, which had ceilings at least forty feet high. In the cave's ceiling was a small pyramid made of glass, which served as a skylight. It was dark outside now, but Rosalyn imagined how vital it must have been for those living down here to know when the day had dawned, even if only through a tiny window forty feet overhead.

"Rosalyn, I thought you would never make it!" Gaspard called out after spotting her near the entrance. "Don't tell me Emma finally ceded to good sense and stayed home?"

"Does 'ceding to good sense' sound like Emma?" Rosalyn asked with a smile. "No, she sent me on ahead while she arranges a way to join us. Knowing Emma, it won't be long."

He chuckled and shook his head. "That Emma. She never gives up. But you know what they say: *Tant qu'il y a de la vie, il y a de l'espoir.*"

While there's life, there's hope. It seemed a little melodramatic, but considering they were standing in caves in which people had found refuge from wartime violence, it felt appropriate.

Gaspard pressed a flute of champagne into her palm, held her elbow lightly as he introduced her to some local vintners, and then gestured to a massive bas-relief frieze carved into the chalk on one side of the cave: a bacchanalian scene of nymphs frolicking with grapes and wine. "In the nineteenth century, Madame Pommery wanted to beautify the chalk pits, to make them more than mere storage space. She commissioned many beautiful tableaux such as this one. And that tradition is continued today, with exhibits of modern artists throughout the cave galleries."

"I saw several on my way in," said Rosalyn. "I liked the elephant standing on its nose. And the upside-down bouncy castle was . . . interesting."

Gaspard threw his head back and laughed. "Modern art, my dear. Not to everyone's taste—I prefer the classic bas-reliefs, myself. But art seeks its own truth, does it not?"

"That's what they say."

"You know, Rosalyn, Blondine mentioned you're quite the artist yourself."

"Oh, I'm really not." She felt herself blushing. "I just sketch and paint a little."

"I am sure you are too modest. Perhaps you will show them to me sometime. I would love to see the world through your eyes."

"Mmm," she said noncommittally, taking a deep gulp of champagne. As ever, she would

have preferred a nice glass of red, but the bubbly that was so adored around the world would have to do. "Is Blondine here yet?"

"She's on her way. She had to visit a few clients."

They mingled with the crowd, and Gaspard introduced her to still more new faces. In the world of champagne, there were two main groups: the growers and the producers. Sometimes those were one and the same, but most growers sold their grapes to the big houses, who then made the wine. Rosalyn exchanged business cards and did her best to remember names, but meet and greets had never been her strong suit, not even before Dash died. Her smile muscles started to ache.

"And this is the famous—or should I say infamous?—Monsieur Jérôme Comtois," said Gaspard. "Jérôme, this is Madame Rosalyn Acosta."

Accustomed to seeing the farmer in his work clothes, Rosalyn was surprised to see Jérôme Comtois in a well-cut suit and a tie, his wild hair more or less neatly combed. She wondered whether she would have recognized him immediately if they hadn't been introduced.

"*Nous nous sommes rencontrés,*" Jérôme said, then repeated in English: "We've met."

"*Ah oui?*" Gaspard raised his eyebrows.

"A few times, as a matter of fact," said Jérôme. Rosalyn smiled. "Monsieur Comtois was my

328

knight in shining armor when I ran out of gas over the holidays. I have an American card."

"Ah yes, I've heard about the problem with the American card," Gaspard said. "But I thought you and Emma wanted me to introduce you to Monsieur Comtois?"

"Emma's the one looking for an introduction. She'll be here any moment, I'm sure."

Jérôme gave her a ghost of a smile. "No avoiding it this time, I suppose?"

"Emma's a force of nature," Rosalyn said. "There's really no avoiding her. I suggest you do as we do: Accept it."

"This is true." Gaspard nodded. "Now, if you will excuse us for a moment, Jérôme, I must introduce Rosalyn to some others."

Jérôme raised his glass and nodded, and Gaspard continued ushering Rosalyn around the large room, making introductions, until she came face-to-face with Ritchie James, her competitor from Bottle Rocket Imports. Hugh had warned her Ritchie would be attending the gathering. He was a good-looking man, in a slick, too-much-hair-gel kind of way, with dark hair and sparkling blue eyes.

"Well, if it's not the lovely Rosalyn Acosta! How amazing to see you here," Ritchie gushed in his unctuous way. He greeted her with a kiss on each cheek, reeking of aftershave.

"Nice to see you, Ritchie," Rosalyn said, and

gestured to Gaspard. "Do you two know each other? Ritchie James, Gaspard Blé. Ritchie James is one of our biggest competitors at Small Fortune Wines, and I promise you, Gaspard, you'll be sorry if you shift your business to him."

Gaspard let out another loud laugh. "She doesn't beat around the bush, this one, does she?"

Ritchie frowned. "Now, Rosalyn, you make me sound awful."

"Not at all," Rosalyn said with an insincere smile. "But you're no Hugh Small, either. We've done very well by Blé Champagne, and he by us."

Ritchie smiled and gave her an odd look.

"Anyway, I suppose I should be more subtle, but I wanted to make that clear. I hope you enjoy the upcoming festivities."

Rosalyn glanced at her phone; she had been at the party barely half an hour, but she was already exhausted from wearing the mask of the sociable American wine rep. She yearned for her little cottage in Napa, or her *Chambre Chardonnay*. She ached for solitude.

Last night's lightheartedness with Emma and Blondine was gone—the typical up-and-down roller coaster of grief. As the crowd grew, flowing around her, voices chatting in French and laughing, Rosalyn struggled to understand

and to respond in kind. She understood French well enough when she concentrated, but forming the words herself was another thing entirely. In French she wasn't witty, couldn't make sly references or engage in the sort of repartee that distracted others from realizing that she was one of the walking wounded.

More than once she caught Jérôme Comtois watching her from the other side of the crowded cellar. She barely knew the man, so why did she imagine such profound understanding in those light grayish green eyes?

The crowd parted, and she again found herself near Ritchie James, who was absorbed in a discussion with a couple of the local vintners whom Rosalyn had yet to meet. Suddenly, she overheard one producer say, "Wait. Isn't Acosta the name of an importer . . . ? What was his name? Lovely fellow, life of the party."

"Unusual name," said another vintner. "Dashiell, went by Dash."

"Ah, yes. He went bankrupt, didn't he? This was a few years ago—he never paid me for my shipment."

Rosalyn froze, scarcely breathing. She knew she had to say something, but this whole scene felt so otherworldly, and when she opened her mouth to speak, nothing came out. Waves of heat seemed to radiate through her, but deep inside she felt ice-cold, and for a moment, she feared she might faint. Then she felt a presence beside her: Jérôme Comtois.

". . . a very important client I want to introduce her to," he was saying, one arm lightly encircling Rosalyn. "*À plus tard.*"

Rosalyn felt tears welling up and kept her gaze on the floor as Jérôme guided her away from the crowd, toward the entrance of an adjoining tunnel.

"What happened?" Emma appeared, swinging nimbly on her crutches.

"Someone mentioned her husband," said Jérôme in English.

"Oh, *damn,*" Emma said. "Divorce is the worst."

Rosalyn couldn't bring herself to respond.

"I do not think that is the problem," Jérôme said in quiet French to Emma. "If Dashiell Acosta was her husband, he died a few years ago."

"He . . . ? Oh, good *God.* That explains a lot," said Emma. She grabbed a bottle of champagne from a buffet table as they passed, and handed it to Jérôme. "C'mon, this way."

Ignoring the velvet cordon that signaled the tunnel area was closed, Emma led the way past another gallery and into a small chamber filled with racks of champagne, the bottles covered in dust, cobwebs, and grime. Just beyond the *pupitres*, they found a clearing hidden from view by the bottles. Half a dozen small barrels were arranged in a semicircle, and a few empty champagne bottles and cigarette butts littered the floor. The space was dim, the only light spilling in from the corridor.

"This is where the workers take a break," explained Emma, sitting on a barrel with a grateful sigh. "I spent some time here, a while ago. I'll tell you the whole story one day."

At one side, in a niche that looked like a half shell carved into the chalky wall, stood a two-foot-tall Madonna. She was clad in royal blue robes, her hands pressed together in prayer, her serene countenance looking down at them in perpetual understanding.

"That Madonna there?" said Emma. "She's called the Virgin of Deliverance. According to the story I heard, she was taken by American soldiers during the Second World War, but they brought her back and installed her in that niche."

"Why did the soldiers take her in the first place?" Rosalyn asked, glad for the distraction. She sat on a barrel and gazed at the little statue.

"Maybe they needed a little extra virgin power," Jérôme said. Rosalyn and Emma looked at him, and he shrugged. "Sometimes you need some Madonna energy in your corner. Anyway, I should return to the party."

"Why?" Emma asked.

"She is all right with you, is she not?" he said in French.

"Oh, come on, you seriously want to return to that dull party? Listen, Jérôme Comtois, of Comtois Père et Fils, I can tell just by looking at you that you know what it is to have been wounded. Like the Madonna there. Now, be a good man—open that bottle, and let's have a drink."

Jérôme hesitated for a moment, as though about to say something, then shrugged, took a seat on a barrel, and started twisting the wire off the champagne cork. After easing the cork out with a soft sigh, he held the bottle out to Emma. She took a big swig and passed the champagne to Rosalyn.

Rosalyn shook her head. "As you know, I'm not a fan."

"In the immortal words of Bette Davis," said Emma, " 'There comes a time in every woman's life when the only thing that helps is a glass of champagne.' Take a drink, sweetie. A big one."

Rosalyn gulped some down, feeling the bubbles dance on her tongue. She passed the bottle to Jérôme.

Jérôme held the bottle in front of him for a moment, studying the label. Finally, he nodded, took a long pull on the bottle, and passed it back to Rosalyn.

"Try it again, Rosie. More slowly this time," Emma said.

Rosalyn glanced at Jérôme.

"As you said, she is a force of nature," he said. "We must accept this."

She smiled despite herself and took another drink. Rosalyn was enough of a wine person to realize that most wines could not be appreciated with a quick swig. This time she closed her eyes and concentrated.

The champagne was silky, not heavily carbonated like a soda; rather, the bubbles were a shimmer on the palate. She rolled the wine around in her mouth for a few moments, trying to calm her mind, to let go of preconceived notions. Searching for a dominant impression, she concluded that the wine felt opulent and mature. Creamy and complex.

"Wasn't it Oscar Wilde who said that only the unimaginative can fail to find a reason for drinking champagne?" Jérôme asked Emma.

"I believe it was," Emma said, holding the bottle up high for a moment before taking a big draft. "To you, sir, a gentleman and a scholar, and a man who knows his Oscar Wilde. I salute you."

"What's that?" Rosalyn said, pointing to a seam in the rear wall of the chalk cave. "It looks almost as though something was walled up."

"It probably was." Jérôme nodded. "There are hundreds of kilometers of tunnels and galleries and pits down here. The Romans dug it out to use the stone, so there was no particular rhyme or reason to the excavation—they followed the veins of stone wherever they led. When the caves were converted into wine cellars, some areas were widened, and some areas were closed up."

"And some of the champagne houses walled up their best vintages to keep them out of German hands," said Emma.

Jérôme let out a laugh. "Not just the Germans. They were the most despised, of course, as invaders. But French and Allied soldiers also used these tunnels during the war, and practically bathed in the stuff. You won't hear the champagne houses complain about that because it was all for the cause, but it took years to overcome the loss of inventory during the wars."

"Champagne makers are required to keep a certain amount in reserve, right?" asked Rosalyn.

Jérôme nodded. "It is important not to flood the market one year and have too little to sell the next. And champagne is unlike other wines because the vintage—the year of production—isn't a primary consideration; most champagne producers mix their vintages. The goal is to create a consistent product so that the Pommery house is known for a certain flavor and level of bubbliness, as is Taittinger, or Mumm, or any of the others."

"Is that true for the smaller houses as well? Like yours?"

"Less so, but yes. Our flavors are drawn from

the terroir, of course—the earth, the land, and the weather conditions—which means the grapes grown in one field taste different from those grown in another. The large houses mix grapes from many different areas to achieve a signature flavor, whereas my wine tastes only of my grapes." He paused, took another sip from the bottle. "It can be like tasting the earth, imbibing of life itself."

"Ever think about getting an investor for your winery?" Emma asked. "I'm filthy rich, you know."

Jérôme looked surprised. "I hadn't really thought about it. Have you even tasted my wine?"

"No," Emma said. "But I like you. And knowing you as I do, I'm going to assume you make a good product."

He chuckled. "You've 'known' me for all of half an hour."

"Your reputation precedes you."

"That's a frightening thought."

They sat in silence for a while, passing the bottle around. Rosalyn took another sip, closed her eyes, swirled it in her mouth, thinking of the earth, the terroir. Now she noticed the soft tang, as well as notes of apricot and wild rose, fern and truffle. The minerality and . . . a note of burned toast?

Warmth flowed through her, despite the cool, damp walls.

"I have to say," said Rosalyn, "this champagne isn't half bad. I'm liking it more and more."

"No wonder. We drank the whole bottle," Jérôme said.

Emma brought out her phone. "I'll call André and have him bring us more."

"Phones don't usually work in the caves," Jérôme warned.

Sure enough, Emma wasn't able to get a signal.

"Allow me, ladies." Jérôme stood and wiped the dust off the seat of his pants.

"Why can't we just drink one of these?" Rosalyn asked, reaching over to the stack of hundreds of bottles hiding them from the gallery. "You suppose they'd notice if one went missing?"

Emma laughed. "These bottles are not ready. They still have the sediment and lack the *dosage*."

"Brut is great," said Jérôme. "But not *too* brut. I'll be back."

The women watched as he disappeared behind the bottles.

"You think he'll come back?" Rosalyn asked.

"Oh, I have a sense he will. We're a lot more interesting than that party."

"Don't you want to find where Lucie and her family were living down here?"

"Of course I do. You know, I used to think I was strange to be so intrigued by Émile's letters, but now I see it's contagious. I think you might even be more obsessed than I am. You certainly know the letters better than I do, at this point. Maybe *you* should write the book."

Rosalyn laughed.

"I'm serious."

"I'm not a writer, Emma."

"Are you sure? Judging by your e-mails, you have a flair for the written word—and you studied marketing, right? So you probably know how to write copy, at least."

"You flatter me. But I think you need a historian to do those letters justice. I don't know enough about the context of what was going on in the world at the time."

"Maybe. But you see, there are these things called 'history books' that you can read to fill in some gaps. And we're not talking about writing a textbook—it's a story." She nudged Rosalyn with her elbow. "Maybe the story needs a little *dosage* to sweeten it up, give it that *je ne sais quoi*."

Rosalyn smiled. "I'll be happy to work with whomever you select to write the book, when the time comes. But I'm a wine rep, not a writer."

"No offense, Rosalyn, but if your performance back there at the party was an example of your wine-repping skills, you might want to look into a different line of work. Successful sales-people *enjoy* going to parties, socializing, getting to know people. They like nothing better than working the room—like that sleazy Ritchie James fellow."

"You think he's sleazy?"

"He's a sales guy, just not my style. But my point is, being a wine rep is damned hard work, but a true salesperson loves it—and you clearly don't. It's your life, of course, but I don't see that this is a profession that plays to your strengths."

Rosalyn shrugged.

"Do you know that in all this time, you haven't asked to taste the champagne from my vineyards?"

"You told me you were already represented in the U.S."

"I am, but that fact wouldn't have stopped someone like Ritchie James, is all I'm saying."

Just then Jérôme returned, saving Rosalyn from having to respond.

"Success," he said, holding three bottles—two in one hand, one under his arm—and three flutes hanging from the fingers of his other hand.

Emma gave him a broad grin. "Just how much of a party do you think we're having?"

"Never hurts to have a backup," Jérôme said, taking a seat on his barrel, setting two bottles on the floor, then removing the foil wrapping from the neck of the third. "We can always take a bottle home with us."

"Sure," Emma murmured, "because there's no champagne to be found there."

Rosalyn watched, intrigued by the grace of his calloused hands, as Jérôme skillfully untwisted the wire and removed the cap. He pointed the bottle away from them and pushed on the cork with his thumbs, resulting in a satisfying muted *pop*. A little mist escaped from the bottle, but the precious wine didn't spew out in a frothy explosion of bubbles. He poured them each a glass.

"You're not half bad, Monsieur Comtois," Emma said, raising her glass in a toast.

"Call me Jérôme. Please. Otherwise I think you're talking about my father."

"Here's to your father," Emma said, holding her glass high.

Rosalyn noticed Jérôme's mouth tighten, as though he wasn't sure that he wanted to drink to his father. But he joined them nonetheless. They chatted companionably for a long while, Emma describing the wine business in her region of Australia, Rosalyn comparing it to Napa, and Jérôme comparing it to Champagne.

After a while, the muffled sounds drifting down the corridor suggested the party was winding down.

"Okay, I suppose it's time to bribe some hale young men to hoist me back *up* one hundred and sixteen stairs," said Emma, rising and hopping on one foot, careening slightly to one side before getting her bearings on her crutches. "Either that or we steal the key to the freight elevator again."

Rosalyn stood up and felt the champagne go to her head.

"Are you sure you're okay on those crutches, Emma?" Jérôme asked as Emma led a slightly crooked path down the corridor.

"Oh, sure," said Emma. "You know, F. Scott Fitzgerald said that too much of anything is bad, except too much champagne is just right."

Jérôme let out a low chuckle and met Rosalyn's eyes. "Let's just hope that holds true in the morning."

Chapter Thirty-five

On the way home, Emma sat in the front passenger seat while André drove, and Rosalyn sat in back. Emma lowered her seat and tilted her head back to make eye contact.

"So, you've been holding out on me," said Emma in a gently teasing tone. "You let me think you and your husband had split up. Not that he'd *died.*"

"I wasn't keeping it a secret, exactly. It's just . . . hard to talk about. It's been nice not having to carry that weight for a while."

André met Rosalyn's eyes in the rearview mirror. He didn't say anything, but she read sympathy and understanding in his steady gaze.

Emma blew out a long breath and looked out the windshield for a moment. "Did you know the word 'grief' comes from an old French word, *grever*, which means 'to burden'?"

"I didn't know that."

Emma nodded. "From the Latin word *gravare*, meaning 'to make heavy.' Something impossible to carry, and yet carry it we must."

"You just happen to know the etymology of the word 'grief'?"

"Long story, not worth going into. The point is, losing someone you love, such as your husband . . . that can be a crushing burden. Do you want to talk about it?"

Rosalyn felt tears well up, but otherwise was surprisingly composed. Perhaps it was the lingering effects of the champagne; perhaps she felt safe with Emma, and André, too.

"It was cancer, caught too late. We tried everything, from chemo to power smoothies to acupuncture. He didn't last long. Only ninety-seven days." Her breath caught in her throat. "Ninety-seven days, from diagnosis to death."

"Tell me something about Dash."

"Dash was . . . larger than life. He found joy in everything; everything was a cause for celebration. I'd never met anyone like him. He was older than I was, and a lot more worldly; we married right after I graduated from college. He had made money in an Internet start-up, and invested in a small winery in Napa. That's how we met. I was a marketing intern in his company."

"Married an older man, eh? The boss, no less."

"I know people thought the age difference was strange, but it was lovely. He taught me so much."

Rosalyn remembered that while her mother had

been overjoyed that Rosalyn had "found a good man to take care of her," a few of her friends had voiced concerns about their different levels of life experience. Such arguments bounced off Rosalyn like water droplets off a waxed finish. She wanted Dash with a kind of mania, studied his fingers and thought of what they could do, inhaled deeply of his scent whenever he was near. She desired him not only physically but with her whole heart; she wanted to cleave to him, to go through the world with him boisterously inviting fellow patrons to dine with them, creating a party everywhere they went, taking care of hotel rooms and rental cars and tickets. Dash had taken care of her, taken care of everything. Except he hadn't.

"He taught you about wine?" Emma asked.

"Wine and the world, and . . . *everything,* really. I'm from the Central Valley of California, and my father left when I was young, so it was just my mother and me. She had to work, of course, but never made much money, so we just scraped by. I had never been to a nice restaurant, never traveled anywhere. I didn't know much about anything except what I'd read in books. Dash opened up new worlds for me."

"Sounds lovely."

Rosalyn nodded. "I used to paint in the vineyard while he worked, and it was . . . heaven. You know that saying 'You never appreciate what you have until you lose it'? That wasn't true for me. I knew how lucky I was, every moment. I felt like I was living in a fairy tale. Everyone in Napa knew Dash. He was larger than life."

"A 'great man'?" Emma asked.

Rosalyn was startled by the idea. "I . . . He . . . I mean, I suppose so, in some ways."

"What was your relationship with your dad like?"

"Look, just because Dash was older doesn't mean I was working out daddy issues." Rosalyn felt a surge of annoyance. Emma hadn't known Dash, much less her deadbeat father. Emma didn't understand. She couldn't understand.

"Did I say you were?" said Emma. "I was just asking."

Rosalyn blew out a breath. The flash of irritation ceded to frustration that she couldn't find the words to describe all she had lost. Even those who had known and loved Dash hadn't known him the way Rosalyn had, hadn't experienced the relationship she'd had with him. They couldn't know. She couldn't put it into words; she couldn't explain it.

"Dash brought the joy, that's all," Rosalyn said. "And when he died, he took it with him. He took everything with him."

They drove in silence for a long while.

Then Rosalyn added: "He took everything with him. But he didn't take me."

• • •

Although it was late when they returned, Rosalyn didn't even try to sleep. Instead, she dove back into translating Émile's letters. She no longer tried to find the correct order, but enjoyed the roulette of picking up letters no matter their date.

August 16, 1917

My dearest *marraine*, Mrs. Whittaker,

I am sending you sincerest thanks for the lovely package! I don't have to tell you my comrades were jealous at the sight of my new scarf, and the tobacco has, I believe, saved my sanity. The playing cards were put straight to use, and my pal Rémy was so moved, he began to sing and play on a funny little fiddle he made from scrap metal.

We left the trenches at xxx on August 5, and marching back nine or ten miles, we eventually reached a village called xxx for the purpose of allowing us a brief respite from the trenches. The signalers thought an orchard would be very convenient to erect our bivouacs in, but an old man appeared at the scene, raising objections. It seems his orchard had been in his family for generations, and he feared the blood and trenches that he had seen marring the fields of others.

After much discussion, we were able to work something out, and traded some tins of confiture for a little fresh milk and a bit of cheese, and the old fellow sold us some apples from his cellar. The fruit was old and slightly soft, but the sweetness most welcome. And after too many months of soup and bread, the cheese was heaven, indeed.

We are back in the trenches now. In fact we seem to spend about three times as much time in them as we do out, and at the moment, we expect heavy fire. It was this area toward the end of last summer that witnessed some of the fiercest fighting of the war. The countryside is now a veritable maze of trenches, and sometimes we are only about twenty yards from the *Boches*. The air is thick with bombs, grenades, and trench mortars. These last are a diabolical kind of toy. Their explosion feels like ten earthquakes rolled into one.

I hesitate to tell you this story, my dear *marraine*, but you insist that I should tell you all and in truth it has been worrying my mind. The fighting at one time was so fierce that there was only time to bury the dead in the sides of the trenches, but due to rain and bombardment the trenches sometimes start to collapse. So now one is constantly seeing not only boots but the bones of men's legs or even skulls sticking out from the sides of the trenches. It is not the sight itself that so disturbs me but rather the sense that this has begun to seem normal. I have ceased to see those bones as the sign of a mother's agony or a wife's despair or a child's lifelong anguish, but as the building blocks of the trenches in which I live.

[xxx whole paragraph censored]

I wonder whether these poor fallen *poilus* will be given proper burial one day, when our collective nightmare is over. Otherwise, how will families come to know of the fate of their loved ones? Even now, as we are live men, there are mistakes made. Apparently I look a lot like a man—a boy, really—who comes from Belval-sous-Châtillon; thrice now the officer in charge has mixed us up. When we correct him, he seems to think it is a thing of conceit, but believe me when I say it is not. I simply want my remains to be sent back to my loved ones, if the worst happens. I suppose this is the business of war; perhaps those who are running things have a plan. It is hard to believe from here, just now.

With respectful affection, your "god-son,"

Émile Legrand

February 1, 1917

My dear Mrs. Whittaker,

This day I fear I have nothing much of optimism to say; please be forewarned! You may not wish to read this letter at all; none could find blame if you burned it, sight unseen.

Here in the trenches we *poilus* descend to primal man. There is no time or water to wash or shave, and the most basic demands of nature are answered as quickly as possible in the handiest shell hole. We are beset by lice and rats, and even trench mouth, where the gums rot and teeth become loose. And of course there are unburied bodies, not only men but also horses, everywhere.

I try to think of pleasant things: of Lucie's face, the clicking of her mother's knitting needles. I think of the scent of the lavender sachets the good lady makes for those too sensitive to the acrid smells of the caves. I remember the scent of the ointment Lucie made for me, concocted of rosemary and thyme. But of course, any mental transport I can achieve is soon overrun by my hideous reality.

At present we are billeted in a ramshackle barn, and negotiate a sea of mud to get in and out. We have no boards, so sleep on straw on the wet ground. Fires are not allowed and at night the cold cuts through our winter fur coats. We huddle together like puppies in an attempt to keep warm and, I believe, to hear the beat of another human heart.

Lately in the trenches we have stood knee-deep in water for days at a time, our gum boots filling with water and offering little relief. With every moment we all fear the dreaded trench foot; many so afflicted lose their feet and legs altogether.

xxx found ourselves under assault, and as it was impossible to make any advance in our quarter, I dug myself in and awaited events. It was a horrible suspense; I recited poetry to myself, but it hardly calmed me. As the hours passed with aching slowness, I seemed to be the only man untouched; all around me were dead and wounded. Being personally acquainted with each man made the loss that much worse.

In fact, it's wrong to call them men, as they are mostly boys. Rémy xxx is quite fit and, now, the only pal I have left in the platoon. We have been resting since getting information about the xxx but by all reports we shall be up again soon.

No rest for the wicked, as they say; if true, we must surely be a wretched lot.

Within two days we were back out digging trenches at night when the *Boches* let us have it for five hours with trench mortars and gas shells. We wore our masks to protect from the poison, but two poor souls were hit directly with the gas shells and dropped just that easily. Another eight were put out by mortars in the first ten minutes, reducing our number from twenty-two to ten.

The sights and smells are awful, as the bodies of the *poilus* lie just as they fell during the advance. It is impossible to stop and bury them. Also there are a dozen dead horses in the mud, killed by shell fire while bringing up ammunition for the guns.

As we started forward again, one young boy fell at my side. I heard him call, "*Maman!*" as he dropped. Then on the other side a boy of eighteen had both legs blown away at the knee. I bound up his wounds as best I could and ran with him on my back to the nearest dressing station.

"Émile," I heard him say as we neared the medics, "don't leave me, will you, pal?" And with that he was gone. I became so enraged I do believe I went a little mad. With the next advance I ran amok in the enemy's trench and with rifle, bayonet, and mortars took the lives of at least twenty Huns. My savage rage has earned me a medal.

I hope you understand, my dear *marraine*, that I write this last not with the least bit of pride, but with a dull, trembling fear for my own humanity.

Your war godson and doomed friend,
Émile Legrand

May 18, 1917

Dear Mrs. Whittaker,

In the midst of horror come strange tales—some strange enough even for our beloved Monsieur Edgar Allan Poe, I do believe. A British engineer who spoke very decent French told me a story, and I wonder if it might be true.

There was intense fighting, and many of his comrades had fallen from bullets and gas when, out of the mist, walking across No Man's Land, came a figure. The man walked straight through the poison cloud, though he wore no mask. Indeed, he was clad in the uniform of the British Royal Army Medical Corps.

The engineer remembered that the stranger spoke English, but with what seemed to be a French accent. He carried a bucket of clear liquid and on his belt hung a number of tin cups. As he joined the men down in the trench he began filling the cups and passing them out to the soldiers, urging them to drink.

The engineer said the potion was almost too salty to swallow, but he and his friends obeyed the stranger. When the gas cloud had blown over and things calmed down, they found that not a single one of the soldiers dosed with the elixir suffered injury from the gas. No explanation for the strange visit could be given, and the Royal Medical Corps claimed they knew of no such man. But thousands died or were gravely injured in that terrible attack, save the soldiers who took the cup from the stranger.

Do you believe it? It seems it could hardly be true. But I have to say that sometimes there seems to be a strange pause—not in the shooting or shelling, because that is unceasing. But sometimes it feels that all the noise quiets, and I wait, scarcely breathing, for something. It seems to be long minutes, but it might be mere seconds. And then it comes— invisible, intangible, but nevertheless very real. Something comes to that place of desolation, stops a moment beside me, comforting as a mother placing her hand on a child's head, and then it passes on again.

I know you are not a priest, my dear *marraine*, but I believe you are a wise woman who does not suffer fools. Do you think what I see and feel could possibly be real?

Could it be a spirit or a sign, do you think? Or could it be that the desire for godly interference is so strong that it affects our eyes and ears?

How do the angels stand it? I wonder.

As always, I am your affectionate

Émile Legrand

The next morning Rosalyn encountered André as she left the *Chambre Chardonnay*.

"*Bonjour*," said Rosalyn.

"*Bonjour, madame*." André hesitated, as though he wanted to say something more.

Rosalyn waited.

"I lost a brother, when I was a teenager." André spoke slowly in French, as though to make sure she could understand. "He was killed in a car accident."

"I'm so sorry."

"He was my big brother, and I idolized him. It was very hard for me, for my family. I don't think my parents ever recovered. I went off to university. I know I did things, but I have almost no memory for more than two years after he died."

Rosalyn nodded. They stood together in the foyer of the *gîte* for a long moment, neither speaking, neither making a move to leave or to force the moment to pass. Allowing the kindred knowledge of loss and pain to fill the space, the slightest delicate comfort found in the sharing of it.

"I just wanted you to know that in some small way, I understand," André said. "As Emma says, it is very heavy to carry."

"André, would it be all right to give you a hug?" Rosalyn asked.

"Of course."

They held each other for another long moment, and then they each went on with their day.

When Rosalyn made her way into the kitchen for coffee, she found Blondine and Emma sitting at a table, eating breakfast.

"*Bonjour.*" They traded hellos.

"Rosalyn, Emma told me your news, about your husband," said Blondine, rising to face her.

"News travels fast in small towns." She meant it as a joke, but there was a bitter tinge to her words. Not that her widowhood was a secret; it just hurt to deal with it, even at this level.

"I had no idea," Blondine continued. "I am so very sorry."

"Thank you."

"Guess what," said Blondine, changing the subject. "Emma's taking us to Paris!"

"I'm sorry?" Rosalyn was in grave need of coffee, and her discussion with Emma last night—and the encounter she'd just had with André—left her feeling raw and vulnerable. Also, she was a wee bit hungover from last night's champagne.

"I have an appointment in Paris that I can't reschedule," said Emma. "So I was thinking, why not make it a girls' road trip?"

"Oh, I . . ." Rosalyn busied herself in the kitchen, putting the water on to heat and prepping a mug. "I don't think I can make it."

"It's all of an hour's drive from here," said Emma.

"More like two, depending on traffic," Blondine said.

"It's not far, is my point," said Emma. "What's the holdup?"

"I'm not really fond of Paris," said Rosalyn.

They both stared at her.

"I'm sorry. I just . . . I went there once, a long time ago. That was enough."

"I thought you were kidding when you said that before," said Blondine. "First, you don't like champagne, and now you don't like Paris? *Everybody* loves Paris."

"And maybe I will, someday," said Rosalyn. "But I only have a couple of weeks left in France, and there's a lot still to do here in Champagne. I'm not being paid to traipse around Paris."

"Are you sure I can't convince you, Rosalyn?" Emma said, her voice so full of gentleness and understanding that it grated. "A road trip might be just the thing."

"*No,* thank you," said Rosalyn. "Truth to tell, I could use a little time by myself. But take pictures; I look forward to seeing them, and hearing your stories. And if you need bail—do they have bail in France?—anyway, if you do, I'll be happy to deal with the gendarmes on your behalf. I'm sure André and I will have you out of the slammer in a jiffy."

Rosalyn had been looking forward to a return to solitude, but she found herself missing her friends: the late-night talks around a bottle of wine, cooking together, sorting through the letters. It was lonely at the *gîte* without them.

It wasn't like her hermitage when she first arrived, however. Rosalyn knew people in Cochet now. Gaspard and Pietro were often around, as well as the Blé Champagne office manager.

When she walked to the store for supplies, she chatted with Dominique, then stopped to say hello to Monsieur Bonnet as she passed by the mechanic's shop. Waving to familiar faces on the street, Rosalyn realized she had made connections almost despite herself. She had also become attuned to the rhythms of village life: the shouts of the children at the end of the school day, the regular chiming of the church bells, the growing number of tractors in the fields as more townsfolk returned from their vacations.

Rosalyn meandered through the little cemetery, and even slipped into church when she noticed a service being held, letting the words of mass in French slide over her in an incomprehensible stream, smelling the mingled scents of old damp stone and incense, reading the walls engraved with the names of the deceased.

In the pews were only Rosalyn and half a dozen elderly women, all dressed in black. Looking around at them, she realized she was starting to long for color.

Chapter Thirty-six

Lucie

I have neither seen nor heard from Émile for a very long time.

In one large pit of the *crayères* is a chapel with pews made of champagne cases. There is a virgin here, rescued from the ruins of the cathedral. Each champagne pew is full every Sunday. The priest tells us that Champagne—both the region and the drink—has become a symbol of France's determination to survive. But despite bringing in the harvest, and setting up schools, and having enough food and shelter to survive, we are miserable.

Together we recite the Lord's Prayer:

> *Notre Père, qui es aux cieux,*
> *Que ton nom soit sanctifié,*
> *Que ton règne vienne,*
> *Que ta volonté soit faite*
> *Sur la terre comme au ciel. . . .*

As my mother would say, before we start thinking we are particularly devout, it should be noted that our underground cafés and bars are full as well. And throughout the caves, many people become drunk on the only thing we have plenty of, champagne. I do not judge.

Give us this day our daily bread.

> *Donne-nous aujourd'hui notre pain de ce jour.*

I felt great joy, not long ago, when I married my beloved, Monsieur Émile Paul Legrand. My mother, now ailing in earnest, stood up with us, as did my brother. Topette was my flower girl; despite my admonishments, she snuck out one day to gather wildflowers and made me a crown of white and yellow blossoms. The baker managed to create a few dubious-looking cakes from flour made of potato and turnip, but somewhere he found a bit of sugar, and they were much appreciated. Many of our cave-dwelling neighbors joined in the festivities, and of course, we drank our fill of champagne.

Émile and I spent our wedding night together in my little cave within a cave. Our dubious bridal chamber, complete with gargoyle.

But our happiness was short-lived. After we'd spent only a few brief days together as husband and wife, Émile was called back to duty. We mounted the one hundred sixteen steps hand in hand toward what we call the mouth of hell—but is hell at the top of the steps or below?

We kissed, and then he turned to leave. My husband looked over his shoulder and smiled at me as he walked away through the rubble.

My heart felt like it shattered.

We repeat the Lord's Prayer when the shells fall and the *crayères* tremble, raining dust down upon us in a grisly parody of the priest tossing earth upon a casket at burial.

> *Pardonne-nous nos offenses,*
> *Comme nous pardonnons aussi*
> *À ceux qui nous ont offensés.*
> *Et ne nous soumets pas à la tentation,*

But it is the last I recite whenever I think of my beloved Émile facing what no one should ever have to face:

> *Mais délivre-nous du mal.*

Deliver us from evil.

Chapter Thirty-seven

Rosalyn pulled up to the gas pumps, dismayed to see the store was closed. *Again.* Why? What possible reason could there be for closing today? It was a random Thursday, for heaven's sake.

At least this time she wasn't running on fumes. The gas could wait until tomorrow.

She was about to leave when a familiar truck pulled up on the other side of the pumps. Jérôme Comtois. Her heart sped up. A young boy sat on the passenger side of the truck, just tall enough to look out the window. She waved at him, and he smiled and waved back.

"Need me to buy gas for you?" Jérôme asked as he climbed out of the cab.

"Not this time, thanks. I'm fine," she lied. "I just wanted to clean the windshield. But why isn't the store open?"

"Saint's day."

"*Another* saint's day?"

He nodded. When he smiled, crinkles appeared at the corners of his eyes. The last rays of sunlight peeked over the horizon, painting the whiskers of his face with an orangey light.

"Just out of curiosity, do the stores close for every saint's day? I mean . . . isn't there a saint for just about every day?"

"There is, as a matter of fact. But the stores only close for the saints that are important to the region, or sometimes to the owner."

"Clearly, I need to keep track of such things. Is there a calendar of when businesses are closed? Or maybe an app for my phone?"

He shrugged and began pumping gas. "I suppose it's something one grows up with around here."

Rosalyn used the squeegee to scrub her windshield, carrying through with the charade. "I guess I need to learn to plan ahead."

"I remember when I was in New York," Jérôme said, leaning back against his truck while the numbers on the pump ticked by. He wore work clothes and his muddy boots. "Things were open all the time. There was no need to plan ahead. I found it convenient, but also . . . disconcerting."

"That's New York City. Small-town America is more like Cochet, where the sidewalks get rolled up at sundown. Looks like you're hard at work, though. Isn't that going to offend the saint of the day?"

"The vines don't allow many days off. And the saints don't seem to mind. So, where is Emma? Isn't she your—what is the expression?—your 'partner in crime'?"

"I guess she is, in a way." Rosalyn smiled at the thought. "She's out of town at the moment. Is there something I can help you with? Us being partners and all."

"She was asking about my father's collection at the party, and I assumed she would follow up. But I haven't heard from her."

"She and Blondine went to Paris."

"Really?" Jérôme pushed out his chin in a classic Gallic move. "They should have talked to me; they would have been welcome to use my flat there. But perhaps it wouldn't be nice enough for them."

"Emma does seem to have champagne tastes, so to speak."

"You didn't want to join them?"

"I'm not that fond of Paris."

"I'm surprised. Most people like Paris."

"Once was enough for me. I didn't enjoy the tourists."

"Then you weren't with the right tour guide. One of the great things about Paris is that although there are a lot of tourists, it's also a city where people live, and work, and raise their families. There are many neighborhoods, restaurants, cafés, where you rarely see tourists."

She used a paper towel to dry the edges of her windshield.

"You were there with your husband?" Jérôme asked after a moment.

She nodded. "Honeymoon."

"Ah. Well. That makes sense, then."

"Did you know him?" Rosalyn asked suddenly. "Dash?"

"I wouldn't say I knew him. We met once, briefly, years ago, when my brother was still involved in the vineyard. Your husband approached us about representing our champagne in the U.S."

It was on the tip of her tongue to ask if Jérôme had turned Dash down because, like the man she had overheard at the party, he didn't trust Dash to pay his bills. But that made no sense, she thought. Jérôme had refused Rosalyn's offer of representation, too. But what she had overheard at the Gathering of Vintners had rattled her, and she found herself wondering if everyone had known what she learned only after he had died—that their lavish lifestyle was a sham; that when it came to money, Dash was well intentioned but unreliable. Was that his reputation? Should she have realized that earlier?

"Your husband was very well liked, Rosalyn," said Jérôme. "He was kindhearted, and charming."

She forced a smile. "That he was."

There was a long pause, but as before, it didn't feel awkward.

"Well," said Rosalyn as she finished wiping the windshield and tossed the dirty paper towels in

366

a trash receptacle, "fun running into you here. We'll have to do it again sometime."

"What will you eat?"

"I'm sorry?"

"Tonight, since you are alone at Gaspard's *gîte*. What will you eat?"

"I . . . haven't thought about it."

He tilted his head. "Come dine with us."

"Oh, no, thank you. I wouldn't want to bother you."

"I'm cooking anyway; we just bought groceries—at a store that *is* open, by the way, in Foucrault. My son is with me." He called out, "Laurent, *viens ici*. I would like you to meet someone."

The boy crawled out of the cab. His cheeks were rosy, and he was dressed in a little green wool sweater that looked handmade.

"This is my son, Laurent. Laurent, this is Madame Acosta."

"*Bonjour, madame. Enchanté.*"

Laurent tilted his head up to her, and she leaned down so they could kiss on both cheeks.

"*Enchantée, Laurent,*" replied Rosalyn. "*C'est un grand plaisir de te rencontrer.*"

"You're the American?" Laurent asked in lilting, slightly accented English.

"I am, yes."

He looked up at his father. "*Elle mange avec nous?*"

"You see?" Jérôme asked Rosalyn. "Even Laurent knows you should come eat with us. This isn't California, you know. In France, one cannot just skip a meal. It simply is not done."

She fiddled with the locket at the base of her neck, and looked up to find his eyes on hers. Was it just her imagination, or did she find a kindred sadness there?

"Will you show me the collection?"

"You are a very stubborn woman, Madame Acosta, if I may be so bold."

"You're not the first to notice." Rosalyn smiled.

"Come, then, allow me to cook for you and to show you my family's collection. And then perhaps you will find something else you would like me to do for you. I am at your service."

She laughed. "I'll try to come up with something. You, sir, are a true ambassador for your people."

"*Bon*. It's settled, then. Please follow me. *Allez, en route, Laurent*!"

The boy ran and climbed into the truck, and Rosalyn drove after them in her car, down the highway toward Cochet before turning left onto a long lane just before the town limits. She noticed something she hadn't before: a sign had been covered over. They passed through a gate, and the pitted pavement gave way to gravel, which in turn yielded to mud. The last of the snow had melted, leaving behind puddles and small ponds in the gullies.

Rosalyn said a fervent prayer that her rental car wouldn't get stuck in the thick mud, then realized a farmer like Jérôme would have more than enough equipment to pull her out if need be. She forged ahead.

At last the path widened in front of a large two-story house with small dormer windows in the attic. The thick stone walls and rusted ironwork made the house look ancient. To one side was a clutch of outbuildings that housed the tractor and other pieces of heavy farm equipment. She recognized the fruit press, a large device that crushed grapes to capture their juice.

The garden in front of the house was an overgrown and tangled mess, but when she looked closely, she realized it was laid out in a four-square pattern, with a fountain in the middle. It would probably be beautiful in full summer.

A sign on a gate in a stone wall to the other side declared: MUSÉE DE VIGNE ET VINS, COMTOIS PÈRE ET FILS. Museum of vines and wines, Comtois Father and Son. Beyond the wall was a building the size of a small house.

Rosalyn pulled up behind Jérôme's truck and watched as Laurent bounced out of the cab of the truck, carrying a tote bag with a baguette sticking out, and ran to open the front door of the main house.

Jérôme climbed out with two more shopping bags full of groceries. They passed several large rectangular boxes as they walked toward the house; Rosalyn could hear the buzz even at a distance.

"Are you a beekeeper as well?" Rosalyn asked.

"Yes, a lot of vintners are. It's very little trouble, because the bees do all the work. They are important for the grapes, with the extra added benefit of producing honey. I also keep chickens, ducks, and goats, and we use the fertilizer."

"*Bienvenue chez nous, madame*," Laurent piped, holding the door open and inviting her in.

"*Merci*," Rosalyn said. "*Très gentil.*"

"Actually, would you mind speaking English with Laurent? He doesn't get a chance to practice as often now. . . ." Jérôme trailed off. "It's good for him to converse with a native speaker."

"I'd be happy to. Much easier for me, anyway," Rosalyn said, stepping into the foyer and taking it all in. The thresholds were high and the doorways so low that Jérôme had to duck to pass through them. Ancient artifacts and antiques were everywhere, from solid mahogany credenzas to a baroque gold-framed mirror so old, the silver was flaking off the back.

But in among the classic antiques, the décor had been playfully reimagined, with a chartreuse wall here and colorful modern paintings there, whimsical racks made of deer antlers and strings of holiday lights. It was charming, an eclectic mix of old and new.

She followed Jérôme into the kitchen, which was separated from the large living room only by a counter. A huge fireplace held pride of place along one wall. Jérôme crouched down to light the paper and kindling already laid out in the grate.

"This will take the edge off the chill soon enough."

"I love your house," said Rosalyn. "It's gorgeous."

"It's quirky—I think is the best euphemism. It's an old family home, and now a work in progress," he said as he strapped on an apron and started extracting things from the fridge. "I brought some of my favorite art pieces from Paris. I'm no collector, but I enjoy the contrast of old and new."

"May I help with dinner? Blondine's got me well trained as a sous chef."

He smiled. "At the moment, just take a seat and keep me company—if I need chopping, I'll let you know. It's nice to have an adult conversation."

Jérôme lined several chilled bottles of champagne up on the counter. "These are my private labels. May I pour you a glass? Or would you prefer red?"

"I'd love to try your champagne," she said. "At long last. So, where did Laurent go?"

"Up to his room, I'm sure. He'll be back soon, carrying any number of books or games he'd like to show to you, unless I miss my guess."

"He's adorable."

Jérôme nodded as he poured champagne into two flutes. "Six-year-olds are pretty cute."

They *tink*ed their glasses in a silent toast, and Jérôme's eyes never left Rosalyn's face as she took a sip of the champagne.

"You're right," she said. "This is very different from what we were drinking in the caves."

He nodded. "This is a *blanc de blanc*, which means it is made of only Chardonnay grapes. We have a lot of minerality in the soil here, which comes through, so there's very little sweetness. It's not to everyone's taste."

"I like it. Very much."

"Not bad for champagne, eh?"

She smiled. "Indeed."

"Good. Help yourself." Jérôme picked up a sharp knife and started chopping *mirepoix*—the classic combination of onions, carrots, and celery that was the basis of many French dishes.

"Speaking of adult conversations, I don't think I'm telling anything out of school, but there are a lot of adults in town who would be happy to converse with you anytime," Rosalyn said, taking a seat at the counter. "You seem to have developed a reputation as a solo act."

"It's complicated. I left the town when I was barely eighteen, with very different plans for my life. It was hard to come back after . . ." He trailed off and let out a long breath. "After that. It's not that I dislike the town or anyone *in* town—just that we don't have much in common. There's a reason I left in the first place; I wanted something else from my life. Not necessarily better, just . . . something different."

Rosalyn nodded. "I understand. What's that old saying—'Life is what happens while you're making other plans'?"

"Quite right. Plus, I despise gossip—and since, as I imagine you have heard, I have already provided the townsfolk with plenty to gossip about, however inadvertently, I'm determined not to give them any more."

"That sounds like something of a short-term plan."

"I'm not certain how long I'll be around."

"You're leaving?"

Jérôme shrugged but did not elaborate, so she continued. "I take it the gated area next door is the infamous Comtois collection?"

He nodded distractedly, rummaging through a shopping bag. "*Damn.* I forgot shallots. Ah well . . ."

"You know, in America we have these places called convenience stores. . . ."

"We have those here, too. Like Dominique's."

"Yes, but our convenience stores are actually open when it's convenient. Including saints' days, and nights."

"That might be convenient for the customer, but not for the people forced to work on holidays."

"That's a plus of being a nation of immigrants. A Hindu works on Christmas no problem, I work on Tet no problem, and so on and so on."

He gazed at her with a small smile playing on his lips. "Is that how it works?"

"Theoretically." She shrugged. "Although I suppose a lot of people do wind up working on holidays they'd rather be celebrating."

Laurent showed up clutching three books and a game of tic-tac-toe.

"What have we here, eh?" Rosalyn asked. "I'll have you know, my dear sir Laurent, that I am the Napa Valley tic-tac-toe champion."

"Really?" Laurent asked.

She nodded. "Care to try me?"

Rosalyn was able to lose the first game, but Laurent was a smart child, and after that, the best she could manage was to tie several games in a row.

"Papa! Did you see? I won! I am the champion!"

"Well played, Laurent," Jérôme said, with a wink at Rosalyn. "Why don't you be a good host and offer *madame* more champagne, and perhaps she will play another game with you?"

"It's a deal," Rosalyn said.

"It's a deal," Laurent echoed.

Rosalyn then dealt out a deck of cards and taught him how to play war, a simple card game that she explained was *la guerre*. Each player took half a deck of cards, then placed their top card, facing upward, on the table at the same time. Whoever had the higher card won that round, and whoever had the most cards at the end of the game won the war.

"*J'ai gagné la guerre.*" Laurent ran around the kitchen crowing upon taking Rosalyn's last card. "*J'ai gagné la guerre!*"

"In English, Laurent!" Jérôme called out.

"I have won ze war! I have won ze war!"

"I admit it. I am defeated, young sir," said Rosalyn. "Now, how about you wash your hands before dinner?"

"You have a way with children," Jérôme said as Laurent trotted off.

"I find a game of war almost always wins over the under-ten set."

Dinner was a slow, drawn-out affair. They began with a chicken liver pâté served with cornichons and a crusty baguette, followed by a saffron-based bouillabaisse, and *blanquette de veau*. Following this was winter salad with buttermilk dressing, and a plate of four cheeses alongside more bread.

Laurent became fidgety and whined a bit

toward the end of the meal, not wanting to linger at the table while the adults chatted about everything from literature to the Napa wine scene to the formation of the European Union. Rosalyn could hardly blame the child; she wondered if they ate this formally every night, just the two of them, and decided they probably did.

Early training for a lifetime of Taking Dinner Seriously.

Afterward, Laurent helped to clear the dishes; then his father sent him upstairs to brush his teeth. Rosalyn helped Jérôme clean the kitchen while classical music played softly in the background.

When Jérôme excused himself to give Laurent his bath, Rosalyn sank into a comfy chair by the fire, enjoying the feeling of fullness and the slight tipsiness from the wine.

Fifteen minutes later Jérôme came down with Laurent in his arms, wrapped in a towel, to say good night. Rosalyn's heart just about broke at the sweet sight: Laurent looking so young and vulnerable in Jérôme's strong arms. A surge of anger took her by surprise: *Of course Dash never wanted children.* If they'd had a child, he would have had to share the spotlight, would no longer have been the center of her universe.

After she bade Laurent good night and Jérôme took the boy back upstairs to tuck him in, Rosalyn studied the three different Comtois Père et Fils champagnes, tasting them, one after another. The color ranged from straw yellow to antique amber. She took the time to swirl them around in her mouth, feeling the creamy, sumptuous fizz.

Yep. Rosalyn was definitely developing a taste for champagne. She wasn't ready to abandon her heavy reds yet, but these honeyed bubbles were growing on her, no doubt about it.

But what *was* it with the French and their boring wine labels? The Italians, the Spanish, and the Australians had fun with theirs. Some California labels might have been accused of being downright silly, but they were memorable, and wasn't that the point of a label?

"You're enjoying the champagne?" Jérôme asked, startling her.

"Very much, as a matter of fact," Rosalyn said. "I was just thinking to myself that I'm becoming a fan after all."

"That would be quite a coup, to bring a Californian red wine lover to worship champagne."

She let out a bark of laughter. "Not sure I'd carry it that far. But I'm definitely appreciating it like never before."

"Not the highest compliment I've ever heard, but I'll take it," he said, and started to prepare some dessert.

"Oh, please, none for me."

"Just a little fruit tart? My mother made it. It goes great with champagne."

"Twist my arm."

"Pardon?"

"It's an expression. I'd love a small slice. Thank you." She smiled and allowed herself to sink into the warmth of the home. The looseness inspired by the champagne. To embrace the openness she so rarely felt anymore.

"Any specific thoughts about the champagne?" Jérôme asked.

"Mostly about the labels."

"What about them? I think they're very simple, very classy."

"They are classy, yes. And there's a place for that."

"But . . . ?"

They carried their dessert plates to their seats at the table.

"But Americans like something pretty, a bottle they can stick a candle into."

"Excuse me?"

"The French labels are very elegant, which makes them perfect for special occasions. But otherwise they're a little . . . stiff."

"Stiff?"

"Stuffy."

"Stuffy?"

"I know you take your wine seriously, and for good reason. But if you ever do want to sell your wine to the U.S. market . . . Well, I know a little about marketing. Most customers in the U.S. don't know much about the different regional characteristics of wine, that sort of thing— though at least with champagne they understand the designation better than usual. But in the end, a lot of people buy wine because of the label."

"A nonstuffy label."

She nodded.

"So you can put a candle in it," he continued around a bite of tart.

She nodded. "I mean, you said you're not interested in branching out to the U.S. market, and you might not even be here for much longer, so maybe I'm just wasting my breath. But if you ever change your mind, I suggest you invest in some original art for your labels, like you did for this house. It could still be classic and elegant, but with a pop of something new. Personally, I've never understood why every French winemaker doesn't have a beautiful Art Nouveau–style label, since that's such an iconic style and it *never* goes out of fashion."

He pushed the crumbs of his tart away, leaned back in his chair, and fixed her with a gaze. "Fascinating."

"Also, you might include your personal story."

He frowned, and she was beginning to understand where those worry lines came from between his brows. "What about my personal story?"

"For the back of the label. In California, anyway, more and more wineries are owned by big corporations out to turn a profit."

"We make a profit as well. At least, that's the dream."

"Of course it is, and there's nothing wrong with that. I'm talking about how to sell the wine so you can make that profit. A family winery, handed down through the generations—from a marketing perspective, that's pure gold."

"It's not gold of any sort. My father, I'm sorry to say, drove this place on the ground. He cared more about his bloody museum than the business. Didn't notice when the American 'champagnes' started gaining a foothold in the market, displacing the French wines."

"Yeah, sorry about the encroachment on the champagne designation."

"The only thing worse than inheriting a family winery you don't want is inheriting a family winery you don't want and then running it on the ground."

"*Into* the ground."

"Pardon?"

"The expression is 'running it *into* the ground,' not *on* the ground."

"Thank you. You see, it has been a while. I am losing my English."

"Your English is remarkable. Prepositions are always tricky."

They lapsed into silence for a moment. Chopin played softly in the background; the candle burned down. Flames crackled in the giant fireplace, keeping the living room warm and cozy.

"You mentioned you spent time in the U.S.?" Rosalyn said.

"I taught at NYU for a semester on a faculty exchange, and spent a summer touring California a little. But I did most of my studies in England."

"If you study English literature, it's the place to be."

"There's nothing quite like walking the moors, following in the path of Heathcliff or Jane Eyre."

She smiled. "So you're a romantic, underneath it all."

He stuck out his chin and gave a little Gallic shrug. "I do enjoy the Romantics. But I would say I'm more of a modernist."

"I don't know much about literature."

"You studied marketing, apparently."

"Sorry. I didn't mean to offer unsolicited advice." Rosalyn hiccuped and set down her glass of champagne. " 'Scuse me."

"Not at all."

"You know, I don't know Emma all that well, but everything I've seen indicates that she's the real deal. If she's offered to invest in your winery, you might consider it. It might be the influx of cash you need to turn things around. And one thing I love about Small Fortune Wines is that

Hugh wants to keep a viable business, sure, but he's also truly interested in keeping small family wineries afloat, and . . . sorry. More unsolicited advice."

They held each other's gaze for a long moment before Rosalyn looked away. She wondered if a part of Jérôme *wanted* the winery to fail, so that he could walk away with a clear conscience and return to his life in Paris.

"As I'm sure you've gathered," said Jérôme, "my family has a bit of a fascination for the old— the ancient, actually."

"And you don't share their passion for history?"

"I do, in fact. Quite a bit. But I prefer to live in the modern world, appreciating the beauty and innovation of the past but staying firmly planted in the ethos of modernity. So, what about you? You mentioned the 'crossroads in your life,' I think was the phrase you used."

"I hate my job." What *was* it about being around Jérôme that inspired her to blurt out the truth? "I mean, I don't *hate* it. It's a good job. . . ."

"But you don't enjoy sales."

She shook her head.

"You said you studied marketing?"

"I was more of a branding person, dealing with the design side of things. My true love is painting."

"So you're an artist."

She felt herself blushing. "I wouldn't go that far. I had hoped to be, but . . ."

His gaze did not move from her face. She let out a shaky breath and continued. "Then Dash died. I discovered the life we were living was a sham, our land was mortgaged, and the business was underwater. I'm still trying to dig my way out of debt."

"And art doesn't pay the bills."

She shook her head. "Not my art, anyway. And the truth is . . . it's hard to explain, but I haven't wanted to paint since Dash died. I know everyone thinks an artist would find refuge in her art after something like that, but for me it's too . . ." She trailed off.

"Too close."

She nodded, not fighting the tears.

They sat there for a long time, in comfortable silence.

Chapter Thirty-eight

"C̲ome," Jérôme said after a while. "Please follow me down to the cellars, to the *in*famous collection of Comtois Père et Fils."

They ducked through a low door and descended to the cellars. Jérôme flipped on switches, revealing several low, broad, arched tunnels that branched out in different directions.

Rosalyn understood why he was reluctant to let the public in here: The electricity was not working in several sections, there was obvious water damage in others, and in one area the roof was caving in altogether.

The caves were lined with barrels and baskets, bottles and wineskins, massive wooden wine-presses and smaller corking machines. There was old wine-making equipment, a bottle-glass-blowing exhibit, and a wooden *pressoir* from the seventeenth century so large, Jérôme told her they had to remove a wall to get it in. One entire room was dedicated to a display of carvings made from the twisted remains of vines, and another held corks: lots and lots of different kinds of corks.

Despite the air of abandonment and neglect,

Rosalyn liked being in the cellars. It felt like being privy to a secret.

"Did people hide down here during the shelling, like they did in Reims?" she asked.

"It wasn't as bad here. Reims definitely had it worse. But still . . . it was good to have the shelter. The Germans invaded the village during World War Two, and my great-grandfather had to construct fake walls to save at least some of the wine. The Germans do love their champagne—I should say, they love *our* champagne."

At long last, Jérôme led the way into a storage room, deep in the bowels of the earth. He switched on a light, and a bare bulb glowed in a wire cage overhead.

"There's just about everything down here," he said with a shake of his head. "But no correspondence from an Australian woman."

"You looked?"

"Of course. The first time Emma wrote and asked about it, I searched to see if I had anything of use for her. But while my grandmother enjoyed collecting books, I didn't find historical documents. My family members weren't archivists. I think my father's ultimate goal was to own the largest, most difficult-to-move winepress of all time. And he accomplished that much, at least."

"Is your father still with you?"

"He passed away last year—died of a heart

attack, down here in the cellars, as a matter of fact."

"I'm so sorry."

He nodded. "We had a difficult relationship. He found me . . . *disappointing,* I suppose is the best word for it. When I was a child my nose was always in a book, not the wine making, or this collection. I was always closer to my grandmother. She was a teenager in World War Two, but she used to tell me stories of her own father, who was a veteran of the Great War. This stuff lives on around here."

"I love that sense of history," said Rosalyn. "It's harder to find where I'm from. But I'm sorry you and your father weren't able to reconcile before he died."

"As I said, he found me a disappointment. But then, I found *him* disappointing as well. I suppose he would be happy to see me now, covered in mud, tending the fields and even more so his ridiculous museum."

"You'd rather be in Paris?"

He let out a harsh bark of a laugh. "If you'd asked me even two months ago, I would have said *oui* without hesitation. But . . . the land gets to you after a while. I was raised here, and as much as I tried to escape it, it's hard to think about letting it go, allowing a stranger to tend to it." Jérôme shrugged and flipped off the lights as they left the collection and started to climb the flight of stone steps. "Maybe my father was right. Maybe it's in my blood."

"Do you want to hand it down to Laurent, a new generation of Comtois Père et Fils?"

"Part of me does. But at the same time, I don't want him to feel tied down, to leave him no options, the way I always felt."

"Oh! I've been meaning to ask: What is biodynamic agriculture? You mentioned it the first time we met, and I've been wondering ever since."

"My brother, it turns out, was suffering from a brain tumor, and several of our neighbors have had similar struggles. It hasn't been directly tied to pesticide use, but for those of us who live this close to the land, it's a concern." Jérôme led the way back to the living room, where they took seats by the fire. "When I brought Laurent to live with me here, I decided to try doing without pesticides. The biodynamic method doesn't make a lot of scientific sense, but it seems to be working. I want to give it a year or two, at least, to see if it makes a difference."

"How does it work?"

"A man named Steiner developed it in the twenties. It views the farm as a living organism made up not only of land but also air, animals, plants, compost. . . . I know it sounds mystical, but in many ways this is what winemakers have always done. This is the magic of wine: the way the taste of the grapes reveals the spirit of the land."

"That doesn't sound all that woo-woo."

"Woo-woo?"

"It's a term that means 'supernatural,' sort of different."

"Well, I've given you the short version. There are some bits that are a little more *woo-woo*—stuffing a cow's horn with manure, burying it for six months, then digging it back up, mixing the contents with water, and then sprinkling it over the land. Every time I do that, I wonder whether Dr. Steiner is looking down on me and laughing at the gullibility of those who follow his method."

"I don't suppose it could hurt, though, right?"

"That's what I tell myself, as I drag myself out of bed at three in the morning to apply manure according to the movement of the cosmos."

They shared a laugh. Silence reigned for a few moments as Jérôme stoked the fire. Rosalyn studied the photos on the mantelpiece: several of Laurent, but also others she assumed were of relatives. There was one of a young Jérôme with his arm around another young man who shared a strong family resemblance.

"How's your brother doing now?"

"He's been given a clean bill of health, thank goodness. But . . . I don't know if it was the tumor itself or the lengthy recovery, but the ordeal changed him."

"Is that why he ran off with your wife?"

Jérôme looked surprised. "Is that what the rumor is?"

"Oh my Lord, I'm so sorry I just blurted that out. Too much champagne, maybe."

He shrugged. "In a small town, rumors are inevitable. Anyway, I mention Raphael's health as an explanation, not an excuse."

"And your wife?"

"*She* had neither excuse nor explanation."

"Is that her?" Rosalyn asked as she looked at a photo of a striking blond woman holding a baby.

He nodded. "Naomi."

"She's very beautiful," she said.

"She is." A muscle worked in his jaw as he looked at it. "I keep that photograph for Laurent."

"How did you two meet?"

Jérôme sighed, relaxed into the sofa, and put his feet up on a low table. "It could not have been more of a cliché. We met in Paris, at Shakespeare and Company. Have you heard of it?"

"The famous bookstore?"

"The very one. It's an iconic place, especially for those of us with a love of English literature. With Notre-Dame visible out the window, no less. The store had this friendly black dog that would greet the customers, and a huge sign saying: 'Be not inhospitable to strangers, lest they be angels in disguise.' "

"And did you think Naomi was an angel in disguise?"

"I blush to say it now, but at the time I did," he said with a wry smile. "She had fallen asleep on one of the cots—the store has these cots left over from when exhausted students needed to nap—and she was lying there with a book of Yeats's poetry splayed open on her chest. She was a vision, her hair strewn out behind her. . . ."

"That's very romantic."

Jérôme gave a bitter laugh. "Are you familiar with Yeats? He's one of my favorite poets. 'I have spread my dreams under your feet; tread softly because you tread on my dreams.' It was only much later that Naomi confessed to me that she wasn't a poetry lover after all. She simply wanted to nap and had chosen the book by chance."

"Well, she's resourceful, at least."

"She was that. The worst of it? She was napping because she'd been up all night drinking and dancing in a discotheque."

"That's hardly a crime," Rosalyn said.

"I suppose. But I thought she loved Yeats."

"At least the beauty wasn't a lie."

"Amazing how little that can matter, over time. Don't get me wrong. She isn't a bad person. We were both at fault—I thought Naomi was a beautiful poetry lover, and she thought I was a Parisian English professor. Turns out, we were both wrong. Cochet, as you may have noticed, isn't Paris. Naomi wasn't cut out for village life."

"That's no excuse for running off with your brother." Rosalyn put her hand to her mouth, as though she could get the words back. "I'm sorry, again. That was over the line."

"It's the truth, though. Turns out, she was . . . *déloyale*. Is it '*dis*loyal,' in English?"

Rosalyn nodded.

"And it wasn't just that Naomi didn't like poetry—she didn't even like to *read*. We had almost nothing in common, except Laurent. He came along quickly. Otherwise we would have broken up long before."

"He's a charmer."

"He's my everything. It breaks my heart to see him miss his mother, despite everything."

"I missed my father after he left, even though he didn't deserve it." Rosalyn stared into the fire, remembering running after her father's car as he drove away; she had screamed and cried, begging him not to leave. The image was so vivid, she sometimes wondered if she had seen the scene in a movie and superimposed it over her own memory. After that, their only contact was an annual birthday card, holding a ten- or twenty-dollar bill. She hoarded the money in a jar on her bookshelf, imagining taking him out to lunch the next time she saw him, impressing him with how grown-up she had become. But he never visited. Dash had managed to track him down and flown him in for their wedding; she used the opportunity to give him his money back. It was the last time she saw him.

"So, Naomi moved back to Paris?" she asked.

"Last I heard, Berlin. She's living with a fashion designer there. She shows up when she feels like it."

"She looks like she's a lot of work."

Jérôme let out a bark of laughter. "That she is."

Rosalyn remembered the time and effort she used to spend making herself look good for Dash: getting hair extensions, going to Pilates class, having her nails done every few weeks. Constantly burnishing the external shell. Her mother's words rang in her ears: Men liked pretty girls, and since she was not a natural beauty, she would have to work at it. Stay on the diet, endure the plucking and waxing, never "let yourself go," never dare to relax and just be herself because her real self was not good enough.

After Dash got sick, Rosalyn had dropped the unyielding beauty regime and hadn't looked back. What was the point? No matter how hard the external shell, life pierced through to the soft core.

"Your hair looks different, by the way," said Jérôme. "I noticed it at the party."

"Blondine trimmed it for me." She brushed her fingers across her forehead, feeling self-conscious. "She decided I needed bangs."

"It's very . . . becoming. That's how you say it in English?"

She smiled. "Works for me."

His eyes locked with hers for a moment.

"Well. It's getting late," Rosalyn said. "But may I ask one more favor before I go?"

"Why stop now?"

"May I see your family library?"

"It's my favorite room in the house."

The library was something out of her childhood fantasies. Two stories tall, complete with a spiral staircase in one corner that led to a catwalk that encircled the room. Floor-to-ceiling shelves were lined with books, some with old leather bindings, others with glossy new covers. The air held the same slight mustiness as Émile's letters.

"This is amazing," Rosalyn said, her voice breathless.

"My great-grandfather was self-educated, and had a passion for books. He built this library, and then his daughter, my grandmother, added to it. According to family lore, the villagers were invited to borrow books, which was a boon before the mobile library started coming to town."

"And do you do the same?" she asked as she pulled a tome from a shelf. Victor Hugo's *Notre-Dame de Paris*. She opened it and recited:
" '*Il y a aujourd'hui trois cent quarante-huit ans six mois et dix-neuf jours que les Parisiens s'éveillèrent au bruit de toutes les cloches*

sonnant à grande volée dans la triple enceinte de la Cité, de l'Université et de la Ville.' "

He smiled. *"Très bien fait."*

"This is the first book I ever read entirely in French," she said. "I was terribly proud of myself."

"You are welcome to borrow it, if you would like," he said, leaning one arm on a shelf, gazing at her as if perplexed by her actions.

"Would I have to sign in blood, or anything like that?"

He frowned. "I do not understand."

"I'm joking," she said. "Sorry. Thank you for the kind offer. I would love to borrow a book, if you truly wouldn't mind. But maybe one in English? I finished the books I brought with me my first week here. I had an e-reader, but it broke right before I left home."

He let out a *bof*, to let her know what he thought of her e-reader. She loved the device, which would have been especially useful on a trip like this one, allowing her to take dozens of books with her, one to suit every mood. But there was nothing quite like the sensation of a real book in her hands, the thrill of discovery when perusing the shelves, as she had after her father left, when she found refuge—and fantasy—in her local library.

"Do you speak all these languages?"

"Oh no. My Latin is rusty, and my Arabic

is close to nonexistent—I know a few words, but never mastered the alphabet. I speak only English, Spanish, and German. I get by in Italian and Portuguese, but I wouldn't win any awards."

"Only six languages? My estimation of you is plummeting, *monsieur*."

He looked surprised, then chuckled when he realized she was teasing. "You like to joke."

She smiled in response, perusing the spines of books written in Arabic. "All these books, all these stories, but we don't have the key to open them."

"Rilke."

"Pardon me?"

"Rainer Maria Rilke said something similar: 'Be patient with all that is unsolved in your heart and try to love the questions themselves, like locked rooms and like books that are now written in a very foreign tongue.' "

Their eyes met and held.

"Do you believe that?" Rosalyn asked.

"It's as useful a philosophy as any other. Rilke also says that we would not be able to live the answers, so we should live the questions. Something along those lines."

Live the questions. For some reason the phrase reminded Rosalyn of her therapist's insistence that pain wasn't optional but suffering was.

"There is an English section over here," Jérôme

said, leading her into one corner and running his hand along the spines.

His hands were large and brown, the fingers long and capable-looking, calloused from farm-work. Rosalyn leaned toward him, close enough to smell his scent, something green, like the earth. Who knew naked grapevines carried a fragrance? She noticed the way his honey-colored hair curled on his tanned neck, had an urge to lean closer, to put her mouth right there, on that spot. . . .

Rosalyn reared back, shocked at her own reaction.

"You know, I—I have to run," she said. "I'm sorry. I totally forgot I was supposed to return a very important e-mail before bed."

"Don't you want to take a book with you?"

"Thanks. I'll take this one." She grabbed the nearest book in English. "I don't have time to find more right now. I'm sorry. Thank you so much for dinner."

And she hurried out, compelled by cowardice, just like she had that one time, the last time, at the hospital.

Chapter Thirty-nine

That night, Rosalyn dreamed she was back in front of the medicine cabinet in the cottage in Napa.

This time she tried to slam the door closed, but something was blocking the way. When she looked to see what, she found Dash tucked inside—Dash, but not Dash. He reached out for her, swollen fingers grasping, as she backed away, reliving the betrayal of running from his hospital room, unwilling to go with him but forever after steeped in regret and remorse and fear.

Rosalyn awoke crying, awash with the awareness of death.

Three a.m. Dash died at four twenty-seven in the morning. She stared at the smooth ceiling of *Chambre Chardonnay* and did the math in her head: In an hour and twenty-seven minutes, it would be nine hundred thirty-nine days since Dash died.

Her sheets were damp with sweat, and she shivered.

She remembered one rare occasion when

she had been at a wine event and come home later than Dash. He was already in bed, asleep, but when she slid under the covers, he turned and reached for her, spooning her, sharing his warmth. It was the safest feeling in the world, being held in his arms as she let sleep take her.

Later, it was she who cradled *him,* slipping carefully into bed so as not to wake him, when he'd lost so much weight that he felt skeletal in her arms, a bag of bones. She lent him her warmth then.

Perhaps she had given him all of her warmth. Perhaps she still was.

Rosalyn gave up on sleep, turned up the heat in the room, and took a long, hot shower, feeling the reflexive guilt of a native Californian for wasting water, but doing it anyway.

One of the techniques she used when grief threatened to consume her was to concentrate on mundane things. The scent of the shampoo. The slipperiness of the bar of soap. The small sky blue crackle-glazed mosaic tiles lining the shower stall. Slowly, she allowed her mind to wander, prepared to rein it in should it stray too far into the minefield of grief. She wondered if Emma had to hold her leg outside the stall to shower without getting the cast wet. She imagined Blondine arguing with Gaspard as they had built this new *gîte*, the frown on her face as she picked this towel, the determination to create a large shower that would please demanding American tourists.

This American, at least, was grateful.

Rosalyn quickly dried off and dressed, noting the rough grain of the thick towel, the softness of her favorite blue jeans and sweater, the warmth of her wool socks—then opened her journal and started to draw.

She thought of the *séchoirs*, the barbed wire that hung young soldiers out to dry. She drew a sketch of herself like that: injured, bleeding, stuck. She thought of the look on Dash's face in the nightmare. The baby in her locket.

It was too much. She shut her journal and turned back to Émile's letters.

September 2, 1917

My dearest *marraine*,

Just a brief note because it has been too long since I wrote last. I know you will be overjoyed for me when you learn that I have secured another pass to visit my dearest Lucie. My wife.

I scarcely believe I can call her this. Ours was the humblest of ceremonies; a few friends, and Lucie's family, gathered to share champagne and special "cakes" made by the baker for the occasion. But I did not care if we drank only water and ate hardtack. I cared only for my dearest, loveliest, strongest Lucie.

Our wedding chamber was in the attic of Dakar, through a rabbit's hole, strewn with flowers and candles. We had only a few days together, a painfully brief honeymoon. When the fighting is over, I hope to take her to Paris, where she has never been.

Rosalyn sat back, elated that Émile, the poetic farm boy, had married his astonishing Lucie. That they could find joy together under such grim circumstances. Unfortunately, the missive ended abruptly and without a farewell, as though this page had been separated from the rest of the letter. She searched for its fellow pages.

Her hands stilled when she found a letter written in an unfamiliar hand.

December 18, 1917

My dear Madame Whittaker,

My name is Lucie Maréchal Legrand.

I am so very sorry, sorry beyond belief, to tell you what I must.

Émile has fallen. I received official notice that he has been buried at Châlons-en-Champagne. He lies beneath one of the millions of horrifying white crosses marking the final resting places of too many young men, studding the land in a painful mockery of the vines.

I am told his mother is inconsolable; I doubt she'll survive the final blow after so very many others. Émile was so vital a person, the repository of so many dreams for the future. He was beloved.

He *is* beloved.

A soldier who passed by the old Legrand farm told me his beehives still hum with life.

My only consolation is our child, safe in my belly. It breaks my heart that Émile never knew he was to become a father; I waited to tell him when next I saw him, selfishly wanting to see the light in his beautiful, sad eyes as he heard the news.

I wish to thank you for being such a solace to him. We in Reims are often cut off from the rest of the world, and not all of my letters made it to my dear Émile. But each time he visited, he would read yours to me. Your care and sympathy were a balm to him at the very worst of times.

I wonder if we shall meet one day? I used to dream of sailing away on the ocean I have never seen, perhaps all the way to Australia. But I no longer dream.

Cordialement,
Lucie Maréchal Legrand

Rosalyn sat with the letter clutched in her hands for a very long time as tears stung her eyes. After all this . . . how could Émile have simply *died?* Disappeared, just like that.

Just like Dash.

Leaving in his wake yet another grieving widow.

Chapter Forty

Doris

1918

Doris swept the contents of the table to the floor with a crash, then hurled her silver-handled brush into the vanity mirror. It shattered, sending shards flying, bullets of silvery glass showering onto the plush Aubusson wool carpet.

Sally the maid rushed into the sitting room. "Is everything all right, ma'am?"

"Get out!" Doris screamed.

"Seven years' bad luck," Sally muttered with a shake of her head, taking in the damage. The servants were no longer cowed by Doris, having become accustomed to her mercurial temper. "I'll fetch the broom."

"Later," Doris snapped. "Close the door—and bring me some tea."

As if the threat of bad luck would frighten me, Doris thought. What were seven more years of misery to crown the wretchedness of a wasted lifetime? Bitterness filled her, leaving an acrid taste in her mouth. Sally had best not dawdle with that tea.

Émile. Gone.

Impossible.

Doris had never shed a tear for her husband, and her stoic acceptance of God's will had earned her accolades at Richard's funeral. She should have been praised for not bursting out with glee and tap-dancing on his coffin. Losing Émile, on the other hand . . .

She collapsed into her chair, dropped her head onto her arms, and sobbed, hot tears and mucus flowing unhindered down her face. She wailed and keened, made wretched by the death of a young man she had never met.

For years, Doris had been waiting hungrily for the daily post, hoping for one of his missives, wishing her money could somehow make them come more frequently. Often weeks passed with no letter from France, and then a bonanza of three or four arrived at the same time. Doris sequestered herself in her study and devoured the letters all at once, absorbing Émile's descriptions of war: the carnage and the beauty, the butchery and the moments of grace. Then she would ask Sally to bring her tea and cakes, and would read the letters over again, more slowly, this time searching for meaning in how Émile had formed each sentence, the emotions conveyed by his choice of words.

She had been so happy for Émile when his Lucie said yes, when they found each other—

and love—in the middle of the blood and the violence. Doris had had Sally bring her a bottle of champagne and she had drunk to the young couple's connection and their joy. She had drunk to their future.

And then it was snatched away, just that quickly.

Just like that.

Still crying, Doris moved to the other side of the room, to her most unusual and most recent dollhouse. It was a series of caves, complete with a little school within the muddy walls, and a little cave within a cave leading off the nook labeled "Dakar." There was a tiny, fierce gargoyle, and a wedding bed of clean white linens, encircled by candles.

Two figures sat on the crude steps, drinking champagne as they toasted each other and their future. A future stamped out by cruelty, by a war that had no reason.

Doris returned to her desk and reread the letter.

> My only consolation is our child, safe in
> my belly.

A child. Now here was something Doris's money *would* be good for. Émile's widow, and her dear child, would never want for anything.

Doris would make sure of it.

Chapter Forty-one

Lucie

My dearest husband,

I shall never believe it. I think I shall go to my grave not believing it. How could someone like you disappear from this earthly plane?

Since this war began, I have made a game of asking myself: What was the worst moment? The head of the Smiling Angel crashing upon the pavement. The breaking of the blind woman's teacup. The look on your face at that very last moment, when you turned back to smile at me.

Never before had you turned back.

This page is stained with tears, as yours are with blood.

I wipe the tears from my swollen eyes. According to the notice from the war department, my dear husband, my Émile, had been dead nearly a month by the time I received word. I cannot accept that: How could I not have known? I am appalled by my betrayal. I had carried on living, eating, sleeping, organizing a play with the children—all the while my Émile, my husband, had departed this world, and yet I did not know it.

Now everything makes me angry: the need to ingest water, to relieve myself. To breathe. Every breath makes me angry.

I don't know why I am writing a letter to a dead man, except that I cannot believe he is truly dead. Would I not feel his absence in the world if he were?

But there is nowhere to send my letter. If I post it to his military address, it will come back, forwarded to me as his wife.

Still. I have to speak to him. I have to share my news.

I have stared at the butcher knife, pondering death. I know they would say my death was a victory for the enemy, but I know differently. My death would not be an escape but a triumph, a statement of my power. I would lay down my arms and walk into the arms of the abyss.

But I cannot, because our child keeps me here. Did you know, *mon amour*? Did you sense it, somehow? Our child grows within me. I wish I had told you.

I hold out hope that this has been a

mistake, that you are out there, some-where, still. Your Australian *marraine* writes you still, and I will keep the letters for you. She has yet to receive the terrible news, to read the words that cannot be taken back.

You must be out there. Wouldn't I feel it if you were not?

The bubbles continue to buoy us. The vintage holds its promise of a future. So I have hidden a package for you: bottles of Victory Vintage champagne, and a sweater—one of my mother's last, as her health is fading—in our special nook.

All awaits us in the attic of Dakar.

Until we meet again,

Your loving wife,

Lucie

Chapter Forty-two

Emma and Blondine were scheduled to return from Paris that afternoon. Rosalyn steeled herself, knowing she would have to tell them about Émile. *She should be good at this.* After Dash died, she had been forced over and over again to share such words, the ones that cannot be grasped or taken back.

The words that, once uttered, meant the world had changed.

Rosalyn was in the tasting room fixing a cup of coffee when their car pulled in. Blondine carried several shopping bags, and through the window, Rosalyn could see André taking packages out of the trunk. Blondine was effusive and flushed, but Emma seemed subdued, not her usual ebullient self.

"I take it you had a good time," said Rosalyn, as they came into the tasting room, "or at the very least, an *expensive* time."

"Smell this," said Blondine, thrusting a slender, pale wrist toward Rosalyn. "Is that not the most divine scent you have ever smelled? *Absolument divin.*"

"Parisian perfumeries," said Emma. "Hard to get any sweeter than that."

Dutifully, Rosalyn took a sniff. The scent was woody but subtle and sophisticated, precisely what one would expect from a Parisian perfume.

"You're right. It's divine."

"Emma got one for you as well," said Blondine. "A different kind, though, so we don't smell the same."

"That's so generous, and completely unnecessary," said Rosalyn.

Emma waved her off. "Nonsense. Why bother visiting Paris if you're not going to buy perfume? And you know how those salespeople can get, *très snob. Qui se la pète*? I love shocking them by buying the place out. What's money for if not to embarrass snooty salespeople? Anyway, we tried to guess what would suit you, but if you don't like it, feel free to regift it to a friend."

"*Que-ce que c'est* 'regift'?" asked Blondine.

Emma explained the concept to a confused Blondine while Rosalyn dabbed a bit of the amber liquid on her wrist. It was heavenly, a blend of jasmine tones over a base of bergamot and amber.

"I love it. Thank you so much. Did you get some for yourself? A signature scent?" asked Rosalyn.

"I already have more perfume than I can use in this lifetime," said Emma.

Again, Rosalyn sensed a slight dampening of Emma's usual upbeat nature. Was it the conversation they'd had before she left? Rosalyn should speak to her alone and clear the air; the only thing worse than experiencing grief was taking those feelings out on other people through anger. Emma had offered nothing but friendship and support; she certainly didn't deserve that.

"One more thing," Emma said as Blondine handed her a bag from Magasin Sennelier, an art supply store.

Rosalyn peeked inside to find a set of oil paints, brushes, and solvent.

"André insisted," said Emma. "Drove us all over the Marais searching for just the right set. We found plenty at Rougier and Plé Filles du Calvaire, but they weren't good enough. He wanted you to have the perfect one. He's got several blank canvases in the car as well."

Wordlessly, Rosalyn ran her hand over the beautiful set of paints. The gift of perfume was touching, but this was something else entirely. She glanced out the window, but André had long since disappeared.

"The shower's great in the *gîte*, so I'm not about to complain about the accommodations," continued Emma. "But good heavens, we need something to spruce up those guest rooms. Blondine keeps mentioning your sketches, and André noticed them the other day as well. Maybe you should make the walls your canvas, leave a little of yourself behind."

"That's a great idea," said Blondine. "My mother helped with the decorations here in the tasting room, but my father and I don't have much of a sense of these things. You should feel free to paint champagne on the walls!"

"Are you sure about that?" Rosalyn asked. "Wouldn't you like to approve a sketch first?"

"Why?" Blondine said with a shrug. "I trust you. Besides, we'll just have Pietro paint over it if we don't like it."

Rosalyn laughed. The idea appealed to her; it felt like permission to be a naughty child, painting the walls.

And then she sobered, remembering her news about Émile. She was on the verge of telling them when Emma announced: "*Well.* I'm beat. I'm heading to my room to root through my acquisitions, and perhaps take a *petite sieste.* Rosalyn, lovely to see you, as always. We'll catch up soon. We have some stories to share, do we not, Blondine? *Parisian* stories."

She limped out of the room on her crutches, two sets of eyes following her.

Rosalyn turned to Blondine. "What's going on?"

"She sent me shopping one day," said Blondine. "She didn't want me to know where she was going, but André told me they went to the hospital."

"Is there a problem with her leg?"

Blondine shrugged. "I can't get a thing out of her. When I asked, she said something about André and beans—does that mean anything to you?"

" 'Spill the beans' means 'to reveal a secret.' "

"Ah, that makes sense now. In any event, Emma said it was just a routine checkup, but . . ."

"But what?"

"Her appointment was at the Hôpital Universitaire Pitié-Salpêtrière—Charles Foix."

"Is that good or bad?"

"It is a teaching hospital, known for research." She paused. "I worry when people go to research hospitals. My grandmother was sent to one. It usually means they have something that can't be easily cured."

"You know how Emma is," Rosalyn said, as she felt a stab of fear. "Probably just demanded the best physician in all of Paris look at her leg."

"Maybe," Blondine said, looking doubtful. "But if she wants to keep it to herself, I suppose that's her choice. After all, we keep our own secrets, *non*?"

Rosalyn decided to wait to share the news of Émile's fate until the three of them were together again. They had explored Émile's journey together, and should grieve his death together. Returning to her room, Rosalyn paused in front of the door of *Pinot Meunier* but heard no movement. She didn't want to disturb Emma if she was napping. Could Blondine be onto something? She had noticed Emma taking pills a few times, which she had claimed were vitamins.

Rosalyn had seen enough pills in her life to know that what Emma was taking were not simple nutritional supplements. Still, many people took medications for high blood pressure and a myriad of other ailments; Emma was in her fifties, old enough to have developed a few chronic issues. The thing was . . . Dash hadn't told Rosalyn he was feeling ill for a very long time, until it was too late. Why hadn't he confided in her?

She carried her gifts to *Chambre Chardonnay* and set the beautiful perfume bottle on her bedside table so she could sniff it at will. The new paint set she placed on the table, running her fingers over the tubes of pigment with reverence, reading the names aloud. "Phthalo green, barium yellow, bremen blue, celadon green, alizarin crimson . . ."

The thought of Emma being sick, really sick, filled Rosalyn with dread. She remembered the look on the doctor's face when she referred Dash to a research hospital to explore experimental treatment options.

Still, it wasn't any of Rosalyn's business. Not to mention she had known Emma for only what—a few weeks? Was it simply being someplace new, or the fact that they were living together, that fostered this feeling of closeness to someone she hardly knew? There was an intensity to the relationship that made her understand why so many people had affairs while on vacation.

Affairs. Her mind went to Jérôme. After the lovely evening at his house, she had fled without explanation.

The truth was that he had stirred something in her that Rosalyn thought had died along with her husband. From the very first time she saw Jérôme in his fields, in the barely dawning light, something had drawn her to him . . . a yearning, a craving, a desire for closeness.

Intimacy. This was a loss that even the young widows' support group had trouble discussing.

Rosalyn used to hunger for Dash's touch. Even after they had been married for a while, their connection still burned, not as hot as it was in the very beginning but more intense, buoyed by their closeness, the experiences they had shared.

How could she hunger for another?

Jérôme had introduced her to his son, had noticed her new haircut, had shown her the Comtois collection and his family's library. He was sending her signs, wasn't he? She wasn't even sure what that felt like anymore.

She should seek Jérôme out, to apologize for her abrupt departure.

And yet a part of her longed to remain in her

cold little cocoon, insulated from the world. Rosalyn fiddled with the locket around her neck and recalled her horrific nightmare, Dash not allowing her to close the door of the medicine cabinet.

She made her decision.

Chapter Forty-three

Rosalyn dressed in warm clothes and set out walking. Jérôme wasn't in his fields near the highway, but she spied plumes of smoke from small fires staining the sky, and a team of half a dozen workers bustling like busy ants, high on the hill.

She hiked up and found an impossibly old man, a middle-aged woman, and a few younger people clad in heavy wool sweaters and wearing fingerless gloves, with mud caking their rubber boots. They sat on little rolling stools, moving along the rows as they tended to one vine after another. In oil drums at the ends of the rows burned the clippings, providing warmth for cold fingers.

The scene reminded her of the battlefield *séchoirs*, and she felt an urge to capture the scene on canvas with her new paints. The impressionist painter Édouard Manet once said there were no true lines in nature, only areas of color coming together. She would prepare her palette with zinc oxide, cerulean blue, burnt umber, viridian green. . . .

"They're tying up the vines," said a voice behind her.

Heart thudding, Rosalyn turned to see Jérôme, dressed like the others in muddy boots and a heavy parka over a sweater. His cheeks were shaded by whiskers, and his mouth drew her attention. But as always, it was his eyes that captured her.

"I've seen the process, in Napa," Rosalyn said. "But isn't it early?"

"It is, yes, but we adjust our calendar to accommodate the weather." He crouched down and pointed to where the canes were tied to the horizontal wire. "We use biodegradable twine to train the plant."

She nodded, leaning over to see.

"The pruning cuts down on mildew and stimulates the buds to encourage new growth, which replaces the old wood." Jérôme looked up at her for a long moment. "Rosalyn . . . I apologize."

"For what?"

"For whatever I did to make you run away."

Rosalyn felt her cheeks burning. She straightened and focused on the steeple of the church rising out of the sea of red-roofed homes in Cochet, far in the distance.

"You have nothing to apologize for, Jérôme. Honestly. I'm what we Americans call 'a hot mess.' "

He chuckled.

Despite the cold, she felt warmth flood through her as they stood side by side, looking across the fields of neat parallel grapevines.

"Did I say something funny?" Rosalyn asked.

"One thing I have learned from all of my reading over the years is that we're all a mess," Jérôme said in a quiet voice. "Hot or otherwise. Every single one of us. Even my little Laurent."

"How is he? I'm surprised he's not out here learning to prune the vines."

"He spent the day in the fields yesterday. But today he is with my mother; they are baking an onion tart."

"Well, of course. Every six-year-old should know how to prune grapevines and bake an onion tart."

Jérôme fixed her with that quizzical look again. "It is a joke?"

She smiled and nodded.

"Oh. It is not very funny, this joke."

"Told you, I'm a hot mess."

He smiled then, and they exchanged another long look, the only sounds the crackle of the fires and the snapping of the *sécateurs*, or clippers, as the workers snipped the deadwood from the vines.

"Do you have a date for the festival of Saint Vincent?" Jérôme asked suddenly.

"Are escorts required? I know the French are

more formal than Americans, but that seems a bit much."

"You don't *need* an escort. I was wondering if you would like to accompany me."

"I . . ." Everything in Rosalyn shrieked *no. No, of course not. I'm a married woman.* But she heard herself say, "I would love that. Thank you."

"Be aware: Escorts are not required but costumes are."

"I believe Blondine and Emma—my partners in crime, as you call them—have rounded one up for me."

"Good, then. We'll be marching with the Cochet growers."

"Marching? What marching?"

"It is a *défilé* . . . a parade. But everyone marches, so there are very few to witness the parade. We carry a small statue of Saint Vincent on a frame—a . . . stretcher, I think you call it."

"Like you would carry an injured person on?"

"It is better than it sounds. But in any case, the *défilé* ends with a grand feast. You know what they say about the *Champenois*: We work hard, but we love to celebrate."

"You're wearing a costume, too, right?"

Jérôme gave her a crooked grin and ducked his head. "I'm told I look very good in tights."

Chapter Forty-four

When she returned to the Blé Champagne compound, Rosalyn found André taking a smoke break at the edge of the parking area.

"I wanted to thank you for the paint set," Rosalyn said.

"It was Emma who bought it, not me."

"But she told me it was your idea, and that you sought out a special one. I can't tell you how much that means to me. Thank you."

"I admire your drawings. I can only imagine them in color. I hope you will share what you paint."

"Only if I produce something halfway decent. But again, thank you." She paused and then said: "By the way, I know you don't want to break a confidence, but I'm worried. Is Emma okay?"

His hesitation said more than his words. "You must ask her directly."

"I will. Is she around?"

He nodded. "In the tasting room, with Blondine."

She kept André company while he finished his cigarette; then they walked together toward the buildings.

• • •

Rosalyn stopped by *Chambre Chardonnay* to pick up Lucie's letter to Doris with the news of Émile's death. Blondine and Emma were in the tasting room, laptops open, surrounded by some of Émile's letters as well as books and photocopies from the archive in Reims.

Rosalyn took a deep, shaky breath. "I have to read something to you both. It's a letter from Lucie to Doris, about Émile. It's not good."

Emma and Blondine listened intently as she read Lucie's letter aloud.

He lies beneath one of the millions of horrifying white crosses marking the final resting places of too many young men, studding the land in a painful mockery of the vines.

Blondine gasped and her hand flew to her mouth. "*Mon Dieu . . .*"

"I take it you never read this one?" Rosalyn asked Emma.

"I never got that far," said Emma, shaking her head, her eyes shiny with unshed tears. "I started reading from the beginning. *Damn.* I knew it was likely Émile didn't survive, as so many did not. But . . . *damn.*"

Rosalyn finished reading them the rest of the letter just as Gaspard came into the tasting room from the office. Upon seeing the women surrounded by papers and books, he made a disparaging sound. "Are we becoming an archive ourselves now?"

"It's *history,* Papa."

"That's the problem with this country," Gaspard groused as he went to the kitchen to make himself a cup of coffee. "There's no room for the here and now. Everything's focused on the past. I thought you had more sense than that, Blondine."

"I'd love a coffee. Thanks," said Emma, though he hadn't offered.

"I really . . . I just can't believe it." Blondine sniffed loudly.

"It's hard to accept," said Rosalyn. "He seemed so alive through all these letters."

"What in the world's wrong with you women?" demanded Gaspard as he measured coffee grounds into the cone.

"It's Émile," said Blondine in a flat tone. "He died. Émile's dead."

"Émile who?" asked Gaspard.

"Émile Legrand."

"I don't know an Émile Legrand," Gaspard said. "Do I know an Émile Legrand?"

"He's the man who wrote these letters we've been reading," said Emma. "The World War One soldier."

"Oh. Well, I've got news for you," Gaspard said, china rattling as he prepared two mugs. "He would be long dead by now anyway. He was writing a century ago."

"Honestly, Papa," said Blondine.

"It is incredibly sad," said Emma, ignoring Gaspard. "But what about Lucie's *happy* news?"

"That she was pregnant?" asked Rosalyn.

Emma nodded. "That's something beautiful, at least."

"But Émile never knew he was going to be a father," said Blondine. "How sad is that?"

"The child might not have survived," said Gaspard. "I read it someplace, a while ago. In the caves a lot of the young died of disease and malnutrition, and without a father . . ."

"Really, Papa." Blondine shook her head and blew out a long sigh. "*Ça suffit, oui*?"

"Is there any way we can find out what happened to Lucie and her baby?" Rosalyn wondered.

"André has tracked down every Maréchal he can find, but no luck. Of course, she may have remarried and changed her name," said Emma. "Or relocated. A lot of people started their lives over elsewhere after the war. Maybe she couldn't stand the thought of remaining in Reims after everything that happened."

"At least you could find this Émile fellow," suggested Gaspard as he set a cup of coffee in front of Emma. "*He's* not going anywhere."

"Oh, Papa . . ."

"No, your father has a point this time, Blondine," said Emma, looking thoughtful.

"Let's find Émile's grave. According to Lucie, he was buried at Châlons-en-Champagne. There are massive cemeteries from World War One, and most of them keep good records. They might even give us a clue as to Lucie's whereabouts, since she was his widow. Who's up for a road trip tomorrow?"

"Count me in," Rosalyn said.

"Me, too," said Blondine.

"Not me," Gaspard said. "I have work to do, unlike some people."

"*You* weren't invited," said Emma.

On the way to the cemetery the next day, Emma asked André to take a detour to a town called Haumont-près-Samogneux.

"We forget how ancient these lands are," said Emma. "This town was founded to celebrate the Gallic sun god. There was an altar here in the first century AD."

As they approached the outskirts of town, a sign indicated that Haumont-près-Samogneux had been designated *Un village mort pour la France.*

"What does that mean—the whole *town* died?" asked Rosalyn.

"It's been unoccupied since the battle of Verdun, in 1916," said Blondine. "And it's not the only one. There're Bezonvaux and Beaumont-en-Verdunois, and lots more. Several others in the region of Meuse alone. The *Rémois* had a tough go of it, but at least the city didn't die altogether."

"Were all the villagers killed?" Rosalyn asked.

"No, most of them fled before the worst of the fighting," said Blondine. "But they were never able to return."

"Something like eighty soldiers were buried alive when the town literally collapsed under a massive bombardment," said Emma. "In addition to that, bombs and gases poisoned the earth, and so many bodies were left to rot—animals and human—that the groundwater was poisoned."

"*Quel dommage*," Blondine said. "I get frustrated with Cochet at times, but I can't imagine if someone told me that I could never go back."

André pulled to a stop, and they got out and walked the area, now curated as a historic site. There wasn't much of the town left to see; a small chapel and memorial had been erected decades after the war, but otherwise all that was left of the village of Haumont-près-Samogneux was a few crumbling walls covered in vines, and small verdant mounds disguising the rubble of collapsed buildings. They passed by the metal hull of a huge reddish bomb sticking up out of the ground, the only tangible sign of the brutality that had been visited on these grounds.

Despite the violence the area had seen, birds chirped, and the damp earth smelled fresh and green.

Rosalyn was reminded of the remains of Mayan pyramids that she and Dash had toured in Yucatán, Mexico. But those ruins were thousands of years old; the once-thriving village of Haumont-près-Samogneux—which had been full of people and businesses, farmers and bakers, where people had fallen in love, had children, endured heartbreak, and lived their lives—had been reclaimed by the hungry forces of nature after only a century.

Here and there cardboard cutouts showed life-sized black-and-white photographs of former inhabitants, now long gone. Their faces beckoned eerily, ghostlike against the green backdrop of encroaching forest.

"Come on," said Emma. "Enough fun for today in the town that died. Let's go look at a cemetery."

They continued on to Châlons-en-Champagne.

"At the American and Australian cemeteries, many of the graves have been adopted by local French families, who bring flowers and tokens of remembrance," Emma said. "Which is about the sweetest thing I've ever heard."

Blondine nodded. "The Americans came into the war late, but they were an essential part of the victory. And of course the Australians were here all along. They bled for France, and people here don't forget that."

The cemetery consisted of thousands of white crosses marching in neat, orderly rows along the softly rolling hills. As Lucie had written, their parallel queues seemed to mock the grapevines.

At the reception center, Blondine looked up Émile Paul Legrand on a public computer database.

"He's not listed," she said, shaking her head.

"He must be," said Emma. "Surely Lucie was notified correctly as to where her husband was buried."

"Not necessarily," said Blondine. "Didn't you see the memorial outside for ten thousand unknown soldiers? Things were chaotic. There must have been many families who never learned the fates of their loved ones."

"True, but Lucie mentioned this cemetery specifically," Rosalyn pointed out. "Maybe it's an oversight?"

"Let's ask," said Emma.

The man in charge, Monsieur Dervin, was a balding fellow in a sweater vest and thick spectacles. They gave him Émile's name and town of origin, and he had them wait for twenty minutes while he did some research.

When he emerged from his office, he declared: "There are scratch outs."

"What does that mean?" Blondine asked.

"A lot of people were misidentified during the battles and immediately following the war," said Monsieur Dervin.

"Didn't they carry identification of some kind?" asked Blondine.

"*Bien sûr.* Soldiers wore a *plaque d'identité*, a bracelet with a metal disk that was engraved with the soldier's name and rank. Unfortunately, many fell off or were switched. There was so much blood and mayhem, you see, and many of the bodies were not"—Monsieur Dervin lowered his voice—"complete. Other brave men died in a manner such that their bodies could not be retrieved for some time, and were thus rendered unrecognizable, even to their comrades. Injured soldiers were often misidentified, their papers lost or mixed up during a hurried evacuation, for example."

He pointed to names that had been crossed out and replaced with other names. "Like this one, here—you see?"

The three women leaned in to study the hand-written records that had been scanned into the computer. A few of the names had lines through them along with notations.

"Émile Paul Legrand . . . Legrand . . . ," Monsieur Dervin repeated, as he scrolled through the lists, searching the names. "Yes, here he is. . . . Émile Paul Legrand was a scratch out. He was at first believed to have been killed in action, but see here? Much later he was found among the wounded."

"Wait—you mean he survived the war?" Emma demanded.

Monsieur Dervin nodded. "I have no idea how *long* he survived, but according to these documents, one Émile Paul Legrand from Reims was not killed in action as initially reported."

"When was this?" Emma asked.

"Toward the end of nineteen seventeen. According to the notation—see this, here?— Legrand was evacuated to a military hospital near Nantes. He suffered a head injury and lost his left hand. Due to his severe injuries, he was unable to communicate."

"When was the scratch out made?" Rosalyn asked. "When did they realize the mistake?"

He shook his head. "This I cannot tell you. However, it was likely after the war had ended, when he had recovered sufficiently to tell them who he was."

Chapter Forty-five

Lucie

I wonder if the history books will record that twenty *petits enfants*, and many more adults, gave their lives for the grape harvests. Is it worth it? That is a question I ask myself every day, every hour, every minute.

Another year, another harvest.

Our baby, Narcissa, is left with a neighbor, as my mother is fading fast. I spoon honeyed tea into her mouth, but she has stopped eating altogether. I'm sure I don't know what I'll do without her.

Émile gone, and *Maman*, too?

Father hardly reacts to anything anymore; I fear he will not long be with us, either. And sweet Henri tries his best, but he spends more and more time with the animals, which is where his talents lie.

At least I have Topette, who has become like my little sister. Mother has taught her how to knit, and she is quite the protégée, knitting sweaters and balaclavas for the soldiers, and for those of us who tend the fields. It is said the war cannot last much longer. When everyone has finally put down their swords, I will go with Topette and Narcissa to find my beloved Émile's grave site, and then we shall visit the ocean. Perhaps one day we will travel to Australia to visit Émile's *marraine*, Madame Whittaker. She writes to me now instead of Émile, and has promised me that our dear Narcissa will be taken care of, always.

She writes that she wants to come visit, after the war.

Topette and Narcissa and I—and Madame Whittaker, too. We will find a way to carry on.

We have no other choice.

Chapter Forty-six

H ow did it go?" André asked when Emma, Blondine, and Rosalyn returned to the car, still reeling from the revelation that Émile Legrand might have survived the war.

"The plot, as they say, thickens," Emma said.

"While you were gone," André said, "Madame Bolze called."

"Why did she call you instead of me?" Emma asked.

"I met with her after you offered my services as chauffeur, remember? She likes me."

"Everyone likes you. What did Madame Bolze have to say?"

"She remembered the name of a woman she knew from school whose mother lived in the caves as a child," said André, referring to a small notebook. "Her name is Madame Jeanne Bisset, and she lives outside of Ay. She might know something about the woman you're looking for. Madame Bolze gave me her phone number."

"That sounds promising," Rosalyn said.

"Ay is en route to Cochet, if you would like to stop," André mentioned.

"Well, then, no time like the present," said Emma, then pulled out her phone, dialed the woman's number, and asked if they could drop by for a visit.

Madame Bisset lived in a well-appointed but humble home on a very busy road. Inside, photographs of grandchildren and great-grandchildren graced the walls, and hand-crocheted blankets covered the backs of the couch and several chairs.

A warm and welcoming woman in her eighties, Madame Bisset reminded Rosalyn of an elderly chihuahua: She was petite and thin, with a well-coiffed head of pure white hair and an abundance of nervous energy. She introduced them to her husband, Gustave, and, when he turned away, whispered that he "has the Alzheimer's."

"You go play the Beethoven now, Gustave," she said in a loud voice, and with a nod he complied. "Come, young ladies—please have a seat. Madame Bolze told me you are looking for information about the orphanage, and life in the caves during the war. And about Lucie Maréchal, in particular."

"We are," said Emma, as Beethoven's "Für Elise" began to play in the other room. "Do you think your mother knew her? I know it was long before your time, madame, but what can you tell us about it?"

"Oh, please call me Jeanne. Otherwise you'll make me feel old," she said, springing up from the sofa to grab a photo, which she handed to Blondine, who passed it around. The photo showed a smiling young woman in a simple tea-length wedding gown. "This is my mother, Topette; she lived with Lucie Maréchal in the caves, as a child."

"She's very beautiful," Emma said to Jeanne.

"Wasn't she? That photo was taken in the nineteen thirties, I think. She left Reims right after the war, and later became a schoolteacher, like Lucie. I followed in her footsteps, and now my daughters are both teachers!"

"That's a wonderful legacy," said Emma. "Lucie was a teacher, then? I heard she was an assistant."

"If I recall correctly, Lucie Maréchal wasn't trained as a professional *maîtresse*, but during the war she helped in the classrooms they set up in the caves. I'm sorry I don't have any photos of that time."

"And did your mother ever tell you what happened to Lucie?" Rosalyn asked.

"What? Oh, I'm so sorry. I thought you knew," said Jeanne, looking troubled.

"Knew what?"

"This is why the story is so famous, why my mother told it to me so many times. It broke her heart."

The strains of Beethoven heightened the emotion of Jeanne's words. Rosalyn was suddenly afraid to hear what Jeanne had to say, not wanting the elderly woman to utter words that could not be taken back.

"Please, madame," Emma said softly. "What happened to Lucie Maréchal? We know part of her story, but not the ending."

"My mother was an orphan; she lost her parents in the war. She found refuge with the villagers in the Pommery caves, and was taken in by Lucie and her mother, Madame Maréchal. Madame taught my mother to knit and crochet—even to tat—and she in turn taught me." Jeanne smiled. "I remember my mother saying that Lucie was terrible at knitting, and every time she tried, they had to rip it all out and start again. She said Lucie's talents lay in other areas."

"And what broke your mother's heart?" Emma asked.

"Lucie and my mother worked the harvest, along with so many others. Women and children, the old people who were still strong enough to manage. They brought in the Victory Vintages, knowing they would have to wait several years for the wines to ferment properly, to effervesce. They believed they were investing in the future of France, a future without war.

"One night of a full moon, the silver light limned the grapevines and everyone was working among the vines.

"All of a sudden, the children started screaming

and flinging themselves into the mud, the way they had been taught to do when they heard gunfire or mortars. It wasn't clear where the sniper shots were coming from. Lucie ran toward my mother and sheltered her with her body.

"My mother said they lay there in the vines for what felt like hours. Finally, the firing ceased, and they remained still for a count of three hundred, as they had been taught. Then they started to crawl toward the hole they used to reach the caves—they crawled along on their elbows, dragging their bodies to remain close to the ground.

"Lucie ordered my mother to go into the caves. Mother didn't want to leave her, but Lucie was very stern. When the survivors gathered back at the caves, they realized three people were missing: a boy and a girl, and . . . Lucie. It was only then that my mother realized she was covered in blood. Lucie's blood."

"Lucie was shot," Rosalyn said, a statement more than a question.

Jeanne nodded. "Her body was recovered from among the grapevines the following night, along with the two *petits enfants*."

"After all this time, we find out Émile survived the war but Lucie did not?" said Emma as they pulled away from Jeanne Bisset's house, waving good-bye to Topette's daughter, who stood in her doorway watching them leave. "I can't believe this."

"Maybe she's wrong," said Blondine. "She's old. Maybe her memory is affected. Or she's making it up."

"Why would she make up such a story?" Rosalyn asked. "I think we all want to deny it happened, but it has the ring of truth, doesn't it? I can easily imagine Lucie giving up her life to save a child."

Blondine shrugged. "I think we should find some proof. Maybe there are lists of the civilians killed in the vines, or something?"

"I didn't think to look for such a thing when I was at the Reims archives," said Emma, sounding tired. She checked the clock on her phone. "The archives are open another half an hour—André, let's see if we can get there before they close."

"*Oui, madame*," André said, and floored it.

They pulled up just minutes before closing time. The well-dressed, perfectly coiffed woman at the front desk was not pleased to see them, but when Emma made it clear she wasn't leaving, the woman agreed to make photocopies of the pertinent documents, then shooed them out, no doubt needing to shop for her intricate French dinner.

Rosalyn was eager to read through the papers, but the mound of handwritten documents was daunting. The three women were tired and hungry, and overwhelmed by all they had learned that day.

"I suppose it's like my father said," said Blondine after they'd arrived back in Cochet. "They would have been dead for years, anyway. For now, we have dinner to make."

"You're right, Blondine," said Emma. "We'll tackle this in the morning, when we're fresh. For now, hand me that bottle of champagne."

The next morning in the Blé Champagne tasting room, the three women took their seats at the document-strewn table, divided up the photo-copies from the archive, and began reading through the faint handwritten names and explanations entered into the archive's database.

"*Bouge pas*. Wait. . . . Wait," said Blondine. She looked stricken.

"What is it? Blondine?" Rosalyn asked.

She held her hand to her mouth and breathed a shaky breath. She handed Rosalyn a paper.

"What is it?" demanded Emma, frowning.

"A list of those killed bringing in the harvest." Blondine's voice was flat. "Every year from nineteen fourteen to nineteen eighteen."

"And?" Emma looked at Rosalyn, who was holding the paper tight in her hand.

She blew out a long breath, and read aloud: " '*Le seize septembre, mille neuf cent dix-huit. Sont decedés deux petits enfants*: *Armand-Jacques*

Pelletier, âgé de sept ans, et Marie-Suzanne LeFleur, âgée de dix ans. Et leur maîtresse, Lucie Maréchal, âgée de vingt-trois ans.' "

Emma sighed. "So Topette's daughter was correct. Lucie was shot and killed by a sniper while bringing in the harvest, along with two children under her care."

They sat in dazed silence, sharing the strange, sacred space of grief.

Blondine sniffed loudly, tears in her eyes. "I knew it was a possibility, of course. We all did, with the terrible number of casualties. It wasn't just the soldiers who died. . . . One in twenty of the total population of France was killed in the war."

"Wait. What was the date?" Emma asked.

Rosalyn looked at the photocopy. "September sixteenth, nineteen eighteen."

"Lucie would have had her baby by then," Emma pointed out.

"So what happened to the child?" Blondine asked.

"Was there any record of births in the caves?" Rosalyn asked.

"Good question," said Emma. "Short answer: I don't know. The war ended two months later, in November of that year. Most of the city had been destroyed, and people scattered. In all the chaos, I doubt anyone was keeping track of who went where."

"Lucie's mother, of course," Blondine said. "She would have taken care of her grandbaby."

"Except, according to the letters, Lucie's mother wasn't well," said Rosalyn. "What if she couldn't take care of the baby?"

"The orphanage," Emma said, excitement in her voice. "I wonder if the child ended up there. One of the million French war orphans."

"Wait," Rosalyn said. "We know Lucie wrote to Doris and told her she was expecting Émile's child. If Doris knew Lucie was pregnant, don't you think . . . ?"

"Wild horses wouldn't have kept her away," Emma said with a nod. "Once the war was over . . ."

"She would have come to help Lucie," Rosalyn finished her thought. "Doris would have come for the child."

Chapter Forty-seven

The next morning the trio stood out in front of Madame Bolze's house, Vieille Ruche, leaning against the car, feeling frustrated all over again.

After their discoveries the day before, Emma had called Jeanne Bisset to ask if her mother, Topette, had ever mentioned Lucie Maréchal's baby. According to Jeanne, her mother had referred to the child, but she did not know what had become of the infant.

"We need to look at that ledger," Emma had said, "the one you two found in Madame Bolze's attic, with the names of all the orphans. Let me give her a try."

If Madame Bolze was home, she wasn't answering her phone, so on Monday morning Blondine drove them to the Vieille Ruche. A neighbor boy informed them that Madame Bolze had left two days ago to meet with her daughter outside Tours.

"Well done, Emma," Blondine said. "You had to convince her to reconcile with her daughter *now?*"

"I could hardly have foreseen this eventuality," Emma said, then lit a cigarette and leaned back against the car. She closed her eyes for a few seconds, looking weary. "But you're right. It's more than a little maddening. We're so close."

"Now what?" said Blondine.

"Do you suppose it would be crossing the line to break in?" Emma asked, her dark eyes searching the house's façade as though she was assessing possible points of entry.

Blondine looked at Emma, alarmed.

"I . . . do, yes," said Rosalyn, when it appeared Emma wasn't kidding. "I think breaking and entering would be crossing a line. I'm not ready for a meet and greet with the local gendarmes at this point."

"Honestly, Rosalyn," said Emma. "Here I think we're on the same wavelength, and then you go and say something like that. But I suppose Gaspard was right after all. These people lived more than a hundred years ago; we can wait a little longer to learn their fate."

"Right now, it's time for lunch," Blondine said, checking her phone. "I know a place. *C'est pas mauvais.*"

"As you know, *pas mauvais* means 'not bad,' " Emma explained to Rosalyn as she stubbed out her cigarette and they piled back into the car. "But here's a helpful hint: The French apply it to *everything,* and depending on the inflection, it can mean anything from 'terrible' to 'terrific.' "

"And in this case?" Rosalyn asked. "Terrible or terrific?"

Blondine shrugged. *"Pas mauvais."*

They stopped at a corner bistro in the nearby town of Fleury-la-Rivière. The busy bistro was filled with workers in muddy boots and overalls, sipping champagne with their *menu du jour* the way folks in Napa might have had a beer with their sandwich.

"So, let's recap," Emma said as they savored their *entrées*, or appetizers, of smoked salmon and duck terrine. "Émile made it through the war alive, which means Lucie wasn't a widow after all."

"No, she was the one who died," Blondine said, dejected.

"And Émile was listed as dead, but must have been in some sort of coma, unable to tell anyone who he was," said Rosalyn. "Was there any way he would have known Lucie had a child?"

"Not according to the letters," said Emma.

"He must have come back to search for Lucie, but . . . ," Blondine said.

"By then all the people who had been living underground had dispersed," said Emma. "Either they took part in rebuilding Reims or they left town. André and I have found references to a few Legrands around Reims, but no sign of an Émile

Legrand. We've checked tax rolls and census reports, but like I keep saying . . ."

"It was chaos after the war." Rosalyn finished her thought. "It's possible we'll never find out."

On their way back to Cochet, Rosalyn noted the unusual traffic and number of people milling about in the villages.

"They are all coming for the festival of Saint Vincent. It's great fun," Blondine said. "Wait until you see your costume."

"Oh, good," Rosalyn said, trying but failing to stir up much enthusiasm. "Thank you."

"We should go early," Blondine continued. "Emma, if André is willing to drive us, we won't have to worry about parking. But then *he'll* have to worry about parking."

"I don't think that will bother him; festivals aren't really André's thing. Should we say we'll leave at nine?"

"Perfect," said Blondine.

"Actually, I'm . . ." Rosalyn blushed. "I sort of made plans to go with Jérôme."

"*Quoi*?" Blondine said, staring at her in the rearview mirror.

"With Jérôme?" Emma gaped.

"Jérôme Comtois," Rosalyn clarified.

"Yes, we're familiar with Jérôme Comtois," Emma said with a smile. "Well, well, aren't you just the scamp? You remind me of Doris with all your secrets."

"*Qu'est-ce que c'est* 'scamp'?" Blondine asked.

"*Petite coquine, garnemente, chenapane, polissonne . . . friponne, galopine . . .*"

"Emma, for someone who claims she doesn't speak French all that well, you sound suspiciously like you swallowed a French thesaurus," said Rosalyn.

"I like words," said Emma. "And don't try to change the subject. How long have you been keeping Jérôme a secret?"

"He's not a *secret*. I just didn't happen to mention him."

"I think it's great," said Blondine.

"*C'est pas mauvais*," said Emma, and they all laughed. She sighed, laid her head back against the headrest, and closed her eyes.

"Since we're on the topic of spilling secrets," Rosalyn began, "Emma . . . are you all right? Blondine said you had an appointment at a research hospital in Paris."

"I'm fine."

"You seem tired. I mean, not for a normal human, but for you."

"This is true," said Blondine, glancing at Emma. "You are not normal."

Emma chuckled. "I've had a few complications, but nothing to worry about."

"But—," began Rosalyn.

"I said I'm *fine,*" Emma said, an edge to her voice. She added in a gentler tone, "I'm frustrated that we don't know what happened to Émile, and the baby, and I need a smoke. But otherwise, I'm fine."

Blondine dropped them off at the *gîte,* telling Rosalyn she would be back at eight in the morning, costumes in hand. Rosalyn helped Emma into the entry since her crutches made navigating through the door a challenge. Emma looked wan and weary; Rosalyn knew it wasn't her imagination.

"How are you feeling about the festival?" Emma asked as they paused outside their respective chamber doors.

"*Ugh.* Ritchie James will be there, I have no doubt. And I'm not big on costume parties."

"But Jérôme is taking you. That will be fun."

"True. But you saw what happened at the last party. I just hope I can hold it together this time."

"Why are you so committed to going, if you hate it so much?" Emma asked.

"Attending the festival is the reason my boss sent me to France in the first place."

"This Hugh character—he sounds like more than just a boss. I mean, you're unusually committed to him."

"I owe him."

"Why? Sorry to be blunt, Rosie, but wine reps

are a dime a dozen, and you're really not all that great at it. Surely he could replace you?"

"Thanks. I feel so much better now."

"I didn't mean it that way."

"Hugh's been an incredibly good friend to me. He was so supportive when Dash got sick, and after I learned just how much debt we were in. And on top of that, do you have any idea how much medical treatment can cost?"

"I got a crash course in it when I broke my leg in San Francisco," said Emma. "Pardon the pun."

"Even with insurance . . . Dash had to take all these pills," Rosalyn said, realizing she had never told anyone about the medicine cabinet. "He was supposed to take one every morning and evening. One hundred dollars apiece. And then the antinausea meds so he wouldn't vomit them up. And the blood thinning meds and the painkillers . . ."

"So Hugh helped you with the medical bills?"

Rosalyn nodded. "And it wasn't just the medical bills, but our regular living expenses—the credit card debt, the car note, the mortgage—and the business itself was underwater. . . . Hugh bought our inventory, and the land, for more than they were worth. He gave me a job and let us live in the caretaker's cottage on his estate."

There was a long pause. "He sounds like a kind man."

"A very kind man. And a little pushy. You should meet him. I have the sense you two would get along well."

Emma smiled. "Are you calling me pushy because I think researching and writing this book would be a better use of your talents than sales? I just want you to be happy. Dash wouldn't have wanted you to suffer like this, especially for *his* sins, would he?"

"How am I supposed to know what Dash would have wanted?" Rosalyn snapped.

Along with "He's in a better place now," this was one of the things well-meaning friends said to comfort the grief-stricken. Rosalyn found it deeply annoying, though she couldn't put her finger on exactly why. How could she, or anyone, presume to know what Dash would have wanted? He had always said he wanted her to have a lifetime of laughter—but then he had gotten sick. And left her. And that had made laughter impossible.

"I'm just saying you don't owe Hugh your whole life, and if he's half the man you suggest he is, he wouldn't want that, either. First you lived for Dash, Rosalyn, and now for Hugh. Does that sound smart to you?"

"You'd rather I live my life for you?"

"Heaven forbid," Emma chuckled. "I'm offering you an opportunity, Rosalyn. Creating a life is on you. But maybe we see this differently.

What's the expression in French? *Chacun voit midi à sa porte*."

"Meaning?"

" 'We all see noon on our own doorstep.' In other words, everyone sees things according to their own perspective. All I know is that in the end, no one can make you happy but you." Emma let out a long sigh. "Anyway, I'm exhausted. I'm going to lie down."

"Rest well, Emma. And thank you."

"For what?"

"For your thoughts."

"It didn't sound like you enjoyed hearing them."

"I didn't. But I appreciate them. I'll see you at dinner."

"After that lunch? I don't know that I could eat another bite."

"Can't skip meals in France. If I've learned one thing, it's that."

Chapter Forty-eight

The exchange with Emma left Rosalyn agitated. She gazed out the window, fiddling with the silver locket around her neck.

She glanced at Émile's letters—there were still dozens she hadn't yet read, much less translated. But after what they had discovered about Lucie today, she didn't have the heart to face Émile's handwriting, to think of him in those god-awful trenches, carefully composing his thoughts and hopes and dreams for the future.

Instead, she opened the new paint set. *Sap green, Payne's gray, Vandyke brown, turnsole red lake, burnt umber . . .*

She gazed at the pristine cream-colored walls of *Chambre Chardonnay*. Did she dare?

Pietro could always paint over it.

Without a plan or preliminary sketches, she started painting, right there on the walls. Before long, green champagne bottles took shape under her brush, their fat corks flying. She painted golden flutes of the bubbly, spattered pigment on the walls to create the impression of effervescence escaping, then added painted bunches of purple and green grapes and, just for the heck of it, a few birds flitting by. She dragged a chair over to the wall, climbed on it, and painted a loose border of grapevines just below the ceiling.

Ever since Dash died, Rosalyn's life had been nothing but gradations of gray. But now she felt the urge, the *space,* for color. Great splashes and splatters of color, washes and opaques and glazes. She wanted it all.

She needed the beauty.

Exhausted after hours of painting, Rosalyn sat down at her computer to e-mail Hugh. She remembered a time when the paint splatter on her hands would have bothered her, but now she enjoyed it.

She worked on the message for a long time. What would she do if she didn't work for Hugh? She had terrible credit and still owed money to Hugh and many others. But she had to trust herself to figure that part out; if worse came to worst, she could always go back to waiting tables, and she could pick up a second job. Right now Rosalyn knew, in her core, that she needed to make a change. She had to save herself.

She concentrated on finding just the right words to express to Hugh all that she felt: profound gratitude for the generosity he had shown her and Dash, as a friend and a mentor, and why attending tomorrow's festival of Saint Vincent would be her last official act as a Small Fortune wine rep.

Somehow she doubted Hugh would be surprised.

The next morning, Blondine arrived early with a bag of fresh croissants, a pot of strong coffee, a cold bottle of champagne, and four colorful costumes.

"I have one for you, me, and Emma, and Dominique will come here to dress as well. It's more fun that way. I hope they fit. . . ."

"Oh, great. Thank you. So . . . what do you think?" asked Rosalyn, anxious to hear Blondine's opinion of her artwork on the walls.

"What do I think about what?" Blondine asked, setting the croissants out on a plate.

"The walls," said Rosalyn. "I've been painting your walls."

Blondine looked up. "Oh! I didn't even notice! You see, this is why I can't be in charge of decorating. Oh, Rosalyn, this is—"

"*Pas mauvais*?"

Blondine laughed. "*Pas mauvais*, truly. Not bad at all. In fact, I love it. Look at the glasses of champagne. They're dancing! And the vine border, and the grapes and birds—it is enchanting."

"I hope you mean it. If not, it won't hurt my feelings if you want to paint over it. I had a lot of fun doing it."

"I love it, but now you must paint Emma's room. Speaking of whom, has Emma seen it yet? She should be up by now."

Rosalyn felt a pang of fear as Blondine went to bang on Emma's door, requesting her presence in *Chambre Chardonnay*. But soon enough she heard Emma yelling at Blondine to "hold your horses, already."

Dominique arrived not long after, smelling of cigarettes. She admired the painted walls, but then asked, "What happened to the poor ornament?" gesturing to Rosalyn's cracked ornament in its evergreen nest.

"She likes it that way," said Emma as she joined them. She popped the champagne and poured it into four flutes.

"It's true. I like it that way," said Rosalyn, relieved to see Emma looking whole, if tired.

"If you like broken ornaments, there are plenty more where that came from," said Dominique. "I have two cats, and they have a way with Christmas trees."

Emma handed them each a flute of champagne, which they held high in toast.

"In answer to a question Rosalyn posed long ago, today's the day we all drink champagne for breakfast!"

For the next hour, the women chatted, feasted on croissants, drank champagne, and helped one another to don the traditional dress of this area of Champagne: long red skirts and red capes fastened by gold clasps at the throat. The white bonnets were trimmed in lace, with long sides that fell to the shoulders, and reminded Rosalyn of van Gogh's paintings of peasants in Brittany. Rosalyn's skirt was a snug fit—too many croissants?—but the cape hid a multitude of sins.

"Do all the women wear the same costume?" Rosalyn asked.

"No, of course not," said Blondine. "Some wear more white, some green. I have even seen some brocade."

"Rebels," murmured Emma.

"We're all cheating, though," said Dominique. Her robust form looked surprisingly at home in the traditional outfit. "If we were really committed, we'd be wearing wooden shoes."

"I tried that one year, and *aye-yi-yi*," said Blondine. "I'd rather wear high heels. They must have developed calluses or something; I can't imagine working in the fields in those wooden shoes."

"You aren't going to be a stickler about me rolling around in a wheelchair, are you?" said Emma. "Because I suppose my crutches are more traditional, but my armpits will never last the whole day."

As Rosalyn adjusted her bonnet in the mirror, tilting her head this way and that, she realized that for the first time in a very long while, she cared about her appearance. She wasn't about to construct a false shell as she once had. But as she swept on a hint of mascara and lip gloss, she was glad to see that a glow had returned to her cheeks, and now that she was sleeping more, the dark circles under her eyes had receded.

Jérôme seemed happy to take her as she was, but still—she wanted to look nice for him. And also for herself.

And when her date arrived to take her to the festival, she learned he was a man of his word: Jérôme really did look good in tights.

Chapter Forty-nine

Lucie

Here's what I remember: climbing out of our hole into the blessedly fresh air of the vineyard, treading lightly to muffle the sound of our wooden shoes on the rungs, handing up the baskets.

I remember the hills glowed in soft silvers and golds, and even the ugly barbed wire was painted in lunar light. I remember the stars twinkling on that crisp, clear night. My little Topette, smelling of the lavender sachet my mother had given her to wear around her neck to shield her from the foul smells of the caves.

I remember breathing deeply of the aroma of dusk, feeling the warmth of the dissipating heat, the smells of earth and leaf and *les raisins*, the sweet grapes. The children stole a few of the little jewels, popping them into their mouths as though the grown-ups did not notice.

The rustle of the drying leaves in the soft breeze.

Turning my face up to the full moon shining above us. Still wondering if Émile might be looking up at the same moon, somewhere, somehow.

That is what I remember.

I heard a loud pop and saw a boy fall. The sheer terror, the taste of metal in my mouth. In the dim light, I couldn't tell who it was—Édouard or Charles or little Marcel? I turned to go to him, only then realizing the pops were continuing. Another child fell.

I grabbed Topette's arm roughly in my panic, and threw her to the ground, covering her with my body, hoping the vines would hide us.

As I lay there, I tried to envision the sniper. Had he once been a sweet red-cheeked boy? Did he have a doting mother and a warm hearth waiting for him in a charming gingerbread-decorated Bavarian hamlet? Did his loved ones fret and pray for his safe return? Did they realize that he lay in wait, exhibiting the patience of a spider, until women and children crawled out of their holes, emerging from their underground refuge in search of grapes, and in that moment, he took aim and fired hot lead into the vulnerable body of a child?

I thought of my precious Narcissa with her rosebud mouth and bright eyes so like her father's. I thought of my dear Topette, crushing her as I was. I thought of joining my beloved Émile, holding his hand as we ascended the steps, toward the light, toward a world without war.

I wondered if I would forever wander these vineyards, meander through these caves, remain a friendly spirit haunting these beloved lands.

That was all I wondered.

Chapter Fifty

"Why Saint Vincent?" Rosalyn asked Jérôme as they made their way to the designated meeting spot for the marchers. Reims had been decorated to the nines, with banners, flags, ribbons, and flower baskets hanging from lampposts and telephone poles. They stopped short as half a dozen excited children dressed in colorful aprons and caps ran by them, screaming and laughing.

"Pardon?" Jérôme asked.

"Why is Saint Vincent the patron saint of wine?"

"No one knows, exactly. His saint's day coincides with the lunar phase for commencing the new growing season, but the explanation might be even simpler: he has a *vin* in his name, as in 'wine.'"

Rosalyn nodded, feeling mellow from the champagne she had enjoyed with breakfast. "As good a reason as any, I suppose."

"The festival is held in a different part of the region each year—last year it was in Épernay. So obviously the *Rémois* are excited to host this year. It was organized by the *Archiconfrérie de Saint Vincent des Vignerons de Champagne.*"

"That's a mouthful. Gaspard is proud of being on the committee this year. He's mentioned it a few times. But isn't that a lot of infrastructure for a regional festival?"

"We French excel at bureaucracy," said Jérôme. "But it's not just for the festival, of course. The officials set the standards for pruning, dictate the amount of reserve each vintner must carry, determine how long we can pick, and when. . . . They do important work for an important industry. You'll see groups from every town and part of Champagne represented here today."

In her red skirt and headgear, Rosalyn felt like a woman from another time and place. She thought of Lucie, and wondered where she had been buried; she thought of those thousands of small white crosses sprinkling the landscape in Châlons-en-Champagne. The losses of war were enormous, yet too easy to forget.

But Gaspard was right: Lucie had died over a century ago, and she would have been long gone even if she had lived a full life. Still . . . What had happened to the baby? Had Émile been reunited with his child?

At long last they found the group from Cochet and the surrounding area, who would be marching together in the parade. Gaspard and several other local growers were there; Michel Bonnet and Dominique and Dani, and Pietro and his wife. Blondine was chatting with several friends her age, and André—who also looked very good in tights—was pushing Emma in her wheelchair. Rosalyn spotted other familiar faces, including those of Gilbert Schreyer and Valérie Trepot, whom she had met at Dominique's shop the first day it opened after the holidays. That day seemed a lifetime ago, though it had been a matter of only weeks.

"Where's Laurent?" asked Blondine.

"He's with my mother," said Jérôme. "He'll join us later, when the parade begins. He likes the marching part, but not so much the standing-around-waiting part."

"A boy after my own heart," said Emma.

It took another hour to get organized, but at long last, the parade commenced, led by a marching band, with a cohort of costumed dancing children following behind.

Four men from Cochet hoisted up a stretcher carrying a carved wooden figure of Saint Vincent, dressed in humble brown robes and sitting on bunches of grapes, and Laurent ran to join them just as the group from Cochet began to march. Despite Jérôme's warning that there would be few to witness the parade, the streets and squares were full of hundreds of celebrants. Most of the men wore red capes similar to the women's, but their caps were black. Some people carried old-fashioned cone-shaped baskets on their backs, reminiscent of the historical photographs of the region, and a few even sported wooden shoes.

Two women filled small plastic glasses with champagne from a massive oak keg, handing them out to the cheering crowd—and to the grateful marchers.

A large tractor rumbled by, towing an old-fashioned wooden *pressoir* like the one Rosalyn had seen in Jérôme's cellar. Another trailed a massive wine bottle—Rosalyn tried in vain to remember the name: Jeroboam? Methuselah? Balthazar? Madame Bolze would have known. Some floats were strewn with flowers and grapes, and topped with kegs of wine, while others featured mounds of bread, old-fashioned beehives, and miniature windmills.

It was raucous, silly, good-natured fun, and as Rosalyn marched alongside Jérôme and Laurent and the others from Cochet, waving and throwing candy to the bystanders, she felt it again: that sense of not-quite-unhappiness. Her smile muscles didn't even ache.

At last the marchers ended up in the large square in front of the cathedral. As each group arrived, they stopped and sang songs from their region. Rosalyn did her best to sing along, though she had no idea of the words. Finally, they took their seats at one of the long lines of tables set for an elaborate feast.

"As I told you," Jérôme said loudly to be heard over the crowd and the band, "we work hard in Champagne, but then we celebrate."

"With champagne."

"*Mais oui*. But of course."

When a roving accordionist stopped to ask for requests, Rosalyn shouted out: " '*La Vie en Rose*'!"

Jérôme winced. "You're such an American. '*La Vie en Rose*' is about the most stereotypical tourist song ever."

"I don't care," Rosalyn said as the beautiful notes of the song filled the air. "I'm ready to be sappy, and stereotypical, and see *la vie en rose*. I'm ready for a little color in my life, pink or otherwise."

"If it was good enough for Édith Piaf," said Emma, lifting her glass in a toast, "it's good enough for us. Here's to seeing life through rose-colored glasses."

"I have a surprise for you," said Jérôme, hours later, after they had eaten—and drunk—their fill.

"I don't love surprises," replied Rosalyn.

He laughed.

"I'm serious."

"I believe you. But you'll like this one. Fancy a walk?"

"I think I need one." She was feeling the effects of the champagne and the meal, and she surreptitiously loosened the top button of her red skirt. Leaving Laurent in the care of his grandmother, they headed down the Rue du Barbâtre and onto the tree-lined Boulevard Victor Hugo.

Rosalyn recognized the route. "We're headed to the Pommery champagne house?"

Jérôme nodded. "I know one of the cellar masters there, a fellow named Marius. He got permission for me to take you exploring in the *crayères*."

"Are you serious?"

"I thought you might want to replace the memory of what happened the last time with a nicer one."

Rosalyn smiled. "That's sweet, though the overriding memory is of you and Emma saving me, and then making me tipsy on champagne for the first time in my life."

"In French we have a saying: *Bien fol qui ne s'enivre jamais*. It is only a fool who never gets drunk."

Rosalyn laughed. "That's a handy excuse for indulgence, isn't it? So, have you ever written poetry yourself?"

"As a young man, I poured my heart out on the page on more than a few occasions. Wretched stuff. True 'dreck,' I think is the word?"

"That is a word, yes. But I'll bet it wasn't as bad as all that."

"Oh, I assure you, it was. I hate to admit it, but I think farming is a far better use of my time. And reading, of course."

Upon arriving at the champagne house, Jérôme spoke briefly with a security guard, and they were permitted into the reception area. They crossed over to the entrance to the caves. Descending the steps with Jérôme by her side, dressed in their costumes, felt so different from when she had come by herself, for the party. *She* felt different. And she saw the caves in an altered light now, knowing what she knew.

"You told me Lucie's family stayed in a niche called Dakar," Jérôme said. "It's down this way. I have a torch."

The *crayère*'s main corridors were lit overhead, but many of the smaller tunnels were dark. He switched on his flashlight as they got farther away from the stairs, turning this way and that.

"Like I was telling you before, all kinds of valuable things were hidden in these caves, to keep them from the invaders."

Jérôme squatted to show her a rough opening in the wall, close to the floor. It was just big enough for a person to crawl through.

"This opens up to a private stash, for example. Marius showed it to me."

He handed her the flashlight; she crouched

down and pointed the beam through the hole. Inside were stacks of ancient-looking wine bottles, covered in grime.

"This is amazing. How did they find it?"

"Over time, the old mortar tends to crumble under these damp conditions, so occasionally bricks fall and walls open up."

"And they just leave the bottles there like that?"

"They'll categorize it when they get the chance; according to Marius, it's not a priority. There's no urgency to remove the bottles. Where would they even put them?"

"Is the champagne still drinkable?" she asked as they continued farther along the dark corridor.

"Highly unlikely. Red wine can age well for decades, but not champagne. If it's drinkable at all, it might taste a bit like a sherry, or some kind of fortified wine, but not like champagne as we know it. The champagne houses usually use such old bottles for display, though occasionally they'll auction one off to raise money for charity. It's a novelty item rather than an enjoyable wine. This way."

They turned to the right, and a large sign attached to the wall told them they had arrived at Dakar.

The niche didn't look any different from the others in this stretch of the caves; it was dark, and dank, and filled with bottles. Jérôme cast the flashlight beam over the whole area, but there wasn't much to see.

"It's sort of . . . disappointing," Rosalyn said.

"You haven't seen the best part," he said, leading her around the stack of bottles, where they had to squeeze by. He shone his light on the wall. Etched into the wall was: "*La Famille Maréchal: Raymond, Eugénie, Lucie, Henri.*" And below this, in crude letters: "*et Topette.*"

Rosalyn ran her fingers over the carving. "Incredible."

"This is the family you've been looking for?"

She nodded. Words failed her. Lucie had lived right here, in this nook, with her family. Rosalyn could practically hear the clicking of Madame Maréchal's knitting needles, smell the lavender from her sachets and ointments. She imagined Lucie breezing in, exhausted but satisfied after bringing in the harvest.

She used her phone to snap some pictures.

"And look," Jérôme said, pointing the beam of light toward the back of the niche. "Do you see the carving there?"

"Yes! It's . . . a rabbit? In a waistcoat, with a little watch . . . like the White Rabbit in *Alice in Wonderland.*"

"That's what it looks like to me, too."

Rosalyn squinted her eyes and inspected the cave closely. "Wait a minute—look at that, right next to it. Do you see what I see?"

Jérôme peered closely. "This area appears to have been walled up."

Rosalyn nodded. "Do you think there are more bottles behind there?"

"Possibly."

"Or . . . Émile's letter mentions he and Lucie spent their wedding night in the attic of Dakar, 'through a rabbit's hole.' Maybe this is what he meant!"

Their eyes met.

"How good a friend is Marius?" Rosalyn asked.

"Do you mean, would he call the police if we punch a hole in his wall?"

"That's exactly what I mean."

Chapter Fifty-one

As Jérôme had mentioned earlier, it was not difficult to open a hole in a bricked-up wall when the century-old mortar had turned crumbly over the years.

As soon as Jérôme had opened up an area large enough to look through, Rosalyn crouched down and pointed the flashlight beam every which way.

"There's a space back here, for sure," said Rosalyn, "and I see some steps."

"Stand back and I'll widen it a bit more so we can crawl through."

Once they were able to squeeze through, they carefully climbed the crude, shallow steps. At the top, Rosalyn jumped at the sight of a squat, chubby gargoyle.

"I'll bet that came from the cathedral," Jérôme murmured.

They arrived at an opening that was nothing more than a small, claustrophobic loft. Shallow ledges held very old candle stubs, encrusted with dust, and a broken piece of mirror.

But Lucie's humble little "attic" also held a treasure.

The walls had been decorated with bas-reliefs of sirens and sailing ships, clouds and trees and flowers. There were three bottles of champagne, one from each vintage that Lucie helped to harvest. In a folded pile were a heavy wool sweater, a balaclava, and several pairs of socks, all suffering from mold and rot. Next to these was Émile's military kit, sent to Lucie as his wife, along with the official notice of his death.

Rosalyn snapped more photographs with her phone, and then she took the lid off a small wooden box and took a picture of the contents.

Within were six bundles of letters tied with twine, all from Doris Whittaker. One letter from Lucie to Émile, penned after he died, had been added to the stack. Unfortunately, the paper was in terrible condition, spotted with mold and falling apart.

"Doris's letters. At long last."

Tucked into the side of the box was a small book of stories by Edgar Allan Poe, translated by Charles Baudelaire. The frontispiece was dedicated "with much affection" to Lucie Maréchal, with a dramatic signature Rosalyn would recognize anywhere:

Émile Paul Legrand

"I wonder what finally happened to poor Émile," Rosalyn said softly. The space was cramped and not appealing to a claustrophobe, but there was nonetheless something sacred about it. It felt like a chapel. "Did I tell you? We thought he had died in the war—Lucie had received official notification—but it was a mistake. He survived with severe injuries, but no one here knew the truth until after the war."

"That wasn't uncommon. My grandmother's father was a veteran of the Great War. She told me he was referred to as an 'unknown soldier' because he was lost for a while due to his injuries, and only reunited with his family several months after the end of the war."

Rosalyn stilled. "What was his name?"

He shrugged. "I'm not the historian my father was. I never met my great-grandfather, only heard stories. He was originally an apiarist—a beekeeper—but his family's farm in Reims was destroyed in the war, so he worked for one of the big champagne houses for a number of years until he was able to save enough to buy land here in Cochet, which became Comtois Père et Fils.

"Was he missing a hand, by any chance?"

"How did you know that?"

"Jérôme, could your great-grandfather have been the Émile whose letters we've been reading all these weeks?"

"I'm sorry?"

"We've been searching everywhere for more information on what happened to Émile Paul

472

Legrand, but Emma's research didn't find any connection to Cochet or the surrounding area."

"She was probably looking for the wrong name. My grandmother was one of four girls; the family name wouldn't have passed on through them."

"This could mean you're Émile's great-grandson! Do you have a family tree in your library or a family Bible—something that might list his name—to see if I'm right?"

"We can certainly look. Now, what about these letters? They're in terrible shape, as bad as the wine."

He shone the flashlight through one of the bottles, displaying the sediment floating within.

"It's a Victory Vintage," Rosalyn said. "Even at the time, I think it was more about the making of it than the drinking of it."

Rosalyn picked up Lucie's letter from the top of the stack. It had been written by Lucie to her husband, after she had been told he had been killed. The paper was spotted with mold and falling apart. She held it as gently as she could as she read aloud:

> I shall never believe it. I think I shall go to my grave not believing it. How could someone like you disappear from this earthly plane?
>
> Since this war began, I have made a

game of asking myself: What was the worst moment? The head of the Smiling Angel crashing upon the pavement. The breaking of the blind woman's teacup. The look on your face at that very last moment, when you turned back to smile at me.

Never before had you turned back.

Tears bubbled up and spilled over as Rosalyn reached the end of the letter. Wordlessly, Jérôme put an arm around her and hugged her close. She turned her head and let her tears stain his white shirt.

"I'm not even crying about Lucie and Émile. It's that— I don't know. . . . For some reason, I keep thinking about Dash. He always used to promise me a lifetime of laughter."

After a beat, Jérôme said softly, "You Americans are an optimistic people; I suppose we Gauls seem melancholic in comparison. But personally, I don't believe you can truly appreciate laughter without experiencing tears."

She sniffed, pulled back, and looked up at him. "Live the questions, not the answers?"

He gave her a sad smile. "Rilke was no slouch."

"Do you suppose Émile quoted Rilke to Lucie down here, in their little cave?"

"I wouldn't be surprised."

She let out a long breath. "I think I've been

grieving not just Dash's death, but finding out he wasn't the person I thought he was, after the fact. That he'd put us into debt, that his grand life was a sham. He even kept his illness from me, at first. Why couldn't he confide in me? It makes me doubt everything that we shared, everything my life—*our* life—was, before."

Jérôme opened his mouth to speak but hesitated, as though searching for words. "I know it's nothing like what you've been through, Rosalyn, but I grieve the loss of my marriage. It's difficult letting go of dreams, of what we had—or, more precisely, what I *thought* we had."

"Letting go of the people we used to be."

"And embracing the people we are yet to become."

The spirits of Lucie and Émile swirled around them as they sat together in that peculiar chapel-like vault in the earth, their red capes enveloping them. With her bonnet and his cap, it was easy to imagine they were two lovers from another era sheltering deep beneath the surface of the earth, hiding from their chaperone . . . or the German bombs.

Rosalyn became acutely aware of Jérôme's arm around her, his thigh pressing against hers. Ignoring the musty, chilly air of the caves, she focused on his masculine scent: of freshly tilled earth and woody grapevines. She leaned into the warmth of his body, matching her breathing to his, feeling the steady beat of his heart. He was so vital, so alive.

And so was she.

Rosalyn tilted her face up to his, and cupped his cheek with her hand, savoring the soft prickle of his whiskers in her palm. He gazed down at her for a long moment before slowly lowering his face to hers.

They kissed.

It was the sweetest, gentlest touch. He nibbled at her lips, landed tender butterfly kisses along her cheeks, left a trail of heat as he made his way down to her neck. Her skin tingled under his caresses; something deep down began to awaken. She hadn't felt anything like this since . . .

Dash.

She pulled away. Jérôme went still.

After a moment, he put his hand over hers. In a voice so soft it made her want to cry, he said: "Stay with me, Rosalyn. Stay here with me. We don't have to do anything; just stay with me."

Breathing heavily, she gazed around Lucie's hidden attic room, the walls carved with sirens and sailing ships, flowers and trees. Were these things Lucie longed to see and to experience when the war was at last over and she and Émile were reunited? Rosalyn's heart broke at the thought of a beautiful life cut so very short.

Don't think, Rosie. Just let yourself feel. Let yourself live.

She turned back to Jérôme. His sad eyes, his quiet way. Her attraction to Dash had felt like a lightning bolt, but this was different. This was soft, hushed. Jérôme was safe, and kind . . . and just looking at him made her want him with an animal fierceness she had forgotten she possessed.

Leaning toward him, seeking his heat, she sank into his embrace once more. She kissed him, this time deepening the connection, allowing herself to experience what she had denied for years now: the yearnings and desires for connection, for sensual pleasure. The aching hunger for the touch of a man's hands, and for all the wild, untamed sensations they elicited. She let herself go, embracing aspects of herself she had hidden—and denied—for so long.

When Jérôme eased back onto the little chalk floor of the strangely poetic attic of Dakar, Rosalyn followed him, tumbling impetuously down the rabbit hole.

Much later they ascended the main stairs of the *crayères*, climbing the hundred sixteen steps, leaving the caves behind.

They had agreed to leave everything as they had found it in Dakar's cave within a cave for the time being; Jérôme would speak with Marius to determine how the winery wished to proceed. Rosalyn hoped that professional archivists might be able to salvage what was left of the letters, and that she would be able to revisit their discoveries soon. She wanted to read through Doris's letters, especially.

"There's one more thing I would like to ask from you," said Jérôme as they left the Pommery cellars and headed back to the festivities.

"More?" she asked, trying to keep her tone light.

In truth, her mind was a jumble of contradictory emotions and sensations: the trace of his lips on her skin still tingled, and her limbs were languid and sated, but she felt wildly guilty, even disgusted with herself. Her mind screamed at her, *What have you done?* More precisely, what had *they* done?

She didn't know how to make sense of it; she wanted to be alone.

"Let me take you to Paris," said Jérôme.

Rosalyn shrugged. "Maybe."

"I don't mean right away. One day." He paused. "Rosalyn?"

"Mmm?"

"Are you okay? Did I say the wrong thing?"

"It's not that. It's . . . I just need to get back to the festival. I can't believe how late it's gotten."

Back at the plaza in front of the cathedral, they found that their little group from Cochet had dispersed. The feast had become a party as the afternoon turned to evening; strings of

478

lights added a festive touch. They searched for Emma and Blondine and the others, but everywhere Rosalyn turned, it seemed to her that all she saw was Ritchie James, schmoozing vintners and snatching up accounts *she* should have been trying to secure for Hugh.

Her stomach clenched. She was on that roller coaster again: from the heights of giddy joy while lying in Jérôme's arms to feeling guilty and confused and overwhelmed, all at the same time. She glanced up at the strong, bewhiskered jaw of her escort, and remembered the sensation of his mouth on hers, moving down her neck, and then . . . *How could she have done what she did?* She barely knew this man.

She fiddled with the silver locket around her neck. She had been unfaithful to Dash, to his memory.

"Rosalyn, please tell me what's wrong."

"It's Ritchie James—I can't stand that guy," Rosalyn muttered. "He's probably signing the accounts I should be going after."

She chided herself; she hadn't been fulfilling her responsibilities, had been running after ghosts and exploring the caves with Jérôme. And worse. Even though she had given her notice to Hugh, she was still officially employed as a Small Fortune wine rep, and this festival was the main reason Hugh had sent her to France in the first place.

"Well, think of it this way: You can always have *my* business," Jérôme said with a small smile. "Maybe I should seek representation in the U.S. after all. Or . . . maybe you could stay awhile, and redesign my labels."

"All I had to do was sleep with you and you give me your business?"

He stopped short and frowned. "That's a hell of a thing to say."

"Sorry. I didn't mean that. . . . I didn't mean . . ." Rosalyn trailed off with a frustrated shrug. She had no words for the emotions pummeling her.

"Why are you suddenly angry at *me?* You have nothing to feel guilty for because of what happened in the caves, Rosalyn. We may have gotten a little carried away, but it wasn't that surprising, was it? This sort of thing is inevitable."

She snorted. "How very French of you."

"Maybe I *am* being 'very' French, but a few intimate moments together—however wonderful—does not constitute a contract. I made you a business offer, nothing more." He ran a hand through his hair. "I think perhaps I have misjudged things. Forget I mentioned it."

"It's just— Why does everyone seem to have an idea about how I should spend my life?" demanded Rosalyn. First Dash, then Hugh, then Emma . . . Rosalyn felt disloyal, inadequate, and so incredibly sad. At that moment, all she wanted was to be back in her hermitage. Solo. No connections, no expectations, no words. "Why doesn't everyone just leave me alone?"

"Whatever you say, Rosalyn," said Jérôme. "I certainly wouldn't want to stand in your way."

Full of regret and weathering an onslaught of unnamed emotions, Rosalyn caught a ride back to Cochet with Monsieur Bonnet. But as soon as he dropped her off at Blé Champagne, she found that her desire for solitude was not to be satisfied.

Blondine was waiting for her, and the look on her face made Rosalyn ask, "What's wrong?"

"I'm sorry to tell you, Rosalyn, but Emma is sick."

"What happened? Where is she?"

"André took her to Paris. She wouldn't give me any details, but something's very wrong. I wanted to go with her, but we have a huge sales meeting tomorrow that I can't miss. Also, she yelled at me and told me not to come."

"Sounds like Emma."

"Rosalyn, I think it is very serious."

Chapter Fifty-two

Rosalyn tried both Emma and André on their phones, but neither answered. Then she called the Hôpital Universitaire Pitié-Salpêtrière, where Emma had gone the last time she was in Paris; they confirmed that one Emilia Kinsley had indeed been admitted that evening. Visiting hours began at eight in the morning.

Rosalyn arose early the next morning and drove to Paris. Consumed with worry for her friend, she scarcely noticed she was facing down the ghosts of Paris that had kept her away before.

On the third floor of the hospital, she spotted André standing out on a large terrace, smoking. They shared a hug without speaking.

"How is she?" Rosalyn asked when she finally pulled away.

"*Grincheuse,*" he said, which meant "grumpy."

She smiled. "I'll bet."

"She won't be happy to see you," he said in that measured, thoughtful way of his. "She does not like people to think of her as being sick. She is always so full of life; she wants people to think of her that way."

As she went to find Emma, Rosalyn wondered: Was it just human nature to wear a mask?

"Knock, knock," she said as she strode into Emma's room. The accommodations were very nice, for a hospital: Hers was a private room, with a sitting area and a window that looked out over the rooftops of Paris. Emma wore a hospital gown with a blanket over her knees, and she was seated in an armchair by the window. She looked pale and tired.

"You are quite the intrepid investigator, Rosalyn Acosta. Or did André spill the beans?"

"No, I figured it out all by myself."

"Like I've been saying all along, you really are in the wrong business."

Rosalyn sank into the chair opposite hers. "Emma, what's going on? Why are you here?"

"Well, I adore those little Parisian boutique hotels, but with this cast, they simply won't do. . . ." She trailed off with a shake of her head. "Nothing quite like elevators when you're out of commission."

"That's not what I meant, and you know it."

"Care for a drink? André snuck in a bottle of Scotch—it's a nice change from champagne."

"It's ten o'clock in the morning."

"Stickler." Emma laid her head back and closed her eyes.

"I want to be a friend to you, Emma," said Rosalyn. "Please let me be."

Emma let out a long sigh. "I hate to heap things on, Rosalyn, what with what happened to your husband and all. But I fear I'm not much longer for this world. That's why I was in San Francisco. I had a consult with a specialist at U.C. San Francisco Medical Center. But that was pretty much my last attempt."

"What is it?"

"A rare form of cancer, lymphoma—sarcoma—something or other." She waved a hand in the air. "Not worth going into. A lot of this sort of thing is curable, but apparently not my version. In this, as in all else, I like to think of myself as a maverick."

"Is it connected to what happened to your leg?"

Emma let out that raucous party laugh again. "No, as a matter of fact, that really was a dastardly taxi, though I would no doubt recover more quickly were it not for this other thing."

"But surely there's something that can be done?"

"Remember how you told me how people say stupid things when you're grieving, and they try to give advice? Just try being sick and having people ask you: 'Have you tried coconut oil? Crystals? The finest medical care money can buy?' "

"Excellent point. I apologize."

Emma shook her head and gazed out the window. "The doctors here insisted on running more tests, and are urging me to try yet *another* experimental treatment that is about to start clinical trials in San Francisco, but at some point, I'm going to have to call it quits. And truly, I'm not afraid of death; it's what's next. Circle of life and all that. What I despise, though, is leaving things unfinished—like getting someone to take over my wine business. Say, you're sure you don't want to take the reins? Great excuse to come visit a certain cute vintner in France."

"I'm not sure that particular vintner wants me darkening his doorstep anymore."

"Lovers' spat already? You work quick, Rosie. I'll give you that."

Rosalyn smiled and shrugged, looking away and trying to act casual, to ignore the screaming in her head, but of course Emma noticed.

"Seriously, Rosalyn? What happened?"

"It was just too much, too fast, I guess. Maybe. I don't know, with Lucie's cave and everything. . . ." She trailed off.

"Maybe it's the meds, but I'm not following you, sweetie."

"I *slept* with Jérôme," Rosalyn finally blurted out, letting the tears come, and turn into sobs.

"Crikey, was it that bad?"

"*No.* It was *wonderful.* More than that. Absolutely amazing. I had forgotten how it could be."

"But?"

"But as soon as it was over, I felt . . ." Rosalyn's voice wavered. "I feel like I've betrayed Dash. I *know* he's been dead for years now. I know he's never coming back, but it still feels like a betrayal, as if I'm forgetting him, letting him go."

"I think it's more than that."

Rosalyn sniffed loudly, and Emma passed tissues.

"I think you need to forgive yourself for loving Dash," Emma said. "For loving him despite the fact that he screwed up royally. He left you in debt, and given that he was human, I assume there were a few other thoughtless or stupid things he did."

"Like hiding from me the fact that he was sick."

"Dash didn't tell you?"

Rosalyn shook her head. "Not until he had to. Sometimes I wonder . . . maybe if he'd gone to the doctor earlier, if he had taken better care of himself, if he had let me help him . . . maybe things would have been different."

"Maybe. But then, maybe not. My point is this: It's all right to love deeply flawed people. You can be angry at Dash and yet still love him; you can love other people and still honor what you had with him. In a way you're betraying *yourself* by seeing Dash as perfect."

She could love Dash even though he was flawed. She could mourn him even though she was angry at him. Rosalyn was going to have to ponder that one further. Still, she felt like a weight was lifted off her back—not the boulder she usually hauled around, but a stone, at the very least.

"But I really didn't come here to talk about me," said Rosalyn. "Back to you, and your wine business . . . I could . . . I mean, if you really need someone to take over for you . . ."

The weight settled right back on Rosalyn's shoulders. She would do this for Emma; she would do anything Emma wanted her to do. But running a wine business, going back into sales . . . Her heart dropped at the thought. It was one thing to bring in the harvest, maybe even to try her hand at *making* wine, but never again did she want to have to sell.

"For the love of *God,* Rosalyn," said Emma, "you are incapable of keeping the emotions from your face. Listen, it was just an idea. You don't want to do it, I'll find someone else. I've got a little time, several months, at least, maybe more."

An idea occurred to Rosalyn. "What about Blondine? I could help out until she gets her feet under her—I don't mind consulting. I just don't want to *run* the thing. I was planning on introducing her to my boss, Hugh; maybe you three could form a partnership of some sort. An international concern, with Blondine as liaison, and André here on the ground in Champagne."

Emma smiled. "I like the sound of that. I'll

look into it. But back to you: If you don't want to work for Hugh, and you don't want to stay with that luscious vintner Jérôme . . . what is it that you *do* want, Rosie? You want to go back to Napa?"

"Not permanently."

Rosalyn's life in Napa had been all about Dash: what he'd wanted and what he'd needed. And she had loved it. But she realized now that even if Dash hadn't gotten sick, things would have changed. He would have had to admit the money problems, and given their different approaches to the world, their dynamic would have shifted. Perhaps they would have weathered the storm; perhaps it would have put them on a more even keel as partners. But things would have changed, no matter what.

Fairy tales didn't last. But maybe that was okay.

Her life couldn't be about what Dash wanted anymore. It had to be about what *she* wanted.

"Hey, you'll never guess what Jérôme and I found in the Pommery caves," said Rosalyn, eager to share her news—and to change the subject. She brought out her phone and scrolled through to show Emma, but it was hard to make out very much in the photographs.

"What am I looking at?"

"It's Dakar, the niche Lucie's family lived in, in the Pommery caves. Jérôme got us permission to explore. See? They had carved their names into the wall! And at the back, there was a crumbling section of wall, and we busted through and found the little area Émile wrote about, the 'attic' of Dakar."

Emma sat up straighter. "Are you serious? You broke through a wall in the cellars? I knew we were on the same wavelength."

"It's hard to tell in the photo, but we found Doris's letters."

"Finally!"

"They're in terrible shape, though. And it felt like stealing to take them, so they'll have to go through official channels before we can get our hands on them."

Emma made a *tsk*ing sound. "Drawing the line at stealing, are we? Now you've disappointed me."

"But here's the best part: Jérôme's great-grandfather was a veteran of the Great War, and he was severely injured, and believed dead for a while, and *lost a hand.*"

Emma blinked. "You think Jérôme's great-grandfather was Émile Legrand? *Our* Émile?"

"We don't know for sure yet; Jérôme said he'd try to find his name in a genealogy or family documents to confirm it. But it seems awfully coincidental, doesn't it?"

Emma nodded. "It certainly does. So, if true, Jérôme and I are cousins. A few times removed, but cousins nonetheless."

"I'm not following."

"While you were destroying private property and canoodling with Jérôme—"

"Canoodling?" Rosalyn asked with a smile.

"—*I* made a discovery of my own. André got his hands on the orphanage ledger from Madame Bolze."

"How did he manage that?"

"The man has a way with old women—I'm a case in point. I don't ask questions."

Rosalyn stilled. "Have you looked through it?"

Emma nodded slowly, a smile on her face.

"What did you find?"

"It's over on the nightstand, by the bed. Check out the bookmarked page."

Rosalyn rose to retrieve the ledger and flipped through its ancient pages. Where the bookmark held the place, she ran her finger down the names, pausing at: *Narcissa Emilia Maréchal LeGrand, Reims*; *agée moins d'un an, adoptée, Madame Doris Whittaker, veuve, Australie.* Narcissa Emilia Maréchal LeGrand, less than a year old, adopted by the widow Doris Whittaker from Australia.

"You're kidding me." Rosalyn stared at Emma. "Doris adopted Lucie and Émile's daughter? But I thought . . . Didn't you say Doris didn't have any children?"

"She didn't. Not according to the family tree, anyway."

"Would she have kept the adoption a secret for some reason?"

"I can't imagine why. She was a wealthy widow, and known to do pretty much as she pleased. But I started thinking about the timeline. . . . Doris didn't live past forty. We know that Narcissa was born in nineteen eighteen, which means she would have been only a few years old when Doris died."

"Oh, the poor thing," said Rosalyn. "She lost *another* mother? What happened to her then?"

"Ah, that's where things get even stranger. Doris had one brother, Louis. He and his wife—my great-grandparents—had ten children. The youngest child, who was my grandmother, was named Narcissa."

Rosalyn stared at Emma. "That's not a very common name, is it?"

Emma shook her head. "And here's the kicker: My full name isn't Emma—it's Emilia. It was my grandmother's middle name."

"Emilia . . . as in Émile? So this means you are Narcissa's granddaughter, and the great-granddaughter of Émile and Lucie," said Rosalyn, a note of wonder in her voice. "No one in your family ever said anything about Narcissa being an orphan from France?"

"I'm sure they were aware of it at the time, and I always knew we had French blood in the family, but I never heard about it. Then again, my great-grandparents had ten children, so I imagine they just folded her into the brood and raised her as one of their own. Maybe that's why I was so fascinated by the letters—maybe I was meant to find my cousins, *eh?* I have two brothers who can follow up on that. They'll like Jérôme; I bet they'll get along like wildfire."

"What does your mother say about all of this?"

"I haven't spoken to her yet. I . . . I don't want to call her until I know what's going on with my health situation, and decide what my next steps are, assuming there are any." She let out another long sigh, and closed her eyes. "By far, the worst thing about all of this is imagining what my death is going to do to my poor mother. But I can't do anything about that—death is the ultimate relinquishment of control, after all. And she's got lots of grandchildren to console her. Still, I always meant to leave a legacy of some sort. I never had kids, so it should have been something else. Something . . ." She left off with a shrug.

"Maybe part of your legacy is bringing Émile and Lucie's story to light, however tragic it might be."

"Is it tragic, though? I think Gaspard had a point: We want Émile and Lucie to have lived, but they would have been dead by now no matter what. All stories have to end sooner or later, and there's really no 'right way' to exit, when you think about it. Ultimately we're all just the

492

contents of our own letters, which someone in the future might read; everyone dies eventually."

"That's very philosophical," said Rosalyn, leaning forward and putting her hand over Emma's. "And I accept any decision you make, of course. But, Emma, if the doctors think this new experimental protocol might work, I hope you'll try it. And I want to go with you. I need to take care of a few things in Napa, but it's not far. I can be there for you, Emma. I *want* to be there for you. And if you still want to pay me to write Émile and Lucie's story, I would love to accept. Turns out, I really need a job."

"You're hired, on one condition: Apologize to Jérôme. Don't be an ass, Rosie. The man's adorable; he works the fields during the day, reads poetry at night, and busts through walls. Assuming he's good in bed, he's the real deal."

Rosalyn laughed. "I will. But hey, you're going to want to stick around long enough to read my book—*our* book—when it's done. With all these new revelations, it ought to be a bestseller. I see Hollywood blockbuster written all over it."

Tears in her eyes, Emma squeezed Rosalyn's hand and blew out a long breath. "Are you sure you can handle this, Rosie? The great likelihood is that I'll die, just like Dash did. Just like we all do, eventually."

Rosalyn had fled from Dash's hospital room at the last moment, so fearful was she of facing loss. But loss was part of life; it was inevitable. She was no longer afraid of death. As a matter of fact, she was no longer afraid of facing life, either.

"I want to be there, if you want me to be."

"All right, what the hell? If the tests reveal I'm a good candidate for it, we'll head back to California. I want to meet this Hugh character I've heard so much about."

"I promise you won't be disappointed."

"One more try, Rosie, but if this doesn't work . . ."

"If it doesn't, I'll be there till the bitter end."

"It won't be bitter, Rosie. It's just the next step."

Chapter Fifty-three

When she didn't find Jérôme out in his fields, Rosalyn drove up to the old stone farmhouse. She sat in the car a moment, hesitating. She probably shouldn't disturb him—what if he was napping after waking up at three in the morning to tend his vines?

Get a backbone, Rosie, she told herself. *Awkward never killed anybody.*

She knocked. When she got no response, she knocked again. Finally, she heard some muffled sounds, and Jérôme opened the door, looking rumpled and gorgeous. He didn't say a word.

"I know your English skills are impressive." Rosalyn jumped right in. "But I'm not sure you completely understood when I told you I was a hot mess."

Jérôme gazed at her for a long moment, his head tilting slightly, those tiny lines forming between his eyebrows. Not long ago Rosalyn would have assumed he was angry with her, or annoyed with the ever-problematic American. Now she knew different: He was confused. Hurt. Perhaps even . . . feeling betrayed? Before long he would give a little shrug and turn away.

How had she come to know him so well in such a short time?

"Could I come in for a moment?" she asked.

He stepped back so she could walk through the doorway. Once again she was impressed with the feeling of being at home and comfortable, despite the wildly awkward situation she found herself in.

"Coffee?" he offered. "I was just making some."

"Thanks. I'd love a cup." She leaned back against the kitchen counter. "I'm sorry, Jérôme. Again . . . this is a lot for me. I'm doing the best I can, but I think things moved a little fast between us. I wasn't sure I was ready to start something new with someone. And I got caught up with the stories of Émile and Lucie, and the First World War, and thoughts of Dash, and—"

"I understand. It was fast for me as well." He set a mug of coffee in front of her. The cup was chipped, as though it had been in the family a long time. She ran her finger along the groove and decided she loved it even more for its imperfection. *None of us makes it out of this life unharmed.*

"Emma's sick," Rosalyn said. "She has to go back to San Francisco, to try a new therapy."

He nodded. "I heard something about that, at Dominique's store."

"Since when did you start listening to gossip?"

"Since I started caring about who—or is it 'whom'?—the gossip was about."

Rosalyn smiled. "Our flight leaves for San Francisco tomorrow."

"Tomorrow? You are escorting Emma back to the hospital there?"

"Yes, but it's more than that. I have to go back to California for a little while," Rosalyn continued. "I have things to do in Napa."

"You have to get back to selling wine?"

"Actually, I quit my job. I don't want to sell wine anymore. But I have to finish up with my boss and help train my replacement. And, most important, I have to clean out my medicine cabinet."

The lines between his eyes deepened. They reminded her of the vineyards, carefully laid out in their parallel rows. The worries of war and harvest, the preoccupations of Champagne and the *Champenois*, now and forever.

"The medicine cabinet?" he asked. "Is that a metaphor?"

"In a manner of speaking. I'll explain it to you one of these days, I promise." Rosalyn's mind went to the aqua bath mat, the vials lined up on the shelves. They no longer felt like a temptation, just a sad reminder of what Dash—and she—had gone through toward the end. "I left a life behind in Napa, Jérôme. Not one that I want anymore.

I realize that now. But I have to go put things right."

Their gaze held for a long moment.

"I was going to call you," Jérôme said. "I have something to show you in the library."

As they carried their mugs of coffee down the hall, Rosalyn studied the stone of the floor, the chartreuse molding, the surprising modern art hung on the ancient walls, splashes of color everywhere.

They stepped into that fantasy library.

Jérôme took a book off a stack on the desk and handed it to her. "Look inside."

She opened the crumbly leather cover and saw the signature she had read so many times: *Émile Paul Legrand.*

Rosalyn let out a little gasp. "Where did you find this?"

"Right here, in the library. After what we found in the Pommery caves, I started looking through the books in earnest. There are many inscribed with the name Émile Paul Legrand—the man who built this library."

"So we were right? Émile—*my* Émile—was your great-grandfather," Rosalyn said, a note of wonder in her voice. "Among other things, that means that you and Emma are cousins."

"Pardon?"

"Emma discovered she's the granddaughter of Émile and Lucie's daughter. Everyone thought

498

Émile had been killed in the war, so when Lucie died their daughter, Narcissa, was adopted by—"

"The Australian woman who corresponded with Émile during the war?"

"The very one."

"I don't understand. . . . Why didn't Émile search for their baby?"

"He didn't even know Lucie was expecting a child," said Rosalyn. "She hadn't told him yet when he went missing and was presumed dead. I suppose by the time he was well enough to return to Reims, everyone had dispersed, and he couldn't find anyone who knew her, or who knew what had happened to her."

"I also found this, tucked into a book of Charles Baudelaire's poetry." Jérôme handed Rosalyn a very old newspaper clipping, in which one Émile Paul Legrand, of Reims, was searching for anyone with knowledge about one Lucie Camille Maréchal Legrand, whose last known address was in the Dakar niche of the Pommery caves.

"So he *did* search for Lucie."

Jérôme nodded. "I wonder how long he looked before giving up, assuming he ever did give up."

"Why didn't he write to Doris to let her know what happened, after he'd recovered?" Rosalyn asked herself as much as she asked Jérôme.

"I doubt he even still had her address; he had no personal items with him. Or perhaps he simply didn't want to remember anything that would remind him of the war."

"And yet he remarried, and started another family, kept his bees, planted a vineyard, and built this library. That's quite a spirit of resilience. I wish I could have known him."

"I have a feeling you know him better than a lot of people, because of his letters."

Once again their eyes met, and held. Jérôme reached out and took Rosalyn's hand, traced the faint blue veins, toyed with her fingers. Her skin felt hot under his touch.

"I'm sorry you're leaving tomorrow," he said in a low voice. "I wish we had met earlier."

"You met me my first morning here. Out in the fields, at dawn."

"Yes, but I thought perhaps you were a crazy woman."

She smiled. "Perhaps I am."

He gave a quiet chuckle. "Let me be more precise: I wish you weren't leaving."

"I have to go, for Emma's sake. But I was hoping—" Rosalyn took a shaky breath. "That is, I wanted to ask you . . . Could I come back in the fall, to help you work *les vendanges*?"

"You want to work the harvest?"

"I do."

"It is hard work. Most grapes here are still picked by hand, since the grapes must be whole and undamaged when they go into the *pressoir*."

"I know that. And the grapes come ripe all at once, so there are only a few weeks in which to work, as determined by the *comité*. You see? I've been learning all about the *méthode champenoise* while I've been here."

"I'm impressed."

"The point is, if you tell me when you need me, I'll come. If you want me, I'll help bring in the harvest."

"Is the harvest the only reason you will come back?"

"Well, I'm in charge of bringing the *galette des Rois* for Epiphany next year. And besides"—she smiled—"I do believe I've developed a taste for champagne."

Chapter Fifty-four

In the offices of the Small Fortune winery in Napa, Hugh held up his flute of champagne, tears in his eyes. His voice rough with emotion, he said, "Here's to Emma Kinsley. A grande dame, if ever there was one."

Blondine and Rosalyn held up their glasses and chimed in solemnly: "To Emma."

"Oh, *please*," said Emma as she returned from the restroom to join them. "Hugh, for the love of God, you sound like you're toasting me at my funeral."

They all laughed and took deep quaffs of the golden bubbly, noting their impressions of the sample sent by a winery Rosalyn had connected with while in Champagne. Several thick green glass bottles, topped with their bulbous foil-wrapped corks, were chilled and just waiting to be tasted. But this morning, Hugh had insisted on raising a champagne toast to Emma's latest prognosis of "guarded, but positive."

"Hugh, when this child first came to France, she wasn't accustomed to drinking champagne in the morning," said Emma, gesturing to Rosalyn.

"I want to know: What in the world have you been teaching her all these years?"

Hugh grinned at Emma, and their gazes lingered. As Rosalyn had predicted, the two got along famously—so well, in fact, that lately Hugh had insisted on chauffeuring Emma to and from San Francisco for her treatments. After a few weeks of inpatient care, Emma had been discharged from the hospital and now needed to visit the medical center only once a week, so she had rented a beautiful home in the Napa Valley so she could be closer to Blondine and Rosalyn—and Hugh.

Hugh had helped Blondine to get a work visa, and she was staying with Emma and attending English classes at night school. Blondine loved Napa, and was thrilled to soak in the California sunshine. Back in Cochet, Gaspard was not at all pleased to lose his best salesperson, but after a long phone call from Emma, he had acquiesced with as much grace as he could muster. One of Blondine's brothers had stepped in to help fill the considerable void Blondine had left at Blé Champagne.

"I should have made a bet with Rosalyn that she'd love Champagne," said Hugh with a chuckle as Blondine topped off their glasses of champagne. "Could have made a little cash."

"I don't have any money, remember?" teased Rosalyn. "I'm still in debt, and Emma pays me a scandalously low wage."

"This is true," said Emma. "How do you think I stay so rich?"

In fact, Emma had offered an embarrassingly large salary, which Rosalyn could not in good conscience accept. The two finally settled on a comfortable but not exorbitant retainer, and they agreed to share in any proceeds from the future book, should it sell. Rosalyn was able to cover her debt-repayment schedule, and was well on her way to reestablishing her credit.

Best of all, when she wasn't training Blondine as her replacement, Rosalyn had been able to devote her energies to deciphering Émile's letters, finally in chronological order, and was now working on interpreting the scans of Doris's side of the correspondence as well. The papers from Lucie's niche had been donated to the archive in Reims, which had made them available to the public through a computer database. Even though the paper had deteriorated in the dank cave, they were mostly legible; the archivists noted that Mrs. Doris Whittaker must have used very high-quality paper and ink, indeed.

Though Rosalyn would have preferred to hold Doris's actual letters in her hands, at least the Australian widow's handwriting was easier to read than Émile's—or Lucie's, for that matter. The knitted items they had found in the Dakar "attic" had been donated to the local Reims museum, and Jérôme had recently informed them that the gargoyle had been remounted in its original place on Notre-Dame de Reims. He sent a photograph of the squat little fellow, high on the north side of the cathedral, looming over the city. Rosalyn planned on painting a picture of it.

"Ah, but you're a published author now, Rosie," said Hugh with a wink. "Don't authors make a load of cash?"

Rosalyn laughed. She had been thrilled to publish her very first article, entitled "The Widows of Champagne," about her experiences in France. It had paid very little, but the article had been well received, and she hoped her book telling the story of Émile and his correspondence with his *marraine de guerre*, and Lucie and the caves, and baby Narcissa's fate, would find its audience. She might even include a little bit of her own odyssey on the page, if she felt brave enough.

And at long last, Rosalyn had cleaned out the medicine cabinet and, in a dramatic but cleansing gesture, burned the aqua bath mat.

Emma had hired an experienced winery manager to assist André in operating Emma's wineries in France—and the two had fallen in love. They were planning on getting married next spring in a village not far from Cochet. Emma was determined to make it to their wedding.

And, as promised, Jérôme had called Rosalyn when it was time to bring in the harvest.

Rosalyn hesitated to leave Emma, but Emma

insisted that she was far *too* well taken care of by Blondine and Hugh. She gave Rosalyn a clumsily wrapped package, with the strict instructions that she wasn't to open it until after her flight to Paris had taken off.

"Okay, a less somber toast!" declared Hugh, lifting his glass high. "To Blondine's new job—she is *so* much better at this than you ever were, Rosie girl, sorry to say—"

"Hey!" Rosalyn interrupted, and they all laughed.

"And to Rosalyn bringing in the harvest," added Blondine.

"To Hugh," said Rosalyn, "who forced me to go to France in the first place."

"And to Dash," Emma said, "without whom none of this would have happened."

"Thank you, Hugh," said Rosalyn the following day, as her former boss drove her to the San Francisco airport.

"No problem. I had a lunch planned in the city anyway."

"I'm not talking about the ride as much as . . . *everything*. Your support when Dash got sick, and all your financial help . . . I can never repay you. And you wanted nothing at all from me."

"I made you sell wine."

She laughed. "Just barely."

506

He chuckled. "Anyway, it's not true that I wanted nothing. I wanted you to be happy."

"That's what Dash used to say."

"I'm pretty sure he's still saying it, wherever he is."

"Well, I'm not one hundred percent happy, but I'm working on it. Still, Hugh, not many people would have been so generous, or so understanding."

"Oh, I wouldn't bet on that." He shrugged. "I went through some tough times as a kid, and some folks helped me out. If I didn't pay it forward every once in a while, I wouldn't be able to live with myself. Do me one more favor?"

"Name it."

"Give this Jérôme character a chance. According to Emma, he's the real deal."

Jérôme and Rosalyn had been carrying on a correspondence since she'd returned to Napa. Theirs were long handwritten letters full of news and thoughts, longing and poetry. Being able to take time to explain her thoughts and emotions on the page allowed Rosalyn to open up more than she might have been able to face-to-face, and Jérôme seemed to feel the same. *An epistolary relationship has a lot going for it,* Rosalyn thought every time she thrilled at finding the telltale international envelope in her mailbox.

Émile's letters had given her insight into the

past, while Jérôme's offered her a promise of the future.

When the airplane bound for Paris reached altitude and the seat belt light pinged off, Rosalyn eagerly unwrapped Emma's gift to find a ridiculous floppy, striped hat.

A note in Emma's distinctive scrawl read:

My dear Rosalyn:

Here's to bringing in the harvest, and drinking the wine. Because nobody's story is written until the day they die.

Epilogue

Champagne in early September was a different world from the frozen landscape Rosalyn had known when she was last here, in January. She was struck by the region's muggy heat, the sudden rainstorms, the plethora of bugs, and the verdant beauty of the region's lush rolling hills.

The teams of grape pickers, called *hordons*, were made up of workers primarily from Turkey and North Africa, as well as several locals and a few unpaid volunteers like Rosalyn, who stayed in a separate section of Jérôme's house referred to as "the dormitory."

If Rosalyn had anticipated a sun-drenched bacchanal, or an *I Love Lucy*–style escapade stomping grapes with her bare feet, she had seriously miscalculated. Instead, clad in rubber boots and rain slickers and wide-brimmed hats, gripping their *sécateurs*, the workers left at dawn in vans that transported them to their daily section of the vines.

Foliage rustled, birds chirped, frogs croaked, and *sécateurs* snapped as Rosalyn pawed through dew-wet vine leaves in search of the correct stem to cut, which was tougher than it looked. The plants were laden with fruit, the warm air redolent with the honeyed scent of ripe grapes. She reached up to touch the silver locket she still wore around her neck; it had become her talisman.

Dash would have loved this.

Rosalyn carried her late husband with her still, a constant companion. His presence was no longer a burden, but a memory she embraced, a balance of contradictory emotions, both happy and sad at the same time.

Dash—through Hugh—had brought her to Champagne, where she had met Emma and Blondine and Jérôme and had uncovered the story of Émile and Lucie and baby Narcissa.

It was because of Dash that Rosalyn had come to savor champagne, and to love the region of Champagne, with all the secrets and stories hidden within and beneath its lush vineyards.

A bunch of grapes tumbled into her hand, and she placed it in a bucket, which would then be dumped—gently—into a thick plastic box at the end of the row, its contents later to be tipped into the *pressoir*.

Kneeling, stooping, and bending over the plants, she thought of Lucie doing the same, somewhere among the grapevines, bringing in the harvest no matter the circumstances. She pondered Émile putting one foot in front of the other after the war, heartbroken and maimed, but making a new home, setting up his beehives, planting the vines, and starting a family. She reflected on the terrible pathos of Émile losing not only his first wife but also his unknown daughter. She also thought of the joy of learning that Narcissa had grown up strong with Doris's brother in Australia, safe from the destruction and ruins of war-torn Champagne.

Her bucket grew heavy as she crept down the row, but Rosalyn was happy to be part of the *hordon*. They would bring in the harvest; they would make the wine.

And then they would drink their fill.

The skies began to clear, the sun peeking out from behind steel gray clouds, sunlight reaching the vines in streams like heavenly spotlights. Rosalyn straightened to stretch her back just as Jérôme came by to retrieve her full bucket of grapes, dropping an empty one in its place.

"*Bon travail*. Are you doing okay? Need a break?"

"No. I'm doing great."

Their eyes held for a long moment, and they shared a small secret smile. Jérôme had insisted on picking Rosalyn up at the airport in Paris, and their reunion had been sublime, both of them feeling excited and shy, especially after the intimate revelations in their letters. They passed two romantic nights together in his flat on the

Left Bank of Paris, not far from the Sorbonne, and spent their days walking, sightseeing, eating at brasseries, and walking some more. Pausing in front of the Cathedral of Notre-Dame de Paris, closed for renovations to repair damage from a devastating fire, Rosalyn couldn't help but think of the Reims Cathedral after the First World War: how the stained glass had been replaced, the wooden features carved anew, and the Smile of Reims restored and returned to her rightful place.

As Lucie said, the human spirit is a resilient thing.

On the third day, as they drove from Paris to Comtois Père et Fils, Jérôme stopped in Cochet to show Rosalyn yet another discovery, this time in the little village cemetery adjacent to the church. In a Comtois family plot, listed alongside numerous names of the extended family, was one Émile Paul Legrand, 1895–1976. Jérôme brought a jar of honey in lieu of flowers to place at the grave, and suggested he and Rosalyn return to plant narcissus bulbs, which would rise and bloom each spring, in recognition of the daughter Émile had never known.

After all the time they had spent searching for him, it turned out Émile had been right there with them in Cochet.

As Rosalyn bent over the vines, she sent out a whispered *merci* to Émile and Lucie for reaching out over the years, beyond the veil, to help her to come to peace with death and, most especially, life.

Two rows over, a man started singing in a language Rosalyn didn't recognize.

Turning her face up to the sunshine, she let the graceful, sonorous notes of the tenor voice slip over her. She didn't need to understand the words to recognize their beauty.

She would be patient with all that was unsolved in her heart.

She would live the questions.

Author's Note

A few years ago I traveled to Reims on a champagne-tasting jaunt. It was only then that I began to understand the extent of the destruction heaped upon the beautiful region of Champagne during the First World War, and learned how the remaining populace of Reims had sheltered within the wine caves in an attempt to escape the bombs. I highly recommend a visit to the Vranken Pommery champagne house, among others—and don't miss the chance to tour the caves.

Needless to say, I was fascinated by the history and soon consulted many books and articles about World War I. The following are key sources I relied upon as background material when I was writing the stories of Émile in the trenches and Lucie in the caves:

Forsant, Octave (Inspecteur primaire à Reims). *L'école sous les obus*. Paris: Hachette, 1918.

Hanna, Martha. "War Letters: Communication between Front and Home Front." 1914–1918 -online. International Encyclopedia of the First World War. https://encyclopedia.1914-1918 -online.net/article/war_letters_communication _between_front_and_home_front (last updated 8 October 2014).

Kladstrup, Don and Petie. *Champagne: How the World's Most Glamorous Wine Triumphed Over War and Hard Times*. New York: Harper Perennial, 2006.

Lestienne, Camille. "Des marraines de guerre pour les soldats (1915)." *Le Figaro Histoire* (22 August 2014).

Mazzeo, Tilar J. *The Widow Clicquot: The Story of a Champagne Empire and the Woman Who Ruled It*. New York: Harper Perennial, 2009.

Rolt-Wheeler, Francis. *Heroes of the Ruins*. New York: George H. Doran Company, 1922.

Spencer, Luke. "The Secret World Hidden Beneath the Vineyards of Champagne." Messy Nessy (23 August 2017). Messynessychic.com /2017/08/23/a-secret-world-hidden -beneath-the-vineyards-of-champagne.

Acknowledgments

As always, many thanks are due to my wonderful agent, Jim McCarthy, who is always in my corner. And to my editor, Kerry Donovan, who always helps keep me on track and helps transform my books into the best stories they can be—here's to the next ten years together!

To Michel Dervin at Champagne Dervin, Cuchery, for hosting us at his wonderful *gîte* and introducing me to families with stories about the wars. Thanks to everyone at Champagne Colin in Vertus, Champagne-Ardenne, for the explanations of the *méthode champenoise* and how to tie up the vines. Many thanks to John Charles Ricciuti at Champagne J. C. Ricciuti in Avenay-Val-d'Or for sharing the fantastical true story of his grandfather and father. Special thanks are due Jacques Calvel of Domaine J. Laurens in Limoux, for his friendship, for sharing his love of the bubbly, and for inviting us to witness the harvest of 2019! And to Madame Pommery: Thank you for your artistic legacy, and for taking some of the sugar out of champagne! Finally, to Vranken Pommery champagne house, and so many others, for sheltering the Rémois during the war.

As ever, many thanks are due to my sister

Carolyn Lawes, professor of history and dealer of truth. I wouldn't know where to start without you—much less where I'd end up. You shared with me the phenomenon of the *marraines de guerre*—which sparked this champagne odyssey—and you were still there at the bitter end as I tried to whip the manuscript into shape. I can never thank you enough!

Thank you to my dear friend the "Plot Doctor," Adrienne Bell, who helped me mash amorphous ideas into something akin to a story line. To fabulous professor Nicole Peeler, who read four hundred pages in *one night* and gave me astute, clever, very constructive criticisms that made *Vineyards* a much better book.

Merci beaucoup à Jacquie Weisner for reviewing my French! I like to say that I stumble through the language passably well, especially with a glass of wine in hand, but it takes a French teacher to get all those accents right—not to mention the spelling!

For teary, heartfelt discussions of sudden "out of order" loss, thank you to Anna Cabrera, Muffy Srinivasan, Christine Jurisich, Megan Devine, and the Compassionate Friends network.

As always, to the friends, family, and colleagues who have helped keep me sane by making me know I am loved despite despair, depression, and deadlines: Rachael Herron, Sophie Littlefield, Bee Enos, Mary Grae, Karen Thompson, Pamela

Groves, Jan Strout, Wanda Klor, Susan Baker, Kendall Moalem, Bruce Nikolai, Faye Snowden, Chris Logan, Brian Casey, Sharon Demetrius, Suzanne Chan, Sara Paul, Dan Krewson, and Susan Lawes. To my son's friends who have helped me through a very dark time, especially Anna Kenney, Maja Magnussen, Sailimanu Willis, Mario Gallardo, Jonathan Fishman, Joe "Stingray" Ross Riggs, Lena Ringstrom, Cady Mura, and Danielle Glick-Scroggins.

To Robert Lawes, a proud veteran and the best dad in the world. Thanks for sticking around; I couldn't have done it without you.

And to my precious "daughter" Hanna Toda, such a bright light in my life.

Finally to Eric, *toujours, et encore*.

Questions for Discussion

1. If you could have coffee with one character from the novel, who would it be and why? What would you like to discuss with this character?

2. Would you say the dominant theme of *The Vineyards of Champagne* is about love or about loss?

3. In the first part of the novel, Rosalyn is searching for a "hermitage." What does she mean by that? What are the benefits of her retreat and what are the drawbacks? Have you ever felt or experienced a similar inclination?

4. How would you characterize Rosalyn's relationship with Dash? Why was she angry with him? Was that anger justified?

5. In what ways were the challenges Rosalyn faced unique to her personality and circumstances? In what ways were they similar to what many women face as adults?

6. Did you find Rosalyn's story depressing, uplifting, or some combination of the two?

7. Wartime is horrific in so many ways, but— like grief—it sometimes reveals new depths of character and strips away falseness.

Without romanticizing the past, can you think of any positives to living through a war?

8. Which character did you relate to the most? Why?

9. Were there any characters you didn't like? If so, what was it that you found unappealing?

10. The working title for this novel was "The Widows of Champagne." How has widow-hood affected characters other than Rosalyn, such as Doris and Lucie and other war widows, or the "Champagne widows" Louise Pommery and Barbe-Nicole Clicquot?

11. Grief is an intensely personal experience. Does Rosalyn's journey ring true given your own experience of loss and mourning? If not, how does it differ?

12. Why do you think Lucie and her family decided to remain in Reims after the war began? What do you think you would do if faced with a similar scenario?

13. What did you think of Blackwell's use of language? Did the characters "sound" different from one another in your mind?

14. Since *The Vineyards of Champagne* is set in France, did you like that the author included French words and phrases?

15. Imagine you were in Lucie's situation. How do you think you would have coped with the confinement and the lack of natural light and

fresh air while living in the caves under the House of Pommery? How would caring for your family and handling daily needs pose new challenges? What would have sustained you?

16. What did you know about the First World War before reading this novel? About the city of Reims or the process of champagne making? What was the most interesting or surprising thing you learned from reading the book?

17. *The Vineyards of Champagne* deals with female friendship, specifically that of the somewhat offbeat trio of Rosalyn, Emma, and Blondine. How is each character influenced by her friendship with the other two?

18. If you were making a movie of *The Vineyards of Champagne*, who would you cast for each role?

19. Have you ever run into a problem in a foreign country and ended up "stranded"—for instance, in need of gas without a functioning credit card? How did you feel in that moment, and how did you find a solution? In what ways does it feel different to be stranded abroad compared with encountering difficulties in one's own country?

20. Lucie says that her mother sees beauty in necessity, whereas Lucie sees a necessity of beauty. What do you think she means by

that? Which perspective better reflects your own?

21. Have you ever visited the Champagne region and/or traveled to another part of France? Did the cultural aspects of the book feel true to life for you? Did anything feel different compared with your own travel experience? For instance, did you notice an obsession with preparing and eating dinner?

22. Emma's great-great-aunt Doris was embittered and disappointed by life but found new purpose as a *marraine de guerre*. How did Doris's connection to Emile, and then to Lucie, offer her a kind of redemption?

23. The Champagne region of France has been a theater of war for many centuries. What impact do you think such a history has on the people who live there, and on the regional psyche? How might such a legacy resonate through generations?

24. The women living under Reims brought in the harvest every fall despite the dangers, hoping their champagne would be a "Victory Vintage" that would be ready to drink after the war had ended. Why do you think they took such big risks?

25. What do you think Rosalyn decides to do at the end of the book, after finishing the harvest? Does she remain in France, return to Napa, or make a different decision

entirely? What do you wish for her—and for Jérôme?

26. Have you read another book by Juliet Blackwell? If so, how did it compare to *The Vineyards of Champagne*? Do you see any similar themes among the books?

About the author

Juliet Blackwell was born and raised in the San Francisco Bay Area, the youngest child of a jet pilot and an editor. She graduated with a degree in Latin American studies from the University of California–Santa Cruz, and went on to earn master's degrees in anthropology and social work. While in graduate school, she published several articles based on her research with immigrant families from Mexico and Vietnam, as well as one full-length translation: Miguel León-Portilla's seminal work, *Endangered Cultures*. Juliet taught medical anthropology at SUNY–Albany, produced a BBC documentary, and served as an elementary school social worker. Upon her return to California, she became a professional artist and ran her own decorative painting and design studio for more than a decade. In addition to mainstream novels, Juliet pens the *New York Times* bestselling Witchcraft Mysteries and the Haunted Home Renovation series. As Hailey Lind she wrote the Agatha Award–nominated Art Lover's Mystery series.

She makes her home in Northern California, but spends as much time as possible in Europe and Latin America.

Connect Online
JulietBlackwell.net
Facebook: JulietBlackwellAuthor
Twitter: JulietBlackwell

Center Point Large Print
600 Brooks Road / PO Box 1
Thorndike, ME 04986-0001 USA

(207) 568-3717

US & Canada:
1 800 929-9108
www.centerpointlargeprint.com